A DROP INTO

Memling shifted again and tugged on the parachute harness until the offending buckle came away from his spine. He started to curse, but gave it up, having already run through his entire vocabulary several times, and looked at the watch again. Twenty-five minutes. Of a sudden, that damnable surge of fear slashed through his chest. After two years' active service in the Royal Marine Commandos he thought he was finished with that pervasive terror . . . Yet Memling also knew from experience that the fear would continue, growing more intense, until he was safely out—or dead. It did no good telling himself he hadn't wanted this mission: no one ever did.

Also by Joe Poyer in Sphere Books:

NORTH CAPE
THE CHINESE AGENDA
OPERATION MALACCA
THE DAY OF RECKONING
HELL SHOT
THE CONTRACT
TUNNEL WAR
THE BALKAN ASSIGNMENT

Vengeance 10

JOE POYER

SPHERE BOOKS LIMITED
30-32 Gray's Inn Road, London WC1X 8JL

First published in Great Britain by Michael Joseph Ltd 1981

Published by Sphere Books Ltd 1982

TRADE
MARK

Printed and bound in Great Britain by
©ollins, Glasgow

For Nick Austin

HEERSVERSUCHSSTELLE PEENEMÜNDE
(Army Research Center)

Based on the Map Drawn by
Maj. Jan Memling, RM, DSO, OBE,
August 6, 1943

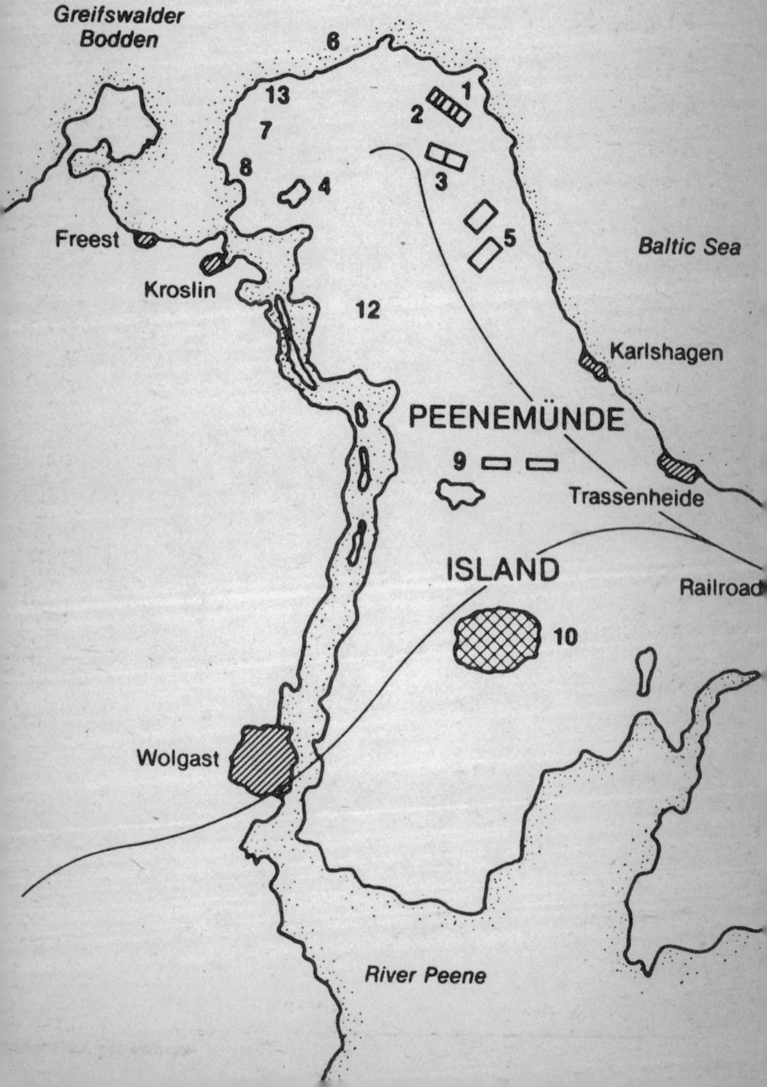

LEGEND

1 A-4/V-2 Launch Complex
2 A-4/V-2 Test Stands
3 Peenemünde East Development Center (Army)
4 Liquid Oxygen Plant
5 Preproduction Works
6 FZG-76/V-1 Test Site
7 Peenemünde West (Air Force)
8 Main Power Station
9 POW Camp
10 A-10/V-10 Launch Complex
11 Gestapo Headquarters, Zinnowitz
12 SS Barracks
13 Tank Farm

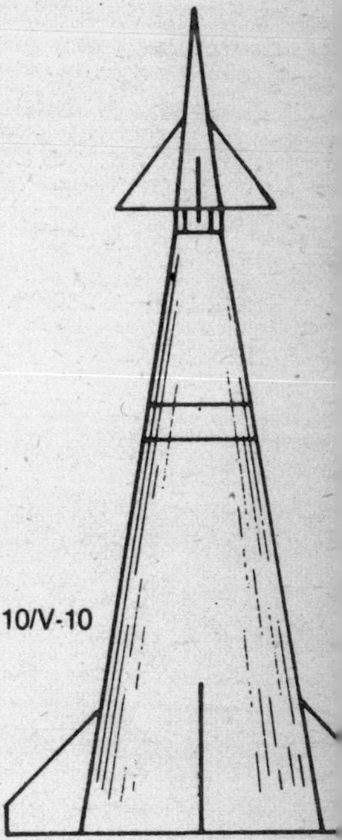

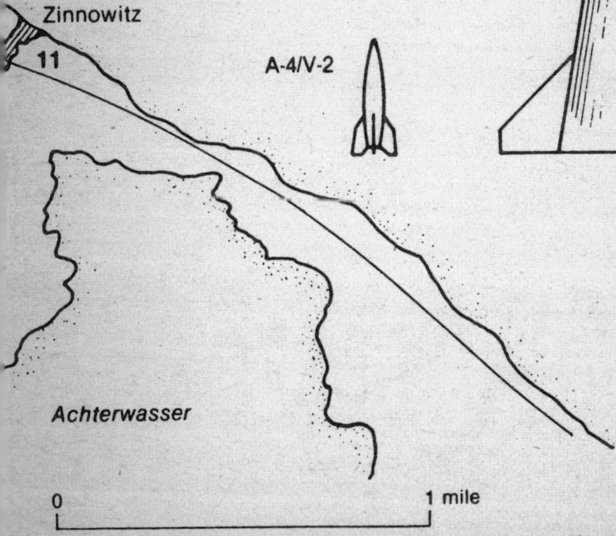

Map drawn by Bob Michae

AXIOM: *A "nine days' wonder"*
is taken as a matter of
course on the tenth day.

AXIOM: *A "common sense" prediction*
is sure to err on the side
of timidity

AXIOM: *The more extravagant a*
prediction sounds the more
likely it is to come true.

Robert A. Heinlein, PANDORA'S BOX

Prologue

Lunar Appenines 6 May 2009

Now that they were out of the plains and into the foothills, the terrain was becoming rugged. Gently rounded hillocks were giving way to craggy hills, and here and there a rough stretch showed ahead along the route that led up towards the ridge they had selected a few hours previously. The changing lunarscape now provided sufficient reflecting surfaces to relieve the dense, formless shadows which the tractor's powerful floodlights could do little to resolve.

Douglas Cummings eased the speed down a trifle to feed more torque to the rear tracks. He scratched his jaw, then reached around for a persistent itch beneath his shoulder blade. They were a hundred and five hours out of Armstrong Base at Taurus-Littrow, and he badly needed a bath.

Don Wayne slid into the co-driver's seat and swivelled so that he did not have to look at the sun-blasted lunarscape. Cummings raised a single eyebrow.

'A possible. Selenography is good.' He shrugged. 'The satellite magnetometer readings are strong and consistent. If there's iron ore, it should be an extensive deposit.'

'Should be,' Cummings echoed. 'If I had a dollar for every should be . . .' He let the thought trail off. 'All right. This one, then we go home. I've had it.'

Wayne turned to face the rear of the cabin. 'Flip to see who goes out?' he asked hopefully.

'Like hell. I went last time.'

'Shit.'

'You wanted to sleep, remember?'

'Okay, okay.'

An hour later Cummings eased the big tractor up a narrow gorge that led through sheer, jagged walls. Terrain this rough was unusual short of the mountains, still some ten kilometres distant. The gorge opened out on to a wide, featureless plain that dipped towards the centre to form an irregular bowl. He eased the speed up again and sat contemplating the route ahead, searching for the smoothest way across to the long ridge that was their destination. Fifteen minutes, he judged, and used the intercom to warn his partner to get into his pressure suit.

The airlock display winked red ten minutes later to indicate that Wayne was inside and cycling. Cummings swore under his breath. As many times as he had warned Don against that practice, he persisted. The time saved just wasn't worth the possibility of a blow-out. He sealed the driving cabin and turned the heater up.

Cummings had begun a sharp turn along a crevice that he hoped would lead to flatter ground, when Don shouted. He slapped the engine switches to cut the power, and as the tractor eased to a stop he caught sight of Wayne sprinting across the surface in long, even bounds. What the hell, he thought, and reached for the transmitter switch.

'Doug, get your suit on and get out here,' Don shouted, beating him to it. 'I saw metal glinting, about ten o'clock and three hundred metres out. It's either an old Saturn S-IVB stage or that Russian cargo container they lost last month.'

Cummings hooted and snatched his suit from the locker. God damn, he thought. If it was the cargo carrier and if it wasn't smashed to hell and gone, they might find some vodka, real vodka and not that musty sludge the Chem lab cooked out of the algae-oxygen system.

As he left the tractor he picked up Wayne's transmission narrating a running commentary for the tapes: '. . . elongated cylinder split down one side. It seems to have tipped on landing . . . hard to . . . yes, it's crushed across the centre, as if it fell over on landing.'

'What the devil are you talking about, Don?' Cummings demanded as he jog-jumped towards the slight irregularity barely visible in the sun glare. 'Russian cargo carriers are spherical . . .'

'It ain't Russian, Dougie. And it ain't ours. And it ain't Indian or the British or the Martians either.'

Cummings reached him a moment later. 'What do you . . .'

The spacecraft was, as near as he could judge, approximately ten metres long and four or less wide. The skin, where it was intact, was smooth metal, slightly hazed by micrometeorites, indicating that it had been there for some time. Its shape was streamlined, rather like the old-fashioned concept of a spacecraft. Lying nearby, and clearly identifiable in spite of its battered and crumpled condition, was a wing. A hell of a long wing, he thought, and the idea occurred to him that the spacecraft was, or had been, intended to make an aerodynamic, gliding-type landing – which suggested in turn that its makers had intended it to return to Earth – or elsewhere?

Wayne had moved to the other side of the spacecraft as he arrived, and Cummings heard him grunt in surprise.

'Doug. Come here.'

Wayne's voice was hushed in astonishment and Cummings found him kneeling beside a gash in the metal skin, looking into a cabin.

'What . . .'

'Take a look.' Wayne pointed.

The cabin was in shadow, but there was sufficient reflected sun to relieve the interior. At first the impact was so overwhelming that he had to deal with each impression in turn. There was the twisted control panel mounted on a swivel arm covered with old-fashioned dials and switches. The walls, once a light greenish colour, had cracked, and the veneer had splintered long ago under periodic temperature fluctuations of two hundred and more degrees Celsius. Plywood, he thought. I'll be damned!

The body shocked him. Hunched half in the seat, half against the main console, the pressure-suited figure seemed asleep; except he knew it could not be. The leather and rubber material – leather and rubber! – of the suit had cracked in places, and a long tatter trailed along one arm. Obviously the pilot had not died in the crash but later. Good Christ in heaven, how much later? A chronometer had been dismounted from the cabin wall and was propped against the sloping console where it could be seen. It had stopped at 0800:20. The thought gripped him. What year, for God's sake?

A pencil lay near the gloved hand, and he picked it up. A sheaf of paper was half-concealed beneath the body, but the writing had faded long ago and he knew if he touched it, the paper would crumble to powder. Whatever the pilot had written was gone for ever.

Wayne tapped him on the arm and pointed to a medallion mounted in the centre of the console. Cummings peered at it, then, not believing, found his flashlight. The beam of light glinted from the silver and red and black enamel of the stylised eagle clutching the swastika. Printed neatly in pencil beneath was a date: 31 January 1945.

Four Horsemen

Germany–England February 1938

The train was less than fifteen minutes from the German-Belgian border when the two men entered the carriage where Memling was seated. They found places at the end of the aisle facing him. The one to the left shook out a newspaper and began to read. Memling could see the banner *Das Eizenblatt*, which suggested they had come from Berlin. The second man, clad in a shapeless black suit, was staring out the window, apparently oblivious to the stale air and the crowded train. Winter light carved deep hollows in his cheeks, making him appear tubercular. Their eyes met as the carriage jolted over a set of points, and the man smiled a death's-head leer.

Memling knew then they were Gestapo and had come for him.

Jan Memling had arrived in the Ruhr town of Arnsberg two days earlier to keep an appointment with the manager of the manufacturing concern of Zemwalt GmbH. This was his first trip abroad and the first time he had been entrusted with dealings of such importance. In spite of his nervousness, the initial meeting had gone well enough, he thought, and the following day, to his immense surprise, agreement had been reached. A contract was drawn up with delivery of the required washing-machine parts promised for mid-May.

Memling was in a euphoric mood, and despite the icy rain which had persisted for days, he strolled the three miles back to the Hotel Husemann, whistling happily and peering into shops along the way. Depending on continental insouciance, he had even dared a ladies'-wear establishment where a pretty young clerk, under the maternal eye of an older woman, embarrassed him mightily. Even so, he left with a frothy lace blouse for his fiancée. Not even the outrageous price could dampen his mood.

Back at the hotel, he hurried to his room to change into dry shoes and trousers, brushed up, and went down to the lounge for a celebratory drink. He had been sitting at the bar practising his German on the bored waiter when a hand descended on his shoulder with a thud that almost knocked him from his seat. 'Jan

Memling!' The words exploded in his ear, and he was spun around to see a square face topped with a shock of unruly long blond hair grinning at him.

'I thought it was you!'

'Wernher!' Memling gaped. 'Wernher von Braun! I don't believe it.' He stumbled to his feet and wrung his friend's hand. 'My God, it *is* you. How long has it been?'

'Four years. Paris, 1934, remember? Ah, did we get drunk that last night.' Von Braun stepped back to take a good look at Memling. 'Are you never going to add some weight? Do the English never eat? You all look half-starved.' Then, remembering his manners, von Braun turned to the man with him. 'But allow me to introduce my good friend and associate, Herr Doktor Franz Bethwig.'

Bethwig was as tall and blond as von Braun, Memling noted as he extended his hand. A lock of hair slipped over his forehead, and he brushed it back with a quick, nervous gesture, then shook Memling's hand once and contrived to bob forward from the waist at the same time. His expression was noncommittal as he said, 'So pleased to meet you, Herr Memling.'

Von Braun signalled the waiter who hurried over with two more chairs. Bethwig sat down, his posture suggesting quite plainly that he hoped they would be staying no more than a moment or two.

'This is amazing,' Jan Memling said, struggling in his excitement for the correct words. 'Do you work in Arnsberg?'

Von Braun chuckled. 'In a way. Franz and I have been here for three weeks.' He lowered his voice to a whisper and leaned across the table. 'And we are heartily sick of it. There is nothing to do but walk in the hills and drink. As it has been raining so much . . .' He shrugged. 'Why, there is not even a decent cinema in the entire town. Thank God we leave tomorrow. But enough of us. Why are you here, of all places?'

Memling also shrugged, striving to appear nonchalant. 'Nothing much. A few days on business. To settle a manufacturing contract for my company.'

'Then you have taken your engineering degree,' von Braun exclaimed. 'I recall that you were studying when you came to Paris. Let me see' – he tapped his forehead – 'the Imperial College of Science and Technology, was it not?'

Memling looked uncomfortable for a moment. 'No, I did not finish. The depression ruined my father's business . . . I was lucky enough to find a position with a manufacturing firm in their quality control department. I have since been moved to production engineering. But I do plan to finish my degree when I am able.'

Bethwig's expression was sceptical, and to break the sudden silence, von Braun leaned back and called to the barman for three steins of beer.

'But you, Wernher, I heard that you not only earned your doctorate but are employed by the army as well. That's wonderful!'

Von Braun looked at him with a quizzical expression. 'Where did you hear that, Jan?'

Memling's cheeks flamed a sudden red. 'Isn't . . . isn't it true? I mean . . . I . . . Arthur Clarke did have a letter from Willy Ley. He mentioned it.'

At the mention of Ley's name, the two Germans exchanged glances. The barman arrived at that moment, and Memling looked from one to the other as the beer was served, his cheeks still red with embarrassment.

'Willy, my God, I haven't heard from him in years, not since he left Germany,' von Braun exclaimed a shade too heartily. 'I was just surprised that you knew. One is always amazed at how word gets about.'

'How do you know Arthur Clarke and Willy Ley?' Franz Bethwig asked Memling. His expression was guarded, and there was something a bit disturbed, or disturbing, in his eyes, Jan could not tell which.

'I am a member of the British Interplanetary Society . . .' Memling began, but von Braun whooped suddenly.

'Franz, didn't I tell you? Jan is one of us! He has been a rocket experimenter as long as you and I.'

Bethwig's expression relaxed immediately, and he grinned. 'Well, then, that is different.' He raised his stein in toast. 'To us, everywhere!'

'After the VfR failed in 1932,' von Braun went on, 'as I think I told you before, the army offered to pay my university expenses if I would work for them. Naturally, I jumped at the opportunity.'

'I should think so.' In spite of himself, Memling could not keep the envy from his voice. 'Arthur was correct, then. You are working full-time with rockets. I think that's wonderful. Our people refuse to pay attention to us. They consider us nothing more than cranks. We have so little money, we can barely afford to buy petrol for fuel.'

'I had heard that the British Interplanetary Society had fallen on hard times,' Bethwig remarked in his precise English. 'It is unfortunate, but then we ourselves have discovered that a private venture is simply not practical. Rocket development is an expensive undertaking, and only the government has sufficient resources to fund such work. It was not until the National Socialists took power that we were provided for. Perhaps if you too had a National Socialist government . . .' Bethwig smiled and let the sentence trail off.

'Perhaps,' Memling replied somewhat uncomfortably, 'but in – '

Von Braun interrupted, banging his empty stein on the table and shouting for the barman. 'Please, please. No politics. Politics give me a headache. I do not care where the money comes from so long as I am allowed to build bigger and better rockets. Then one day soon, God willing, we will travel to the moon and beyond.'

Memling instantly forgot his uneasiness. A warm sense of companionship sped through him, and when the barman had departed, he drank off the second stein in one long gulp. They were three young men who shared a dream, and that was all they needed to understand one another.

'Wernher and I were about to celebrate a very successful day,' Bethwig told him. 'We are intent upon the finest supper and the best bottle of hock this hotel can supply. Will you join us?'

Memling did not think to hesitate.

'. . . And so, after we poured the liquid oxygen into the tank through a funnel, just as we used to in the old days at the Raketenflugplatz, we ducked behind the logs that formed our shelter and waited three minutes for the vapour pressure to build. Franz ran out and opened the fuel mix valve. You should have seen him trying to scramble back up the slope in that rain.' Von Braun was roaring with laughter and had to wipe his streaming eyes. Bethwig was laughing even harder, and Memling could not remember having such a good time since the Paris congress.

'Anyway' – von Braun pushed himself up, hiccupped, and gulped another mouthful of wine – 'he . . . he threw himself over the barrier just as the fuse burned down – can you imagine? we forgot to bring a fuse with us; I had to go all the way to the army base at Cassel to borrow some – and the rocket lit off with a bang.'

'It sounded like a cannon,' Bethwig chortled.

'I was certain,' von Braun went on, 'the explosion had destroyed the motor, but when the smoke cleared away, there it was, working perfectly. The flame was almost four metres long and already settling down into a clear, white torch in which you could see the most beautiful diamond shock waves, one right after another. It was truly a wonderful sight. If only we had known this morning that you were here, Jan, we would have taken you along with us.'

Bethwig leaned forward and tapped the table with his bread knife. 'And do you know, Jan, that engine ran perfectly for a good four minutes and might have done so longer if we had not run out of liquid oxygen. All our previous motors in that series burned through in three minutes!'

With careful concentration, Memling succeeded in setting his wine down without spilling it. 'I do not believe it!' He enunciated each word carefully. 'Pardon my scep-ticism, gentlemen. But four – four minutes with liquid oxy – oxygen' – he grinned in triumph – 'and alcohol is imposs – imposs – can not be done. *Our* best engine burned up in two.'

'Ah.' Von Braun leaned closer and lowered his voice. 'But now we know how. When the motor cooled, Jan, we took it back to the machine shop and cut it in half. Not even a discolor – discoloration in the area of the throat.' He smacked the table with his hand and flipped up the empty bread plate. Bethwig caught it, and as he tried to bow, the waiter moved in swiftly and cleared away the rest of the dishes.

Memling made a rude noise, and Bethwig laughed.

''S true, damn it.' Von Braun had lapsed back in German. 'Franz has designed a new combustion chamber.' He leered at Memling and pushed his glass away. 'He drilled small holes in the walls leading to the throat area. The fuel . . . fuel is pumped down to the combustion chamber . . . pardon me . . . pumped down to the combustion chamber where a little bit is bled off and sprayed through the little holes.'

Memling's face wrinkled in an effort to visualise what his friend was saying. Bethwig impatiently sketched the design on a napkin. 'See, here. The fuel comes through the side and cools the combustion chamber walls by absorbing heat here, about the throat, where it always burns through. The extra fuel also adds to the combustion process and . . . and raises chamber pressures.' He paused dramatically, but the effect was spoiled when he fell off his chair.

'And the best part, Jan' – von Braun took up the story, ignoring his friend's struggles to regain his seat – 'is that the motor was machined entirely of brass! If Franz's new cooling system works that well in a material with such a low melting point, then we should have no trouble at all with a rocket motor made of steel!'

Memling's face glowed as he listened to von Braun's recital of the day's events. Bethwig's new cooling technique was sure to revolutionise rocket motor design; it was as big a technological step forward as change from powder to liquid fuels forecast by Tsiolkovskii and Oberth.

'The main concern of all rocket experimenters, whether British, American, German, French, or Russian,' von Braun went on, 'is to cool the combustion chamber so that the flaming gases at 2900 degrees centigrade do not destroy it.'

Memling shook Bethwig's hand so vigorously that he upset the wine carafe, which von Braun just rescued with a well-timed catch.

'My God, I believe you may have given us the future, Franz. Imagine what can be done now! Huge motors utilising your cooling technique to power cargo and passenger rockets across the oceans, into space, even to the moon. Why, we could build a landing aerodrome – no, no, that's wrong – not an aerodrome but a lunardrome, on the moon. My God, think of it! A matter of a few years. Why, if we all worked together – '

Memling stopped abruptly as political realities overcame his enthusiasm.

'Jan' – von Braun had sobered quickly – 'you must understand that what we have discussed here must never be spoken of again.' He glanced around the room and bit his lip.

In an attempt to salvage the mood of the evening, Bethwig poured each of them another glass of wine. 'Mem-ling' – he pronounced each syllable. 'It is not an English name?'

'No.' Jan hesitated a moment. Von Braun's warning had troubled him, causing him to remember the real reason for his trip to Germany. 'My grandfather emigrated from Belgium. He was a gunsmith.'

Bethwig nodded and asked a few more questions concerning his background, the type of questions new acquaintances ask, more out of politeness than any real interest. But the spectre of political considerations stayed with them, and shortly the party broke up. Von Braun and Bethwig were leaving early to begin the drive back to Berlin, and Memling had morning train connections to make to Ostende and the cross-channel steamer. The excuses served admirably.

Had he seen the man hiding behind the newspaper the previous evening in the hotel dining-room? Did they know he was an agent of MI6, or was it just a coincidence they were on the same train?

Memling looked at the old steel watch that had belonged to his father. The Belgian border was just a few minutes away. Customs and passport control had been accomplished at Aachen where he had boarded the train, so there would be no reason to stop this side of the border. Yet . . .

He shook his own paper and folded it to a new page. The movement caused the man at the window to glance the length of the carriage. So they were watching him! Memling shifted the newspaper until he could just see over the top. The two Gestapo agents exchanged quick glances, and Memling was certain he saw one nod to the other.

The fear that coursed through him was so intense, so unexpected, that he thought he would vomit. In all the training sessions he had endured, there had never been anything so overpowering as this. He found he could not catch his breath, and an ugly blackness was threatening to overwhelm him. He had only one thought, to leave the train as quickly as possible. That nod could only have meant his arrest before the frontier. As if to endorse his terror, the train began to slow.

The carriage was crowded; students returning from Christmas holiday filled the aisle. He had studied the maps carefully, as he had been taught, and knew that they would cross the frontier deep in the Ardennes forest, a relatively uninhabited area with few roads. The driver would not dare stop on a slope this steep with the tracks certain to be icy. At the crest, then, or in the valley on the far side. Ten minutes, five minutes? Who was waiting? Political police, civil police, or soldiers. Mounted or afoot?

Memling wasted no more time in useless speculation. The only thing that might save him was the unexpected. He lowered his paper and stood up casually as if going to the lavatory. Excusing himself, he stepped over the legs of a fellow passenger and pushed his way along the crowded aisle. He knew without turning that at least one of the Gestapo agents was following. As he approached the end of the compartment Memling risked a glance behind and saw that the thin-faced agent had also pushed his way to the aisle. Desperate to force a way through the crowd, he began to use his elbows. He stumbled through to the draughty platform and shoved a young girl away from the door. Someone yelled at him, tried to grab his arm, but he flung the hand off and yanked up on the handle. It refused to move, and he threw his weight on to it, cursing. He yanked a third time and the handle gave way. Memling lost his balance as the door swung outwards, and was sprawled in a snowbank before he realised what had happened. The train rushed by, and pushing himself up, he saw the Gestapo agent leaning far out of the doorway, shaking his fist in frustration. Scrambling up the side of the cut into the icy wind, he stumbled into the forest.

Memling was half-asleep in his chair, stupefied by heat and exhaustion, when his superior officer, Charles Englesby, entered the room. He gave Memling a distant glance and sat down behind the desk. Memling roused himself with an effort, and Englesby took a cigarette from the open box but did not offer him one. Memling lit a cigarette of his own, ashamed and angry that he could not keep his hands from shaking, even now.

He had not slept in thirty-six hours, and the overheated office, after the intense cold of the forest and the unheated aircraft, was threatening to overwhelm him at any moment.

'I would like to know why,' Englesby began in sudden, clipped tones that startled him fully awake, 'you felt it necessary to create an international incident. Both the German and the Belgian authorities have been on to the Foreign Secretary about your behaviour, and he is quite angry. An illegal exit from a country, in full view of hundreds of witnesses, is not characteristic of an intelligence agent, or did you not know that?'

Memling made an effort to gather his wits. 'I'm sorry about the disturbance,' he began, 'but I felt . . . felt it was quite necessary. You see, sir, quite by accident I came across some information that may have drastic military implications. I was being pursued by two Gestapo agents when I jumped from the train.'

Englesby pushed his glasses down and stared over the tops at Memling. What he saw was a tall, gangling young man in a badly cut, muddy brown suit and well-worn shoes, one of which showed a gaping hole where the upper and sole had parted company. The man certainly does not display the type of breeding one is used to, he thought, or he would have had a brush-up and a wash before coming in. But then, the new regime . . . He sighed inwardly. The service seems to be taking in a number of his sort these days.

'Explain,' he snapped.

Memling did so. He talked for ten minutes, reviewing his cover as an engineer for a London manufacturing concern, briefly reporting on his contacts with certain members of the Belgian and German engineering societies – his real reason for travelling to Germany – and finally explaining his accidental meeting with Wernher von Braun. He sought to impress upon Englesby the importance of the German scientist's position and summarised the details of Bethwig's cooling design for rocket motors. He kept it as simple as possible, sensing that Englesby would not understand the technical details, would in fact be put off by them.

Even before he finished, however, he realised he was wasting his time. Englesby sat staring at him over the pencil with which he had been playing.

'And you say the German government has given these two scientists all the money they need to develop rockets for use in war? Preposterous! I would certainly expect that you would realise when someone was exaggerating his own importance. Even Hitler and that crew would not waste time and money on such foolishness. Of what use would a giant rocket be? I dare say they do not even celebrate Guy Fawkes Day.' Englesby permitted himself the trace of a smile.

Memling ploughed on doggedly. 'To replace artillery and even bomber planes for long-range attacks. The importance of Bethwig's design is beyond belief. His development will lead to massive rockets that could bombard cities from long distances. Paris and perhaps even London itself.'

'London!'

'Yes, sir. The importance of this discovery must not be underrated.' He knew that he was repeating himself but could not help it; he had to make Englesby understand. 'In a few years' – Memling had leaned forward to speak earnestly – 'using Bethwig's discovery, it will even be possible to build a rocket powerful enough to travel to the moon. You see . . .'

This was too much for the civil servant in Englesby, and he threw down the pencil. 'Enough of this nonsense. Next you'll be asking me to believe in fairy castles and death rays. I don't know whether or not you made up this ridiculous tale to cover your mistakes, but I intend to find out. You have, in any event, disgraced the service and yourself by botching your first assignment, which, I may say here and now, I had great misgivings in allowing you to attempt. I do not believe you are suited for this type of work, and you have proven me correct. The minister is displeased, and I dare say the Prime Minister will be livid.

'Appropriate disciplinary action will have to be taken, but until then you are on ten days' leave of absence. Before you go, write out a complete report of your activities from the moment you left Dover. Do you understand?'

When Memling nodded, he pushed a button under his desk and the door opened silently. 'Please show Memling here to the writing-room, Peters,' Englesby snapped, not bothering to look up.

It was a long drive from Arnsberg to Berlin, and it was quite late when Bethwig wheeled his Lancia into the deserted car park. The thin drizzle that had accompanied them since midmorning had increased as they neared the city until it was a steady downpour slashing at the buildings of the Heersversuchsstelle Kummersdorf (the Army Research Centre at Kummersdorf) in the southern suburbs of Berlin. Wind rushed through the pines surrounding the Centre and sprayed sheets of water from the immense puddles that had gathered on the metalled surface. They snatched their bags from the boot and ran for the administration building where, in spite of the late hour, a lamp was burning in the office of the superior, Colonel Walter Dornberger. The door was open, and Dornberger entertaining a guest, but he waved them in.

'Ah, there you are. I was beginning to think you might not arrive tonight in this rain. Come in, come in!'

Dornberger's expression seemed to harden a bit as he turned to his guest. 'Allow me to introduce Herr Doktors Wernher von Braun and Franz Bethwig. Their work has been invaluable to the programme. Gentlemen, may I present Captain Jacob Walsch.'

Walsch unfolded his gaunt body just far enough to extend a hand, which Bethwig clasped with reluctance.

'Pleased, gentlemen.' His voice was quite resonant, in contrast to his appearance. The ceiling lamps served to deepen the hollows beneath his cheeks and eyes.

'Well, and what have you to tell me?' Dornberger's voice was eager. He motioned them to chairs and produced glasses and a bottle of cognac from his desk. He held the bottle up to the light with satisfaction. 'A gift from Colonel General Brautisch.' He accented the name and title just the slightest bit and glanced covertly at Walsch, Bethwig noticed, before he poured.

'Your wire arrived this morning and, of course, I have been waiting impatiently for details.'

Von Braun started to speak, then hesitated and glanced at Walsch. Dornberger nodded.

'You may speak freely before Captain Walsch.'

Von Braun then began the recital of the events of the past two weeks, and Bethwig sank down in the comfortable chair to nurse his cognac. He eyed Walsch, wondering just who he was. *Hauptmann*, Dornberger had called him. The title captain implied a military connection, but the man was not wearing a uniform and did not look like military material. As von Braun talked on, Bethwig gradually became aware that although Walsch was listening politely, there was no comprehension in the man's expression. So then he was not an engineering or an artillery officer. One could also eliminate the Luftwaffe, as air force officers would certainly be familiar with enough technical terms at least to follow what von Braun was saying.

Wernher talked for nearly fifteen minutes, interrupted occasionally by his superior's exclamations of delight. And each time this happened, the captain transferred his measuring stare to Dornberger for a moment, before returning to von Braun.

Von Braun suddenly leaned over and clapped his friend's arm, startling him. Bethwig had been so engrossed in watching the strange captain that he had lost track of what was being said.

'So I would say that Franz here was completely correct, as usual.'

Dornberger jumped up to shake his hand. 'By God, Franz, I don't know what I would do without the two of you!' He slapped a fist into the palm of his other hand. 'This may well solve the last major technical problem. Now we can proceed with the A-Three design.'

'A-Three?' Walsch murmured. 'I do not . . .'

'Our first large rocket,' von Braun explained, his voice eager. 'You see, we have not been able to build a rocket motor that was powerful enough or would last long enough to raise a really big rocket vehicle. But with Franz's development we could build one large enough to travel to the moon if we wanted to!'

'Ah.' Walsch nodded and turned back to Dornberger as if von Braun's statement was of no consequence.

'You see, Captain,' Dornberger said, glancing uneasily at Bethwig, 'I told you these two are the most valuable on my staff. I had word yesterday that General Werner Fritsch, the army commander, will attend a rocket firing demonstration when we are ready. That means that we will probably be allowed to proceed to full-scale development shortly.'

Bethwig exchanged a puzzled glance with von Braun. It was not like Dornberger to gush so, and to a total stranger.

'Perhaps the general will reconsider when he discovers that two of his most valuable scientists cannot be trusted to control their tongues.'

Bethwig looked around so sharply that cognac spilled from his glass. 'Captain,' he said slowly, frowning as if the word left a bad taste in his mouth. 'Captain of what, may I enquire?'

Walsch favoured him with the ghost of a smile. 'Certainly. I am with the Secret State Police Office, Division Three.'

'Gestapo,' von Braun exploded. 'What have we to do with such people?' he appealed to Dornberger.

The scientist had jumped to his feet and now advanced on

Walsch who snapped, 'Sit down, young man. You are in serious trouble.'

Von Braun stopped short, face flushed, breathing heavily. He towered over the Gestapo agent who stared grimly back. 'Trouble? How could I be in trouble with . . . you?'

'Division Three is, if I recall correctly, counterespionage, is it not?'

Walsch nodded in reply to Bethwig's question.

'And how should that concern Wernher and me? Surely you do not suspect us of being foreign spies?'

The Gestapo officer gave him a sour look and took a small notebook from his jacket. He thumbed through it deliberately until he found the proper page, then shifted to a more comfortable position and began to read aloud.

'Your full name is Franz Hans Bethwig. You were born in Hamburg, 8 January 1909. Your father is a well-known banker and has been a party member since 1923. You yourself were enrolled in that same year. You were graduated from the Berlin Technical Institute in 1934 and have been employed since then by the Army Research Centre. So you are surely aware of the danger to the fatherland, surrounded as we are by enemies. Yet you deliberately chose to betray Germany.' Walsch uttered the last sentence without inflection. Dornberger, obviously unaware of the exact nature of the charges, goggled at the man. Bethwig laughed. He was thoroughly familiar with Walsch's tactics.

The Gestapo agent was taken aback but only for a moment. He shot forward in his chair and pointed a finger. 'You have betrayed Germany by speaking of classified military matters to an agent of a foreign power last evening in Arnsberg!'

At that, von Braun joined Bethwig in laughter. 'Is that all, Captain? Then you are quite mistaken. The young man with whom we dined last night is an old friend and also a rocket enthusiast. He is a member of the British Inter – '

'You fool!' Walsch shouted. 'We know exactly who this Jan Memling is. He is a member of the English secret intelligence service. He was sent to Germany to spy on our scientific progress. He is a scientist who was trained specifically for this task.'

Von Braun stared at Walsch in consternation. 'No, you must be wrong. How . . .'

'I assure you, Herr Doktor, we are rarely wrong. I myself followed this man on to the train at Aachen. Just before the frontier he was warned by an accomplice and jumped from the carriage. He crossed the border illegally before we were able to apprehend him. Several arrests have been made among the passengers, and we will know more shortly.

'There are two questions' – Walsch scowled at them – 'which you are required to answer. First, how much of what you told this man concerns classified military secrets? And was it done deliberately?'

This was too much for Dornberger. 'Captain Walsch,' he roared, 'you forget yourself. I protest these unwarranted accusations. I have known these men – '

The Gestapo agent waved a weary hand. 'Colonel, I am very tired. I was forced to fly through this miserable weather to Berlin to speak with these two . . . gentlemen. I would rather do so here than at my headquarters. However, if you persist in interfering with my investigation, I shall have no choice but to summon assistance.'

'I can assure you, Captain,' Bethwig said evenly, 'that not only did we not have the slightest inkling that this man was a spy, as you claim, but we did not pass on anything of military significance. I would, however, like to know why, if you were aware of his identity at the time, you did not intervene? It would seem that if there are questions to be answered, you have your share to contend with. For instance, the matter of the man escaping from the train? I would suggest not only that you make certain of your facts but that you be sure of the grounds on which you raise this ridiculous story to cover your own incompetence. Otherwise, you may find a lawsuit, or worse, lodged against you personally and your superiors as well.'

Walsch returned his confident smile. 'Young man, by law the Gestapo is immune to civil proceedings. You would do well to curb your own tongue. I am aware of your father's position in the party, and it does not deter me in the least. Do I make myself understood?'

Bethwig stood and bowed stiffly. 'Completely, sir. We shall, however, have to wait for another time to see how this all turns out.' He turned to a worried Dornberger. 'Good night, Colonel.'

Memling fumbled his key into the lock and entered. Although the walk from the bus was less than two blocks, he was chilled through. The parlour was cold, but coal was piled on the grate, and the house was spotless. The newspaper and magazines he had left beside the chair were now in the rack, and his sweater, he saw when he opened the cupboard to hang up his overcoat, had been washed. So, Margot had looked in while he was gone. Smiling, he slipped it on and stooped to touch a match to the shredded newspaper under the kindling. The fire caught immediately, and he adjusted the draught. While he waited for the fire to warm the room, he lit the kitchen gas ring and put a kettle on.

The clock showed five-thirty. He had spent most of the day in the writing-room completing his report, and he was too tired to be hungry. The small piece of ham and the cheese, which he found in the pantry, dry as they were, were sufficient. The kettle began to whistle, and he fixed a cup of tea and took the ham and cheese back to the parlour.

As he stood before the fire he glanced at the gleaming walnut and shining blue metal of the over-and-under-twelve-bore shotgun which his father had made. The old man had been well known for his fine shotguns, much good that it had done him. The old, dingy house was his only legacy, that and the gun and his own skills at making firearms.

The room was warming quickly, and Memling pulled the chair up to the fire and sank down, weary beyond belief. A black mood that he could not shake had settled over him. 'What the hell have I done?' he muttered aloud. His main assignment had been carried out satisfactorily. In addition, he had brought back information about a possible new military weapon, *and* he had escaped from the Gestapo, using all the skills that he had been taught. Another agent would have been welcomed home with the certainty of a CBE in the not too distant future. Instead, he had been accused of damaging relations with Germany. Nonsense, he snorted. But even so, his actions were to be submitted to the scrutiny of an enquiry board, which would surely support Englesby.

And Memling knew why it had turned out the way it had. He was not a gentleman, moneyed or well connected, all of which were prime requisites for a successful Foreign Office career. What's more, he had a foreign sounding name and lacked the educational essentials provided by a good school and university. In fact, he lacked a degree of any kind. A month after his father's business had failed, the old man had shot himself with one of his own shotguns. Memling had often wondered since then if he and his mother could have managed on the small pension. Had he again given in too easily, frightened by future unknowns?

Along with his hopes for a degree, he gave up his activities in the British Interplanetary Society. No more than a few amateur scientists were scattered among the usual collection of astrology buffs, fantasists, and spiritualists attracted by the grandiose name, but those few were dedicated to a dream, an overpowering vision of man's future in the vast reaches of the universe. Memling was gathered in during his first year at college. His scientific training stood him and the society in good stead but did not inhibit his dreams of space, the frozen, sun-blasted lunar plains, the wonders of multistar planetary systems, or the heights to which man might aspire once freed from the green but confining hills of Earth. Until his father died, every moment and penny Memling could spare were dedicated to one or another of the BIS projects. Then the demands of his mother's failing health and a succession of part-time jobs cut short these activities, and he was left with only the pages of science-fiction magazines to sustain his dreams.

One of his father's oldest customers was Admiral Sir Hugh Sinclair. After the old man's death, the admiral visited the house to express his sympathies and, on leaving, pressed a card into Jan's hand and urged him to call at his club. It was a month or better before he screwed up sufficient courage to do so. His reception was exactly as expected; ignored by the members and treated with disdain by the servants, he was on the verge of leaving when Sir Hugh appeared. He led Jan into a private parlour and opened to him a new vista that he had never imagined to exist outside the novels of Somerset Maugham and Joseph Conrad.

'I have asked you to come and talk with me so that you can consider whether or not you would be willing to serve your country.'

'I beg your pardon, sir?' Jan was completely confused.

The admiral smiled. 'I have just begun the direction of a certain department in the government that has to do with intelligence matters. The old-fashioned word is spying. I would like you to join that department.'

'Become a . . . a . . . spy?' He brushed a hand across his forehead, an old gesture signifying his confusion. 'I don't know anything about being a spy.'

The admiral shrugged. 'Neither do I. Perhaps we could learn together.'

'But why me, sir? I don't see that I have any qualifications . . .'

The admiral held up a hand. 'My boy, the days when individuals might ferret out the secrets of a mighty nation as did Davies and Carruthers are fast coming to an end. Today spying, a distasteful but accurate term, is a huge business and takes a good many people to make it go. Now, you take our own spies, of which, I might add, there are more than a few. For the most part they are professional enough. My predecessor saw to that. But since 1918 we've tended to go a bit slack. You have a technical education. If ever we must fight another war, that kind of background will be invaluable. Great Britain requires something more than adventurers and titled younger sons. You speak Flemish and French like a native, and I am certain you can improve your German. I was a good customer and, I like to think, friend of your father's, and so I had a chance to watch you develop over the years. I have a feeling you will do a creditable job on His Majesty's Service.'

And Jan Memling, thus rescued from a dreary succession of menial posts, began his training two weeks later. He had skills the admiral wanted, but apparently no one else did. When Sinclair died the following year, a new man, Stewart Graham Menzies, also an outsider but of another kind, took the unofficial title of 'C'. If he was aware of Memling's problems, he was far too busy fighting his own battle against the 'old boys' to do anything about them.

The service was prepared to tolerate Menzies – and to a lesser extent, people like Memling – as long as they remained quietly out of sight. He should have realised, he thought with bitterness, that he would never persuade Englesby. And by mentioning space travel and moon rockets, he had given him just the excuse he needed to justify dismissing everything Memling had to say as too fantastic to be believed. He clenched his fists in a spasm of involuntary embarrassment at the memory. How in the name of God had he expected Englesby of all people to understand the promise of space travel?

Memling must have fallen asleep because he woke with a start when the front door closed. Footsteps sounded in the bare hall, and he turned to see Margot standing in the doorway, a frightened look on her face.

'Oh, Jan! You gave me a start. I didn't know you were back.' Margot sighed in relief, took off her coat, and flung it over a chair. She was a tall, lithe girl of twenty-three with soft brown hair, a fair English face, and a figure that reminded Memling of the Wyeth illustration of Maid Marion. She was wearing an old but neatly-pressed wool skirt, a sweater, and sensible shoes. The sight of her caused the breath to catch in Memling's throat.

'It's so cold in here. You've let the fire go out,' she reproached him, but with a smile and a kiss. Then she knelt and placed several lumps on the grate and blew up the embers with the old leather bellows until bluish flames were licking the undersides of the coals.

'You're back,' she repeated fondly. 'Have you had anything to eat?' When he nodded, she shook her head. 'It couldn't have been much. There was only a bit of ham and some cheese.'

Memling was comfortably warm and relaxed, and to have her in the house made everything complete. The Westminster clock on the mantelpiece chimed seven, and he found he had not the slightest inclination to move. Margot went into the kitchen, and he could hear her filling the kettle. She was back in a few minutes with a tray, which she placed beside him. The light scent she wore drifted about the room, and he caught her hand and pressed it to his lips.

'Tea and biscuits,' she said archly, disengaging her hand. 'And I must leave in a few moments. Mum thinks I've just popped across to check the gas.' She drew up a cushion and perched before the fire to pour his tea. 'Tell me about your trip. Was Manchester cold and snowy?'

With a start, he was aware again of the necessary gap between them. So much had happened in the past two weeks that she could never know. Memling sipped his tea before answering.

'A bit of both,' he replied, hoping the indefinite answer would serve. 'Very depressing this time of year.'

'At any time of the year, I should think.'

He smiled again and took the biscuit she offered. 'My luggage was lost somewhere along the line. I brought you a gift but it was in my suitcase. I'm to call at Euston tomorrow to see if it has been located.'

'What a bother, but I suppose I must wait. Did you learn anything that will be of any use in your position?'

Memling hesitated before answering. He and Margot had grown up together in adjoining houses. When they were younger, his father had even installed a small gate for them in the fence separating the two gardens. There had always been the understanding they would marry some day, and he had been more than content to accept it as so. Margot was a very attractive and intelligent young woman, and he felt they would be very happy, but lately she had shown a tendency to push. Gently of course, as she did everything. But at times like this he wondered if the tendency might not intensify after they were married. And he wondered how she would react when he finally told her what he really did for a living. As far as she knew, he had just been promoted from the quality control department of a small electrical appliance manufacturing concern. They had given him that cover, he reflected bitterly, as he did not have sufficient polish for the Foreign Office, the usual sinecure for MI6 personnel.

'I doubt it,' he answered truthfully enough. 'Anyway, as things are slow, they've given me a fortnight's leave.'

Margot sat up suddenly, alarmed. 'With pay, I hope?' Both were all too familiar with the implications of a sudden leave without pay in these times.

He nodded, chuckling at her expression. 'I've told you often enough, I'm much too valuable an employee for them to do without.' At least part of that was true, he thought. Once taken into the fold, you were with them for ever. No one ever quit or was dismissed; in extreme cases, you would be shuttled into a safe job somewhere in one of the ministries where you could be watched.

'You work long enough hours, at any rate.' But her expression was still troubled.

The clock struck the half-hour, and Margot stood up reluctantly. 'I'd better go. Mum will be expecting her cup of tea and a read before bedtime. You know how cranky she gets if anything disturbs her routine.'

Memling helped her into her coat and, as she reached for the latch, took her hand and pulled her to him. 'I'll wait outside the store tomorrow evening and walk you home, all right?'

Margot nodded, smiling, then threw her arms around him with sudden passion. He pressed her body to his, holding her, experiencing the all-too-familiar ache. They had waited so damned long. She crushed her mouth to his for a long moment, then pushed away shakily. 'I'm so glad you're back,' she whispered. 'Things go so much better.'

Memling knew Margot was referring to her mother, a bedridden arthritic who would try – deliberately – the patience of a saint. They would have been married three years ago if it hadn't been for the old woman.

Margot gave him a quick, final kiss and ran lightly down the path as he remained in the shadows. The block of semi-detacheds was full of elderly gossips, and Mrs Cummings's only remaining delight was the long whispered conversations with her cronies. If the gossip concerned her daughter, Margot's life became a hell for days. Thinking of the predatory presence propped up in the front room next door, waiting for her daughter's return, he found it hard to reconcile the nasty old crone with his memory of the sweet-voiced, plump, and laughing woman who used to serve them biscuits and cocoa when they were children.

Germany August 1939

The Baltic island of Greifswalder Oie was a scorched speck in the placid sea. Shimmers of heat rose amidst the gaunt concrete structures scattered throughout the pine forest. Roads snaked among the sprawl of buildings, disappeared into the forest, and reappeared along the coast, all leading to a single open space one hundred metres in diameter overlooking the beach. Several sandbagged bunkers delineated its landward periphery, and set squarely into the middle of the clearing was a sheet-metal tower now tipped to one side. A squat, pencil-shaped rocket painted yellow and red stood beside it on a metal table.

A loudspeaker spewed instructions, its iron voice bouncing across the island to the sea. Overhead a small aircraft flew in monotonous circles at a thousand metres.

Two lines of folding chairs had been set out beside an elaborate silver bowl from which a uniformed Luftwaffe mess attendant ladled well-laced punch into crystal cups for the various dignitaries. From where he was standing beside his instrument panel, Franz Bethwig could hear their conversation only as a meaningless buzz, clarified now and then when a breeze whispered past. Colonel General Hermann Goering, commander in chief of the Luftwaffe, a corpulent figure in tailored uniform, was surrounded by sycophants. He had already greeted Bethwig profusely, more to demonstrate that he was a hail-fellow-well-met than to show respect for Franz's father.

The A-5 rocket squatting on its launch table in the centre of the cleared circle would be the vindication of his hard-fought theory, the deciding factor in his continuing arguments with Walter Tuchman, the stubborn old scientist who disregarded all ideas but his own, who alienated everyone who worked for him, yet who was undeniably a genius. Tuchman maintained that Bethwig's cooling system would so weaken the combustion chamber walls that they would burst long before full power was achieved.

Bethwig, improving on his original idea, had designed a series of injectors mounted in the inner wall of the combustion chamber. Where originally the fuel had been sprayed in, it was now forced through the ports under just enough pressure to form a thin film along the chamber walls. To test his theory under actual flight conditions, he had installed a series of pyrometers inside the motor. Dr Tuchman had refused him more than a single radio channel, and he had been forced to wire each pyrometer in series, hoping to obtain useful data by means of a small integrator he had designed and built to average the temperature readings and transmit them through the Siemens radio control equipment. He finished his work, noted the results, climbed out of the bunker, and walked across to the shade of a service lorry. Across the way, he could see the technicians removing the tarpaulin from the bunker housing one of the three cinetheodolite cameras, which would photograph the rocket during flight. A patrol launch idled across the bay, and the sun continued to pour down.

A plume of vapour twisted above the fuel bowser, and the liquid-oxygen hose snaking up to a valve in the side of the A-5 glinted with frost crystals. On the other side of the test area a door in the main bunker opened. Bethwig shaded his eyes and saw Wernher von Braun turn to speak to someone inside, then hold up an instrument to measure the inclination of the rocket on its launch table. Von Braun saw him and waved. The loudspeaker's hum increased abruptly, crackled, and announced five minutes to firing.

A green flare arched over the test site to warn the aircraft and patrol launches to take stations. Bethwig walked back to the bunker for a last check of his instruments.

A hand descended on his shoulder, and he turned to see the bloated face of Goering peering at him.

'The scientist at work. Gentlemen, see how the Reich's young men are so totally engaged. Not like those foolish children in England and France who protest and march for pacifism. Come, Franz, can you not spare a moment to describe your work?'

With difficulty Bethwig refrained from shrugging off the pudgy hand. He tried to explain his experiment, but the combination of heat and champagne punch had glazed the Luftwaffe commander's eyes. An aide stepped in to divert Goering's attention, and Bethwig, scanning his dials, cursed the lost seconds under his breath. The radio transmitter signal was strong, showing a temperature reading near normal. The sensors attached to the combustion chamber walls were on-line, and the integrator seemed to be working properly.

A lorry engine racketed to life as a technician stripped the shroud from the rocket's nose and descended the ladder. The lorry drove towards the gap in the high concrete wall, leaving the launch area clear. Two minutes to launch.

The fuselage was captured in a sheath of glistening ice crystals as the minus-two-hundred-degree-centigrade liquid oxygen sucked moisture from the humid air. A thin plume of vapour shot from a vent half-way up the rocket's side to signal that the oxidiser tank had reached full pressure. The red flare indicating an imminent launch arched up from the control bunker. At minus twenty seconds the merest wisp of vapour appeared beneath the rocket, and a collective sigh of relief went up from the technicians in the bunker. Bethwig heard Dornberger explaining to Goering that the vapour had been vented through the fuel feed system to make certain that everything was operating properly and that no valves were stuck.

At minus ten seconds sparks showered from the nozzle as the pyrotechnic igniter went off. A gout of reddish-black flame belched from the rocket's base, steadied, faded to yellow, and a sound like a giant blowtorch gone mad swept the island. The flame turned an incandescent white impossible to watch without protective glasses, and clouds of smoke and dust sprang up to obscure the rocket. For a moment, only its nose was visible, and then, like some prehistoric monster rearing slowly above a primeval fog, the A-5 appeared. Bethwig could see it turn slowly on its axis as its fins cleared the smoke. It tilted slightly and was gone, a fast-dwindling dot of flame directly overhead.

Silence held the launch site for a moment, then cheers and shouts erupted. Bethwig turned to see the officers gathered about Goering pointing upwards, shading their eyes against the sun, all talking at once. His instrument panel was registering perfectly, and the whir of the cinecamera focused on the gauges surprised him. In the excitement he had not recalled having turned it on. The temperature gauge was holding steady at 2902° centigrade, five degrees below his prediction. Satisfied, he turned his glance upward and, after a moment of practised search, found the white dot now moving slightly to the east.

'Thirty-five seconds,' blared the loudspeaker.

Even through his powerful Zeiss binoculars Bethwig could not resolve the pencil-shaped A-5 completely. This was far better than they had hoped, and he glanced quickly at his instruments again. No change.

'Forty-five seconds,' and a moment later, '*Brennschluss*, end of combustion.' The white dot disappeared.

'Rocket motor burning time was forty-six seconds,' the loudspeaker intoned, 'and altitude at burnout was eight point one kilometres.'

Through the glasses Bethwig watched as the rocket continued to climb under the momentum imparted by the engine until the shape elongated and he knew it had reached its peak altitude. At any second von Braun would press the button that would send a radio signal to deploy the parachute. The rocket was tumbling now, and sunlight flashed from the alternating squares of red and yellow painted on the fuselage. Abruptly the tumbling stopped. He could make out a hazy stream behind and the main parachute deployed in a perfectly-shaped canopy.

The missile hung quiescent in the shrouds, and the air was so still, Bethwig could follow its descent until foreshortened trees appeared in his binoculars and the rocket splashed into the Baltic. There was a puff of yellow smoke as the explosive charge cut away the parachute, and the A-5 bobbed, stern up, like a child's bath toy The patrol launch described a sharp turn and raced across the harbour.

For a moment Bethwig remained standing on the lip of the bunker, glasses pressed against his eyes, wanting to impress the picture on his mind: the colourful rocket, paint bright against the intense blue sea, gleaming wakes, the tiny Storch aircraft swooping low over the tilted gnomon surrounded by the creamy parachute. There had been dozens of launchings, and hundreds were yet to come, but none, he knew, would ever be as important, or as perfect, as this.

Colonel General Hermann Goering had departed as darkness crept in over the Baltic. The evening brought cooling breezes that were gratefully received, and Dornberger ordered supper served on the roof of the canteen, overlooking the tiny harbour.

Bethwig had noticed the man earlier, standing a bit apart from the officials and officers fawning about Goering. He was of medium height, balding, and he wore a simple but expensive summer suit. His eyes missed nothing, Bethwig thought. He arrived shortly after Goering's plane had landed, and Dornberger hurriedly introduced him as Albert Speer, mentioning something about a post as Hitler's personal architect. How did one go about becoming a personal architect? he wondered. Yet Dornberger had seated Speer on his left, a position that would have been given to Goering had he remained.

Bethwig and von Braun were seated further along the table, but several times during the meal Speer leaned forward to ask them questions. Each time, others engaged in conversations of their own stopped to listen.

'Colonel Dornberger tells me,' Speer said to Bethwig as the waiters removed the last course, 'that today's test flight of the A-Five rocket vindicated one of your developments.'

Bethwig coughed to hide his embarrassment and stole a glance at Tuchman. The old man was watching Speer and Dornberger in tight-lipped silence.

'Come now, young man, no modesty please,' Speer prompted.

'Well, yes, the test flight did bear out a few of my thoughts.'

'I would like to hear about them.'

Bethwig appealed silently to Dornberger, who chose to misinterpret the glance. 'You may speak freely, Franz. Herr Speer has the highest clearances.'

'Was it the graphite vanes?' Speer asked.

'Ah . . . no, sir. We knew they would work.' Bethwig was surprised that Speer knew that much.

Speer laughed at his expression. 'You were correct, Colonel. Herr Doktor Bethwig is a modest young man. He reduces the cost of the vanes from one hundred fifty to one point five marks and claims to have known it would work all along.'

Dornberger grinned at Bethwig who was now flaming red. Von Braun chuckled, nudging him with an elbow as Tuchman stalked away from the table without an apology. Under prompting by Dornberger and von Braun, Bethwig explained the film cooling system, and Speer listened closely, asking occasional questions.

The military officers and civilian officials invited to watch the launching filtered to the far end of the table as the talk became increasingly technical, and the scientific staff gathered about the head. Bethwig thought it strange that Speer, who for all his interest seemed a lightweight in scientific matters, should prefer to indulge in what must have been a boring discussion of velocities, specific impulses, radio telemetry techniques, and a myriad other engineering concerns.

When he finished, Speer turned to Dornberger. 'I understand, Colonel, that another purpose of today's launching was to test a guidance system?'

Dornberger nodded and folded his napkin. 'Our A-Three rocket was cursed with the problem of maintaining directional stability. The rocket would turn on its axis during powered flight, thus making it impossible to keep a proper course. At first we thought this a result of wind acting upon the fins, but wind-tunnel tests disproved that. It was due rather to fluctuations in the exhaust stream. To correct the problem, Wernher developed a gyroscope system that controls the movement of the vanes in the exhaust stream. Now, when the rocket begins to veer, the gyroscopically controlled vanes bring it right back by bending the exhaust in the opposite direction.'

'I see. Exactly how does the system work?' Speer asked.

Dornberger began to sketch on a napkin. 'It is really quite

similar to a child's top spinning inside a metal cage. Like a top, it always remains upright, no matter which way the surface on which it is mounted tilts. To take advantage of this natural phenomenon, a metal rod fixed to the rocket is passed through the top's centre. A series of electrical switches are placed along the rod, and as the rocket begins to veer off course the rod turns with it, thus touching the top and closing a switch, which sends an electrical impulse to the motor controlling the graphite vanes extending into the rocket's exhaust. The rocket is thus turned back on its proper course.'

'My congratulations, Herr Doktor.' Speer rose and bowed to von Braun.

Von Braun laughed and shook his head. 'Thank you, Herr Speer, but the credit goes to spy work, not to us.'

'Spy work?'

The others at the table groaned. It was an inside joke that had grown hoary with age but always drew the expected reaction from outsiders.

'Yes, the system was developed by an American named Robert H. Goddard who developed the first liquid-fuelled rocket in 1923 and is now working with a small grant from the American government somewhere in their western states. Dr Goddard published a paper in 1937 which was ignored by nearly everyone in the world, including the Americans. But one of our embassy employees in Washington obtained a copy from the Library of Congress and sent it on to the Army Weapons Development Centre at Kummersdorf on the chance that it would be of value. Dr Goddard was actually the first to use vanes in the exhaust stream to control flight, and I would say that his work has saved us at least three years. Fortunately for us, his own people have ignored him entirely.'

The rowdier members of the party had begun to stagger off to bed, and the table grew quiet. A soft breeze blew landward, drawing its cooling breath across the parched island. Speer asked a few more questions about technical problems, then leaned back in his chair and regarded Dornberger for a moment.

'Where will you go from here?'

'To the A-Four,' Dornberger replied without hesitation.

'A-Four? I must admit that I was curious as to what intervened between the old A-Three and today's A-Five.'

'The A-Four is a very ambitious step forward and has been our objective all along,' von Braun told him. 'We did not realise just how ambitious until we were rather far along in its design. We saw very early that we needed a great deal more information than we possessed or could ever hope to gain from the A-Three. So, we dropped it and designed the A-Five as our test vehicle.'

'Wait just a moment.' Speer clutched his head in mock despair. 'You are making me dizzy with so many numbers. Tell me, just what do you intend the A-Four to do?'

All eyes turned to Colonel Dornberger. 'It will carry a thousand-kilogram high explosive warhead three hundred kilometres.'

An artillery officer, who had remained, whistled in amazement. 'What do you intend its accuracy should be?'

'Plus or minus two kilometres. And,' Dornberger added, 'we hope to improve that to within half a kilometre.'

The officer calculated the range in relation to impact deviation on his slide rule and shook his head. 'Impossible,' he said flatly.

'I do not understand the technical details of artillery ballistics,' Speer murmured, ignoring the officer, 'but even I can recognise the value of such a weapon. How long would it take to produce one operational by troops under field conditions?'

'That depends upon the priorities and budget restrictions under which we would have to operate. And of course, approval from the chancellory. The Führer visited us early this year at Kummersdorf and seemed not in the least impressed with our rockets.'

Speer only murmured a noncommittal response to Dornberger's probe, and during the long silence that followed they could hear the gentle slap of waves on the sand.

An hour later Franz Bethwig and Wernher von Braun walked along the beach as they often did before retiring. Usually they reviewed the day's events, discussed new ideas, or speculated idly about the future of rocketry. Tonight von Braun was quiet, resisting Bethwig's attempts to draw him into conversation. Finally, in exasperation, Franz swore at him.

Von Braun grunted and shoved his hands deeper into his pockets. 'I have a feeling that everything is about to change, and I don't know if for better or worse. It seems to me that today we took the first real step towards space. The A-Five performed beautifully under control. We've proven what we knew all along, and now we have only to build ever bigger versions until we are there.' He waved a hand vaguely at the sky and shook his head in exasperation. 'But I . . . I just have a feeling that we are being sidetracked. Walter talks only about war rockets, and this Speer character agrees with him. Did you see how they all listened whenever he said anything? I don't want to waste time building war rockets. Let the army find someone else to do that. We've shown them how.'

'Don't forget' – Bethwig grinned – 'you are in the army, my friend. Or at least paid by them, which amounts to the same thing.'

'Don't remind me.'

'Why not? So far you've just wasted a great deal of energy kicking against the inevitable. You know as well as I why the army wants rockets. Goering was here today to see how much of a threat they might be to his precious bombers. I have a feeling this Speer is more than he seems; in fact, I suspect he was sent to keep an eye on Goering. Who knows what's going on in Berlin these days? Even my father has gotten to be quite vague about it. But whatever, our salary is paid by the army, and if they tell us to build war rockets, I don't see that we have any other choice. Do you?'

'I guess not,' von Braun mumbled.

The moon was nearly full and hung in mid-sky, a silver beacon strong enough to light the beach. Franz stared at it, trying to imagine as he had done a thousand times since childhood what it would be like to walk across its surface. It was not only that barren desert of frozen, airless stone that drew him, but rather the promise of what was to follow. The moon and the various planets of the solar system were only the beginning. There was a universe beyond to be explored and bent to man's will. Mankind needed something greater than itself to challenge, if for no other reason than to refocus selfish thoughts and petty concerns. Space travel offered the ultimate goal, stars in their billions with unlimited room for the race to grow and expand.

Bethwig and von Braun shared that dream, had done so since the early days of the Verein für Raumschiffahrt (Society for Space Travel), a small group of dedicated amateurs with a common goal: the realisation of space travel. The VfR was formed in 1929, and in the ensuing months he and von Braun had forged an uneasy alliance – this despite his own shyness and von Braun's unconscious arrogance – as they were two of the very few members with sufficient private resources to allow them to devote endless hours to society projects.

Their friendship had grown, and when the Gestapo disbanded the society in 1932 and the army seduced von Braun in return for a university degree and a well-paying job building rockets, it was Bethwig he had hired first. Franz still remembered the excited telephone call, could still hear von Braun shouting over the static: 'I tell you, they will actually pay us to build rockets!'

Bethwig broke the silence. 'I talked with an army officer this morning. He told me that troops are gathering along the Polish border and have been doing so for weeks now. He thinks we'll attack Poland before summer is out. If that's true, we could be at war with England and France within a few months. And if that happens, the Reich will need war rockets, as many as we can build, and the fatherland will not be able to afford the cost of building a moon rocket. At least not for a good many years.'

Von Braun went on a few more steps. The night was growing cool, and they both shivered when a vagrant wind slid landward.

'Perhaps you're right,' he murmured. 'I don't know. How can you believe anything they tell us? You would think we were surrounded by bloodthirsty enemies just waiting to destroy Germany for ever. First it was the Czechs and now the Poles. Who'll be next? The French, the Russians, the British?'

'But, they *are* waiting to destroy us,' Bethwig protested. 'Didn't they try in 1919 and almost succeed? We were sold out then, but there were still enough loyal Germans to resist total destruction. Then they tried to destroy our economy by insisting on unjust war reparations. And now the Jewish merchants and bankers have joined with the capitalists to urge the slavic nations to attack our blood-German people held prisoner within their borders. Only, we will fool them. The Führer has seen to it that Germany is much stronger than they expect. I tell you, Wernher, the coming war means the life or death of Germany, and to win it we will need war rockets.'

'Damn it, Franz, you sound like one of those radio propagandists.' Von Braun turned away, plainly anxious not to be drawn into another political argument. 'I . . . of course, you're right' – he relented 'but still, it seems such a waste of time and energy.'

'Not really.' Franz grabbed his arm and brought him to a stop. 'If we go about it correctly, we can turn it to our advantage.'

'Is that so? How?' Von Braun was teasing now, but Franz remained serious.

'If war comes, it is certain that England and France will be drawn in by virtue of their alliance with Poland. Unless we can defeat them immediately, the war will go on, and ultimately the United States must be drawn in. Her sympathies have always lain with England and against us. Everyone in Berlin says that Hitler is frightened of the United States becoming involved again and is determined the mistakes of the last war will not be repeated. But even so, it is almost certain the Americans . . .'

'Franz, get to the point. Politics give me a headache.'

'Just a moment, Wernher, it is important to follow the reasoning. War has become a matter of who can produce the most and best weapons and maintain adequate supply lines. English and French industries are exposed to our bomber aircraft, American factories are not. If we are to fight America, we must destroy her industrial capacity – you've heard Dornberger and others say that a hundred times. Now, if our rockets had a transatlantic capacity . . .' He let the thought trail off.

Von Braun shook his head. 'A range of up to six thousand miles would be needed. The guidance problem alone is almost insurmountable. You know we are a long way from there.'

Bethwig knelt and drew two circles in the sand, one large, the other a metre away and smaller. The moonlight was so bright that von Braun had no trouble seeing as Bethwig wrote their Latin names beneath each circle: *terra, luna*. He then drew a curving line to connect the two.

'This is the ballistic trajectory of a rocket flying to the moon. We are agreed there is no way to carry sufficient fuel for powered flight the entire distance, so the rocket will coast under its own momentum once it enters space.' He drew a deep breath.

'The main difficulty will be in climbing out of Earth's gravity well. Once out, as long as sufficient velocity is achieved – on the order of eleven point two kilometres per second – the rocket will be pulled by the moon's gravitational attraction towards itself.' He reinforced the curving line with a finger. 'In short, as long as proper velocity is achieved, there is no way the rocket can miss the moon. Agreed?'

'Of course. Why . . . ?'

Bethwig held up a hand for patience. 'Reverse the process.' And he described another, flatter curve from moon to Earth. 'The same laws of physics hold true. The flight will be faster, as Earth's gravitational pull is much stronger than the moon's. But the result is the same.'

'True, within reason . . .' von Braun began, but again Bethwig shushed him.

'You and I once calculated that a lunar rocket must carry at least a five-thousand-kilogram payload and have a total thrust equal to three million kilograms. Now, when you come right down to it, there is no need to separate the military and civilian aspects of space travel. The oldest military axiom in the world requires that you always hold the high ground. Therefore the objective is the same: to transport a human being to the moon.

'A speed of eleven point two kilometres per second is required to overcome Earth's gravity in order to reach the moon. But to escape from the moon requires only two point four kilometres per second. In short, we need only double the speed attained by the

A-Five. Tonight Dornberger described that rocket to Speer – the A-Four.'

Von Braun studied Bethwig's smug expression. 'I'll be damned,' he said slowly. 'Are you suggesting we fire rockets from the moon to Earth?' The thought took hold, and he exclaimed, 'Good God, Franz, that would be an invincible weapon, wouldn't it!'

'Exactly!' Bethwig shouted in triumph. 'Only the simplest of guidance controls would be required. The speed of such rockets could vary between two point four and eleven point two kilometres an hour, and we could still shower them on to an enemy nation. There would be no way to stop them. And in two years, if all goes well, the A-Four will be perfected. We need only build a more powerful version of the A-Four to take us there to begin with.' He hesitated only a moment. 'I've already assigned it a project code, A-Ten. Are you game?'

Von Braun shot his hands above his head and roared with delight. 'Of course. My God, think of it. The moon. We really can do it, Franz!' He wrapped his friend in a bear hug. 'You have the rationale for the moon landing programme. A weapon to end all weapons, perhaps even to end war! Think of it. Whoever controls the moon controls the Earth! Why, with our A-Ten the Reich could enforce a veritable Pax Germana!'

Bethwig untangled himself and brought von Braun's Indian dance to a halt. 'We will need someone to sponsor us,' he said in a quiet voice. 'Someone with stronger political connections than anyone in the army possesses.'

'Speer?'

'Perhaps. But we have to know more about him first. Does he have access to the Führer? Is he sufficiently high in the party? Such a project will be damned expensive and we will need someone very high up to back us.'

Von Braun grinned at that. 'Franz, for a chance like this I'd make a pact with the Devil.'

Occupied Belgium December 1940

The ruined citadel frowned over Liège. SS guards, rifles slung muzzle downwards to keep out the insistent rain, eyed the line shuffling towards the dirty brick building. Barbed wire was strung to a height of three metres, and red signs warned in Flemish, French and German that it was electrified. A young officer watched, his expression one of ill-disguised contempt. In spite of the cold wind and the rain, he appeared comfortable enough in his black leather overcoat and uniform cap.

Jan Memling had ridden his decrepit bicycle to the first checkpoint at the intersection of the rue Saint-Léonard and rue Marengo to join the throng moving towards the factory gates. The rain slanted down without respite, splattering cobbled streets, soaking threadbare coats and trousers, shoes and boots.

The officer looked his way, spoke to an aide, and Memling cursed silently. An SS officer's interest almost always led to deportation and labour service – slave labour. Deportation was the terror of Memling's life. Once he got to Germany, it would only be a matter of time before his identity was uncovered.

The aide went to the sergeant supervising the checkpoint guards and spoke to him, again glancing in Memling's direction. Jan clutched the bicycle as his fear grew; he was helpless, there was absolutely nothing to do but play it to the end with as much dignity as he could muster. It would be useless to run.

The sergeant shouted, and three soldiers vaulted the barricade and grabbed the man ahead of him. The officer watched, his expression bored, and, after a moment, lit a cigarette and resumed his scrutiny of the line as the unfortunate worker was dragged away.

There was not even a mutter of protest. Memling shuffled forward and the line followed. The man had ceased to exist.

This was Jan Memling's first field assignment since February 1938. He had been sent to Belgium in early May to investigate rumours of German troop movements along the Belgian border. But von Reichenau's sudden panzer attack on the tenth of that month had come as a complete surprise. The following day Fort Eben Emael was captured by glider troops, and the city of Liège occupied, cutting off any possibility of escape. It was not until late June that a courier had found him, issued a set of ambiguous instructions from London, and arranged an emergency contact with the fledgling Belgian underground. Since then he had lived in a nightmare of constant terror. There was no foreseeable way that he could get out of Belgium, and if Great Britain surrendered, as was rumoured likely . . . he did not want to think about that.

Those elderly Belgians who remembered the relatively benign German occupation of 1914–18 expected much the same in 1940. But with the conclusion of the French armistice on 22 June at Compiègne, army troops had been replaced by SS units and the occupation stiffened. Stern reprisals were meted out for the most absurd infractions of the stringent rules. Curfew violators were executed on the spot. A priest who had received an urgent call to attend a dying man had not waited to telephone the occupation authorities for permission. An SS patrol had stopped his bicycle, pushed him against a wall, and shot him. His body had been left as an example.

Memling had found his position in the quality control department of the Manufacture d'Armes in mid-May, before the occupation forces had established themselves. He had been lucky to find it, but the army officer running the factory was desperate for trained technical personnel and not overly inclined to ask questions. Jan had given his birthplace as Barchon, a small town east of the Meuse destroyed by German artillery. As long as he gave the Germans no reason to investigate his background, he felt safe enough.

In the meantime the factory was run efficiently, and some consideration was even given to the workers. In contrast with their counterparts in other German-run factories, they were provided a bowl of hot if watery soup at midday to supplement their rations, were released from work at mid-afternoon on Saturdays, and, if lucky enough to work in an office, enjoyed a measure of heat in the winter. Memling's current task was to prepare quality control inspection procedures for two new German machine-gun designs, the MP40 and MG42.

'Ah, Memling, here you are. Good. I must have you go down to the director of production's office and bring back the latest MG–Forty-two estimates for the coming year.'

Hans Belden, his superior, was a fat, timorous, and self-pitying German civilian who enjoyed the rank and privileges of his position as director of quality control in a factory of great importance to the Third Reich. He was not inclined to pamper his Belgian subordinates – except for Memling. For some reason he had taken a liking to Jan, even to the extent of occasionally inviting him into his own office, which had an electric fire, and offering him coffee and cigarettes. He like to pat Memling on the shoulder or put an arm about his waist. Belden was Nazi to the core, and Memling did not trust him for an instant. Instead, he treated his boss with a deference – verging on sycophancy – to which Belden responded with privileges now and then.

Memling showed his pass to the sentry and went out on to the vast production floor. A dirty, nearly opaque skylight allowed only the palest version of daylight to filter through. The Manufacture d'Armes, or the Gun Factory, as it was known locally, was the largest in the world. Beneath the endless glass roof, in carefully-guarded areas, were manufactured and assembled a wide variety of weapons ranging from the Browning nine-millimetre automatic pistol to the panzer tank. Hundreds of lathes, milling machines, and polishers ran twenty-four hours a day to feed the insatiable maw of the German war machine.

The German production director occupied a spacious suite with a carpeted reception area. His amply endowed Belgian secretary attracted German officers like flies. When Memling entered, an oberleutnant in the dark blue of a Luftwaffe dress uniform was leaning on the counter above her desk staring into the front of her blouse as she reached for a folder. He said something that Memling could not hear, and the girl hesitated, half-twisting to smile at him so that her blouse opened a bit more. Memling walked to the desk and, ignoring the German officer, handed over the requisition.

'What do you want?' the officer snapped in annoyance.

Memling turned to him, pretending not to understand German.

The lieutenant tried to repeat the question in halting Flemish, then in French, and gave up as Memling continued to stare.

The secretary made a remark in German, and they both laughed before she turned to Memling.

'Director Belden asks for the summer production figures on the MG–Forty-two.' His voice was steady enough and devoid of any emotion.

'Oh, all right,' she answered petulantly. 'But it will take a moment. Wait over there.' She indicated the far side of the room.

The girl stood up, brushing her dress smooth across her hips, and with practised movements swayed across to the filing cabinets. The drawer she wanted was in the lowest tier, and rather than kneel, she bent forward so that her skirt drew tight across a shapely bottom. It took her several moments to find the correct folder, and during that time Memling could have removed the officer's sidearm and boots.

She found it at last and, turning, dropped the folder. This time, when she bent down to retrieve it her blouse opened far enough that even Memling, across the room, was aware of soft breasts barely restrained by wisps of silk. The lieutenant grunted as if hit, and Memling closed his eyes, stricken suddenly with the memory of Margot's soft, strong body.

'Here,' she snapped, and Memling came to the counter. He signed the register she pushed towards him, and when she handed back his identity card from which she had recorded the numbers, she gave him a slight wink. Memling's answering nod was barely visible.

'Next time, you are to advise me ahead of time which file you wish to see.' She turned away, dismissing him. The lieutenant's hands twitched as she slid into her chair.

Lucky bastard, Memling thought as he left the office. He knew where the German would sleep that evening.

He had been gone long enough for Belden to begin to fret, and so he hurried along the aisles between the machines. He had eaten only a hard crust that morning, and there were rumours that the meat and sugar rations would be reduced by a third in January. Perhaps Belden would offer him a cup of tea and possibly even one of those tinned biscuits. The idea was overwhelming.

Preoccupied, Memling almost missed the tall muscular man in civilian suit escorted by the director of production and a high-ranking army officer. As he glanced back, his heart turned over, but the civilian had continued on without a sign of recognition. Memling had last seen him in 1938, in Arnsberg, Germany. He was not surprised that von Braun had not recognised him; he was twenty pounds lighter, his hair was twice as long, and there was still a bit of newspaper stuck to his chin where the worn-out razor had nicked him again.

But what the devil was Wernher von Braun doing there? He was a rocket scientist. Had he been drafted to work on more conventional armaments? Memling puzzled over the question, so absorbed that the sentry had to ask twice for his pass. He delivered the folder, accepted the half-filled cup of tea, fending off Belden's arm with what grace he could, and listened to the familiar complaints concerning changes and revisions to plans about which they were never consulted. He soon escaped to his own desk against the windows overlooking the vast production floor.

From his vantage point he could see across and down into the various partitions that divided the factory floor and made it such a warren. Against the far end of the building the Germans had built a tightly closed and guarded section roofed and walled with plywood. Uncharacteristically, they had used their own engineering troops for the job. The area was guarded by heavily armed sentries, and rumours spoke of a miracle weapon under development. But like all rumours under the Nazi occupation, these were both contradictory and fantastic. The quality control department was the pivot in any production facility, especially one dealing with mass-produced weaponry. Vast quantities of specialised materials were demanded, and specifications were rigid. Tolerances between parts were often no more than hundredths of a millimetre. If any kind of weapon were being developed within those plywood walls, they would know about it in quality control – unless, he thought, it was so secret that the Germans had installed a separate quality control department.

But that was absurd. Belden, as fretful of his standing as he was, would hardly have remained unaware of such an operation. And if that was the case, Memling could hardly have failed to hear of it. Or could he? Suppose it was so important that even Belden was keeping his mouth shut? He glanced at the mock-up of the MP40 machine pistol lying on his desk – a cheaper version of the MP38, he knew; compared with what might be hidden behind those walls, it was nothing. Was that why von Braun was in Liège?

It was still raining hard when the final whistle blew. This winter gave every appearance of being much like the previous one – the hardest in Europe for nearly two hundred years. Memling rode his bicycle slowly, lost in the silent, sullen crowd. The wait at the checkpoint seemed longer than usual.

Memling lugged his bicycle up the steps of his boarding-house and nodded a greeting to his landlady who was waiting beside the doorway. Tomorrow night she would want his weekly rent. Arrests were so common these days that rents were demanded on a weekly basis. A few, like his landlady, determined not to lose a penny due her, had tried to collect daily; but someone had complained to the civil authorities, and a man had come round to forbid the practice.

In his room at the top rear of the ancient house, he shed his wet pants and coat and wrapped himself in a blanket, then set about heating his half-can of soup over a tiny gas ring. As had become his habit, Memling remained huddled in the chair to conserve warmth and energy, reviewing any information he had memorised. But tonight his mind refused to concentrate, insisted instead on speculating over the presence of Wernher von Braun in Liège until he fell into an exhausted sleep.

The clock chimed eleven as Hans Belden opened the door and motioned him inside. Memling could see that Belden was angry and knew there would be no tea this morning and probably precious little time to warm himself by the electric fire.

'I've just had a telephone call from the production director's office. Raw material delivery schedules have been delayed again, and all production figures must be revised this week. Take this folder back to his office. We shall have to wait until they are finished, and do it all again!' He slapped the desk with his hand and flung himself around in the chair to stare at the rain spattering the window.

'A miserable country. It does nothing but rain,' he muttered.

Memling varied his route to the director's office, to pass the closed-off section, but there was little to see except plywood walls and unsmiling guards.

He returned the folder to the blonde secretary, who sniffed at him but did not speak. Returning by the same route, Memling noticed as he turned into the corridor that one of the plywood sections had been moved aside to allow a cart carrying a large canvas-shrouded object into the area. The man directing the operation was wearing a white laboratory coat – the Germans allowed no one but their own people to wear white coats. His own was a dirty brown. The cart snagged on the edge of the door, and one of the soldiers swore. The guard stepped forward to help push, and while all eyes were on the cart Memling, who had stopped behind the guard, leaned forward to peer into the opening. He was back in position an instant before the guard straightened and returned to his post. He had seen all he needed.

Sunday was cold and windy, and rain fell intermittently. Jan Memling pedalled into the Parc d'Avroy past the monument to Charles Rogier. In spite of the rain and cold and the late season, the park was crowded with shabby citizens sitting on benches, examining the great equestrian statue of Charlemagne, or wandering the paths and eyeing the food stalls affordable only to German soldiers and their well-dressed collaborators. There was little else to do in the city. The shops were empty, and those theatres that remained open were too expensive, and full of Germans in any event.

Twenty minutes later he crossed the boulevard Piercot and rode up the rue Saint-Jacques. The gardens of the Place Emile-Dupon at the end were practically deserted. Tall Flemish-style houses from the 1700s frowned across the lovely miniature park. Its once immaculate gardens went untended, but the long rows of trees leading one inevitably to Pollard's bronze group, *The Forsaken*, were still magnificent. As he found a bench the sun slipped through the cloud briefly, and he soaked up its warmth in gratitude. Two old men huddled on a bench across the way, oblivious to him and each other. An officer in Luftwaffe uniform strolled past, hands behind his back, a contented expression on his face. In one of the houses opposite, Memling caught a glimpse of a small child peering out.

Memling saw her coming along the footpath and grunted in relief. She was wearing a shabby overcoat and a scarf that hid her blonde hair. Her collar was turned up, and she wore the heavy rubber galoshes that had become mandatory in the winter, now that the trams had stopped running.

'It was dangerous to contact me at the factory. Don't do it again.'

Memling nodded, knowing she was right. Maria Kluensenayer, the production director's secretary, was his sole contact with the Belgian resistance movement.

'I have to see Paul.'

Maria frowned at that. 'It is far too dangerous.'

'What I have to tell him could be even more dangerous if ignored.' Even as he spoke he realised how melodramatic that sounded.

The girl nodded after a moment. 'All right. I will see, but it will take time. I will meet you here this evening, at eight.'

'No. The gates are closed at six.'

Maria bit at her lower lip, indecision plain on her face, then shook her head. 'It cannot be done. It is far too dangerous.'

'Look,' he said, striving to keep the desperation from his voice. 'I've never asked for anything from you people. I could have made a nuisance of myself, but I haven't. Now I am telling you, I have to see Paul!'

Her fingers were tapping nervously on her thigh, and for an instant he had a vision of the smooth, satiny skin the threadbare coat concealed. He swore at himself and jerked his mind back to the problem at hand.

'All right. Meet me in the Parc de la Citadelle at four-twenty-five exactly. Make certain that no one follows you.'

Memling started to ask where in the park, but she turned quickly, slapped him hard, jumped to her feet cursing in French, and was gone. What the hell was that for? he wondered. Then he caught sight of one of the old men grinning slyly, and understood.

A thin spatter of rain drifted across the cobbled street, and he glanced at the sky apprehensively. He had no money to buy lunch at a food stall, but if he went back to his room to eat, the landlady would wonder when he went out again, and there would be a thousand questions to dodge. Cursing the Germans and Maria, he mounted the bicycle and turned into the boulevard Piercot, trying to ignore the rhythmic bumping against the end of his spine as the patched tyre revolved on the cobbled street.

The original citadel was designed and constructed in the

seventeenth century by Prince-Bishop Maximilian Henry of Bavaria. With each succeeding war or threat of war, the fort was expanded and strengthened until by 1914 it was thought to impose an impenetrable barrier to German designs.

The Imperial German offensive was begun on 5 August 1914. On 7 August General Erich Ludendorff entered Liège, and that same day, under bombardment from Krupp's sixteen-inch howitzers, nicknamed the Big Bertha, the citadel surrendered. It would not be the last time an impregnable static defence position was overrun by superior technology. In 1914 it had been accomplished with giant cannon; in 1940, by glider-borne parachute troops.

Memling entered the gracious city park that had been constructed on the grounds of the old citadel and wandered about idly, examining the overgrown ruins of the strongest in a chain of twelve forts once thought sufficient to defend the city below. Liège, Namur, Mons, Maastricht, ancient citadels in the most fought-over area in Europe. His stomach protested its emptiness, and he was shivering in the chill breeze and wet clothes.

'You must be the Englishman?' A hand fell on his shoulder and squeezed. 'No, no. Keep walking. Just greet me as an old friend you expected to meet. Your cover name is Pieter Diecker, I believe?'

The shock of the unexpected approach, of being called an Englishman, had almost unnerved Memling, and he faltered. The hand held tightly to his shoulder, and he tried to smile but failed, miserably.

'Maria's description was quite accurate. I had no trouble spotting you.'

Memling glanced at the man walking beside him. Rather tall and spare, he had a thin moustache and a three-day stubble of beard. His hair was concealed beneath an army garrison cap that had seen better days, and the uniform greatcoat that flapped about his knees was filthy and carelessly mended. He walked with a pronounced limp – which had probably kept him out of the camps where soldiers of the former regime were required to do a period of labour service. The armistice had been in effect for seven months now, and very few men had yet been released.

'By the way, my name is Paul. I apologise if I startled you, but your reaction confirms your identity.'

Memling's breathing had begun to return to normal. 'And if . . it hadn't . . . ?'

The man shrugged. 'We would have walked into those trees.' He palmed a thin-bladed military fighting knife before sliding it away in the depths of the coat. Memling drew an even deeper breath.

'Where can we go?'

Paul laughed at that. 'Right here, my friend. I do not know you well enough for anyplace else. And we must hurry. The Gestapo and the SD vie with each other for my head.'

They found a bench on the edge of the bluff overlooking the city. Memling struggled to find an opening that would catch the attention of this self-assured man. He knew nothing about him other than that he had been an army officer. How to explain something as complicated as rockets in a few minutes' time? he wondered.

He decided on a straightforward account. 'The Germans are developing a powerful rocket which will have the capability of flying perhaps three hundred and fifty to four hundred and fifty kilometres,' he began. 'It will carry an explosive charge of up to twelve hundred kilograms. The motors for this rocket are being constructed down there.' Memling pointed to the distant roof of the Manufacture d'Armes.

'In the Royal Gun Factory?' Paul asked in surprise. 'A rocket? Like a fireworks rocket?'

Memling shook his head impatiently. 'No. Nothing like that at all. This one will be all metal, perhaps thirty metres high, with a powerful motor in which a mixture of petrol or alcohol and liquid oxygen will be burned. It will be able to climb thirty or more kilometres into the stratosphere and continue on for up to four hundred and fifty kilometres.' Memling became aware that he was speaking much too quickly and drew a breath, fighting to slow himself down.

'If launched from anywhere along the Atlantic or North Sea coasts, it could fall anywhere in London. It could be fired north to devastate Stockholm or across the Mediterranean against Egypt or targets in the Middle East.'

Paul whistled softly. 'How do you know all this?'

The question was logical and at least did not express the complete disbelief he had been expecting. He began to relax a bit. 'I saw the motors.'

'Just the motors?'

Memling nodded.

'Tell me where and when.'

The cloud along the western horizon had broken, and reddish light rushed through to flood the distant hills. Below, the city, shrouded in a century of industrial grime, remained grey and dismal. Memling began by describing his chance meeting in 1938 with Wernher von Braun and Franz Bethwig, his subsequent flight from the train, and the encounter with von Braun three days before, which had led to his glimpse of the sealed area.

'I studied mechanical engineering and was also a member of the British Interplanetary Society,' he continued, noting that Paul did not smirk or grin at the name as so many others had. 'Before the war I helped to develop several small rockets that used liquid fuels. I am quite familiar with some of the problems.'

Paul nodded. 'I think I understand. Tell me about what you saw at the works.'

'There was sufficient time for me to get a good look. It was a bell-shaped object one and half metres high and half that wide. The bottom flared into a bell muzzle as a rocket nozzle would do. Above the nozzle was a spherical container from which a series of pipes depended. The sphere was most certainly the combustion chamber.'

'How can you be certain of the size?'

'The soldiers were moving another one inside. It was on a standard factory cart which stands exactly thirty-six centimetres high on its wheels. I measured one. The rocket motor rose to the level of the soldier's chin. When he stood upright, he was as tall as I am, which is one point eight metres exactly.'

'You are very perceptive. Where did you obtain the performance characteristics?'

Memling cleared his throat. 'An engineer must be a good observer. As for the specifications . . . I – I calculated them from the dimensions of the engine.'

Paul nodded for him to continue.

'From the apparent diameter' – Memling's voice was feverish with the urgent need to make this man understand – 'of the nozzle it is possible to estimate the width of the rocket. From the diameter of the combustion chamber it is possible to construct a series of estimates of specific thrust based on the fuels that might be employed. Given that, the rate of fuel and oxidiser use can be estimated, which suggests the amount of fuel that can be carried and thus the possible range. That, in turn, provides an estimate of the weight of explosive that can be carried. Military considerations would further limit the choice of weights; for instance, it would make no sense to shoot a fifty-kilogram payload a thousand kilometres or a six-thousand-kilogram payload ten kilometres.'

Paul was watching the sunset, and Memling wondered if he was really listening. 'Von Braun told me two years ago that their major problem was to contain the twenty-nine-hundred-degree-centigrade temperatures developed in the combustion chamber. He mentioned at the time they were using liquid oxygen. The only fuels that combine with liquid oxygen to produce that temperature are petrol and alcohol. Knowing the fuel and oxidiser, the combustion temperature, and approximating the rate of propellant/oxidiser feed – which is dictated by the combustion rate – it is possible to calculate speed and range versus payload. The targets are obvious and all within a four-hundred-kilometre range of occupied European territory.

'For instance, a rocket capable of striking London from this side of the Channel will travel approximately two hundred kilometres from, say, the vicinity of Antwerp. If we assume that the rocket must travel at least three hundred metres per second, and the fuel consumption is thirty kilograms per second, or twice the acceleration of gravity, you can calculate to find that the rocket must produce five hundred and sixty thousand horse-power. With that figure you can refine your assumptions and define such characteristics as fuel load, desirable payload in explosives, and so on. These, of course, provide you with the maximum and minimum dimensions of the rocket.'

Paul had remained silent throughout the discourse, and Memling was afraid that he had overdone it. The Belgian was staring out over the city to the western horizon where the storm clouds had regrouped, forcing the sun to retreat.

'You are certain of these calculations?' he asked, and when Memling nodded, he smiled. 'I was an artillery officer, of the rank of lieutenant colonel. I am an engineer by training.' He was silent a moment, then stood and motioned Memling to walk with him. They started back along the path, Memling pushing his bicycle and cursing his rumbling stomach.

'I will do this much,' Paul said after they had covered half the distance. 'A message will be sent to London briefly describing your information and conclusions. They may well want a follow-up report.'

Memling clenched his fists on the handlebars and strove to keep his voice normal. He shook his head. 'That won't do.'

Paul glanced at him in surprise. 'Why not, may one ask?'

Memling described the reception his report had received in 1938.

'Perhaps things have changed . . . new personnel . . .'

'Maybe,' Memling replied doubtfully. 'But my superior, the man with whom they will check, is the same as then.'

Paul nodded. 'I understand. However, there is nothing else I can do. Our contacts with London are as yet quite limited. Your government is only beginning to pay attention to resistance organisations on the Continent. They are still preoccupied with a Nazi invasion threat.' He glanced about suddenly.

'I have spent far too much time here as it is. I will send a report through as soon as possible, and if there are further requests for information, they will be passed on to you. Otherwise' – he paused and laid a hand on Memling's arm – 'everything will remain as before. Do not contact us except in an emergency. You have done quite well to date. If I need any further information, the request will come through Maria.'

Memling could not keep the concern from his face, and Paul chuckled. 'If you doubt her reliability, then she has done well. Believe me when I tell you her attitude towards the Nazi is an act. She is my most valuable source of information. You may continue to trust her with your life.' Paul stressed the word *continue*.

The Belgian clapped him on the arm and walked away without looking back. Memling leaned on his bicycle and found a cigarette. Two in one day was extravagant, but in view of the risk, the tension, the disappointment, and his empty stomach, he felt he deserved it. The sun had broken through in one final gesture of defiance and set the storm clouds afire. The Hôpital des Anglais glowed as did the distant buildings of the Académie des Beaux-Arts. It would require a Constable to capture those colours, he thought; and the homesickness that overwhelmed him then was devastating.

The door slammed back against the stop, and two SS men stamped into the office, followed by a young officer. Work stopped abruptly as the five technicians stared in fear at the sudden apparition. Memling's fingers convulsed, and his pencil snapped, cracking across the silent room like a gunshot. The door to Belden's office flew open, and the director of quality control rushed out ready to protest the intrusion – until he saw the SS flashes on the officer's collar. The officer ignored him and stared at each technician in turn, but it was on Memling that his stare lingered longest.

'Pieter Diecker?'

Memling stood. 'I am Pieter Diecker,' he said, hoping the terror in his voice was not apparent.

The officer glanced at him, then at the partially disassembled machine pistol on the workbench and nodded. One of the SS enlisted men slung his rifle and stepped forward to grasp Memling's arm, and he was led to the door without a word.

Eyes followed their progress as Memling was hustled through

the factory, but not a head was raised. Crammed between the two soldiers who followed the officer, he was conscious of the smell of their unwashed uniforms, the odour of heavy Balkan tobacco that hung about them both, and the red smear of birthmark on the neck of the man to his left.

Even before they crossed the yard, which was swathed in a frigid mist, Memling had been under no illusion about their destination. And he was badly frightened. If they had found him out, there was no hope. The fear that gripped him was like nothing he had ever experienced before. He felt as if he were frozen, as if time had slowed, his body reacting only to autonomic control.

He was taken to a single-storey building, little more than a shed, where a man several inches taller and at least two stone heavier than him, signed a receipt, then pointed to an ironclad door.

The room beyond contained a single chair and a bright lamp fastened to the ceiling. Memling was shoved to stand beneath the lamp. He raised a hand to shade his eyes, but it was slapped away. He heard footsteps and the door slammed.

It was intensely wearying to stand with his hands at his sides, squinting against the glare that grew more painful as the minutes crawled by. His feet began to protest, and the joints of his knees throbbed. When he heard the door open, he actually experienced a moment of relief; an instant later a blow sent him sprawling against the wall.

Memling suppressed the oath just in time and pushed himself up – only to receive a sharp kick in the ribs. A hand grabbed his hair and yanked him up to meet a punch that snapped his head back against the wall. A second punch beneath the heart drove every bit of air from his lungs and left him paralysed and gasping. He rolled on to his side, knees drawn up, and struggled to breathe.

'Please, Mr Diecker,' a quiet, understanding voice murmured. 'You must stand quite still. My friend here has had a bad night and is quite impatient this morning. You have been invited to assist in a police investigation. It is a small, rather unimportant matter, but' – the man's tone was apologetic – 'we are still required to perform our duty. We do hope you will be willing to help. It would save us a great deal of time and trouble.'

Memling regained his feet and staggered away from the wall gasping. He was shoved back beneath the lamp.

'First, I must admit to an unfair advantage over you. I know your name, Herr Diecker, but you do not know mine. I am Captain Jacob Walsch of the Geheimes Staatspolizeiamt. The Secret State Police,' he translated.

There was a pause and then his hand was shaken.

'Perhaps now we can become friends. The German government does not wish to inconvenience Belgian citizens any more than the needs of the occupation require. But in times like these we must be ever vigilant, heh?

'Now.' There was the sound of turning pages again. 'You were seen in the gardens of the Place Emile-Dupon yesterday, about midday? Is that correct?'

The man's French pronunciation had a curiously guttural flavour, overlaid with the intonations of the south. He was clearly a German speaking French in the accents of that area. The only German he had spoken, the name of his police organisation, carried a singsong lilt that suggested the Schwarzwald.

'I asked if that was correct, Herr Diecker?'

'Uh . . . yes,' Memling mumbled, trying to sound dazed even though his mind was working now. The blow that followed was as sudden and unexpected as the first. The man seemed to have mastered the technique of striking high on the spine, just below the shoulders, while kicking the victim's legs away so that he landed head first. Half-conscious, head lolling from side to side, he was yanked to his feet and slapped hard.

'Herr Diecker' – the voice was annoyed – 'I must ask you once more not to provoke my associate. You must speak up immediately and clearly when I ask a question. Please repeat your answer.'

'Yes . . .' he managed to force out.

'Yes what?' the man prompted.

'I was in the Place Emile-Dupon . . . yesterday.'

'Was it not rather an unpleasant day for taking the air?'

'Yes . . . but Sunday is the only day I have, otherwise . . .'

'I see. And while you were at the Place Emile-Dupon did you meet anyone?'

Christ, Memling thought, they know. The bastards were playing a game with him.

His vision was clearing as his eyes adapted to the glare, and the faces were beginning to take on detail.

'Yes.'

'And who would that have been?'

Memling twisted his hands together as if embarrassed, and drew a deep breath. Dissemble, they had told him in the all-too-brief training classes. Confirm enough of their story that they may believe your lies.

'I . . . met' – he took a deep breath – 'a girl.'

'Ah. And why should you be shy? Certainly you are a normal,

healthy young man. Tell me, please, what you and this young lady talked about? By the way, what is her name?'

The Gestapo officer was watching him closely now, and Memling realised with a shock that he had seen that gaunt, skull-like face before: the man on the train! My God, he thought, as fresh waves of fear coursed through him, turning every muscle in his body to water. Do they know who I am?

He struggled against the panic, knowing that if he gave way now he would lapse into grovelling terror, and the thought brought such intense shame and self-loathing that he stopped wringing his hands and tried to stand straight.

As if to encourage him, Walsch chuckled. 'Herr Diecker, whatever you tell me remains in the strictest confidence. Now, what was her name?'

'Maria . . . Kluensenayer,' he choked. There was nothing to be lost by telling him. Walsch was certain to know anyway, probably had known the instant she sat down beside him. He could anticipate the next question, and the answer was beginning to form in his mind as it was asked.

'My my, the secretary to the director of production. Now, what would you two find to talk about?'

Memling took a deep breath. 'We did not talk very long, sir. I . . asked – I asked her to come to my room,' he finished with a rush.

'And?'

'She left.'

'Left? Just like that?'

Memling let his head droop a little more. 'Yes . . . no. She slapped me.'

'I shouldn't wonder. Whatever possessed you, young man? Do you know her very well? Did you have reason to believe that she might agree? What a dog you are! And so hasty. Don't you know you must first court a young woman? They are all prostitutes and whores at heart, and so you must go about it correctly. First a present, then the theatre, and perhaps a meal in a fine restaurant.' There was a dry chuckle. 'Then you take the lady to your bed. Not before – and never, never ask.'

'I . . . I do not have the money for that sir.'

'Not enough money!' Walsch shook his head in exasperation. 'Why, you have an excellent job, a responsible job. Surely you are not complaining about the salary paid you by the Reich?'

'Oh no, sir,' Memling replied hastily, already weary of the game. 'It is not that, only . . . I . . .' He shuffled his feet and rubbed his nose. 'I . . . I am quite shy. You see, I am an orphan – '

'Yes, yes, I know all that.' For the first time Walsch had

departed from the gentle chiding tone. 'Where did you go after the whore rejected your advances?'

Memling took a step towards him. 'She is not a . . . a . . .' He stopped as if unable to pronounce the word. Walsch raised a hand to stay the other man.

'You treated her like a whore, so obviously you must think her one. Answer my question.'

'I did . . . I went to the Parc de la Citadelle. I go there sometimes, to be alone.'

'To the park? I see.' More pages turned. 'This woman, Maria, have you met her before, outside the works?'

'No. No, sir,' Memling answered, astonished that Walsch had not asked about the park and who it was he had met there. Didn't he know?

'But you have met her, spoken to her, inside the works?'

Bemused, Memling did not see where the trap was leading. 'Yes, I have spoken to her . . . in her office.'

Walsch tapped the notebook. 'In violation of the law forbidding personal intercourse during work hours?'

'Ye – yes.'

'Are you not aware that such violations are considered sabotage by the occupation authorities? And that sabotage is punished by hanging?' Walsch's voice had become cold.

'Yes . . . but I . . . thought perhaps a word . . .' What is he doing? Memling wondered. Didn't they follow me to the citadel?

'A word? Just a word? And next time it will be two words, and then several, and perhaps a long conversation will follow while your work suffers and the weapons needed by our front-line troops are not delivered on time and they are killed because you were compelled to speak to a whore,' Walsch shouted.

Memling could only remain silent. He had walked directly into the trap. His mind was in total confusion now. What was Walsch really after? If he had been followed to the citadel, they would surely have seen him with Paul.

Walsch uttered the next words with no hint of threat. 'You do realise that I could have you before a court-martial immediately and hanged before this evening? I can assure you the execution is most unpleasant. Perhaps you would be interested to know the procedure? One's last moments should be meaningful, their significance understood. As sabotage is the worst crime one can commit, the government has decreed that the method of execution should be made a deterrent to others. Therefore the prisoner is stripped to the waist and paraded before his fellows who are assembled to watch. The gallows bar is placed some three metres above the ground, so the victim's struggles are plainly visible to all.' Walsch's voice had taken on a grotesque humour.

'The prisoner is mounted on a footboard. A wire noose is placed about his neck and snugged up so that there is no slack. At a signal the footboard is withdrawn leaving the prisoner to strangle. It can take as long as ten minutes to die if the hangman places the noose correctly. As you might imagine, it is very unpleasant. And that, my friend, by your own admission, is the penalty which awaits you, this very afternoon.'

Even through the intense fear that seemed to have shut out everything else, it was becoming clear to Memling what was happening. The Gestapo knew who he was. The files had disgorged his name in response to his fingerprints. But Walsch could not possibly admit to having overlooked a British spy in a most sensitive position all these months, particularly one who had escaped him once before. So Walsch had waited to see where he would lead them. Somehow the meeting with Paul had been missed, but not the one with Maria, and that meant she was now under Gestapo suspicion as well. Now that they had a connection, there was no further need for him. He could be eliminated and at the same time provide a cheap lesson in continued obedience. The floor shifted and he staggered, nauseated by fear. The thought of strangling to death from a wire noose . . .

'. . . be a way to avoid such a severe penalty,' Walsch continued. 'After all, death is rather a severe penalty for speaking to an attractive woman, a temptation to which anyone may give way.'

Memling closed his eyes, shutting out the light, the sound, everything, as he struggled to understand what the Gestapo officer was saying. 'How?' he choked.

'If you are willing to co-operate with me, I may be persuaded to intercede with the court. It has happened that such charges have been greatly reduced if the service rendered is of sufficient importance.'

Gaunt to the point of emaciation, Walsch smiled. He lit a cigarette and, as an afterthought, offered one to Memling. Feigning gratitude, Memling accepted and lit it from the match Walsch held for him.

'It really is quite a simple task. And quite pleasant, I might add. In fact, I might even be doing you an unexpected favour.'

Memling waited, sucking greedily at the cigarette in spite of the harshness of the German tobacco that must have been half dried oak leaves.

'This woman, Maria Kluensenayer, is of interest to you, of course. You must therefore continue with your suit. Become friendly with her, spend time with her. I am quite interested in knowing what she does in her spare time.'

'Maria,' Memling blurted out. 'But she is . . .'

'A whore.'

Memling blinked.

'A whore,' Walsch repeated. 'That, however, is beside the point. Except,' he added, chuckling, 'as it makes your task easier and more pleasant.'

'That is all you want me to do . . .?'

'Yes. If you agree, I am willing to suspend the charges for the moment.'

'For the moment?' Memling could not keep the bitterness from his voice.

'Do not try my patience,' Walsch warned. 'Remember the wire noose. A few days' grace?' He stubbed out his cigarette and glanced at Memling. 'You do understand?'

'But I do not have . . .'

'You what? Speak up!'

Memling was shaking badly. 'She will have nothing to do with me,' he gabbled. 'I do not have money. I am not the kind she . . .'

'That is your problem.' Walsch waved a hand in dismissal. 'You have three days, until Friday afternoon.'

No one said a word about the blood-encrusted abrasions on his forehead or the stiffness with which he carried himself when he returned to the laboratory. The double vision persisted, and bouts of nausea assailed him. The door to the director's office remained tightly shut. The attention of the Gestapo was the curse of death.

Jan Memling knew he was under surveillance. They wanted him to know. A black Volkswagen followed him wherever he went through the streets of Liège. No one spoke to him or looked at him, and even his landlady hurried inside and slammed her door when he returned in the evening. That first night, in the refuge of his dingy room, he wrapped himself in the blanket and, too frightened to eat, sat staring at the blackout curtains long into the night, waiting for the shivering to stop and the fear to abate to its usual tolerable level. But like the nausea that wracked him at regular intervals, it refused to do so. He was under no illusions that his life would extend beyond his immediate usefulness to Walsch. If the Gestapo agent knew who he was, he would also know that he must have a connection to the resistance. Was Walsch gambling that Maria was that connection?

For the first time in weeks he allowed himself to think of Margot. Her features were there, just beyond memory, eluding him now in a way he had never thought possible. Until tonight he had sought to dismiss her, to ignore the intense longing thoughts of her always induced, and he had done so successfully enough that she was slipping away. They had married a year ago, the previous October, after her mother had finally succumbed to a combination of disease and pent-up bile.

There had been a week's leave for a honeymoon in the Lake District where he had obtained a tiny cottage overlooking the far north end of Lake Windermere. Indian summer was giving way to autumn, and the wind blustered with rain. Inside, Jan kept the fire high, and between long, soothing stretches of lovemaking they had taken walks in the hills, discovering one vantage point after another as the lake displayed its moods: iron-grey under the lash of rain, sapphire in the brief periods of intense sun. Dry leaves under graceful oaks amid golden sunshine had more than once served as a lovers' couch. It had been quite as both expected it would be, loving and companionable after the years of impatient waiting. In the long evenings before the fire they had discovered unknown facets of each other's character.

He had never told Margot for whom he worked. She was still under the impression that he was employed by a small electrical appliance manufacturer. When he had left for Belgium that late April day, he had laughed at her fears about war on the Continent. After all, the war had been nearly eight months old and nothing much had happened since the previous September.

Memling woke with a start. The image of Margot sitting across from him before the fire, the memory of her soft body beneath his in the high, handcrafted bed, her gentle laughter at his attempts to master the kitchen plumbing, were gone. He knew then that he would never see her again.

By mid-afternoon, Thursday, Jan Memling had formulated his plan. It was desperate and full of loose ends, but anything was better than waiting to be slaughtered at Walsch's command. The resistance had to be warned away, and he had to disappear. The Ardennes was the only possibility. There in the forest he might survive long enough to carry out a few acts of sabotage.

Memling knocked on the director's door with his excuse all prepared, a mistake in the projected production figures for the MG42. The director wrote his pass quickly and slammed the door. The mark of death, Memling thought grimly.

Maria glanced up as he entered, and except for a slight tightening about her eyes at the sight of his bruises, she gave no indication that he meant any more to her than any other employee

– and thereby signed her death warrant. Walsch would be watching her. When a woman shows no sign of recognising a man who three days earlier invited her into his bed, and whom she turned down with a public slap, she must be concealing somcthing.

Memling showed his pass and asked for the production estimates. The only other person in the room was an army sergeant. Memling watched her as he would have been expected to, and the German did likewise. As Maria straightened up from the file drawer the sergeant gave him a slow wink, and Memling grinned weakly.

Drawing a slip of paper from his pocket, he unfolded the sheets on the counter and pretended to study them while Maria returned to her desk. After a moment he muttered a curse. Maria glanced up and he called her over.

'These are not the correct sheets. I wanted numbers six to nine.'

With an air of injured patience, Maria obtained a new set of papers. 'Are these the ones?' she asked in tones dripping with sarcasm. She waited while Memling unfolded the sheets and checked page numbers.

'Yes. Thank you.' His sarcasm matched hers, and under his breath he whispered as he bent forward, 'The Gestapo saw us. They called me in yesterday.'

The girl gave no sign that she had heard, but rolled her eyes in exasperation and flounced back to her desk. Just for an instant Memling was tempted to call her back and repeat the message, but it was far too dangerous. He would have to hope she understood. His face was flushed and his heart pounded as he gathered up the sheets and left.

Walsch was waiting in the corridor. 'I hope that you have made progress.' He chuckled and walked away.

The final whistle sounded, and he joined the throng of workers edging towards the gate. The sun was setting in a burst of colour, and it was intensely cold. The line shuffled forward, and as it rounded the building Memling saw with a sinking heart that the guards had been doubled. Troops in full combat gear stood elbow to elbow along the way leading to the barrier. Memling noticed that none of the workers were being motioned out of line. This kind of intense inspection was usually carried out only as a pretext for selecting deportees.

As Memling neared the barrier a civilian stepped from the shed that housed the security offices, and spoke to an officer standing near the checkpoint. Wisps of vapour wreathed their heads as they talked, and then the civilian pointed directly at Memling. The officer turned, nodded, and sauntered towards the line of soldiers. The man went back to the shed, and Walsch appeared in the doorway. He smiled at Memling and nodded.

Walsch motioned again with his head, and Memling turned. A gallows had been erected on a wheeled cart stored in the alley between two buildings. From the crossbeam glinted a wire noose. Memling swung around, anger overriding the shock of fear. His lips formed a single obscenity, and Walsch laughed and turned back into the shed.

'Papers, you stupid bastard,' a soldier shouted at him, and Memling jerked around to see that he was already at the barrier. He braced himself as Walsch appeared behind, grinning his death's-head grin. The soldier had slung his bayoneted rifle over his right shoulder to leave both hands free to handle the papers. With any luck, Memling thought, I could take it from the guard. As he reached inside his coat for the papers he rehearsed the moves in his mind. With the rifle and bayonet he might kill two Nazis before they shot him down. With any luck, one would be Walsch. The guard took his papers, and Memling was suddenly elated. It was over. They would not dangle him from a wire noose today. He drew a breath, drunk with the cold, acrid tang that filled his throat and lungs.

'Pass.'

The barrier was open, and the guard motioned him on impatiently. Memling stumbled through, the sudden reversal draining away the adrenalin to leave him weak and nauseated. Somehow he found, and mounted, his bicycle. A trick, another damned trick to terrorise him, he realised. Walsch was playing with him, keeping him off balance with fear so that he would never know when they might drag him to the wire.

Headlights swept over him, lighting up the street. He glanced over his shoulder at the thin slits of hooded light from the familiar Volkswagen.

The explosion knocked him from the bicycle and spun him against the kerb. Dazed, he struggled to his knees just as the Volkswagen's petrol tank went up in flames. A man flopped half out of a door, clothes burning. A figure dashed across the road, reached into the flames, and jumped back, holding a machine pistol triumphantly aloft for an instant before firing one shot into the burning man's head. Several more shots were fired, and a lorry burst into the street. Figures jumped down, grabbed and hustled Memling into the back. A second explosion blew the Volkswagen to pieces, digging a huge crater in the street. Someone laughed, and the lorry lurched, backed, jerked once more, as it ran up and over the kerb to the sound of automatic weapons' fire and a third, crashing explosion.

The lorry raced through the narrow streets, throwing him from side to side on the splintered floorboards. Two men were framed against the open back as they crouched behind the tailboard, machine pistols pointing out. A match flared, and he turned to see Paul's face illuminated a moment as he lit two cigarettes. He passed one to Memling.

'Surprised?'

Memling pushed himself up on the hard bench beside the resistance leader and took the cigarette. The lorry hit a pothole, and both were thrown against the side. Paul swore and rapped on the glass window above his head with the butt of a pistol; the lorry slowed appreciably.

'Everyone drives like a Chicago gangster,' he muttered.

Memling finally managed to assemble an entire sentence. 'What in hell is going on?'

'The Gestapo was on to you. We could not afford to let you be taken.'

Memling grunted and braced himself. 'Did you get Maria away?'

Paul flung the cigarette on to the floorboards where it exploded in a cascade of sparks, and swore bitterly. 'We knew that you were interviewed by one Captain Jacob Walsch at thirteen thirty-five yesterday afternoon. They had hoped to panic you into doing something foolish, but you appear to have handled them admirably. When Maria's telephone message came we decided to move tonight. Unfortunately it was too late for her. She was arrested this afternoon.'

Memling was shocked into silence. He had not expected that Maria would be arrested, rather that she would be watched and followed to uncover other members of the resistance. Paul sensed the direction of his thoughts.

'The Gestapo would not waste the time watching her. As soon as they were certain she was a member of our group, they took her in for interrogation. They have methods which are much quicker and surer than cloak-and-dagger games.'

'Interrogation,' Memling echoed, remembering the beating.

'It is much worse for a woman,' Paul went on remorselessly. He paused to light another cigarette, and in the glow of the match Memling could see the bleakness in his eyes. 'There are so many more things they can do to . . .'

'Christ, I . . .'

The Belgian was silent a moment, then Memling felt the movement as he shook his head. 'Don't worry about it. It was not your fault. You did exactly what you should have done. They may have been watching her before you made contact. It was probably through her they came on to you. Not the other way round.'

'Where is she now? Do they . . . ?'

'As I said, do not worry. She is beyond their reach, and she told them nothing. Of that I am certain.'

'But how . . . ?'

'It was her decision, made when she joined. Maria had a family. She knew what would happen to them if she were caught, and so did they. She could not run. Therefore she could only wait to be arrested. She will be dead now. All of us carry a small poison pill.'

'Good Christ!'

'You have no idea what they can do to you in their torture chambers.' Paul described a few of their methods, and Memling felt sick. 'They are not human, none of them. They, men like this Walsch, delight in inflicting pain, the most savage pain imaginable. You would have had only a taste. Death is a small price to pay to escape their attention.'

Memling took a deep breath, beginning to recover from the shock. He shook his head as if to rid himself of the knowledge, and his fists clenched so hard, a joint popped. He stared at his hands in the darkness, struck by the certain knowledge they were covered with blood. In spite of what Paul had told him, he knew that he was at fault, that he and he alone had led the girl to her death by insisting on the meeting.

The lorry lurched over a grade crossing and sped on. The canvas flap had been lowered, and the air inside had grown stuffy in spite of the frigid dampness. 'Where are we going?' he muttered.

'To meet an aeroplane. I am having you flown out tonight.'

In spite of his self-loathing, Memling felt a surge of hope. 'I don't understand. Did London agree?' It was inconceivable they would . . . he was far too unimportant . . .

'You could say so. However reluctantly. They do not, understandably enough, wish to give up an agent on the ground. But I convinced them that your information is much more important than any vague plans they have for the future.' The lorry rounded another corner, and in the fading light cast by a lone street lamp Memling could see Paul's cold expression. 'Be thankful they did agree. Otherwise, we would have had to kill you back there.'

'But . . .'

Paul's voice was harsh now. 'You were to be arrested tonight. After interrogation, what was left of you would have been hanged in the factory yard tomorrow morning. Maria would have been hanged beside you.'

He drew an audible breath. 'We could not chance your arrest. Your information concerning the rockets is far too important to be lost. I repeated your calculations and arrived at much the same answers. With such weapons, the Nazis will win this war. If you had been taken, you would have betrayed us. You had no way of killing yourself quickly, whereas Maria did. It is impossible to resist them – if pain does not work, drugs will.'

Jan nodded. The news of independent confirmation of his calculations did much to relieve his indecision. Looked at in that light, his nebulous plans for coursing the hills to inflict damage on the enemy in a series of brilliant, if short-lived, guerrilla actions was more than foolish; it was stupid, little short of an adolescent fantasy.

His thoughts turned inevitably to the woman. She had exuded sexuality as some people did friendliness or hostility. That was a valuable, a priceless, asset that could have provided her a comfortable life under the German occupation. Instead, she had chosen to live on the edge of madness. Why? What was it that drove people like her, like Paul, like the driver and the two men crouched beside the tailboard? He discounted his own activities on the grounds that he had been forced by circumstances. But they had not. Why? Patriotism? He doubted that. Certainly there were other, safer ways to fight the Nazi, ways that did not mean a slow, painful death at the hands of sadists who delighted in inflicting the worst possible pain.

After what seemed hours the lorry slowed and lurched to one side. They had turned off the road and were travelling at a much slower speed now. Memling had the impression that they were moving uphill, up a slope full of turns and twists that caused the motor to labour and the gears to grind painfully. The canvas cover had been rolled up again, and he could see dark masses of trees on either side. The lorry slowed again, and at a word from Paul the two men scrambled over the back and disappeared. They were travelling at a walking pace now, and Paul knelt at the rear, his machine pistol resting stock down on his bent knee. There was silence except for the rumble of the engine. He saw Paul's head lift to search the sky which was filling quickly with broken cloud.

The lorry stopped, and the driver rapped on the window. Paul climbed out, followed by Memling. A torch beam sprang out of the blackness, and Memling jumped. One of the men materialised beside them and made his report to Paul in tones too low for Memling to hear. The man disappeared again, and Paul gestured with his torch, indicating a narrow path through the forest. They walked until the trees fell away on either side, and the Englishman realised that he was on the verge of a large clearing.

'Is this the landing site?'

'We've used it only once before. We're sure the Germans do not know about it. They are scattered thinly in the countryside as yet, preferring to hold most of their forces in the metropolitan areas.'

Memling shifted from foot to foot, uneasy that he could think of nothing to say. His guilt was growing with the realisation that soon he would be going home, flying out of danger, while Paul and the rest had to remain behind. He refused to let himself think about the girl.

The wind was fresher here on the edge of the trees, and the sense of oppression caused by the dense forest had eased. Memling stamped his feet and jammed his hands deeper into his pockets, wishing he had a decent coat and gloves. Paul gave him another cigarette, and they smoked behind cupped hands. Afterwards the Belgian tucked the packet into his pocket without a word. It was nearly an hour before they heard the distant drone of an aircraft. The wind played tricks with the sound, so that he was taken by surprise when the first flare shot up. In the pitch-blackness the orange glare seemed to light the entire horizon. The plane circled once as the pilot lined up on his landing approach. Paul stamped impatiently, turning to stare back into the trees or around the far unseen edges of the clearing as the aeroplane drifted towards them. Memling sensed the air of uncertainty, and his stomach knotted tighter until nausea caught at the back of his throat. He restrained the gag reflex with great difficulty.

The aircraft had reached the far edge of the clearing, and they could see it now as a vague shape over the first of the oil flares. The engine beat changed as the pilot throttled back. It fled past then and settled with an audible thump on to the frozen field. The engine ran up as the plane swung about and, as Paul waved his electric torch, began to taxi back towards them.

Memling followed him on to the frozen field. Paul was shouting to him now over the noise of the approaching aircraft: '. . . damned fools in London we need weapons and food. Impress that on them. No more propaganda leaflets . . .'

The passenger door swung open as the pilot turned around once more, ready for take-off. The sky exploded with light, and geysers of dirt and grass shot upward. Paul shouted for him to run, but the field was uneven and full of grassy hummocks and dead berry vines that clutched at his boots and trouser legs. A heavy machine-gun ripped the surface as he ran, gasping for breath. The Lysander aircraft was painted a flat black, and it was a moment before he realised it was rolling forwards in fits and jerks, propeller turning at full speed, the pilot allowing him every last possible chance by standing on the brakes.

An amplified voice shouted at him to halt, first in Flemish, then in German, and finally in English. There was a burst of explosions at one end of the clearing, and he could see the flicker of small-arms fire. Memling veered suddenly to his right, and a stream of bullets cut a deep furrow past his feet. He stumbled and nearly fell. The pilot saw what he was doing and at the last moment released the brakes. The aircraft jumped ahead. Memling ducked to avoid the strut, and as the pilot stamped the brakes one last time, he jumped and caught the cockpit coaming where he hung, feet scrabbling for purchase on the landing step, while the aircraft bounded ahead. The field was now in continuous eruption as successive explosions sparkled about them; something slicked past his leg as he hauled himself up and into the cockpit. The Lysander bounced one more time and was airborne. Memling could still hear the iron voice roaring at them as streams of tracers hosed the sky and they banked for the protection of the forest. There was just time to look back and impress upon his mind for ever the searchlight playing along the fringe of trees, the two armoured vehicles firing long strings of tracers, the flaring oil beacons at either end of the field, and, from the forest itself, the pinpoint flashes of answering gunfire as Paul's group delayed the inevitable.

Then the engine shuddered and racketed as the Lysander lurched. Tracers whispered past, and for an instant they were standing on the left wing thirty feet above the treetops. The plane came upright with insane slowness, and the trees fled.

Not until the Channel coast had they outflown the anticyclonic disturbance and broken out of the nightmarish winds and cloud. There was nothing to see below, not even the lights of a ship to break the immense darkness. Not until the pilot was lining up for his approach did Memling realise they had crossed the English coast and were home.

Three men in civilian clothing were there to greet him. They introduced themselves too quickly to be understood and led him to a waiting motorcar. They were the immediate debriefing team, they had told him, and a few moments later the car drew up before a darkened building. Vague shapes came and went, and he blinked and closed his eyes as they pushed through the blackout curtain into a lighted hallway. The chatter of voices, the sound of gramophone music, the sight of women in short dresses, their groomed hair and make-up, were overwhelming, and he stumbled after his hosts in confusion.

They took him inside and sat him at a table near the far wall where there was a measure of peace and quiet, and the younger man went to fetch a tray of food. Jan looked around him, fighting down a feeling of naked exposure.

'It is often like this, my boy,' the older man told him in a kind voice. 'You mustn't take any heed. It will all begin to seem normal in a day or so as old habits reassert themselves.'

The younger man returned, placed the tray in front of Memling, and poured a cup of hot tea for him. The tray held buttered toast and some dried American breakfast cereal in milk. He started in on the tray without complaint, wondering if he dared ask for seconds, but found that after the tea and toast he wanted nothing more.

'You aren't used to rich food, my boy.' The older man chuckled. 'Had others before you get quite sick. Fat content's too high. You must build up your tolerance again. Stick to tea and light pastry or wheaten products for a few days. Eggs, some milk, and fruit. No ham or bacon for at least a week, although you will find that easy enough in view of the rationing.'

When he had finished the tea, Memling searched his pockets and found the packet of cigarettes Paul had given him, but the young man nipped them from his hand quickly.

'Thank you. We can always use these. I'm sure you won't mind a trade.' He opened his case, removing a full carton of Player's. 'These for a German export brand?'

Memling took the carton and shook his head. 'I could . . . could live for three months on these . . . just on what I could earn in the black market, a packet at a time.'

The three exchanged smiles, and the third man, who had remained silent so far, leaned across the table as Memling lit one of the cigarettes. 'Tell us, why was Paul's group destroyed?'

Memling jerked up.

'What happened?' the man repeated.

Memling closed his eyes a moment. Of course. They are dead, he thought. He knew the Germans had been waiting . . . Why had he refused to think about it until now? It wasn't his fault . . . but it was and he knew it. How? How had Walsch known? He opened his eyes to see that everything was as it had been, the room still swirled with people, most in uniform, dishes clattered, and the gramophone swung into another record. The three faces were watching him with an intensity he found frightening.

Memling told them what had happened, speaking slowly and distinctly above the noise, smoking three cigarettes one after the other as he did so. He described his relationship to Paul's group, his first request for contact, his meeting with Paul, and his subsequent interrogation. He left out the threat of hanging, his fear of Walsch, the terror tactics employed to break him, and, by doing so, aroused their suspicions. He described the attack on the Gestapo car following him, the wild ride into the Ardennes forest, and Paul's explanations of why he was being taken out. When he finished, he was more exhausted than he thought possible. They asked a few more questions which he answered as well as he could, and the third man nodded grimly.

'Tell us about this report that you felt was important enough to justify the possible destruction of an entire resistance cell?'

Memling swore and stood so abruptly his chair fell over with a clatter. Some people looked in their direction, but most paid no attention. The other two scowled at their companion, and the younger man urged him to resume his seat.

His anger came as much in response to the past eight months in Belgium as to the man's implication. 'Please, Mr Memling' – he tried to soothe him – 'please realise that we must dig into every facet of what happened while it is still fresh in your mind. What we learn may save someone else's life. You have stated that Paul felt you must be got out immediately. Why? Did he give you any reason?'

'Of course,' Memling snapped. 'He knew I was going to be arrested within hours. It was for the protection of his own people. His alternative was to kill me, which I am certain he would have done if he had not thought my information so important. He knew I would never be able to withstand a Gestapo interrogation.' He saw them exchange quick, knowing glances, just as they had when he mentioned Paul's alternative, and for an instant he wanted to smash their smug, well-fed faces.

'You don't understand,' he snarled. 'You think the Nazi plays by the rules, do you? Maria knew better. She committed suicide. You just do not know, you have never been there . . . you just . . .'

'Did you witness the suicide of this young woman?' the older man interrupted. 'Then how do you know,' he went on when Memling shook his head, 'that she actually did kill herself?'

Memling clenched his fists under the table and tried to make them understand. 'Because she would have! Because Paul told me she had!'

'But surely that is not sufficient . . .'

'Damn you.' Memling pounded the table. 'You have no idea what the Gestapo will do to you, especially to a woman. They begin with rape, many rapes, one after another. The beatings, the red-hot blades and electrical shock, the drugs . . .'

The three men were shushing him now as others in the room paused to listen. The young man poured something from a flask into his empty teacup, and they urged him to drink it. It was Scotch, fine old malt Scotch, but it only made him choke and cough.

'Do you want to know what they did to me in a routine interrogation?' Memling demanded, and brushed his hair back so that they could see the massive abrasion that covered half his forehead. But again there was scepticism and disbelief in their expressions. An hour later, after he had refused to talk to them any more, they put him aboard the train for London.

Jan Memling was shocked at his first sight of London. He had come down by train from Hornchurch where the Lysander had landed after an uneventful crossing. The train ran into Liverpool Street Station before dawn, and the fires lighting the skies above the city reminded him of a painting of Dante's inferno.

The station was worse. Sirens wailed an all clear above the battered streets, and people streamed up from subterranean caverns like troglodytes, blinking in the relative brightness of the main hall and mingling in well-behaved, shuffling throngs with the passengers. There was something about them that Memling could not identify for a moment, that made them different from the people of Belgium. As he stood to one side, watching, it occurred to him that many were laughing. Laughter in occupied Europe was reserved for the Nazis.

Memling had expected to find a taxi, but as he came out of the station into the raw, dark morning there was only a single cab waiting with its light off. A military officer jumped in, and it drove off without hesitation. Memling turned back into the station then and went along to the Circle Line to join the long, long queue.

He came up the well-remembered steps. The cold fresh air blowing off the Thames helped dissolve the memory of the interrogation and the smugness of those who had not been there and who twisted facts to suit their preconceptions. He was free of the terror, and that made the rest endurable. No matter what happened now, Walsch could never touch him. He drew a deep, icy breath and laughed.

Memling crossed Victoria Embankment to stand watching the river for a moment. A policeman hesitated, taking in his worn, baggy clothes, then passed on.

The sky was turning from grey to blue as the sun edged up and the cloud eased away; but the wind had also stiffened, and Memling was thoroughly chilled by the time he had walked up Northumberland Avenue to the grey unassuming building that had been MI6 headquarters for so many years.

Inside, the same elderly porter nodded politely to Memling, as if he had seen him only yesterday. There was no recognition in the nod, and no surprise either at his ill-kempt appearance. It was said the porter condescended to recognise the director but only now and again.

Memling gave his name and asked to see Englesby, and the porter consulted a child's exercise book in which he kept a list of appointments for the day.

'I am afraid, sir, that your name is not here. Do you perhaps have the wrong building?'

'Perhaps Mr Englesby has forgotten, or has not been notified. Please telephone his office.'

A marine sergeant stepped from a tiny cubicle and looked Memling up and down. 'Here now. What's this? Lost your way, have you? Off with you now. There's no . . .'

Memling shook his hand off. 'My name is Jan Memling, and I have business here. Who the bloody hell are . . .'

He shut up abruptly as a revolver was pressed against his head and he was surrounded by three other marines, all heavily armed. His wrists were cuffed, and he was shoved into the cubicle and slammed against the wall.

'All right, now,' the sergeant snapped. 'Just you stand right there, mate. Try any more funny moves and I'll break your neck.'

Memling heard a clatter of high-heeled shoes on the stairs, and a moment later a woman's voice was demanding to know what was going on. The officer tried to send her on her way, but she pushed past him.

'Are you Jan Memling?' she demanded, and he nodded, bemused.

'Turn around,' she snapped, and when he did so she compared his face with the photograph in her hand. 'Take those handcuffs off that man,' she told the red-faced soldier, 'and next time, know what you are about.'

Memling rubbed his wrists where the steel rings had bitten deeply. The sergeant glared at him.

For a long moment he said nothing, then, 'There are a lot of people like you, Sergeant, across the Channel. They wear black uniforms and they like to abuse people too.'

The man's face went even redder, and Memling turned to the woman. 'Thank you, miss. I wish to see Mr Englesby.'

'I know,' she smiled. 'I'm his secretary, Janet Thompson. I'll take you up.'

She turned without waiting for an answer and started up the stairs. Memling followed, thinking that her accent was definitely not London. Closer to south-west with the burr and the *zz*'s removed. At the top of the steps she gave him a quick smile and led him along to the well-remembered office. He noticed, as she opened the door and half-turned to see if he was following, that her figure was slim but full and that she walked with a slight sway, all of which reminded him very much of Margot. My God, he thought, I'll see her in a few hours. What a surprise . . . she'll come home from the shop and I'll be there. It was only the strictest self-discipline that had kept him from going straight home as it was.

'Mr Memling?'

He snapped awake as if from a trance, and she smiled at his awkwardness. 'I'm sorry,' he mumbled. 'Don't quite know where I am yet.'

Englesby was waiting for him in the inner office. He looked up as Janet ushered Memling in, then motioned to a chair set before the desk. 'Be with you in a moment, Memling.' He could have been gone only a few hours rather than eight months from the warmth of Englesby's reception, but he was too tired to care.

To cover the lapse, Janet asked him if he would have a cup of tea; and when Memling shook his head, she glared at Englesby and went out. Englesby read on for a moment more, then closed the file and looked up.

'Sorry about that. Too damned much to do. Home safe and sound, I see. Bit of a bad time over there?'

Memling realised the questions were rhetorical, and contented himself with a nod.

Englesby shifted in his chair. 'Had some nonsense come through on the blower that you were asking to be pulled out. Something about vital information. Can't be true, I told the director.'

Memling took a deep breath. 'I did not ask to be pulled out,' he said through clenched teeth as his anger welled up again. 'The head of the local resistance unit made the request – without my knowledge.' Thirty seconds had not passed and already Memling knew exactly what Englesby was doing – if this blew up, he wanted to make certain that the blame fell anywhere but on him. 'As my controller, you had the option of accepting or refusing that request.'

'True enough.' Englesby's stare was empty. 'Now that we have that settled, suppose you tell me what this is all about.'

'It's to do with rockets again,' Memling said quietly. He could not for the life of him have explained why he was deliberately antagonising Englesby, except, he realised, it made no difference either way.

Without raising his eyes from the sheet of paper on his desk, Englesby growled, 'This had better be good, Memling. As I am certain you know by now, you have cost us an entire resistance network.'

Memling stared at his hands, watched them clench until the blood was squeezed away and the roaring grew and grew in his ears. How had the Germans known they would be there in that clearing . . . ? Had the girl, Maria, not been able to commit suicide after all . . . ? But then, Paul was so certain . . .

'Damn it, Memling, answer me. What about these rockets of yours?'

Jan looked up, and the blackness that had threatened to engulf him began to recede. But his face was stark and white, and even Englesby was a bit shaken. 'Are you all right, man? Shall I call for a doctor . . . ?'

Memling shook his head and wiped at his damp forehead. He took a deep, shaky breath and heard Englesby telling the girl over the telephone to bring in some tea after all.

He forced himself to concentrate then, to ignore the implications of his reception. In a strained voice he described the past eight months in Belgium, the position he had held at the Royal Gun Factory, his glimpse of Wernher von Braun, his look at the rocket engines, and his calculations. 'Paul was an artillery engineer, as you are no doubt aware. He repeated my calculations, and when he was convinced, he made the decision to take me out. The first I knew of it was last night' – my God, he thought, was it only last night – 'when they killed the Gestapo people following me.'

Of a sudden, Memling knew how the Germans had found the landing site. Walsch had cared nothing for Maria or for him. They were merely pawns, expendable, as were his own people, the two men in the Volkswagen. By applying enough pressure, Walsch had forced the Belgian resistance to move, to attempt to spirit

Memling away, and he had then followed them to the landing site. Memling felt physically sick as he came to the realisation that he and not Maria was the Judas goat. He had been used to set up the Belgians. The presence of von Braun, the shrouded rocket engines, the closed section of the factory, were all part of an elaborate plot – Walsch, knowing of his friendship with Wernher von Braun, would certainly have guessed that he would be intrigued enough by rocket motors to contact the resistance and send word to London. And it had worked. Ah, Christ. He closed his eyes, wondering how he could have been so stupid.

'I see,' Englesby murmured. 'You say this Paul considered this information you have about these German rockets to be quite important? Then I suppose you had better talk with the ordnance people. I'll try to set something up immediately. And you'd better work up a report right away while everything is clear in your mind.'

He paused, then shook his head. 'I'm certain that what you say is substantially true, Memling. However, you must realise there's bound to be a bit of a flap over the loss of an entire resistance group involved in bringing home one operative with a wild claim to having uncovered a new secret weapon . . . again. Whatever you say will be interpreted in that light. Perhaps in your excitement, or in the pressure of the moment, a bit of exaggeration crept into your estimates? Entirely understandable of course, but you must keep in mind that when the NBBS got the wind up about aerial torpedoes or some such nonsense last August, nothing came of it.'

'The NBBS?' Memling asked dully.

'Heh? Yes, I suppose you wouldn't know about that. The New British Broadcasting System, they call themselves. Run by that fellow Goebbels. Radio station in Berlin, beamed here. Nothing but propaganda by renegade Englishmen. Anyway, like so many of Goebbels's claims, there was nothing to this aerial torpedo nonsense. BBC did an analysis of their broadcasts over several weeks. Found most of them came right from those – oh, what do you call that silly stuff by that man Wells, and Verne . . . and, well, your kind of stuff, rockets to the moon and all that?'

'Science fiction,' Memling answered tightly.

'Ah, yes. Science fiction. Buck Rogers and all that. Most of it seems to be American, doesn't it?'

'Submarines were once considered science fiction,' Memling could not resist adding, but he knew Englesby was right.

'Yes, I dare say. In the meantime I'll just get on to the ministry . . .'

There was nothing for it now but to admit he had been duped and therefore was responsible for how many Belgian lives?

'If you don't mind, sir' – Memling's voice was full of defeat – 'I would like to go home first and see my wife. She doesn't know I'm back yet – ' He broke off.

A strange expression passed across Englesby's face. 'Ah, Memling . . .' He swallowed and took out a handkerchief to touch his upper lip. 'As I am sure you saw, London has experienced a very heavy bombing . . . it began in September. There was a blitz. Caused a great deal of damage and in the first two weeks . . .'

Memling had never seen the man at a loss for words before, and then an ugly thought crossed his mind. 'What are you trying to say, damn you?' He was half out of his chair and shouting.

'Your wife was killed during a bombing two months ago.'

For a moment Memling was certain that he had misunderstood. He stared at Englesby, trying to make sense of the words, but it was no use. He tried to rise, but his knees buckled and he fell back.

'There was nothing anyone could do. The fire brigades were on to it as soon as possible. But there wasn't anything . . . the entire block . . . I know what you must be feeling, old man, but the only thing to do' – he wiped his forehead – 'is to keep on.'

Memling left the office, thrust past the wide-eyed secretary, and raced down the stairs. Afterwards he was never to be certain how he crossed London. He was able to recall that as he approached the avenue everything appeared normal enough. There was no damage to be seen, and people went about their business in the usual manner. Only the absence of children and motor vehicles was remarkable. But when he turned the corner, the devastation was complete. Where had stood half a block of semi-detached houses and, across the road, a school, a police station, a fire-brigade headquarters, shops, and all the normal complement of a South London neighbourhood, now there was nothing. And beyond that, great gaping holes appeared where buildings had once stood, as if selected teeth had been removed from a giant's mouth.

All the landmarks were gone, obliterated. Memling could not even know for certain if he were standing where his own house had been. The disposal crews had cleared the rubble from the road into long rows of broken timber, brick and twisted pipe, smashed furniture and torn cloth. He turned slowly, surveying the block. All the neighbours were gone as well; those not killed outright had been removed, said a sad-faced policeman who stood beside him a while and told him how the German bombers had struck in the early morning hours when people generally took shelter under the stairwells or in their basements rather than going out into the cold and wet. There was no reason to expect bombs here; there was nothing to attract them but shops and homes. The policeman shrugged. That was in the early days of the blitz, before they had all learned what was what.

After a while he left Memling standing before the rubble that had been his home. It was safe enough, the policeman judged. The man did not exhibit any of the usual signs of potential suicide, uncontrollable hysteria or violence. And he was profoundly glad of that. He had been on duty since the first raid at eight the evening before, and he was exhausted.

Peenemünde–Prague September 1941

The scream gained in scale and volume. Franz Bethwig watched, fingers gripping the edge of the bench so hard his knuckles were bloodless. When the needle registered 128,000 kilograms of thrust, nearly five times that of the A-4, a slow grin spread across his face. The noise was deafening, even inside the blockhouse, and he could imagine what it was like outside. The twenty-centimetre protective quartz glass was vibrating so much that his view of the test stand was obscured. That was something he had not thought of; the cameras were sheltered behind such windows and the film would be too blurred to be of use.

The television screen, at any rate, was clear enough. As he shifted his glance he saw a white flare spring the length of the engine casing. Bethwig lunged for the fuel cut-off, but there was no time. Just before the test area disappeared in a whirlwind of flame, he thought he had seen the casing split along its centre line. The concussion slammed the blockhouse with a solid hammer of sound, and the television screen went blank.

Fire raged beyond the windows, two of which had been scarred with debris, but even so, he could see that the test stand was being flooded with sea water. The fire blast would cause little damage to the steel and concrete test area where everything was designed to minimise blast effects. But the prototype A-10 engine would be a total loss.

Exhaustion swept over him, and he turned away to gather the tangles of paper tape spewed from the recording instruments. He stripped the circular graph from the thrust indicator and left the building. A hot breeze enveloped him; Indian summer had settled over the island during the last week in September, raising the temperature well past twenty-eight degrees centigrade. The wind blew from the land and seemed starved of oxygen. The mid-afternoon sun glaring from the concrete produced an insistent headache as he trudged to his motorcar, which was parked beyond the safety barriers.

Bethwig drove slowly along the road, squinting at the glare from the crushed oyster-shell paving. The interior of the Lancia was blazing; he was tempted to put the top down but was even too tired for that. The flat, sandy, pine-covered island with its modernistic buildings reminded him of a Florida travelogue his father had taken him to see when he was much younger. Under the white sun Peenemünde seemed to have much the same ambiance as that bit of Florida somewhere near a place called Pensacola.

He had resolved to take the rest of the day off to go sailing in the little catboat he kept at Trassenheide. It had been months since he had had a holiday, and he was pale and sickly looking while the rest of the staff had grown sun-bronzed over the summer. There had been little enough project work, God only knew. Priorities evaporated as quickly as they were set. Speer had been a great disappointment. Not only had he failed to persuade Hitler of the promise of their work and the dire need to avoid delay, but he seemed to have lost interest himself.

Franz parked in front of the block of sterile reinforced-concrete apartments that served to house unmarried scientific personnel, and dragged himself inside abandoning all thought of sailing. He was too tired even to acknowledge the porter's greeting. The heat seemed to have gathered inside, turning the building into an oven. Air conditioning had been included in the original plans but, like so many other promises, had never materialised. The units had actually been shipped to Peenemünde before being diverted somewhere else. He had seen the cartons stacked on the quay.

A persistent knocking woke him. Bethwig sat up, groggy with the heat and sleep, and swung his feet to the floor, ducking his head at the same time. His blood pressure, always low, had seemed abnormally so of late.

'Who is it?' he demanded, still half-asleep.

'Franz, it's Wernher. Are you awake?'

Bethwig swore. 'I am now, yes! What do you want?'

'I am going out to supper. I would like you to come along and meet someone.'

Bethwig lay back, spread-eagling himself to let the perspiration dry. 'I don't think so, Wernher. Not tonight.'

'Franz, damn it, open the door. I can't keep yelling like this.'

Bethwig stumbled to the closet and drew on a light robe. 'Just a moment, just a moment,' he muttered, and went into the bathroom to rinse his face with the tepid brownish water. Von Braun pounded on the door again and Franz flung it open.

'Damn it, I told you . . .'

Von Braun pushed him back into the room, spun him around, and shoved him towards the closet. 'I know what you told me. Get dressed. We are driving to Swinemünde for supper.'

Bethwig changed direction for the bed. 'Like hell. You go – '

Von Braun cut him off. 'You don't have a choice. It's in the nature of a command performance.'

Bethwig tried to twist away, but von Braun held him securely. 'Whose command?'

'Reichsprotektor Reinhard Heydrich.'

The great windows along the ground floor of the Walfisch Hotel had been thrown open to the sea. A faint movement stirred across the water, bringing hope of a cooling breeze. Bethwig glanced about the room wondering at the political power that could open an hotel and restaurant closed for the season at one man's whim.

Tall, trim in his tailored uniform with silver SS flashes on the collar and SD rank prominently displayed, Reinhard Heydrich smiled and motioned for his aide to hand around cigars and pour the brandy.

Bethwig had drunk too much wine, and even though the heat was diminishing, he was finding it difficult to keep from nodding off.

'How did your test go today?' Heydrich enquired as they finished the obligatory toast to the Führer.

Bethwig came awake instantly. 'I don't believe . . .'

'Come, come,' Heydrich chuckled. 'Surely you do not think you can hide anything from the head of the Security Service, do you?'

Bethwig toyed with his brandy, while von Braun looked from one to the other, his expression thoughtful. Franz was recalling Heydrich's first visit less than a month before. Heydrich had explained his presence by telling them he had been asked by the OKW, the high command, to examine security at the test site. But his visit had not been cleared first with Dornberger's Berlin office. As familiar as he was with the rivalry between the military and the party's own armed service, Bethwig could not quite believe the OKW would ever permit, let alone request, an intrusion by the SD. He had meant to speak to his father about the affair, but in the press of work on the new prototype A-10 engine, he had forgotten.

'The test conducted today concerned an army project, a highly classified army project.'

Heydrich dismissed the reprimand with a laugh. 'Of course. But as I told you, the SD is required by law to be aware of everything that occurs inside the Reich. Why, supposing you had been up to no good, perhaps even sabotage? It would certainly look very bad for me if you succeeded, would it not?'

Neither of the two scientists missed the implied threat, and both stared uncomfortably at Heydrich for a moment. He is obviously, Bethwig thought, letting us see the iron fist beneath the velvet glove. But to what purpose?

'Your test was successful, then, in spite of the explosion?'

Bethwig nodded reluctantly. 'Partially.'

'Partially?' Heydrich prompted; and although the smile continued, the eyes seemed to have gone pale with anger at Bethwig's obtuseness.

'The test proved a new fuel pump and nozzle system' – Bethwig told him the cover story with obvious reluctance – 'that meters fuel more accurately and increases chamber pressure so that more thrust can be obtained. A faulty weld appeared to have opened, and the engine was destroyed.'

'And how do you accomplish this increase in pressure?'

'We have replaced the intricate nozzle system with a simple iron plate into which a series of holes have been drilled at specific intervals. It is a more accurate system and will be fitted to all new rockets during manufacture.'

'I see,' Heydrich murmured with a sardonic glance.

Wernher had been sipping his brandy, and now he set the glass down. 'Franz, do you recall our talk on the beach a few weeks before the war began? Do you remember telling me that if we are to reach the moon, we need backing from the highest party authority? Two weeks ago I had a frank discussion with Herr Speer. He still sees the value of our special project, but, as he readily admitted, he has been unable to convince the Führer. He suggested that I speak to Reichsprotektor Heydrich . . .'

'Please, gentlemen, we are all friends here. You must call me Reinhard.'

Von Braun glanced at him, his expression dubious. 'Thank you . . . Reinhard.' Turning back to Franz, he tapped a finger on the table. 'He has agreed to help us.'

'Help us do what?'

'For God's sake, Franz, stop it. Reinhard has . . .'

'Franz, I may call you Franz?' Heydrich's voice was friendly enough, but his expression was deadly and his eyes hooded, and for the first time in his life Bethwig knew what fear was. What in the name of God had Wernher got them into? This man was as deadly as a cobra and twice as unstable.

'You are right to remain silent . . . to a point. But I am in a position to give you all the assistance you require. You have only to accept it.'

'I have described our plan fully to Reinhard,' von Braun told Bethwig, expression intent. 'He is of the opinion that it can be made to work politically.'

Heydrich chuckled at that, and his menacing expression disappeared. 'Yes, I suppose you could put it that way.'

Bethwig studied them both. 'Let me get this all straight, Wernher. You have described to Reinhard our lunar rocket plans, and you, Reinhard, have accepted them?'

'Of course. Do you take me for an ass? I am well able to understand the military and political advantages of such a weapon. And unlike so many others that infest positions of importance in Germany today, I am not frightened by new technology. This could very well be the ultimate weapon. If all you say is true, a rocket base on the moon would control the destiny of the earth. Germany could establish the new world order under the leadership of the Führer, and we would cease wasting our national treasure on weapons development.' Heydrich leaned towards them, eyes glowing. 'Think of it, gentlemen. A world without war, a world led by the German people, the master race, the chosen ones. Why, there is nothing that we could not accomplish then!'

For an instant Bethwig was almost carried away by Heydrich's oratory. Perhaps Wernher was right. Perhaps Heydrich had the vision as well as the political power to help them. But only for an instant: he had heard too many tales from his father about the power of the SD and its constant misuse.

Heydrich raised a cautioning finger. 'There is, however, one vital element which your project lacks.'

'I don't understand.' Von Braun's voice expressed his puzzlement.

'In the plan you state that explosives up to a thousand kilograms, and even rocks gathered from the moon's surface, can be used to bombard an enemy nation. But rocks accelerated to three kilometres per second will only have the destructive force of ten thousand kilos of high explosive.'

Von Braun nodded. 'That is correct. But . . .'

Heydrich's withering glance stilled the interruption. 'According to my staff, that is insufficient to destroy a broadly based manufacturing economy which is spread across nine point five million square kilometres. In addition, if rocks – which you so cleverly suggested – are used, they must be of a certain size and configuration, otherwise they will burn up like meteors when they strike the earth's atmosphere. There is, however, a way to raise the destructive potential of your rockets from the moon to something on the order of a hundred thousand kilograms or more of high explosive.'

Heydrich paused and snapped his fingers at the waiter, who rushed forward to refill the brandy glasses. When he had retreated, Heydrich smiled and raised his glass, but did not offer a toast. 'You gentlemen lack certain vital knowledge. That knowledge, and the means to put it into practice, will be my contribution to our partnership. You see, I am a very fair-minded man.'

Bethwig, tired and still irritated at his friend for having brought someone like Heydrich into their plans, allowed his irritation to override his caution.

'Herr Heydrich, please stop beating about the bush. What are you trying to tell us?'

It occurred to him that it must have been years since anyone had dared to talk to Heydrich in that manner. The man's face flushed, and his Adam's apple bobbed convulsively. His eyes narrowed, and his lips drew together to form a white streak. Bethwig realised at that moment that he was looking at a man who kept his insanity under very careful control.

'Yes, perhaps I should.' Heydrich bit out the words. 'It seems that my attempt to put you at ease has failed, or been rejected.'

'My apologies,' Bethwig began, but Heydrich slashed a hand down.

'Your lunar rocket must have a uranium bomb warhead attached to it. Then it will be as effective as required.'

'A uranium bomb,' Bethwig started to exclaim into the shocked silence but caught himself and lowered his voice. 'Is there really a uranium bomb project?'

Heydrich gave him a thin smile. 'You see, we *can* be of service to one another. Yes, there is. It is the most highly classified weapons project in the Reich. Less than two hundred people even know such a project exists. Now, would not a uranium bomb make the perfect warhead for your rocket?'

'Of course,' von Braun grinned, 'if it will be as powerful a weapon as postulated. It would only require one or two demonstration weapons exploded into the ocean to – '

'Into the ocean? Surely, my dear Wernher, a more severe demonstration would be required. Perhaps a city or two, New York, London . . .'

'Well, perhaps . . . although an explosion in a desert . . . it might show that we are – '

'Of course, my *dear* Wernher.' Heydrich's smile was even thinner than before. 'An excellent suggestion. I will have my staff look into it. The final condition of his defeated enemy must always be a major concern of the victor. They must either be crushed ruthlessly, to the last human soul, or they must be treated with benevolence and kindness. Anything between the two extremes will only allow the vanquished to rise up once more in revenge. Germany herself is a case in point.

'But to return to the subject at hand.' Heydrich paused to light a fresh cigar. 'I am in sympathy with what you gentlemen are attempting to do. With the understanding that military considerations must always take precedence, I am willing to assist you. With my help there will be no more need to indulge in childish and time-wasting – and what could be interpreted in some quarters as criminal – manoeuvrings for materials and equipment. Under my protection there will be no more need to hide requisitions for A-Ten development among the legitimate needs of the A-Four.'

The two scientists exchanged uncomfortable glances. A strict interpretation of the sabotage laws would see them both sentenced to long prison terms, or even executed, if the full extent of their activities in developing the prototype A-10 rocket engine were known.

Heydrich stared at his cigar a moment. 'I think we understand one another, gentlemen. Do we not?'

Both nodded.

'Then you will please furnish me with a complete set of your plans and a list of your needs, ranked in order of priority. All costs should be fully detailed, special suppliers designated, and the reason for their selection stated. I will then undertake to see that your needs are met at the earliest opportunity.' Heydrich paused and chuckled. 'Even though we will never make public my interest in your project, I think I can assure you that there will be no interference from other, shall we say, interested quarters.'

He paused and tapped the table to rivet their attention. 'As you are no doubt aware, the generals do not stand high in the Führer's favour at the moment. The army is now approaching Moscow after having delayed and complained for weeks. Already the weather has worsened. The rains have come early and will soon turn to snow and ice. When that happens, the advantage must inevitably shift to the defenders. In the spring the army may be able to complete its task, but for now the Führer's disaffection will grow. I am not one who thinks the war will end quickly. If we were to beat Russia, we should have done so by now. The war will be long, and you must give some consideration to your own positions.'

The delicate allusion hung in the air between them, and it was von Braun who broke the silence with a nervous laugh.

'Are you suggesting we join the SD?' he asked.

'It is certainly worth considering. There are a great many advantages. But enough of that.' Heydrich smiled suddenly. 'The uranium bomb project is well along. I tell you this in the utmost confidence. Now that Norway is fully occupied, shipments of heavy water, a vital ingredient in its development, have begun. The total quantity of heavy water to be produced in 1942 has been raised to 4500 kilograms. My staff forecasts that it will be ready by late 1944 or early 1945. No matter the outcome in Russia, our greatest enemy will by that time be the United States. Only a blind man could fail to see that. By then we may also have to deal harshly with England, particularly if we do not gain a quick victory in Russia.'

'You seem quite pessimistic on that score,' Bethwig commented, searching for safer ground. 'The predictions are that the war will be won by the end of next summer and that England will be ready to negotiate an armistice.'

'I admit it. And with what I think is good reason. The Soviet Union has massive reserves of men and resources. They are a strange and insular people who have always contested bitterly any incursion on to their territory. They show a positive genius for defeating invaders, and they have always been willing to make an alliance with anyone who will aid them. That is why I am not surprised that Stalin has concluded a treaty with Churchill.'

'But perhaps that may work to our advantage,' Bethwig suggested. 'Eventually they must fall out. The English fear communism as much as we do.'

Heydrich dismissed the subject with a wave. 'Perhaps. However, our concern at the moment has to do with the lunar project. I take it we are agreed upon the terms of our partnership, gentlemen?'

Bethwig learned at that moment that Heydrich could and would expound his own theories by the hour but was completely uninterested in those put forward by anyone else. The ultimate ego, he thought, and therefore most treacherous. Nothing and no one but himself would ever matter to Reinhard Heydrich.

'I think Franz and I would like to discuss it a bit first,' von Braun ventured.

'Of course!' Heydrich waved his cigar jovially in the direction of his aide, who sprang to the table. 'But I return to Prague tomorrow morning at seven. We do seem agreed on what needs to be done, so why not assume your decision will be favourable? Heh?' He stood up, carelessly stubbing out his cigar on the tablecloth. 'I am certain you will enjoy the advantages of working with the SD. Good night, gentlemen.'

'Finding the moon will be relatively simple,' von Braun went on. 'The basic tools one uses are radio, radio direction finding, and the stars, which in effect become signposts that do not vary in the slightest – at least for our purposes. If one calculates the angular distance between the moon's centre and a certain star before starting, it is possible to measure any deviation in the spacecraft's flight path or orbit as one approaches one's target simply by observing the angular distance.'

'Orbit? I thought only planets travelled in orbits.'

Von Braun chuckled with an expert's superiority. 'They do, but any object travelling in space describes a curved trajectory. You see, the gravitational effect of the Earth, the moon, the sun, and even such major planets as Jupiter and Saturn, all affect the object, causing it to be pulled this way and that. If each of these gravitational tugs is balanced perfectly, the effect is really a curved line.'

'I see.' Heydrich nodded. 'I assumed that once a craft reached airless space it merely coasted under the effect of the target planet's gravity field.'

'Basically it does, providing that such gravitational force is not overcome by one even stronger. Many people reading Professor Oberth's book made that mistake.'

'And how do you make certain that does not happen?' There was a trace of annoyance in Heydrich's voice. Clearly, Bethwig thought, he does not like being talked down to.

'It is a matter of acceleration or speed,' Bethwig broke in before Wernher could make matters worse. Heydrich had surprised him by showing genuine interest in the details of the project.

'The correct speed must be selected to place the craft into the proper orbit. Too slow a speed will cause it to fall back to Earth. Too fast, and it will fall into the sun. Even faster, and it will escape the solar system altogether.'

'Correct,' von Braun broke in. 'As the spacecraft approaches the moon, our observations become more accurate, allowing the speed to be adjusted. The occultation – disappearance of selected stars – behind the moon enables us to determine the exact course of the rocket as it approaches for a landing.'

In spite of the veiled threats of that evening three weeks before, Heydrich had since been polite and considerate, had even invited them to Hradčany Castle, his Prague headquarters, for a weekend. With brilliant autumn sunshine streaming across the pleasant garden beyond the french doors, Bethwig could feel tired muscles and tense nerves relaxing. That morning he and von Braun had strolled around Prague, and the mood of the city had certainly suggested that Heydrich was the model administrator he claimed to be. Bethwig recalled his comment about benevolence versus destructiveness. People seemed content, well fed and dressed, and there was none of the sullenness one encountered in Belgium, France, or even Denmark. The Czechs seemed to have adapted well enough to National Socialist rule – or Heydrich had adapted it to them.

Von Braun had begun to describe the rocket. 'We have determined that a single-stage rocket, a vehicle designed to complete a mission as a single unit, is not practical. It would be far too large, given our present fuels, and cause insurmountable aerodynamic problems. So we have designed a three-stage vehicle, that is to say, three complete rocket vehicles stacked one atop the other. The first rocket, or stage, is the most powerful, as it must lift the combined weights of the others. Once its fuel is exhausted, it will be jettisoned, and the second stage will drive the rocket into space and temporary orbit around the Earth. Then, when it's in the right position, the second stage will fire one last time, sending the third stage on its way to the moon. This final stage will coast along its assigned trajectory, firing its engines only to make course corrections and to brake itself to a landing on the moon. The rocket must then be refuelled from supplies brought up by drone rockets before it can return to Earth.'

Heydrich had leaned forward to listen. 'You find it necessary to build three separate rockets? I thought the guiding principle in engineering was to make things as simple as possible. It would seem that the use of three rockets would increase the chance of failure thrice over.'

'Actually, nine times, Herr Heydrich. But, as Franz said, we have not the fuels to build a rocket that can reach the moon in a single stage. In fact, even with three stages it will barely be sufficient. We must cut everything to the bone to save weight. Our navigational equipment, for instance, will be of the most primitive – a simple sextant. The smallest possible radio-direction-finding set will be used. And the pilot must be able to fix anything that goes wrong, as we cannot afford the mass to carry a spare set.'

'Is it a matter of more money?' Heydrich was smiling as he asked the question, but he was watching the young scientist closely.

'No. Rather a matter of technology. Our fuel experts have been able to find only one or two fuel combinations that are more efficient than the alcohol and liquid oxygen mixture we now use, and they have drawbacks that negate their value.'

'I am not certain I understand what you mean.'

'For instance' – Bethwig broke in – 'the alcohol and liquid oxygen mixture we currently use approaches optimum in terms of energy obtainable from chemical fuels. The power, if you will, of a rocket fuel is measured in terms of specific thrust per second, which is simply the push per unit of fuel consumed. Liquid oxygen and alcohol provide a specific thrust of one hundred and eight kilograms per second. We could obtain a greater specific thrust with a combination of, say, liquid oxygen and hydrazine which provides one hundred and seventeen, or even liquid oxygen and liquid hydrogen which provides the greatest specific impulse of all chemical fuels, one hundred and fifty-two kilograms per second. But we do not have the facilities to manufacture or handle liquid hydrogen. Hydrazine would be ideal, but Germany does not produce it in sufficient quantities, and the resulting performance increase would not justify the added cost of developing a manufacturing capability. Above all, an engineer must be practical.'

Heydrich replied, with a trace of annoyance, 'Yes, yes, I understand.' He got up to pace the room as von Braun took up the briefing again, but it seemed to Bethwig that his patience was nearly exhausted. The more detailed the explanations became, the more restlessness the reichsprotektor displayed.

'. . . will stand fifty-one point eight metres tall. At the base the first stage will measure nineteen point eight metres. The entire rocket will weigh 4,082,331 kilograms, nearly as much as a naval cruiser. We have designed a cluster of twenty-one rocket motors to provide a combined thrust of 3,401,942 kilograms. The motor will consume 3,985,230 kilograms of fuel in less than one hundred and twenty seconds. The second stage will have four motors providing a total thrust of 635,028 kilograms. The third stage will have a single motor providing 158,757 kilograms of thrust and will carry the crew and equipment. It will . . .'

'Please, spare me a recital of further facts and figures.' Heydrich heaved a sigh, then turned and smiled. 'I really do believe you gentlemen know what you are doing.'

He went to the window, and Bethwig realised the man was posing for them. He was dressed in what the English would describe as 'country clothes'. Tweeds made in Scotland and probably tailored on Bond Street or wherever that sort of thing was done. Heydrich was, of course, the party's prototype Nordic – tall, blond, blue-eyed, ruggedly masculine; and standing at the window gazing into the distance as if concerned with all manner of problems affecting the direction of the human race, he certainly looked the part.

'Gentlemen, it is too beautiful a day to remain cooped up inside. You do both ride, of course?' Not waiting for a reply, he threw open the windows and stepped on to the terrace, motioning them to follow. 'I am certain that you will find the course challenging. I laid it out myself.'

Von Braun gave Bethwig a startled look and followed him out. He did of course ride, but it was clear from the set of his shoulders that he would rather have spent the day cooped up in the library discussing the A-10 project, willing audience or not. Bethwig followed both men on to the terrace where the horses waited, thankful that Heydrich had suggested the diversion. It had just occurred to him that he was intensely weary of Peenemünde and the host of new problems that had grown out of Hitler's refusal to grant overall priority to either the Luftwaffe or the army for the development of advanced weaponry. In that single respect Heydrich had been a godsend.

'Come, gentlemen. You will enjoy fresh air not filled with the exhaust of rocket engines.' He laughed at his own joke, swung into the saddle, and, without waiting, urged his mount to a canter. Bethwig waited until von Braun, grumbling and muttering to himself, was safely mounted before following.

Heydrich set a stiff pace, and although it had been four years since he had last sat on a horse, Bethwig found himself falling easily into old patterns. The air was crisp and the sun pleasantly warm. Sunlight glinted on massive chestnuts and oaks in the parklike forest, and not until he noticed the huge trunks did he realise that he was in a medieval hunting park that had belonged to Bohemian kings.

The horses clattered over a small wooden bridge arching a deep brook. Bethwig, who had fallen behind, pulled up a moment to examine the lovely stream, drawn by the mysterious way it disappeared into a stand of willow. He was about to investigate further when his attention was caught by a flash of sunlight on metal in the shadows. Bethwig turned his horse in that direction, curious as to who else might be riding in a park belonging to the protector of Czechoslovakia, and saw a horseman watching. The man stared at him for a moment, then turned and disappeared into the trees. Franz had a momentary glimpse of a steel helmet and carbine. Of course, bodyguards. Suddenly, the day was no longer quite so pleasant. The war had intruded and with it the realisation that they were the guests of a man who must, by all odds, be a major target of any resistance movement in Czechoslovakia. Slowly now he pulled the horse around and followed along the trail after von Braun and Heydrich.

Franz Bethwig mentioned the experience at dinner that night. He and von Braun had been seated to the left and right of Heydrich, and their table formed an elevated T to that occupied by the majority of guests. Beneath the huge vaulted arch of a ceiling the vast dining-hall was lit by thousands of candles. Heraldic banners and burnished armour decorated the stone walls, causing Bethwig to feel as if he had stepped into the thirteenth century.

Heydrich repeated Bethwig's comment to the dining-hall at large, and the guests laughed dutifully. Heydrich finished his wine and motioned for the silver goblet to be refilled. 'Your question is perfectly valid of course. When you reach a position such as mine, you are aware very soon that there is only one defence against an assassin.' He waited, and Bethwig asked the question as expected.

'Keep the people sufficiently happy and pleased with you, and they will not fall prey to the blandishments of malcontents. By making this my rule, I have seen to it that the Czechoslovakian people will support a National Socialist government.' Winking at Bethwig, he raised his voice so that the majority of diners could hear.

'Why, there is every likelihood that as soon as the war is finished, Czechoslovakia will be invited to join the Reich under the same status as Austria, that is, as an integral part of the nation.'

Bethwig could see that the impromptu speech was having the desired effect. Many of the guests he had been introduced to before dinner were Czechs. From their smiles and whispered asides he could tell that Heydrich had made his point.

'As you can see,' Heydrich went on, 'the Czechs already enjoy many of the fruits of our victory. There is certainly no reason why they should not continue to do so.' He paused, then bent towards Bethwig as if to confine his remarks, but spoke loudly. 'Unless of course I were to be replaced and my successor to treat Czechoslovakia as a conquered country.'

A dead silence fell over the hall. Faces turned in their direction as if attached to the same wire. Nationality was obvious by expression. The Czechs were frightened, the Germans interested. Everyone had heard the stories emanating from Poland and occupied Russia.

Heydrich beamed at the upturned faces, and Bethwig knew that he was enjoying himself immensely, and he realised then what it was to have the power of life and death. He shivered, even though the dining-hall was overwarm from candles and close-packed bodies.

It was long after midnight before Bethwig broke free of the favoured few swirling about Heydrich and edged out of the dining-hall. Von Braun was still in there somewhere, smiling and laughing and having the time of his life. Wernher liked people and functioned well in such situations even though he preferred to avoid them whenever possible. The halls were quiet, and Bethwig found his way to the main staircase without assistance. SS guards stood like black statues guarding the corridors. Heydrich was obviously a great deal more concerned about assassination than he pretended to be.

Low-wattage electric lamps burned where candles had once blazed, the only sign so far of wartime economies. The walls of the echoing hallways were panelled in rare woods and adorned with magnificent paintings, most of which, Bethwig was certain, had not been hung in the castle before 1939. Heydrich certainly spared himself nothing.

He found his room again with some difficulty, and the door was unlocked. 'No need to lock doors here, Herr Professor. Who would steal in the house of Reinhard Heydrich?' the footman had observed when he enquired about a key. Who indeed?

It was a three-room suite: sitting, bed, and bath, all in differing shades of blue that were not quite contrasting, not quite matching. The effect was striking but vaguely uncomfortable. An exquisite Botticelli reposed on the eighteenth-century credenza that had been rebuilt inside to house a record player. Over the Empire sofa hung a magnificent Renoir, somewhat out of place but acceptable for itself. He had studied the painting that morning but had not been able to decide if it was real or a clever fake. Bethwig crossed the Persian carpet to the bedroom, switching on the light as he entered. Weary of the day's equal servings of sense and nonsense, he shed dinner jacket and shoes and started for the bath. A muffled whimper stopped him dead, and he turned to see the bedclothes thrown aside to reveal a pale face crowned by a tousled mass of long reddish hair. The apparition was so startling that he halted in midstep.

'What the devil . . .' he began, wondering if he had not got into the wrong room. His shock turned to embarrassment as a woman sat up, unmindful of the eiderdown slithering away. Bethwig's protest stuttered into incoherence, and the girl laughed, a quicksilver sound that filled the room. She turned to look at him, drawing her legs under so that she was kneeling on the white satin sheets. She brushed the blanket aside with a lithe gesture, and Bethwig was struck dumb by her unexpected beauty.

'You are Herr Professor Franz Bethwig, are you not?' she asked with a smile that made him catch his breath. 'They told me you were quite handsome and very athletic. I can see that they were correct.' She shifted her legs, so that she was now sitting, and patted the bed beside her. 'Come, here beside me. I can promise you I will bite.' This last pronounced with laughing authority.

Desperate for something to say, Bethwig cleared his throat. 'What is your name, please?'

'Oh my, so formal.' She pouted a moment, then gave him that heart-stopping smile once more. 'Inge. Do you like it?'

Even though Bethwig was experienced enough to know that her entire manner was a well-practised art, he nevertheless felt drawn to the girl and moved to sit beside her. His hands were shaking, and he clenched his fists to hide his nervousness. Inge touched a fingertip to his cheek and smiled again.

'Do you like Inge?' She postured for him, thoroughly enjoying herself. Her voice was pitched quite high, and as he turned to her the soft light shone into eyes that were little more than dark pupils. 'Men always tell Inge she is beautiful. They always want me to take off my clothes.' She laughed again. Bethwig closed his eyes a moment, in pain as he realised that she was mentally retarded.

'Well,' she demanded.

'Yes, very much so,' he told her softly. 'You are quite beautiful, Inge.'

The girl preened like a cat, arching her back so that her breasts shivered seductively. In spite of himself, Bethwig touched a gentle curve, tracing it upward towards the nipple.

'I have never before made love to a professor,' she whispered. 'Have you ever had a girl like me? No? Well, I can teach you and you can teach me. Would that be all right? Isn't that what professors do?' Her hands were busy unbuttoning his shirt. He made a half-hearted effort to brush them away, but she persevered with a giggle. A musky odour compounded of sleep and French perfume enveloped them, and he drew a shaky breath. In spite of his inclination not to touch this beautiful but helpless woman, his defences were crumbling. As if able to sense his misgivings, Inge sat back and regarded him with the perceptive understanding of a child.

'Please, Franz, I am a woman. Please do not deny me that.' She stared anxiously, willing him to understand. The combination of her appeal, her nearness, and her obvious need for him shattered his good intentions.

'I can help you if you let me. Will you?'

There was nothing else he could do, and he nodded.

They lay quietly side by side, and Bethwig wondered if he would ever again experience anything as emotionally trying yet satisfying. That the girl was an accomplished sexual artist, there was no doubt. Strange as it seemed, it did not trouble him when he thought of how she had learned. There was a sense of giving, of sharing pleasure, that he had always thought represented the state of love, and to find it in an SS prostitute had taken him completely by surprise. Bethwig wondered what would eventually happen to the girl and discovered that he very much cared. He propped himself up and caressed her shoulder until she murmured sleepily, snuggled into his body, and, with her fingernail, began to trace patterns that made him catch his breath. His erection came swiftly, and Inge was astride him before he could protest. She put her hands on his shoulders and rocked and rocked until his thrusts matched hers in desperate need, and, inconceivably, their lovemaking was better the second time, seeming to last for ever until both exploded into exhaustion.

Afterwards, when the girl had fallen asleep, Bethwig got out of the bed and covered her with the eiderdown. He stood a moment, studying her face, then found his cigarettes, filled a large tumbler with brandy, and went through to the bath. Lighting a cigarette, he eased himself into the hot water. Trying to concentrate on Inge, he discovered he was too emotionally exhausted. He took a deep pull at the brandy and then a second, half emptying the glass.

Franz Bethwig was certainly not a virgin; he was far too attractive and personable for that. Inexperienced perhaps; but even so, there had been affairs, and once he had nearly married. He supposed the sum total of those experiences must have taught him something about lust, if not about love. And then there was the contribution of the party to the health and welfare of the

German people, or so the joke ran: the promotion of free love – as long as you were a party member. A perk, one might say.

But never had he been subjected to an emotional assault like this evening's. No one had ever done those things to him nor, literally, begged him to do them to her. And it had all been so free, so natural; Bethwig shook his head. He did not want this; she was a cripple, a mental cripple. He could not afford such an affair. And she belonged to the SS. How in the name of God could he cope with that?

The bathwater had cooled, and the brandy was gone. He got out, dried himself slowly, and returned to the bedroom. The night was warm, and in her sleep Inge had thrown off the eiderdown. A pale moon had risen and was shining fitfully through the curtains, touching her body here and there with silver. Bethwig drew the curtains open and returned to the bed, entranced with the vision. For a moment he had an inkling of the power that drove men to kill for a woman's body.

Thinking of the soft presence beside him and the brief gleam of insanity he had glimpsed twice now in Heydrich's eyes, Bethwig slept little that night.

Norway–England April 1942

Lieutenant Jan Memling crouched behind the pilings of a warehouse, spooning tasteless rations from a tin. A frigid wind flung spatters of rain, and his sergeant cursed. The fjord fled into the fog less than half a mile from where they were sheltering. Beyond that, he thought, anything could be happening. Rumour had it that a German destroyer was on its way from Bergen, but rumours weren't worth a damn. He dug the last of the pasty mess from the can, licked the spoon, and slipped it into the light pack lying beside him. Memling then turned the tin this way and that, trying to read the scratched label in the failing light. It was impossible to know what he had eaten from its taste alone.

They had landed shortly before noon, in full daylight. A diversion, they had been told. 'Need someone to distract Jerry's attention while we drop a load of paratroops up on the plateau. Very important job, hush-hush. Wizards tell us there's a big hydroelectric plant at Rjukan the Nazi needs.'

Their target village was defended by a small army detachment that had grown a bit soft with garrison duty, or so they had been informed. No one, it turned out, had so informed the Germans.

His section had been targeted on the wireless facility, which intelligence had pinpointed in the local school, a single-storey redbrick affair that looked very much like an English village school. It stood on the highest point in town, barring the mountains rising almost vertically from the fjord, and so was a logical choice. Apparently the Germans thought so as well, and no one had checked the information with MILORG, the Norwegian resistance organisation.

Memling had realised there was no radio in the building as soon as the door was kicked in. An elderly teacher and fifteen or so students had stared at them in wide-eyed fright. Ten vital minutes had been wasted before the radio was located in the town hall and destroyed, by which time every German garrison in central Norway had been notified.

The wireless set rattled and the sergeant major took the headset from the operator and pressed it to his ear, muttered something in reply, and shook his head.

'Captain says to watch along the northern road. They've picked up something about SS troops coming down from Hergen.'

Memling nodded and went on staring out over the empty fjord. If he were the German commander charged with ousting a bunch of bastards from a tiny pinprick of a town that made absolutely no difference to anyone but the people who lived there, that is exactly what he would want them to think. In the meantime he would be doing his level best to bring his troops up by boat, especially now that he had the fog for cover. Norway's west coast was long on water and boats, short on roads and vehicles.

'Well?' the sergeant major demanded.

'Bugger the road. If they're coming . . .' Memling waved a hand at the fjord.

The sergeant major was a regular, and even two years in the Royal Marine Commando had not broken him of the habit of holding all officers in awe. 'But the captain . . .'

'Bugger the captain as well. What the hell does he know?' Memling sighed and shifted position to take the strain off his thighs. 'If it bothers you that much, send two men to the end of the road. But no further, mind. I want them within shouting distance when the Nazis come out of that fog. And make damned certain the machine gunners know their fire points.'

The two troopers were sent off grumbling as the rain began in earnest. Visibility was even worse now, especially with the coming dusk. The grey-blue sky seemed to have lowered right to the water. Across the fjord, streamers of cloud billowed in slow motion along the dark mountain slopes, and Memling, who had a fondness for just such days, spent a few moments enjoying the spectacle.

Everything about this raid had been screwed up from the beginning. The chief planning officer was killed by German bombs in London the day before the rendezvous in Dundee. His replacement, a hopelessly inept army officer who had given the plans only the sketchiest of readings, had undertaken the briefing, and consequently they had received a great deal of misinformation. And there had been no proper co-ordination with the RAF or the navy.

Two days earlier they had marched in full kit to the docks, to find the berth for the Dutch navy destroyer that was to take them to Norway empty. Three hours in the freezing rain and they were marched back again, eight miles in each direction. An old British destroyer was finally substituted, one of the American lend-lease four-stackers that lacked the speed to get them in and out quickly. As a result, the landing was made in daylight rather than at dawn. Of course no one had thought to inform the RAF, who were to raid three airfields nearby, of the delay, and so they had gone according to the original schedule. Consequently the Mosquitoes, laid on hastily to provide badly needed close support, were jumped over the North Sea and turned back.

That and the fact that Captain Miles Renson, a regular marine officer with extensive service in Greece and Crete, had proven to be a bungler. Renson was making drastic mistakes, and Memling was damned if he was going to contribute to them. If Renson insisted upon concentrating his forces in the wrong spot, he certainly would not help him commit suicide.

The more he studied the narrow beach, the more he was convinced the German attack would come this way. Renson had already ignored his radioed warning as well as the runner sent to convince him. The captain was going to make damned certain he did not take advice from a junior officer, and a mere volunteer at that.

Memling made up his mind abruptly. 'Sergeant Major, keep the men here and under cover. No one is to move without my express permission. That includes instructions from the captain. Understand?'

The man's expression was apprehensive, but he acknowledged the order.

'I'm taking Corporal Hayward with me to make a sweep along the beach to the north and west. If anything happens, I'll fire a red flare. Either way, you'll know I was right.'

The sergeant major gave him a sceptical look, and Memling

shrugged and motioned Hayward after him as he started up the slope to the road edging the beach.

Thirty yards on, the road swerved inland a few hundred feet. Memling vaulted the low wood fence and jumped down to the beach. The road would have been easier, but there were still snipers about and Renson refused to clear them out, claiming the risk was too great.

They trotted along, keeping a wary eye out for enemy troops that might have infiltrated to test their defences. The beach was littered with a winter's accumulation of driftwood, making progress difficult.

Hayward had fallen behind a few paces and was moving swiftly, scanning to the sides and rear. Memling was glad that he had picked the stubby Yorkshireman. He was probably the steadiest of the lot, and that was saying a great deal. Nearly all of the commandos were regulars chosen from the various branches of the service. If any survived, it would be because of their skill. Most of the men on this job had seen action before, hit-and-run nuisance raids such as this or else with a variety of units in Greece or the desert. Renson had as well, and that made his behaviour all the more inexplicable to Memling.

They had gone about a mile when Hayward hissed at him:

'Listen!'

Rain was falling heavily, and the wind was strong enough to set the trees swaying, so that it was difficult to distinguish sounds. Memling knelt close to the water's edge and cupped an ear. After a moment he heard it too, an oar striking water.

Visibility was now less than a hundred yards in the gathering dusk, but the sound told him that there was at least one boat approaching the town. He swore to himself. Who the devil is in that boat – German troops or Norwegian fishermen? The question had not occurred to him before. If they were fishermen, they might not know of the British raid; and if he guessed wrong and fired the red flare, it could give his ambush away. Yet if he held back until he was certain, there would be no time for Renson to move his troops to meet the threat. The familiar surge of exhilaration coursed through him then, and he laughed. The corporal stared at him in astonishment.

'Hayward, fire a burst towards the boat, high enough not to hit anyone.'

'Bloody 'ell!'

'Damn it, do as you're told!'

Hayward stared at him a moment, then as the puzzle of the boat's identity occurred to him as well, slipped the fire selector button on his Sten to the right for automatic, rested the wire stock against the side of his hip, and glanced to see that Memling had the flare gun out and ready.

Memling nodded, and Hayward squeezed off a short burst.

The result was an instant's silence, followed by shouts and gunfire. They were Germans all right, and Memling fired the flare gun as both he and Hayward dived for the meagre cover offered by the trees.

The German barrage lasted only a few moments. Hayward raised his head, spat a mouthful of sand, and gave Memling a steady look. 'Yer a fookin' idiot . . . sir.'

By the time the two men reached the wharf, the firefight was over. Drifting through the fog were the shattered remains of two fishing boats and several bodies. The shingled beach was littered with debris, and two commandos stood guard over a huddle of German prisoners while a third helped an exhausted soldier from the water. Captain Renson was talking to Lieutenant Peter Driscoll, commander of the second Special Service company. Memling was both surprised and relieved to see that his own company was still drawn up into the perimeter as he had ordered. The rest of Driscoll's people could be seen filtering back through the town.

Memling saluted Renson. Renson returned the salute with a suspicious glare. 'I do not think it was a good idea for you to leave your command, Memling.'

Jan took a deep breath. Renson, it seemed, was not about to give an inch. 'My sergeant major is very capable, sir. I had no doubt that he could hold the position.'

Renson remained silent for a moment, then turned pointedly to Driscoll who was watching Memling with a puzzled expression. 'Then the aircraft are not totally destroyed?' the captain asked.

'Not totally, sir. However, we damaged all those found on the apron and set the main hangar on fire. We got two more as they were being rolled out.'

Renson swore quietly, then turned away abruptly and hurried down to the beach.

Driscoll drew a shaky breath. 'What in hell is going on here, old man? I come back after nearly getting our arses shot off, and he's fuming mad. Claims you ran off down the beach against his orders.' Driscoll stared hard at Memling. The two had barely met before boarding the destroyer.

'Damn him!' Memling swung about as if to follow, then thought better of it. Nothing would be gained by a confrontation now.

'Then it's not true?' Driscoll asked, doubt evident in his voice.

Memling turned back to him, eyes blazing with anger. 'Of course not. That makes it sound as if I had deserted. That fool intercepted a German message ordering a combat party here by road from the north and concentrated everyone in that direction.'

'From the north? That's ridiculous.'

'Exactly. It made no sense to me either. It would have taken them a good two hours to reach us, but Renson withdrew from the waterfront and concentrated on the northern approach to the town. We were wide open to attack from the fjord. I stationed most of my company along the beach, then took a trooper and went along the north shore. When we heard the Germans, we opened fire. That gave Renson enough time to realise what was up and save all our necks.'

'I see.' Driscoll nodded. 'So you are saying that it was your action that saved the party . . .'

Memling stared at him, unable to believe what he was hearing. 'Don't tell me . . .'

Driscoll held up a hand. 'Now, now, don't get excited. I'm just trying to get this straight. Didn't make sense that you would run off down the beach. The old man has probably been in the desert too long. Doesn't really believe in boats any longer.'

Memling laughed ruefully at that. 'Perhaps you're right.'

Renson shouted then, and they started down the beach after him.

It was raining in Felixstowe when the Special Service unit came down the gangway. Memling stood by the railing of the over-age destroyer, trying to ignore the smell of diesel oil, salt air and coal smoke which pervaded the harbour. Grimy docks huddled under the lash of rain. Bits of garbage and wood floated in the oil-slick water. Barely visible as it made for the entrance to the harbour boom, a grey submarine wallowed towards the North Sea. The Luftwaffe had been at work recently. Great holes had been chewed in the line of sheds, and over towards the town the church steeple had been knocked askew. It was depressingly unlike the pretty seaside resort he remembered from before the war.

The last of his company trudged off the ship, and Memling followed down the gangway. A non-commissioned officer wearing the red flashes of the Special Police stepped out from the canvas cover. 'Lieutenant Jan Memling?'

Memling frowned and nodded. 'What is it, Sergeant?'

'I have orders to take you to London at the earliest moment, sir.'

'London? I've just returned from an exercise, Sergeant. I must see to my men and make my report.'

'Sorry, Lieutenant Memling. My orders state you are to be returned immediately.'

'Damn it.' Memling frowned. There was just one reason he would be recalled to London. 'Just where in London are you supposed to take me?'

The SP gave him a long, steady stare. 'If you do not come willingly, sir, I am empowered to place you under arrest.'

'What's going on here, Memling? Why aren't you with your people – this time?' Renson had come up from behind, startling his junior officer.

The calculated insult was too much, and Memling swung around, but the SP interposed himself. 'I am afraid, Captain, that I am to blame,' he said, neatly diverting attention. 'I have urgent orders for Lieutenant Memling that require his immediate return to London.'

'London? Immediately? What's this all about, Memling? Found some way to take yourself off active duty?'

Memling started towards him, but the SP gripped his arm tightly. Driscoll appeared out of the mist at that moment, closely followed by Memling's sergeant major. Driscoll nodded and, glancing directly at Renson, motioned with his head. 'Go ahead, Jan. We'll see to everything here, won't we, Sergeant Major?'

The implication was not lost on Renson who glanced from one to the other, then back to Memling. 'I see.' He nodded half to himself. 'I see how it is now. Perhaps you should go along, Memling. I am certain that we can get along without you.'

'Go along, sir,' the sergeant major urged. 'Lieutenant Driscoll is right.'

Memling nodded reluctantly and handed over his helmet, Sten and kit bag of Mills bombs. 'Do I have time to clean up?' he asked the SP, who shook his head with an apologetic grimace.

'Afraid not, sir. I have a car, and if we hurry we can just make the afternoon train from Ipswich. So if you will follow me.'

Memling had been in Special Services for little over a year, caught up in the first sweep through the forces for officers with special training. Even though intelligence personnel were to be kept out of combat units for fear of capture, his MI6 background had been accidentally overlooked at Portsmouth, and he had managed a transfer from the Home Forces G-2 unit to which he had been assigned. In the months that followed, Memling asked himself why as he was slithering up vertical cliffs or wading chest deep through freezing streams in what was euphemistically called training. And although he knew the answer, he was loath to formulate it to himself. But the Norwegian raid was his third combat mission, and, as before, he felt he had performed creditably. His thinking had been cool and clearheaded, and the cowardly fear kept under control. Not once had he experienced the slightest panic.

The SP led him through a turnstile at Liverpool Street Station and stopped to speak with a man dressed in well-cut civilian clothes. The SP produced a receipt book, which the civilian signed after looking closely at Memling. The SP nodded goodbye and disappeared. The civilian introduced himself and offered a weak handshake. His accent spoke of public school and cricket.

'Lieutenant Jan Memling, I take it. Name's Crawford. Work for the Firm, you know. Asked to pop over and bring you around for a chat. Cup of tea if you come quietly.' He laughed at his own feeble joke and led Memling out to an American car painted army drab. Not a word was spoken as the car began its journey through streets clogged with pedestrians and cyclists.

It seemed that every time Memling returned to London, the city looked ever more dingy and battered. The crowds were larger perhaps, if more ill-dressed, than before – thinner, paler, even dirtier after three years of war. But they still retained that infectious humour that had come to characterise the otherwise dour Londoners the moment the bombs began to fall. Traffic was light, nearly all military, due to petrol rationing.

Finally they drew up before the building in Northumberland Avenue, and Crawford waved Memling out. The car remained in position until he had opened the heavy oak door and stepped in. The hall was much the same, smelling of wax and age. The mahogany panelling still shone from daily polishing, and the porter still sat in his little office, looking less wizened than when Memling had last seen him – as if the war agreed with him. A different marine sergeant watched from the end of the hall. The porter nodded the usual greeting, failed to remark on his dirty battledress, and spoke softly into the telephone.

The hall was cold, as was every building in Britain these days. Jan perched on a chair. His eyes drifted closed as the events of the past few days began to fade. The destroyer had taken them off after dark and had run down the fjord in a nightmare of darkness, fog, and gunfire, which they dared not return. The fog had continued most of the morning before melting away at noon, and RAF Mosquitoes had arrived to provide a semblance of air cover. But by mid-afternoon the planes were forced to leave as the anticyclonic front that had favoured their landing in Norway moved west towards Britain, hauling with it the rain and fog and leaving their particular area of the North Sea in weak sunlight. It had taken the Luftwaffe only an hour to find them.

Fortunately for them, Driscoll had done his work well. The Ju.87 dive-bombers had to come from further north, and the ship's gunners had done a creditable job of holding them off, even damaging one severely enough to send it limping home before dusk caused the Stukas to break off. There had been two submarine alerts during the night, but the threat had never materialised. Memling had snatched an hour's fitful sleep before the seas began to break and he was seasick.

'Lieutenant Memling?'

Memling opened his eyes to see a neat pair of ankles. Momentarily intrigued, he followed them up past dimpled knees which even the heavy lisle wartime stockings could not conceal, past the hem of a victory skirt which caused momentary pause, then past a neat waist, breathtaking bust, and a pert and somehow familiar face framed by long dark hair. He got hastily to his feet, suddenly conscious that he had not shaved or bathed in five days.

'Hello.' Memling was certain he had met her before.

She smiled and indicated the staircase. 'Will you follow me, please?'

As they climbed the stairs she glanced back with an apologetic smile. 'Sorry we must walk, but the electricity to the lift has been shut off.'

Memling shrugged. 'Climbing stairs is supposed to be healthy.' He wanted to say 'good for your figure', but refrained.

'I wouldn't think you needed exercise, Lieutenant. You look fit enough.'

Before he could answer, she hesitated and half turned to him. His head was level with her chest, and he dragged his eyes up to her face with some difficulty. 'You wouldn't remember me, Lieutenant Memling, but we met just after you returned from Belgium. I'm Mr Englesby's assistant, Janet Thompson.'

Even then Memling had to think for a moment. He recalled very clearly his homecoming more than a year before. An image of Margot flashed through his mind, and the pain was still enough to cause him to clench his teeth. Janet Thompson saw the reaction, then turned and completed the climb to Englesby's office. Memling remained silent as she led him down the hall; and when they paused outside the door, she risked a quick look at his face. His expression was composed enough, but his eyes were wide and angry. His stubbled face had put on flesh, firming the chin and creating sagging pouches beneath the eyes. She kept silent and opened the door.

As the war had stumbled on, her boss, Charles Englesby, had also progressed. He was now responsible for all intelligence-gathering activities in occupied Central Europe. He had retained the same office, but the Ministry of Works, never one to be put off by the exigencies of war, had kept pace with his rapid rise. A dark-green Wilton carpet now covered the floor of the inner office, Memling noted. The walls had been painted cream, almost the same shade as aged watered silk. Several original oils in the manner of Sargent had replaced the hunting prints, and the massive walnut desk that occupied one end of the room did more than anything else to establish Englesby's new rank and influence. The man himself looked as prosperous as his office and appeared not to have missed a night's sleep since the war began.

'Well, Memling.' Englesby stood up and motioned to a chair beside the desk. He did not offer to shake hands, and his expression changed subtly as he took in Memling's filthy battledress. His nose wrinkled briefly as the odour of perspiration, cordite and petrol fumes crossed the polished desk. Certainly he has not changed, Memling thought. About to make a remark to that effect, he noticed another man in the room, a middle-aged army officer with a colonel's crown and pips on his shoulder boards.

'I would like you to meet Colonel Oliver Simon-Benet.' Englesby turned to introduce the other. 'The colonel is from SOE.'

Simon-Benet was youngish-looking seen close to, one whose easy grin belied the formality of his name. He shook Memling's hand with a firm grip. 'Englesby here has just been telling me they snatched you straight off a ship from Norway. I can see you must have had a fun time. Successful?'

Memling glanced quickly at Englesby who was looking faintly annoyed. There was no help there, he could see. 'Some. Did what we were supposed to and got back with light casualties.'

Simon-Benet stared at him for a moment, a faint smile lurking at the corners of his mouth, then clapped him on the shoulder. 'Good answer, Lieutenant, could mean almost anything.'

Memling's nerves were on edge, and the colonel's bonhomie was not helping. It seemed that it was always like this whenever he was required to visit Northumberland Avenue. He decided to take the offensive for a change.

'All right, Englesby, what the hell is this all about?'

The MI6 executive started, blood suffusing his face. 'Just one moment,' he began, but Memling cut him off, now beginning to enjoy himself.

'I'm not one of your people any more, Englesby, and I don't have to put up with your nonsense. Why did you drag me all the way to London? And who is this' – he hooked a thumb at the colonel – 'and what the devil is an SOE?'

'I see you two are old friends,' Colonel Simon-Benet murmured. 'Perhaps, Charles, I had better explain.' Without waiting for Englesby to agree, he pulled his chair up to face Memling and chuckled. 'You commando boyos do tend to run a bit roughshod at times. But don't blame poor old Charles here. This is my doing. He tends to frustration, stuck here in London when we all know he would rather be in North Africa or somewhere doing something useful. But then someone has to keep up the home front, hey, Charles?'

Englesby snorted but otherwise paid no attention to the colonel's heavy-handed humour.

Simon-Benet scratched his head, then stared at his fingernails absently as if expecting to see something there. Memling relaxed. The gesture was familiar and indicated that the colonel had spent a great deal of time in front lines somewhere.

'You see, we have a problem, one that requires someone with a rather unique mix of talents to help us out.' He stopped abruptly and turned.

'Ah, Miss Thompson, much as I regret having to ask this, I don't think we need a record of this conversation. Would you mind?'

The girl smiled and got up quickly, unembarrassed by the abrupt dismissal. It had happened many times before. Englesby had an obsessive desire to record every word spoken in his rooms. But his visitors rarely shared that desire.

When the door had closed behind her, the colonel sighed dramatically, then turned to Memling. 'As I was saying, we have a problem and one that must be solved quickly. So, the General Staff came to SOE.'

'And SOE is . . . ?' Memling prompted, sorry the girl had gone.

'Special Operations Executive. We do odd and dirty jobs, mostly behind enemy lines, which these days can be just about anywhere.'

'I see,' Memling murmured. There were all sorts of strange, irregular groups popping up all over Great Britain these days. His own commando unit had started life in 1940 under the sixteenth-century name Independent Companies.

'I am certain you do. In any event, the Czech government-in-exile has reported an alarming decrease in resistance activities inside Czechoslovakia, which they ascribe to three factors: the relatively benign occupation; the belief, heartily encouraged by the Nazis, that the war is nearly over and that we have lost; and finally, the personality of the man heading the occupation, Reinhard Heydrich.'

That name sounded familiar. Memling recalled his pre-war studies of the Nazi party hierarchy. 'Heydrich,' he muttered. 'I believe that he was once the number-two man in the Gestapo, reporting directly to Himmler?'

'Close enough. He was, and is still, in command of the SD, the Sicherheitsdienst, or Security Service, of the party. He has become a very powerful man – some say he will be named to succeed Hitler – primarily because he has the dirt on every official and officer in Germany and occupied Europe.' The colonel paused long enough to light a cigar. When it was going to his satisfaction, he remembered his manners and offered his case to the other two. He could not quite hide his relief when they declined.

'We have been assigned to eliminate Herr Heydrich.' His voice was soft but with sufficient menace to cause Memling to shiver. 'And we need your help to do that.'

'Me? Hell, I don't even speak Czech. How . . .'

'You do not have to speak the language. You are needed for another reason. The agents who will do the actual work are Czech nationals. But they still need a cover. You are going to supply them that cover . . . as skilled technical types assigned to the Skoda arms works. We believe the skilled worker is accorded high status in occupied Europe. And the Germans positively kowtow to quality control technicians. They just don't have enough, and a skilled QC man can literally get away with anything short of murder. Do you see?'

Memling nodded. From his own experience he knew Simon-Benet's theory to be essentially correct. 'And you want me to teach them how to talk and act like quality control technicians?' He felt the slow but inexorable surge of fear expanding in his chest at the thought of being sent back into occupied Europe. It had not left him after all; he had not managed to overcome it, and for a moment he thought he might be physically sick.

'Correct. An easy enough task. You aren't being asked to parachute in with them, only to teach them what they need to know to survive. You spent enough time in Belgium to see how the Nazis work. And too, they will only have to stay long enough to get the lie of the land, do the job, and get out again. What do you say? I know it's not as exciting as a commando raid, but it is rather necessary.'

Memling grinned in relief at the news that he would not be expected to accompany them. 'Of course. Not that I expect I have any choice in the matter.'

'Decidedly not.' Simon-Benet turned to Englesby who had remained silent during the exchange. 'Well then, Charles, you can get on with the paperwork for transferring Lieutenant Memling here on to your ration strength.'

Englesby snorted. 'I expected that you would want him carried on my budget. I tell you, it just cannot be done. We are already seriously over for my quarter and – '

'Now, Charles,' the colonel interrupted as he stood up and motioned Memling to his feet. 'I've always said that no one can figure a way around red tape as well as you.' He glanced about the room appreciatively. 'Why, I was telling that to Stewart just the other day, and he agreed with me.'

Stewart Graham Menzies was the director of MI6 and the man known as C. The use of his first name seemed to do the trick, for Englesby subsided with no more than a grimace.

In the outer office Janet Thompson looked up as they closed the door, and the colonel winked at her. She coloured and bent to her typewriter.

'Look here, Memling, don't be too concerned. This shouldn't take more than two or three days. Then they'll be on their way, and you can return to your unit. In the meantime enjoy a little light duty. I know what you chaps go through. Helped to design the training course myself.' He saw a bit of scepticism creep into Memling's expression, nodded, plucked the Fairbairn knife from its scabbard in Memling's jacket, and whipped it across the room to the door-frame where it thudded directly above an indented nail hole which paint had not quite filled.

'Didn't want to break off the point,' he chuckled. 'Now, Miss Thompson here, who seems to have taken a shine to you, will fix you up with quarters. Your end of the training will be done in London. Miss Thompson will arrange to have a car call for you at 0700 sharp. Cheerio.'

Simon-Benet flipped the knife back as he went through the door, and Memling caught it by reflex.

'He's nothing but an over-age boy.' Janet shook her head in prim disapproval. 'Imagine, throwing a knife in here like that. What if someone had come through the door at that moment?'

'I expect they might be dead by now,' Memling replied

thoughtfully. 'Maybe he did have a hand in designing that damned course after all.'

'Colonel Simon-Benet? Of course he did. Now, suppose we see about getting you fixed up. First you could do with a bath and a shave.' She picked up the telephone and dialled a number.

While she was talking on the phone, Memling went to the window and stood looking down on the street below. Again he was struck by the absence of motor traffic and the tremendous number of pedestrians. It was as if the population of London had doubled. And everyone seemed to be in a hurry.

'Bother!'

He turned to see Janet replace the telephone with an impatient gesture. She glanced at him and her expression softened to a smile. 'I'm afraid there is nothing available at the BOQ until after 2400 hours. Do you have any friends you can visit until then?'

Memling had to think before he realised there were none. In the entire city of London, he doubted if he knew anyone well enough to impose even for a single night. His few friends or acquaintances had all lived in the same road, and all had died in the bombing raid or been resettled elsewhere. His stomach lurched at the memory of the raid, and he struggled to get hold of himself. The girl was watching, her look of concern suggesting she suspected what was passing through his mind.

Memling shook his head. 'I'm afraid not.' He tried to smile. 'It's been too long since I've spent any time in London . . . Look here, that's no problem really. If you can arrange the proper papers for me, there's an officers' club in Curzon Street. I can wait there until midnight. I can also get a bath . . .'

'You will do no such thing. Those places are terrible and overcrowded. Here.' She took a key from her purse and pressed it into his hand. 'You can use my flat. There should be plenty of hot water, although you'll have to buy a razor. I shall have to work late this evening anyway and probably won't be home until nearly eight. You get some sleep, and I'll cook you a hot meal when I come in. And it's only a short walk to the BOQ in Cleveland Street.'

Memling started to protest but the girl would have none of it. She forced the key into his pocket, wrote out directions for the underground, and gave him his new orders, ration book, and enough money to replace his battledress with civilian clothing.

'Now go along with you. I have a great deal of work to finish.' She picked up her notepad and went into Englesby's office, shutting off his protests. He took the key from his pocket, looked at it a moment, then, conscious of his utter weariness, did as he was told.

Memling was still asleep when Janet unlocked the door and entered the flat. She struggled out of her wet coat and for a moment remained in the narrow entry, too tired to go further. In a strange way, she found herself conscious of Memling's presence and realised that she could not have explained to anyone else why she had offered him the use of a bedroom – could not even have explained it to herself. It was more than the fact that he was clearly on the verge of exhaustion. London was full of exhausted soldiers. Now that she thought about it, Janet expected it had something to do with their first meeting and Memling's reaction to Englesby's fumbled attempt to tell him of his wife's death. She tried to recall the young, frightened boy who had come to Northumberland Avenue more than a year before and to compare him with the quiet, tense, and competent man now sleeping in the other room. And she thought of her own husband, how two years in the desert had hardened him, changed him irrevocably from the boy she had once known – before he was killed.

Memling had left tea things set out for her, and she smiled at this bit of thoughtfulness as she heated water and took a plate of cold meat from the refrigerator, the last of her week's ration. She saw a shopping bag full of food and realised that he must have stopped on his way to the flat and used his coupons to buy it. She cleaned up the kitchen quickly, then went through the hall to the bedroom. He had picked her room by the luck of the draw, and she stood just inside the door, the dim hall light spilling over his covered form. He lay sprawled on his back, one arm thrown across his forehead, the other tucked beneath his head; he slept soundly. He did not move when she opened the cupboard door for her night things. For a moment she hesitated, biting her lip, not quite understanding what was happening to her, then went out, closing the door behind her. Janet went back into the kitchen, poured her tea, and picked at the cold tasteless meat until she found herself nodding off. She got up slowly then, recalling her promise to fix him a hot meal. Obviously he needed sleep more at this point.

Janet undressed slowly in the bathroom, shivering in the cold air and grimacing at the way her skin tightened into goose bumps and her nipples grew erect. The last thing she was capable of this night was sex. And she blushed furiously at the thought. Quickly she slipped the woollen nightgown over her head and went through to the empty bedroom. In spite of her exhaustion, sleep did not come quickly. When she did begin finally to drift off, Janet knew why she had offered Memling the room. She needed to feel the presence of a man nearby.

Twelve hours' sleep had done much to restore him, Memling thought as he peered into the mirror and scraped away six days of stubble. The blackish pouches beneath his eyes were still there, however, and unaccountably, there was a great deal of grey in his hair. Or was that just the electric light? he wondered, twisting his head to see better.

It had taken him a few moments to recall just where he was and why he was in a real bed beneath a feather tick. He had remained motionless, knife in hand, while the fear drained away and objects took on a semi-solidity in the darkness. Finally he sat up and found the bedside lamp. Memory returned with the light, and he was again ashamed of his fear. That strange colonel – what the devil was his name? Simon something, damn it, another of those double-barrelled names; in any event, he had been promised a car for 0700 hours.

He rinsed his face and pulled on his shirt. The clothes he had purchased from stores did not fit all that well, but they were clean and so was he – for the first time in more weeks than he cared to recall. In spite of the regulations, he had run a hot bath the day before. The girl – he persisted in thinking of her as such in spite of the fact that she had to be at least his age if not a bit more – had said to make himself comfortable, and he had extended this to include the use of a bottle of bath salts. He smelled like a French whore, but the luxury of the bubbles and the hot water had been worth it.

Memling found an army topcoat in the hall cupboard and slipped it on wondering to whom it belonged. It was a bit too large but would do. He did not think Janet would mind if he used it. He hesitated outside her bedroom door, then changed his mind. She had looked tired enough when he left Northumberland Avenue the afternoon before, and there was no sense in waking her just to say thank you.

It was just seven o'clock and deathly cold when a green Humber stopped at the kerb and he stepped from the doorway into the back seat. The driver gave him a sullen good morning and wheeled the car out into the empty street. Memling lit a cigarette and sat back, huddling into the coat against the penetrating chill. The only competing traffic was military plus a few essential civilian vehicles.

The driver made good time along Uxbridge Road, even though a light rain had begun to fall. Turning on to Greenford Road, they eased to a stop before a barricade. An SP in a yellow mackintosh peered into the car and examined the card the driver held up. Satisfied, he nodded, and they shot ahead. The driver barely slowed for a sharp curve, and then they were driving across a level sweep of brown and lifeless lawn. The car stopped before a bungalow-style building, and Memling got out. He looked about the golf course. Then, as he started to ask the driver a question, the car pulled away, leaving him to his own devices.

Somehow the army had managed to make the luxurious clubhouse look like every other military installation in the world. The interior was nearly as cold as the exterior, and several overcoated clerks worked busily at ancient green desks, ignoring him. The peeling walls were plastered with posters commanding closed mouths, purchase of defence bonds, and increased productivity. An SP came forward to ask his name; his manner and voice were polite. None of the clerks seemed to think that in the least extraordinary, and Memling followed him down a draughty hall lined with closed and padlocked office doors. Standing outside one office was another armed SP who nodded pleasantly to Memling's guide. Memling found it all rather unmilitary.

The SP opened a door and ushered him in. Colonel Simon-Benet was waiting for him, full of questions about his well-being, as if he were really interested. Memling replied, wondering what was going on, and when Simon-Benet discovered that he had not yet had breakfast, he ordered a tray from the canteen.

Afterwards he took Memling across the corridor to a largish room furnished with school desks. Two men were waiting, and they rose and nodded as the colonel made the introductions. 'Good, now let's get down to cases. I have asked the lieutenant to teach you gentlemen how to conduct yourselves as quality control technicians. Lieutenant, you have only three days in which to do so, but they needn't be letter-perfect, as they have only to fool border guards and security patrols, not other quality control technicians.'

It was late evening before Memling returned to Janet's flat for his things. The session had lasted all day and into the evening. Meals fetched by the SP guarding the door were taken in the training room. The two men, both Czechs, were quick to learn. Both had university training and so he was able to cover the concepts of statistical sampling, specifications establishment and production records smoothly. 'In western countries,' he told them, 'the quality control organisation almost invariably reports to the legal department. In occupied Europe it seems to report directly to the occupation forces in the person of the German works manager. In the former instance the object is to prevent undue influence by the production or accounting sections, while in the latter case it is to provide a very close check on the native workers to ensure that sabotage is eliminated or at least minimised.'

They left once for an hour in mid-afternoon, and Simon-Benet came in to question him about their progress.

'Just get them speaking the lingo. All you scientist types have your own jargon meant to confuse the layman and keep him outside your magic circle. By the way, I've arranged to transfer you back to your unit as soon as you're finished here. Unless, of course, you'd prefer to remain and work with me?'

Memling did not hesitate, and he thought afterwards that he may have injured the colonel's feelings by his quick rejection. 'Thank you, sir, but no. I would rather return to my unit. I've discovered that I'm really not cut out for clandestine work.'

Simon-Benet nodded. 'As you wish, my boy.' He hesitated, then said quietly, 'We've just had the news through from MILORG headquarters. The parachute raid on Rjukan failed. Both gliders crashed on the plateau. The survivors were shot. I thought you would want to know.'

The flat was empty when he unlocked the door and entered. Janet had left a note stating that a billet had become available at the officers' club but inviting him to stay on if he wished. When he looked into the bedroom he found his clothing was gone. Another note told him that it had been sent out for cleaning, and gave the address where he could call for it the following afternoon. The notes provided a sense of contact that surprised him. They, like the author, had a certain vivacity that had become almost foreign to Memling. A third note, slipped into the frame of the bathroom mirror, told him that she did not expect to return until after eight o'clock again, but that she would then cook him the meal that he had missed the previous evening. The proposition startled him; its generosity reminded him so powerfully of Margot that he could only stare at the slip of paper in shock. He snatched up his kit then and hurried out of the flat.

Memling finished his course of instruction on Thursday afternoon, satisfied that short of actual practice in a factory, he had taught them all he could. He watched them go and, for some unaccountable reason, shivered. The SP asked Memling to wait, and a few minutes later Simon-Benet came to thank him for his help. Memling had not seen the colonel since the first day, and now he appeared preoccupied.

'Really appreciated your help, Memling. Anything I can do for you, just let me know.' He started for the door, then hesitated. 'None of my business really, but I was in Englesby's office this forenoon. His girl, Janet, asked about you. Pleasant enough little thing. Your orders allow you to stay over until tomorrow evening if you like.'

He gave Memling a wave and, as if embarrassed, went out quickly. The SP motioned for him to follow, and at the front door he was handed a packet containing travel orders and train ticket.

A car and driver were waiting. The weather had moderated, and with the omnipresent stench of coal smoke banished by the war rationing board, the air was springlike. Memling got into the car, and the driver waited until he remembered to tell him to go to the officers' club in Curzon Street.

Janet had asked about him. Then she obviously had not yet received his thank-you note. The mail, like all other civilian services, had been slowed by the requirements of war. He decided to take advantage of Simon-Benet's generous offer of an extra day's leave. He could call at the flat, and perhaps they could even have dinner. He was struck by a powerful longing for her company that was clearly sexual. What the hell, he chided himself, the first damned skirt that shows an interest . . . Yet he knew that there was more than a casual attraction between them. Not even in wartime London did women invite men to share a flat so readily.

For eight months in Belgium and then the intervening year in the Special Services, he had lived a monk's existence. And with good reason, he thought with sudden insight. It was impossible for him to endure the anguish of losing someone again. Those few months with Margot had contained more happiness than he ever imagined existed and somehow left no room for another woman. That's a lie, he told himself savagely. But only partially so.

The car rounded the corner and drew up before the blacked-out bulk of the building housing the officers' club, a former dormitory for one of the many medical schools in the area.

'Will you need me further, sir?'

Memling turned his wrist to catch a bit of stray light from the dashboard. His train left Euston in forty minutes. For a moment the urge to stay was overwhelming.

'Yes.'

The driver waited patiently, and Memling forced the words: 'You can drive me to Euston Station.'

The coward has won again, he thought.

Peenemünde–Prague–Berlin April–June 1942

Wernher von Braun tore the end from the envelope and extracted the letter. He read it quickly, then flourished it at Franz Bethwig and Walter Dornberger.

'You would not believe me,' he crowed, 'but here it is, in black and white and from Heydrich himself.'

Bethwig grabbed the paper. It was true: official recognition from someone powerful enough in both party and government to make it work. He shook his head in admiration. 'I have to admit, Wernher, I would never have believed it possible.'

'And he says that he has the Führer's backing as well.' Von Braun slapped the desk. 'Damn, but this is good news!'

Dornberger tapped his pencil on the desk. 'If you gentlemen are quite through, I have a great deal of work to finish today.'

Von Braun laughed and clapped his boss on the shoulder. 'For God's sake, Walter, I should think you would be as happy as we are. We can proceed with the A-Ten project now and with the full backing of the government. You are in an even more powerful position than before.'

Dornberger looked unconvinced. 'Perhaps,' he finally replied. 'But it is easy enough to get such a paper. And these days everyone uses Hitler's name as if it were a talisman. If the Führer spends as much time reviewing and approving these pet projects as everyone claims, I do not see how he finds time to eat or sleep, let alone to direct the war effort. I have warned you too many times before not to mix in politics, especially at Heydrich's level. The favourite today can just as easily disappear tomorrow. We have all seen it happen. Remember Roehm? They shot him. And he put Hitler in power.'

'But this is Reinhard Heydrich we are talking about.' Von Braun grinned. 'Who in Germany is strong enough to pull him down? The head of the SD has got to be – '

'All-powerful?' Dornberger supplied. 'In today's Germany there is no such person, perhaps not even the Führer himself.' He paused to study each of them in turn. 'The SS never relinquish anything. The A-Ten will come under complete SS control, you two included.'

Bethwig shook his head. 'No, Walter, that's where you're wrong. We have Heydrich's own assurance that is not so. There will be no interference from the SS. It's our show, start to finish.' He smiled at Dornberger. 'Wernher and I swore that we would work with anyone to get this project under way, and you yourself agreed that it might well be Germany's only salvation now that the Americans have entered the war.'

Dornberger gave him a troubled look and picked up several folders from his desk. 'I only hope it does not turn out that you've sold your souls without realising their true value.'

At the end of March von Braun flew from the Luftwaffe airfield on Peenemünde to report to Heydrich in Prague. Bethwig watched the little blue Bf.108 disappear into the low cloud, then drove back to his office, conscious that his initial excitement was dissipating the more he delved into the numerous problems surrounding the new project. But then, it was always like this: intense excitement giving way to the hard work and sheer hell of wrestling with recalcitrant technical problems. He was also worried about von Braun. Bethwig had to admit that for a young man to become the director of a major military project was a heady experience, but more and more the man was acting like a child with a new toy. Particularly when it came to the Messerschmitt aircraft that Heydrich had put at his disposal. Von Braun was an enthusiastic pilot and a good one, but his first itinerary was definitely too ambitious. He would be gone at least two weeks. Following the Prague meeting he would visit contractors' plants from Munich to Stuttgart before returning to Peenemünde. Then there was the side trip to Liège to check on the injector systems being built at the Manufacture d'Armes. As no one high in management had visited the factory since the contract had been established eighteen months before, it was time someone did so, Wernher had told him. Showing the flag, he had called it.

Privately Bethwig felt it all had gone to von Braun's head; yet at the same time he did not feel as if he could begrudge him his fun. Certainly he had an outsized ego. All good scientists did; it was a prerequisite for anyone who wished to accomplish grand schemes. But in the meantime here at home where the work was done, he had several knotty problems to contend with. And now Heydrich was pressuring them to move the project schedule up unrealistically for political reasons. So far, von Braun had resisted his blandishments; nevertheless, the reichsprotektor was pushing them to reconsider. His last cable had been tantamount to an order and was at least part of the reason von Braun had rushed off to Prague.

They were, he thought, beginning to discover that Dornberger might well have been correct in his assessment of Heydrich's support; the priority assigned the A-10 project was more illusion than substance. Dornberger had pointed out to them just the evening before that even in Germany the anomaly of a political policeman conducting his own military weapons project at a research station owned and funded by the army would hardly pass unremarked.

'The political situation is becoming murkier all the time, damn it,' Dornberger had snapped. 'There is no telling which way the winds will shift next. After the army's failure to take Moscow last year, we are all on probation. Another failure, and heads will roll. And I mean that literally. You two are employees of the army – civilians yes, but still employees. So don't think you would be spared if someone took it into his head that we are wasting time, money, and vital resources up here.'

As the spring wore on, von Braun made several flights to Prague and to various contractors in occupied Europe, while Bethwig had managed only three short visits to Hradčany Castle himself. He was left more and more with the day-to-day operations of both the A-10 and A-4 series – the latter now approached flight-test status – and spent long hours in the construction sheds watching the assembly workers closely as the parts were slowly integrated and the first three rockets began to take shape. In the evenings he wrote reports to Heydrich's staff and fended off their demands for faster progress. Dornberger lent a hand whenever possible; but as the test centre had grown, he had moved into the administrative end and was more often than not in Berlin.

In the nights, between his infrequent visits to Prague, Bethwig was tortured by images of Inge. At first he was inclined to dismiss his reaction as simple sexual desire. But then he became convinced, or convinced himself – he was never certain which – that there was more to his feeling for Inge than mere lust. Uppermost in his mind was the intense desire to protect her from – and here Bethwig faltered, embarrassed – the clutches of the SS. It began to sound to him like one of those stage melodramas in which the hero rushes in at the last moment to save the beautiful heroine from a lifetime of degradation.

He could not even bring himself to talk to von Braun about her. Somehow the thought of having his best friend know about the girl was too much for him. How do you explain your infatuation with a retarded prostitute? he wondered. Consequently, the more he thought about her, the more confused he became. And night after night he lay awake trying to understand his feelings for her.

In late April Heydrich arrived by steamer and was met at the wharf by a band and high-ranking officers of the Wehrmacht and Luftwaffe staffs who watched stiffly as the great man and his entourage strode down the gangway. Bethwig did not attend the ceremony. He was too busy in the wind-tunnel lab arguing with Dr Rudolph Hermann, the director, over the meaning of new supersonic test results. Their discussion was interrupted by a messenger with peremptory instructions for him to present himself immediately.

Bethwig did not bother to change from laboratory dungarees but crossed the road to the administrative building white-faced with anger. Heydrich had commandeered the canteen, closing it to the staff, and was holding court.

In the two months that had elapsed since his visit to Prague, Bethwig was shocked at the way the man had aged – dissipated is perhaps a better word, he thought. The head of the SD and the chosen successor to Hitler stopped speaking and glared as he entered. An aide jumped forward, frowning at the interruption, and motioned brusquely to a chair near the front of the semi-circle of attentive listeners. Bethwig ignored him, dragged a chair from the wall, reversed it, and sank down, resting his chin on crossed arms. The aide started towards him, but Bethwig waved him away in exasperation. Heydrich resumed his monologue. Bethwig barely concealed a yawn. He had no idea why he was going out of his way to antagonise the man. Idly he supposed it had to do with his father's opinion that Heydrich represented the almost criminal element that seemed to have captured the party since the war began.

'These people have little concept of the fight the Führer is waging for Germany's chance to resume her rightful place among the world's nations,' the old man thundered at the least provocation. 'Instead, they think only of personal empires, of thrusting as much money and power into their bottomless pockets as possible.'

Bethwig knew his father was correct, and the thought that both he and Wernher could become like them was disturbing. It was a few minutes before Heydrich's voice penetrated the haze of weariness and indifference that had overcome him. When it did, he sat up with a jerk and noticed that von Braun was giving him worried glances.

'. . . and now that the liquid-oxygen problem has been solved, the A-Four is expected to be operational by mid-1943 and the

A-Ten in December of the following year.' Heydrich beamed around at the assembled scientists. One or two here and there nodded and smiled, but the majority exchanged worried looks. Von Braun's fingers tapped nervously on the table for a moment.

'Herr Heydrich,' he said into the silence, 'I am afraid your timetable is off. The A-Four has yet to fly, and the A-Ten engines have yet to be tested. We do not know what problems we may encounter. I have just spent the morning discussing the effects of aerodynamic drag on the rocket's structure as it re-enters the atmosphere. Several new facts have come to light that may – '

Heydrich laughed and held up a hand. 'Please, Herr Doktor von Braun, I certainly do not presume to tell experts how their work should be done.' He chuckled in depreciation of his own abilities. 'But I have observed that the successful scientist never knows when to turn his energies to new tasks.' He beamed at them all like a kindly uncle. 'Once you have fired the first one or two A-Four rockets, you simply must turn the project over to others and devote your attention strictly to the A-Ten.' Heydrich stood abruptly. 'But now we must discuss another subject, gentlemen – the use of slave labour to supplement the work force already at Peenemünde.' Heydrich frowned at the murmur of protest and waved a hand at an SS major standing behind him.

The sturmbannführer stepped around the table, glaring at the assembled scientists. He was tall and thin and wore steel-rimmed spectacles. Points of light glinted on his silver braid and on the death's-head insignia decorating his collar. His very presence was intimidating, and the officer played it like a well-practised musical instrument.

'The Reich can no longer continue to supply the reserves of manpower you demand. They are needed for front-line duty with our fighting forces. In fact, it may soon be necessary to call up some of your technical staff.'

The silence that greeted this last pronouncement was strained, but no one dared protest.

'We are aware that you need manpower, and we will make available to you within the next few months ample supplies from our prisoner-of-war camps. The Reich will no longer feed, clothe, and house these parasites without compensation. As good German citizens, you will be expected to set satisfactory production norms and see they are properly met. Labour will come to you in two categories: those with technical skills and those without. The latter may be used as you see fit, in non-skilled positions.'

The officer continued in this vein for some minutes before he snapped to attention, bowed once, and resumed his seat. The meeting broke up then, and as Bethwig lit a cigarette he noticed von Braun engaged in an intense conversation with Heydrich. He was about to join in when Dornberger sat down beside him.

'You never listen to me, do you?'

Bethwig glanced at him in surprise. 'What are you talking about?'

Dornberger shook his head angrily. 'You put yourself under obligation to Reinhard Heydrich, head of the SD and reichsprotektor of Czechoslovakia, and then you insult him.'

'Insult him? How?'

'By not coming to this meeting, you damned fool! Then, by appearing in work clothes and taking a seat at the back of the room. If that is not insulting behaviour I do not know what is.'

Bethwig grinned impulsively. 'Do you think he deserves any better?'

Dornberger hesitated, then smiled in return. 'Of course not. But he is an extremely powerful man; and if you cross him, neither your position here nor your father's influence will protect you. The concentration camps contain a good many people who thought they could snub high-ranking party members. Do you understand what I am telling you?'

Bethwig did, and for a moment apprehension nudged at him. But he decided after brief reflection that he was safe enough from political manoeuvrings. Nevertheless, as it was worrying Dornberger, he decided to placate his boss. 'All right, I'll play the game. Tell me what to do.'

Dornberger gave him a sceptical look. 'I hope you mean what you say, Franz.' He started to say something more, then thought better of it. 'Heydrich is giving a reception this evening. I have to fly to Berlin in an hour, so he'll be using my quarters. I want you at that reception, on your best behaviour, keeping an eye on Wernher. He is getting in over his head.

'I should be back before the weekend. Fortunately, Heydrich will leave tomorrow for Wolfsschanze. There is a rumour the Führer is giving him a new position. No one knows for certain whether it is a promotion or a demotion.'

Bethwig looked alarmed at that, and Dornberger clapped him on the shoulder. 'Come now, if you wish to play the political game, you must accept setbacks as well as advantages. As far as I am concerned, nothing would please me more than to have that man lose interest in your project.' Dornberger sighed and got to his feet. 'Unfortunately, there seems to be little chance of that.'

*

Bethwig, carefully dressed in his best suit, hurried across the windy common to Dornberger's spacious bungalow. An armed SS guard opened the front door smartly, and Bethwig caught a glimpse of several others stationed about the house. The hall was filled with fellow scientists and high-ranking technical staff waiting in a subdued line. Many wives were present, and they seemed more lively, chattering among themselves, each grateful for a rare chance to show off pre-war finery.

As the line moved forward, taking him into the living-room, he saw a row of SS officers, all resplendent in dress uniform, leading up to Heydrich. All officers above the rank of standartenführer, equivalent to colonel, were in the receiving line, those below were acting as serving staff. Even here there were armed SS troopers evident. Heydrich, at his most charming, was bending over the wrinkled hand of the wife of a Luftwaffe general officer, a shrill-voiced shrew whom Bethwig had encountered before. Heydrich said something to her, and she went into gales of laughter that cut off abruptly as he handed her on to Wernher von Braun who was the next in line.

Von Braun murmured something to the woman, and she returned a frosty glance before stepping away. Not even standing to the right of Reinhard Heydrich made a civil servant acceptable to the wife of a Luftwaffe general officer.

Bethwig shook hands with Heydrich when his turn came, and the reichsprotektor nodded. 'We missed you at the meeting this afternoon. Fortunately, someone found you, I noticed. Perhaps we may talk later.'

Bethwig returned a smile just as cold. 'I am at your service, Excellency.'

Von Braun gripped his hand and squeezed hard.

'Why the hell did you do that?' Bethwig demanded in surprise.

'Keep your voice down.' Von Braun grinned all the harder. 'Because you are a jackass.' Bethwig saw that the smile was fixed, and before he could retort von Braun had turned to greet the next guest. Puzzled, Bethwig stepped away from the reception line and snatched a drink from a passing tray. Turning slowly, he surveyed the room, counting four SS guards. He also noted that each SS officer carried a sidearm, whereas the army and air force officers present did not.

The line was coming to an end; the lower ranking technicians were being sped through now. With the usual attention to status, the guests had timed their arrivals to engage in the minimum of shuffling about as the line formed, always according to rank, imagined or real. Now they stood about in glum little clusters, nursing drinks and chatting about inconsequential topics. Clearly Heydrich's visit and the news concerning slave labour were having a dampening effect.

Bethwig could not understand their attitude. Every section head and administrator had been demanding additional manpower for months, even though they knew it was not to be had. Captured soldiers were an ideal source. And certainly they would find labour at Peenemünde more rewarding than the maddening boredom of a POW camp. There was no reason why they should not be put to work. Most would probably be French, Norwegian, Czech or Danish – good intelligent types. But even Russians and Poles would be acceptable as unskilled labour.

He felt a hand on his arm and turned to see von Braun smiling at him. 'Come, jackass, our master wishes to see us.' Again the smile remained fixed as von Braun steered him towards Dornberger's study, politely fending off two fellow workers who wanted to talk. Bethwig made him stop short of the door and pulled him towards the wall.

'What the hell is this all about, Wernher? Why do you keep calling me a jackass?'

'Because you are. Are you trying to get us both in trouble? Why didn't you come to the meeting?'

'I had something more important to do. The latest tests . . .'

'To hell with them. Nothing is more important right now than keeping that shithead in there on our side.'

'Shithead? Why, Wernher, I don't think that quite expresses the proper respect for our revered – what was it you called him? – master?'

'Stop acting the fool. You know what I'm talking about. There was also that little staring contest between you two a few minutes ago.' Von Braun hesitated, and Bethwig waited to hear what he was nerving himself to say.

'Franz, you aren't in his league. And even if you were, it doesn't make sense to antagonise the man. If you make him angry enough, you could disappear for ever.'

'Ah, so you are beginning to recognise that fact, are you?'

'What the devil are you talking about? Heydrich is a . . . a . . .'

'Gangster?' Bethwig supplied. 'Worse than anything the Americans ever turned out?'

'Of course! So why antagonise him? You are the one who told me we could work with anyone, anyone at all, as long as they made it possible for us to develop the lunar rocket. Remember?'

'Wernher, I do not understand you at all. Did you not publicly disagree with Heydrich at the meeting?'

A grimace of exasperation flashed across von Braun's face. 'Of course I did. But that was entirely different. A matter of disagreeing as to procedures, not outright contempt such as you showed.'

Bethwig recognised the note of entreaty in his friend's voice and gave in. He clapped von Braun on the shoulder.

'You are correct, as usual. From now on I will be on my best behaviour, so you can stop worrying.' Bethwig shook his head as von Braun turned to open the door. He was so damned naïve that he probably did not believe Heydrich would view a difference of opinion as an outright refusal to obey orders.

The reichsprotektor broke off a conversation as they entered and crossed the room to shake hands. Bethwig was again surprised at his limp grasp.

'We have much to discuss, so please make yourselves comfortable.' He motioned for drinks, and they sat down.

'As you know' – Heydrich waved a hovering officer away – 'Wernher came to see me in Prague two weeks ago. As I told you then, my friend' – he smiled at von Braun, but his eyes were on Bethwig – 'I was not satisfied with your report. The entire timetable for the project must be speeded up.'

Heydrich stopped; he seemed to be considering, then, apparently having made up his mind, he turned in his chair and waved at a group of officers. Obediently they trooped from the room, leaving only the aide sitting beside the door, apparently engrossed in a technical magazine he could not possibly have understood. Bethwig noticed that his holster flap was unbuttoned.

'Much better,' Heydrich said. 'Now we can speak freely. There is good reason for the urgency. The Americans are rushing troops to Europe. It is possible that a second front will be opened before the next year is out. Even though you are not military men, there is no need to tell you what that means. The Führer has bitten off more than he can chew in Russia. I was against the campaign at the time, preferring to wait until we had arrived at an agreement with the English. If the Russian attack had been held off until this year, I am certain that we could have weaned Churchill away from Stalin and would not then be wasting resources along the Atlantic coast and in North Africa. But that is neither here nor there. The Führer prevailed, as is correct.'

Heydrich sipped his drink, eyeing them carefully. 'What I am about to tell you must go no further than this room.' Both nodded solemnly.

'Then understand this. We will not prevail in Russia this year and perhaps not the following year either. Our tactics are incorrect as you have heard me state before. The Ukrainians are anti-communist for the most part and could become our strongest allies, but we persist in oppression. I have slight hope of changing the Führer's mind concerning this policy.'

Heydrich paused, and again Bethwig had the feeling that he was gauging their reaction, much as an actor would 'feel' the house. 'I am to be made commander of all SS in France, a position from which I will command unlimited funds, material and manpower.'

He smiled at their surprise. 'Now you know why Peenemünde will soon receive levies of POWs. But that is not the point. I have had occasion to examine our defences in France, and I find them quite inadequate in the event of a major invasion. In fact, no matter what is done to fortify our position along the Atlantic, it will be insufficient. Unless our policy concerning conquered peoples changes, which I seriously doubt, eventually we will be overwhelmed from inside as well as without. To prevent that inevitable day, we must cause the Americans and their English allies to leave the war. As long as the Americans are safe from the ravages of war on their own soil, they will continue to contribute material and men to the Allied effort. After all, it is good business. But let them have a taste of bombing and killing across the Atlantic and they will soon fall out.'

Bethwig squirmed on the sofa. He had made this very point to Heydrich some months before. Obviously the man had forgotten the source.

'Our uranium-bomb project is going ahead at a good clip. We expect to receive large shipments of heavy water from Rjukan, Norway, before the autumn. The Allies made a desperate attempt to destroy the hydroelectric plant, but all of their commando troops were killed. In spite of such annoyances, my planning staff informs me of the following: one, the first uranium bombs will be available for testing by late 1943 and operational in 1944, somewhere about mid to late spring; two, the Allies will not be in a position to invade Europe until May of 1943 at the earliest, with the most likely date of invasion in the autumn of 1944 or the spring of 1945. Gentlemen, we must be ready to knock the United States out of the war by the beginning of 1944.' This last was punctuated by Heydrich's fist descending on the arm of his chair. 'And that, gentlemen, can best be done by throwing the uranium bomb at them from the moon. It is nothing less than the survival of the Reich of which we are speaking!'

Bethwig was surprised by Heydrich's emotion. Perhaps he had misjudged the man. Maybe he was more than an opportunistic gangster after all?

'Therefore, gentlemen, it is time to stop pussyfooting around.' Heydrich favoured them with a cold smile and stood up to pace for a moment, hands clasped behind his back. A tall figure in black. The perfect Aryan, Bethwig thought admiringly in spite of himself, the essence of the Germanic spirit.

'You came to me because you were unable to gain backing for your project from your own employers, the army. You convinced me that farfetched though your ideas seemed, they had a great deal of merit. I therefore placed myself in some jeopardy in backing you. Certain people have been promised results, results based upon a very rigid time schedule.' He paused to stare at them both, and Bethwig knew what was coming next. From von Braun's grunt, it was clear that he did as well.

'Now you both tell me that perhaps it was not such a good idea after all. That more time is needed, that the problems are of such magnitude that time schedules cannot be met.'

'Herr Heydrich,' von Braun began, but the reichsprotektor cut him off.

'Please, no excuses. We allow no excuses in the SS. Only success is recognised. There is no such thing as failure, is that clear? You two gentlemen have deceived me . . .'

That was too much for von Braun. He jumped up and advanced on Heydrich who backed away a step in surprise. The aide came slowly to his feet, one hand on his pistol. 'Just one moment, Herr Reichsprotektor.' Von Braun's voice was cold and his face pale. Bethwig had never heard him use that tone of voice before, and he stared, fascinated by this new aspect of his friend's character.

'We presented to you a technological concept, not a finished product. Our proposals made it perfectly clear that this was the case and that rigid time schedules had no place in the development plan. Obviously your so-called planning staff has chosen to ignore – '

'That is enough!'

In that single command Bethwig and von Braun understood how Heydrich had come to be the number-two man in the Schutzstaffel, the head of the Sicherheitsdienst, and reichsprotektor all at the same time. It was not so much the threat in his voice as the confidence – confidence that any order he gave would be carried out instantly. Bethwig found his opinion of Heydrich undergoing an abrupt change. Perhaps his father had been wrong. Heydrich was correct. If the Americans remained an active enemy, the war was lost, and contrary to the party line, Heydrich had freely admitted it. It occurred to Bethwig then that very few people in Germany possessed such power. Even fewer knew how to use it for the good of the nation, for mankind as a whole. Thank God, Heydrich seemed to.

Heydrich stared at them without concealing his contempt. 'You are boys playing a game, expecting everything to go by the rules – rules you make up as you go along. Well, I must disappoint you. You are no longer boys playing boys' games. You are citizens of a nation involved in a war for survival. If we lose, we will disappear into oblivion in the worst bloodbath the world will ever know. If we win, we become masters of the world. With such stakes, your personal desires and feelings are of no importance.'

Heydrich picked up his brandy glass and stared at them over the rim. 'The schedule I gave this afternoon will be met. It is not open to discussion. If you cannot do so, or do not desire to do so, please tell me now. Others can be found to take your place.' He waited, watching them.

Bethwig knew then how a small bird felt as the snake approached. There was horror, a premonition of what was to come, and, worst of all, the knowledge that there was absolutely no way to avoid one's fate.

'Admirable sentiments,' von Braun snorted, and Bethwig turned to his friend in amazement. Even Heydrich was astonished. 'You can threaten and bluster all you wish, but it will do no good. The dynamics of technological development refuse to recognise fear as an incentive,' he went on dryly. 'Put us in one of your famous concentration camps and threaten us with every punishment you can devise. Perhaps you might gain a day or two, but no more.'

Von Braun picked up his own glass and watched in turn for Heydrich's reaction. The reichsprotektor shook his head and burst into laughter.

'What do you think of this, Karl?' He addressed the aide. 'I am unable to impress Doktor von Braun.' The aide permitted himself the trace of a smile. 'You have convinced me, Doktor. Perhaps my planning staff has failed to take the stubbornness of your technology into account. Let us not argue further. If I can have your assurance that everything possible will be done to speed up the project, I will be satisfied . . . for now.'

Just then the door opened and a senior aide looked in to tell Heydrich he had a phone call from Berlin. The reichsprotektor excused himself and left the room, but not before inviting Bethwig for another visit to Prague.

The two scientists left the reception, exiting through the back of the house a few minutes later. A sentry escorted them out to the road, and they walked along in silence.

'He is even more dangerous than I thought,' von Braun muttered under his breath. 'I thought he was intelligent enough to realise that certain things cannot be made to go faster merely because one threatens and blusters. This business of slave labour – how foolish can one be? Such people are not dedicated workers and therefore cannot be depended upon to do things correctly without constant supervision. In addition, they will show no initiative. You know as well as I how much we depend upon the observations of our own trained workers to solve problems.'

Von Braun stopped. Their path had taken them along the edge of a stand of pines defining the border between beach and sea. He stood for a moment, hands clasped behind him, brooding over the waves thundering against the sand. The wind was fresher here, and the air was sharp and filled with the tang of salt and rain. 'Perhaps you were right when you said I had chosen the wrong man.'

Von Braun's depression was so obvious that Bethwig clapped him on the shoulder. 'Come, Wernher. It isn't that bad. Heydrich is an intelligent and very powerful man, more so than ever now that he is going to France. At least he will be in a position to make certain the group of labourers sent to us contains a large number of trained scientists and technicians. And you certainly showed that you could handle him tonight. He backed off immediately when you stood up to him.'

In the blue light from the hooded blackout lamp above the road Bethwig could see von Braun shake his head. 'I don't think so. My impression is that he never deviates once he has set his path. Your visits to Prague are merely one more element in his strategy. He isolates you in that damned castle and persuades you to do things that you know are impossible.'

'Oh, come now, Wernher . . .' Bethwig objected. Although he knew von Braun was right, the thought of seeing Inge once more overrode his misgivings.

'Don't scoff.' He faced Bethwig. 'He is like the devil tempting Christ; he shows you all the world's treasures, then offers them to you in exchange for your soul. And the damnable thing is, you know that he can deliver. How do you think these people gain and keep the allegiance of so many people? Simply by bribery. What do you want? Money, power, women? Once they have you hooked, they threaten you, and their threats are very real. Very real! No, don't look at me like that. He has done it to us, Franz. He's offered us what we want most; the opportunity to build a rocket capable of reaching the moon. How long have we dreamed of that? Haven't we schemed and connived for more than fifteen years to bring it about? He has given us what we want in exchange for our souls – and he means to collect. Wait and see. And if we refuse to pay, well . . . you've heard the stories just as I have.'

Spring was in full bloom, Bethwig noted as the Mercedes limousine swung through the streets of Prague. Heydrich had sent his own car this time, a singular honour. The reichsprotektor's aide engaged him in polite conversation concerning the amenities and shops available at Peenemünde and opportunities to visit Berlin or nearby Denmark until it dawned on Bethwig that the officer was probing subtly into the condition of his wardrobe. If von Braun was correct in his assessment of Heydrich's reason for inviting him to Hradčany Castle, he could expect a visit from a tailor for which he would never see a bill. Inclined at first to refuse the gift, he quickly changed his mind. Good clothing was becoming expensive, so why not take advantage?

The tailor indeed appeared and departed with an order for three suits, a dozen shirts, a dinner jacket, several pairs of shoes, and a riding outfit. 'A gift from the people of Bohemia and Moravia,' he was told.

Franz had been impatient to get the fittings over with, but now that the tailor was gone, he had no idea what to do next. On his three previous visits Inge had been waiting for him in the suite. He supposed that he could ring down to reception and enquire about her, but that would certainly be considered bad form. The only other alternative was to wait. He poured a stiff cognac from the well-stocked bar and wandered out on to the balcony. His room was on the third floor overlooking the gardens behind the castle. Standing by the railing in the soft sunshine, sipping his drink, he gazed out over the carefully tended lawn and forest thinking that from this vantage point one would never suspect that half the world was engaged in a war to the death.

As the afternoon waned, Bethwig's impatience grew. He quickly exhausted the possibilities of the balcony but was afraid to leave the apartment in case she should come. By four o'clock he was beginning to wonder if he had misjudged the nature of this visit. To occupy his attention, he opened his portfolio and, replenishing his drink, tried to lose himself in calculations for a new nozzle design based on the latest wind-tunnel tests describing supersonic flow.

He found he could not concentrate. His mind kept turning again and again to Inge, recalling every detail of previous visits. She was not, as he had first thought, a mental defective; rather she lived in a world of her own, and he had pieced together enough of her background to understand why.

Inge was born in Thuringia to elderly parents who had died within months of one another when she was quite small. A cousin inherited their farm, along with the responsibility for Inge's care and education. The cousin was a drunkard, his wife a chronic invalid, and before she was twelve, Inge had been raped repeatedly – a not uncommon story in the more isolated rural areas of Germany.

The child was removed from the farm after neighbours protested to the authorities. Silent and withdrawn, she was several times placed in foster homes but continued her slide into a world of silence and inaction. Finally, she was placed in an institution for mental defectives where she remained until it was taken over by the SS in 1939. Because of her physical beauty she was spared the various 'experiments and training sessions' and became instead a plaything for the senior SS officers at the facility. How she had come to Hradčany Castle, Bethwig never found out, as Inge herself did not know. She had no sense of time, cared nothing for anything beyond the parameters of her existence, and was an intensely physical being. Bethwig did not know enough about psychology to do more than guess at an interpretation of her condition, but he had to believe that her nymphomania was in fact a reaction to her treatment as a child and later as an adult by the SS. Whatever, for reasons derived as much from sympathy as sexual need, Bethwig found that he very much cared for the girl.

Yet there was little that he could do to change her situation; the SS, by virtue of their special legal position, were virtually immune to the normal processes of German law. They were a physical and legal entity apart, and only one man, Reinhard Heydrich, had the power to release her. To obtain that release, Bethwig must please Heydrich.

Restlessly he pushed himself away from the desk and went out on to the balcony. The sun had swung deep into the west, and a golden haze lay across the vast sweep of lawn. The air was fresh, and the grass was that incredible spring green. Standing on the balcony, Bethwig thought the setting as pleasant as any on Earth.

'Hello, Herr Doktor Bethwig.'

He turned so fast that cognac spilled from his glass. For a moment he was speechless. Inge, wearing only a flowing, diaphanous negligee, was standing in the doorway, more lovely and desirable than he could remember.

Light was fading outside when Bethwig lit a cigarette and offered it to Inge. He propped the pillows against the headboard and smiled as she shook her head, stretched languorously, and burrowed against him. 'Good,' she murmured.

Her propensity for framing questions as statements intrigued him. She was so certain of herself, and with good reason. He muttered an answer, and she nipped at his ribs with sharp teeth. He protested and wriggled away. Giggling, Inge pursued him across the wide bed until he was trapped on the edge; then she swarmed over him, all legs and arms and teeth, until he was laughing so he could hardly stand it. She stopped then, and they began to make love again, more slowly and with deeper pleasure than before.

'I understand that dinner was served in your apartment last night.' Heydrich smiled. 'I trust you found everything to your satisfaction?' He was obviously enjoying Bethwig's embarrassment. 'Inge is a very lovely woman.' Heydrich frowned, then went to the window and stood with his back to the room.

'This is difficult for me,' Heydrich said with some hesitation. 'I do not want you to misunderstand my meaning. I do not want it to sound like a threat, only a fact, a fact we must all live with.' He turned back to see Bethwig waiting politely and thought to himself that he had not misjudged this one. Von Braun was a brilliant man but a fool where politics were concerned. This one, a realist, seemed to understand the game. Certainly his father was important enough for him to have learned early. And he is also greedy for what I can give, his stupid moon rocket and the whore.

'So let us get down to cases. Your friend von Braun has become an obstruction. He must be removed as the director of the A-Ten project.'

Bethwig laughed in spite of his knowledge that it was dangerous to provoke this man. He could not help himself.

'Herr Reichsprotektor, I would not presume to tell you how to rule Czechoslovakia. You are the expert here. So why, then, do you persist in telling us how to manage a scientific project? In any effort involving groups of people there must always be one person with the ability to make all elements work. Doktor von Braun is that person at Peenemünde. Take him away and your project will never be completed – at least before this war is over.'

'I had it in mind,' Heydrich said, 'to appoint you project director in von Braun's place.'

Bethwig stared at Heydrich in surprise, then shook his head. 'It would do no good. I am not a leader. Von Braun is. Colonel Dornberger will tell you the same thing.'

As if accepting Bethwig's opinion, Heydrich stretched in the chair, yawned, and patted his mouth with one carefully tended hand. 'Then what do we do?'

'We, Herr Reichsprotektor?'

'We, Herr Doktor Bethwig. For if I fail in this, we all fail. For me it will be no more than a slap on the wrist. My position is secure. But for you and your friends at Peenemünde it could be worse.'

'In what way?'

Heydrich gave an elaborate shrug. 'The research centre could be closed. There is already more than sufficient sentiment for that. You and your friends might then find yourselves in combat units, perhaps on the eastern front.'

'Ah, I see.' Bethwig studied him for a moment: let the reichsprotektor win this round and Heydrich would own him for ever. 'Even as head of the SS in France, Herr Reichsprotektor, do you not feel that you are overstating your case?' His question was blunt. 'Certainly the SS is strong politically, and your own position is so secure as to be unassailable. But there is still the army to consider and the party infrastructure. Even the SS cannot dictate to both at the same time.'

Heydrich sat forward with a huge grin, snapped his fingers, and pointed at Bethwig. 'I knew I had judged you correctly. You are a sensible man, and you understand the use of power. It is good to talk things out like this, to make certain that we understand one another.'

Bethwig nodded, not at all relieved by his jovial mood. 'Yes, I agree. I do, however, wonder why you are bothering to explain all this to someone as unimportant as I am.'

'Ah, hardly unimportant, and I think you know that as well as I. Your father is a very powerful man in the party, and your own position as an early party member counts for a great deal in itself. Also I consider you the key man at Peenemünde. I fully believe that you are every bit as intelligent and capable as Herr von Braun. Now, let's stop complimenting each other and get down to business.'

Heydrich leaned forward and tapped out his points on the table between them. 'Number one, in spite of Doktor von Braun's reservations, the project must move forward as close to the timetable I have established as possible. The situation has been discussed with Minister Speer, and he has promised every co-operation in the matter of material and manpower priorities. I have arranged for him to obtain the release of a thousand technically trained people to be transferred from the army to

Peenemünde. They will be reconstituted as a reserve army unit to provide security. In fact, they may be used as necessary.

'Point two, the rocket must be ready as soon as possible. Even if all the safeguards possible have not been incorporated. There will be no end of volunteers ready to risk their lives for the Reich.

'Third, Herr Doktor von Braun must be replaced. I see no other choice. Somehow I must convince you to accept the position.' Heydrich smiled pleasantly. 'There are any number of incentives that can be supplied. However, it must be understood that we are constructing a military weapon which will be less than perfect. That is the sticking point with von Braun. He demands absolute perfection and safety. As long as the task can be done, I am not interested in the cost, in money or lives. My God' – he threw up his hands – 'if we had to wait until our fighter aircraft or tanks were absolutely perfect in every respect, we would still be flying gliders and driving automobiles with tin plates welded on for armour.

'Finally – and this is the reason for haste – ' He paused and stared hard at Bethwig. 'And this information is not to leave this room, do you understand?'

Bethwig nodded, not certain what was coming next.

'In spite of the hindrance of other agencies, this information has been gathered. We have recently learned that the Jew scientist Albert Einstein, who defected to the United States some years ago, has convinced Roosevelt that a uranium bomb is feasible. We believe that work has already begun by the Americans, and perhaps by the British, to perfect a bomb. A number of traitor Jew scientists are working feverishly on the project, and there is no doubt that the bomb will be used against Germany. Morgenthau will see to that. So time is running out. My planning staff, which you disparage, has estimated that the Allies will have a uranium bomb at the earliest in the autumn of 1944 and at the latest the summer of 1946.'

The information stunned Bethwig. He had been so certain of their position that he had never considered the possibility that the Allies might beat them to the uranium bomb. 'Does Wernher know this?' he finally managed to ask.

'No. I did not feel secure in telling him. He is not a party member and I am not certain of his politics.'

Bethwig leaned forward. As he spoke a finger punctuated each word: 'Herr Heydrich, this information does not change my mind. Von Braun is the best man for the job. I will not replace him under any circumstances. As much as I desire the post of director, to accept it would be a major mistake.'

'I do not agree.'

Franz threw himself back in his chair. How to make this man understand? 'There is more than just friendship involved. In wartime there is no room for such considerations. Doktor von Braun is the only man who can do this job.'

Heydrich shook his head. 'You could be as effective. Perhaps more so, as you understand the political considerations.'

'No!' Bethwig slapped the table. 'I must insist that you are wrong in this matter.'

Heydrich stared at him a moment, considering, then nodded brusquely. 'Is there anything else to be discussed?'

'There is another problem.'

'And that is?'

'We are feeling increasing resistance from the army over use of the facilities at Peenemünde for the A-Ten. As you know, our highest priority from the Weapons Development Command is the A-Four rocket.'

'I am aware of that problem, and steps are being taken to solve it. Within a week you should see the interference disappear.'

Bethwig was now conscious of an awkward silence. He did not know what else to say. Although the need was pressing, he knew that applying more pressure could not possibly make the project move faster. He was also aware that nothing under the sun would convince Heydrich of that fact.

For the next hour they reviewed the A-10 project. Bethwig was able to report that the first engines had been assembled for testing and that the instrumentation was nearly all in place. Beyond that, aerodynamic and structural studies were nearly completed, and the shops had already begun fabricating those components with the longest lead times. Any final changes necessary could be made as they went along.

Heydrich professed himself satisfied. Leaning back in his chair, he regarded Bethwig closely. 'You will accept the position of A-Ten project director then?'

The question startled him. He thought that Heydrich had satisfied himself that he would never replace von Braun. Bethwig spread his hands in exasperation. 'How can I, Reinhard? I have given you my reasons for refusing. Von Braun is the only man who in my opinion can do the job. I certainly recognise the urgency but . . .'

Heydrich's expression had become hard and frightening. 'You must do more than that, Herr Doktor Bethwig. You must accept. We will discuss the matter further tomorrow, before I leave for Paris.'

Bethwig nodded, relieved that the inquisition was over, at least temporarily.

His exasperation began to wear off as soon as he left Heydrich's office. The afternoon and evening he would spend with Inge were as much as he wanted to think about for now. He had decided that they would go for a drive during the afternoon, but when he tried to arrange for a car at the reception desk, he was told by an apologetic clerk that all were in use. On the way to his suite he noticed that a guard had been stationed at the end of the corridor.

Inge was gone, every trace. The bed had been made and an antiseptic-smelling deodorant sprayed about the room to cover even the trace of her perfume. When he phoned the reception desk, they of course knew nothing, and the SS guard at the end of the corridor would only stare silently ahead.

Bethwig tried to remain calm, but after the first hour he was pacing from one end of the apartment to the other. He knew what Heydrich was up to – a demonstration. The lesson was bitter but not unexpected. Heydrich meant to show him what it was like to have a favourite toy taken away. The bastard! Inge had become more than a toy. Though why he loved her as he thought he did, he could not be certain.

Inge was returned at nine o'clock that evening. He heard a timid knock and threw open the door and the girl collapsed against him. Franz kicked the door shut and carried her into the bedroom. For a moment he thought she was drunk, but there was no odour of alcohol. Her head lolled to one side as he placed her on the bed, and she moaned when he lifted her arm on to the cover. He pushed the sleeve back and shock jolted through him. Swearing like a madman, Bethwig tore away her light summer dress. The sight was stunning. Her chest and back were covered with purplish bruises. Cigarette burns dotted her breasts. Wire marks encircled her thighs and upper arms, and a livid SS brand had been burned into each buttock.

When Bethwig calmed down enough to lift the telephone to call for a doctor, the line was dead. The door to the corridor was locked, from the outside. An SS guard stood beneath the balcony, and when he looked over, the sentry raised his rifle and ordered him back inside. Unable to believe what was happening, Bethwig lowered himself into a chair beside the bed. Inge seemed to have been drugged. She tossed restlessly but was semi-conscious and totally incoherent.

After a while he wet a towel in the bathroom and began to bathe her carefully. The cool water had a soothing effect, and her restlessness ceased. In the dark hour before dawn she wakened screaming. Bethwig took her in his arms, whispering her name over and over until she calmed. Then he filled a glass with brandy and persuaded her to drink. Afterwards Inge lay back, movements stiff and slow, and as she told him what had happened he examined her body under the bed lamp until convinced that the damage was more painful than dangerous. None of the burns were deep except for the two SS brands, and those seemed to have been treated with an antiseptic.

From what he could make out from her childish narration, it seemed she had been ordered back to her room after he had left for his appointment with Heydrich that morning. Her story was not always coherent, and he had to interpret a lot that she did not understand. Assuming that he had left and that she would be reassigned, Inge had done as she was told. Instead, the matron had sent her to the basement. Though frightened, she had still expected nothing more than a beating. It was not the first time. There were so many rules and a guest's single negative comment was considered reason enough for a whipping. But such punishments were limited to no more than ten strokes with a rubber hose administered by the matron. The hose left no marks and, while painful did no damage. The matron apparently enjoyed the punishments, and they were given liberally.

Only, this time the matron was not in the punishment room. Two men stripped her, then tied her hands to a hook in the ceiling and beat her with hoses. Between beatings they left her hanging from the hook. The day became a nightmare of electric shocks, cigarette burns, and more beatings. She was raped repeatedly and finally branded. They revived her especially for that.

Bethwig heard her out, not interrupting, knowing that she had to purge herself of the ordeal. Then she drifted back into a restless sleep, and he covered her gently with a sheet and stepped out on the balcony. Again the sentry shouted at him, and for an instant Bethwig's sanity came near to snapping. A plaster urn filled with geraniums rested on the ledge, and without thinking, he swept it up and hurled it at the man. The pot burst on the steps, but the soldier had ducked inside. Bethwig shouted a curse after him and went back to the bedroom.

An hour later a doctor came for Inge. With him were a nurse and two orderlies. The doctor examined her, shook his head, and had the orderlies place her on a stretcher. The nurse stared at Franz, eyes blazing, and he knew then what the next step would be.

An SS officer appeared next. A standardtenführer who

introduced himself as Edgar Ullman, he was accompanied by an enlisted clerk and two armed guards. Bethwig was ordered to sit beside the desk, and the officer opened his portfolio.

'Herr Bethwig, it is my duty to inform you that charges of rape, assault, and battery have been lodged against you by one Inge Schuster, employed as a staff maid. She has charged that you forced her to commit unspeakable sexual acts, and that when she resisted, you beat and tortured her into submission. I myself have seen the results.'

The officer's expression of contempt was so real that Bethwig decided he could not be a party to the charade.

'Do you have anything to say in your defence?' the officer asked.

Bethwig remained silent, and after a moment the SS officer stood. 'In that case I must report that you refused to speak to me. I will remind you that Prague is under martial law and that you will therefore be tried by a military court-martial. The incident has come to the attention of the reichsprotektor, who has promised to review the details when he returns from the city this afternoon. He told me personally that if he must delay his departure for Paris he will do so.'

'I would imagine so,' Bethwig replied dryly, speaking for the first time since Inge had been taken away. 'And where have they taken Inge?'

The officer's stare was cold. 'To a hospital, of course.'

Bethwig thought for a moment. 'Colonel, I believe that you are doing what you think is correct. So do this for yourself, not for me. Check and see what hospital Inge was taken to. Then go and ask her who treated her like that.'

'Are you saying you are not responsible?'

'Just do as I suggest.' Bethwig turned his back on them then, and a moment later the door slammed.

For the next four days Bethwig was held a virtual prisoner in the apartment. His door was locked from the outside, and his meals were brought by an elderly man who spoke no German. The guard below the balcony had been supplemented after the flowerpot incident, and he was not allowed outside. During the long hours he rationed his cigarettes, tried to read the few books he could find in German, French, or English, and stood at the window for what seemed ages worrying about Inge. He was safe enough, he decided. All he had to do was agree to Heydrich's demands; and once he had done so, Heydrich would probably agree to release the girl, and perhaps even allow him to take her away from Prague.

But by Sunday he was beginning to wonder if he really did understand Heydrich's game. He had heard nothing since the SS officer's visit on Wednesday morning. Heydrich must have realised he had won by now. A hot bath did not help to settle his nerves, and Bethwig now stood before the bathroom mirror, first wiping the moisture clear and then studying his face. The constant state of uncertainty was starting to tell on him. He combed his hair and wandered into the living-room where he dragged the furniture against the walls and spent a rigorous half-hour doing calisthenics.

Late Sunday afternoon the door was thrown open and the SS colonel stalked in. He glared at the sentry who had tried to follow, and slammed the door in his face.

'We do not have much time,' Ullman muttered as he checked the other rooms in the suite.

'Did you do as I suggested?'

'Keep quiet and listen to what I tell you.'

'What in the name of God are – '

'I went to see the young lady,' Ullman interrupted. 'That is why I am here. It has taken this long to find her. She is being cared for at a nursing hospital in a small town nearby. Held in protective custody would be a more accurate description. She told me what happened.' He stared at Bethwig a moment, his expression quizzical. 'She is halfwitted, you know?'

Franz nodded. 'Go on.'

The officer turned to the window and studied the grounds below, then glanced at his watch. 'It was rather difficult to understand her story, but I finally made sense of it.'

He turned again to face the room. 'I do not know exactly what Herr Heydrich was trying to do to you, but I discovered that you have a distinguished background as a scientist. You are too valuable to the Reich to be wasted in petty political nonsense. If you do as I say, you may yet leave Prague alive.'

'For God's sake!' Bethwig stared at him, not able to believe what the man was saying.

Ullman offered a cigarette and lit it for him. Bethwig drew the smoke deep into his lungs. Something was radically wrong, he realised. 'This is unbelievable. Why would Heydrich want to harm me? He has gone to these ridiculous extremes to force me to accept a position which he is certain only I can fill. Why would he change his mind so suddenly?'

Colonel Ullman shook his head. 'Then no one has told you?'

'Told me what?'

'On Wednesday morning, as Herr Heydrich was driving to his

office in Prague, British agents shot at his car and threw a bomb. The chauffeur was killed and Herr Heydrich was severely wounded. He is in hospital now and not expected to live.'

Bethwig swore in astonishment.

'Soon someone will come for you. You will be taken to the basement and shot. The story will be that your aircraft was destroyed returning you to Peenemünde, or some other such foolishness.'

Bethwig sat down abruptly. 'Shot . . . but why?' he protested.

Ullman shook his head. 'I have no idea. Apparently the game you are playing – were playing, rather, with Heydrich had higher stakes than you were aware. In any event, with his death imminent his personal staff is scurrying about cleaning up any messes. You happen to be one of them.'

'My God!'

'It is not as bad as it sounds – yet. If Heydrich survives, you resume your game. If he dies, you die. It is as simple as that. But if you wish to leave Prague, you must do so now. I cannot promise that you will be left in peace afterwards, but at least your chances will be much better than waiting here for the execution chamber. The decision is yours.'

With a tremendous effort Bethwig pulled himself together. He went into the bedroom, and Ullman followed. 'I assume you have some kind of plan?' Bethwig asked as he began cramming clothes into his suitcase.

The colonel nodded. 'Yes. We will simply walk out of the apartment and down the stairs to the main floor. My car is waiting at the door. I will drive you to the airfield, and if God is with us you should be home by midnight.'

'Just like that? Won't the guards have something to say?'

'About what? There are no charges against you.'

'What about rape, assault, and what was the other – extreme cruelty, or something like that?' Bethwig growled.

'All charges against you have been dropped. I saw to that before I came here. The orders were direct from Heydrich himself. Too bad he will never know about them.'

Bethwig straightened to study the officer. 'Aren't you taking one hell of a chance doing this for me?'

'Only if Heydrich should recover, and that is not likely. Blood poisoning has set in. Now, no more talk. We must hurry.'

Bethwig shook his head. 'There is one more consideration – Inge. She has to come with us.'

'Impossible.'

'Nothing is impossible.'

For a moment the irony of repeating Heydrich's own words struck Bethwig as funny, and he almost laughed aloud.

'This is.' Ullman gripped his arm. 'Listen to me. She is under guard. There is no way that I can get her out. If it is known that I even spoke with her, I will be in serious trouble and might find myself part of the clean-up. I can assure you that she is safe for now. She will be released from the hospital in three days' time, then I can arrange for her to leave Prague. But until Heydrich is dead, it is impossible for me to do more.'

Bethwig hesitated, his mind a whirl of apprehension.

'Make up your mind,' Ullman snapped. 'If you are dead, you can do nothing for her. This way she still has a chance, and so do you.'

Bethwig's face was a study in frustration as he nodded. When they left the apartment, Ullman walked behind and a sentry followed at his nod. The three flights of stairs and the ornate lobby seemed endless, but no one paid them the slightest attention. The chauffeur was stiff and correct as he held the door, and the colonel dismissed the sentry.

A curious silence seemed to have fallen over Prague. Military patrols were everywhere, and on some street corners groups of people huddled together under the hostile eyes of SS detachments. The car stopped at four separate checkpoints where their papers were meticulously examined.

'The round-up has begun,' Ullman observed. 'Orders have come from Berlin to find the assassins at all costs. Examples are already being made. They say that the Führer broke down and cried like a child when the news was given to him. Heydrich was his favourite.'

Bethwig kept silent, troubled by the haunted eyes that had stared at their car as they stopped at an intersection for a convoy of military trucks. The people – men, women, and children – seemed to have been rounded up indiscriminately, and all were clearly frightened. If what had been done to Inge was merely a casual lesson to persuade him, they had every reason to be afraid.

'And I thought the Czech people loved him so much,' he observed bitterly after the car had started up again.

'Who told you that?'

'He did.'

The colonel's laugh was bitter. 'It's hard to love your hangman. That's what they called him, you know.'

Colonel Ullman's estimate was not far wrong. It was just after midnight when Bethwig raced from the Peenemünde airfield to von Braun's quarters. He pounded on the door until he heard a sleepy muttering on the other side.

'Damn it, Wernher, open the door!'

'Franz? Just a moment.'

The door opened and von Braun waved him in. 'Damn it, Franz, couldn't you have waited until morning to tell about the fleshpots of Prague?' He shuffled back into the room, turning on the light and sorting through the jumble of papers on his desk for a cigarette.

Bethwig kicked the door closed. 'Shut up and sit down. This is serious.'

'What the devil are you . . . ?'

'British agents shot Heydrich on Wednesday morning. He is not expected to live.'

Von Braun gaped at him. 'Shot . . . Heydrich?' He swallowed. The packet of cigarettes found, Bethwig then waited while he lit one, allowing him time to absorb the shock.

'There was nothing about it on the wireless . . . or in the papers . . .'

'Of course not. And there won't be until he dies.'

'He isn't dead yet?' Von Braun's voice was hopeful.

'He is dying,' Bethwig said harshly. 'Blood poisoning. And good riddance as well.'

'What are you saying, Franz? Without him, how can we continue the A-Ten?'

'Damned good question. First you had better hear what happened to me. Then you might not be so saddened by our dear patron's imminent departure for hell.' Bethwig told him the entire story, leaving nothing out except the details of Inge's mental history.

Von Braun listened with a growing amazement that quickly turned to grim anger. When Bethwig finished, he stubbed out his cigarette with a vicious twisting motion.

'It's damned good riddance then, as you said,' he snarled. 'Until things clarify themselves, I suppose we had better continue as we have. Try to get as much done as possible in case we have to persuade someone else to support us.'

Bethwig nodded. 'That's my feeling as well. As for finding someone else to back us, we're still not out of the woods as far as the SS is concerned.'

'Perhaps not,' von Braun replied, his voice thoughtful. 'But perhaps it is possible that we have enough results now to persuade the Army General Staff to back us, particularly if we let it slip that the SS, in the person of the soon-to-be-martyred Reinhard Heydrich, was behind it. That would scare the hell out of them.'

'It might also get us shot by our own employers,' Bethwig snorted.

Three weeks later two SS officers accompanied by the Gestapo officer Walsch arrived at Peenemünde to arrest von Braun. Walsch politely introduced himself and reminded von Braun that they had met several years before in Berlin, in the office of Colonel Dornberger. He smiled when von Braun recalled the circumstances, and they flew to Berlin that afternoon, in spite of Dornberger's strenuous protests. The aircraft took off even as Dornberger was trying to get through to Gestapo headquarters.

Bethwig telephoned his father that evening to ask him to use his influence to fix an appointment with Reichsführer Himmler, reasoning that the order for the arrest of Wernher von Braun, an army employee, by the SD could only have come from his office. His father agreed to help, but it was three days before the meeting could be arranged. Dornberger threw up his hands in despair when he heard what Bethwig had done.

'For God's sake, Franz, now there will be two of you to get out of prison, or worse.'

Added to his worry about von Braun was the lack of any communication from Colonel Ullman. Twice he had tried to phone through, only to be told that lines were unavailable. And there was little news of any kind from the protectorate. God only knew what havoc the SD were causing there.

The following day Bethwig, taking a roundabout route through Hamburg, drove to Berlin to consult with his father.

'Hah! British agents indeed,' his father had exploded in anger. 'Mark my words, young man, the deed was done and Heydrich murdered at the express order of that weak-chinned jealous little sadist Himmler.' Bethwig had told him what he knew of the happenings in Praguc.

'Jumped-up chicken farmer!' his father muttered, pacing about his cluttered office. The swastika armband he was never without seemed somewhat shabby on the sleeve of his suit jacket, Bethwig observed. As shabby as the party's morals and mission were becoming. What happened to them? he wondered. It had all changed in such a short time. The war was to have tempered the movement; instead it seemed to be destroying it.

'I do not understand why we must put up with such men as these. Even Goering has become a good-for-nothing drug addict.

Such nonsense brings trouble in the end. Gangsters, that's what they are. Nothing but gangsters.'

He spun and pointed a blunt finger at his son. 'Do not let that little toad intimidate you. He is not quite as secure as he thinks. The Führer said to me not more than a week ago that perhaps it was time for the party to clean house again, and I heartily agreed. You know how he works; first the suggestions to high party members to test their opinion, then intensive planning and decisive action – swift, merciless action. That was the way it was when we got rid of Roehm. I suspect that this time he has people like Himmler and perhaps this Goebbels in mind. Never did like that little cripple. Too shrill.' The old man sighed then. 'Well, Franz, if you have told me everything, I doubt if you have anything to worry about. There seems to be nothing that monster can hold over your head. Be firm and remember your position and your strengths. We are Bethwigs and we are German. And the Führer knows who his supporters are.'

You would never think there was a war, Bethwig mused as he drove along the Charlottenstrasse past the well-dressed crowds. An amazing number of soldiers filled the streets, eyeing equally large numbers of girls clad in summer frocks. The mood was certainly not what one would have expected in the capital of a great nation at war. There were few signs of bomb damage visible, but air-raid shelters were conspicuously marked. Shop windows, although taped, were as full of goods as ever; and with war production in full swing, people had plenty of money to spend. Hitler's promises were coming true, Bethwig thought, even though, by virtue of his father's position and wealth, he tended at times to look upon the Austrian as a fool and a buffoon. Yet one had to admit that he had drawn the German people so solidly together after the disillusionment of the 1920s that the country was totally unified, and willing and able to meet the final Allied offensive against it. This time it will be different, he thought in a sudden burst of grim determination.

Opportunity enough, after the war was won, to clean out the scum that invariably worked its way to the top during periods of conflict. If only the Führer did not show so distinct a predilection for such men.

At the SS headquarters in Prinz Albrechtstrasse an elderly porter checked his credentials against a huge appointment ledger, and an unarmed corporal orderly then escorted Bethwig through quiet oak-panelled hallways to a tastefully furnished outer office where a receptionist offered him tea and telephoned through to announce his arrival.

He was made to wait less than five minutes – a gesture of high respect in Berlin these days, he realised – before an aide stepped through a side door, shook his hand, and in a flurry of meaningless small talk ushered him directly into Himmler's office. A vast expanse of carpet stretched away to the far end of the room which, although the sun was bright outside, was shut into deep gloom by close-fitting curtains. So the rumours that Himmler expects to be killed by the British are true, he thought. Heydrich's death must have sent him into a near panic.

A recessed ceiling lamp shone directly on to a single hard-backed chair set squarely before a large walnut desk. A smallish man bent over a single sheet of paper.

As Bethwig approached, Heinrich Himmler looked up, then removed his gold-rimmed pince-nez, and studied him.

The man does have a weak chin, Bethwig thought in surprise. Everyone said so, and it was rumoured that the Reichsführer kept it disguised by forbidding photographs from low angles. But in person there was no hiding it. Dark, nearsighted, and paunchy, Himmler was hardly the propagandist's classic Nordic. No wonder Hitler had preferred Heydrich.

'Ah, young man. You are the son of Johann Bethwig.' Himmler had neither risen nor offered to shake hands. He inclined his head towards the chair, his manner making it quite clear that he was seeing Bethwig only in deference to his father – a politician storing up small favours.

But Himmler surprised him. He studied Franz from pop eyes for a moment, then flicked the sheet of paper so that it shot across the desk. Franz had to lunge forward to catch it. 'I suppose you have come to see me about that?' He pronounced the word *that* as if it contained all that was contemptible.

Bethwig began to read the sheet of double-spaced typing, but the accusations were so absurd that he had to start over again and read each sentence deliberately, like a lawyer. It bluntly accused von Braun of complicity in the plot that had resulted in the murder of Reinhard Heydrich by English espionage agents. Further, von Braun was accused of diverting scarce raw materials to his own ends, and establishing liaison with an enemy foreign power to destroy the German Reich. When he finished reading, he placed it back on the desk.

'These charges are patently ridiculous. This entire document is the work of an incompetent ass.' Bethwig was both calm and assured, and Himmler was clearly surprised, having expected either fearful denial or indignant argument.

'An ass?' He pushed his chair back and half swivelled away,

only to spin back immediately. 'That indictment was prepared by an officer of the Gestapo. How dare you call him an ass?'

'Because he is.' Bethwig stared at the reichsführer, thinking of what had happened the last time he had challenged a high security official. 'Wernher von Braun is one of the brightest and most loyal scientists in Germany. There is not one shred of truth in these accusations. Perhaps, Herr Reichsführer, the man who composed this is your real traitor.'

Himmler's face flushed. 'How dare you insult one of the finest officers of the State Police . . . ?'

'How dare he insult one of Germany's finest scientists?' Bethwig shot back. 'Your man has disrupted a carefully thought out plan of research that can make Germany impregnable. The very man Doktor von Braun is accused of murdering commissioned this project and took an active interest in its development, with the express permission of the Führer.'

Himmler stood up and came around the desk. Bethwig could see that he was barely controlling his temper. 'And that, Herr Bethwig, is the only reason I agreed to speak with you at all. Reinhard Heydrich was a close personal friend of mine. I was aware of his interest in the work being done at Peenemünde. I do not mind saying that he was so excited by it that I was obliged to counsel him against overeagerness. He, of course, was convinced that his plan was correct and chose to ignore my counsel.' Himmler turned away then and paced around the desk.

'That was his choice. But he is dead now, murdered in a conspiracy organised and directed by British intelligence. In a routine review of the circumstances the name of your friend von Braun came up. It was noted that he travels freely about Europe in a private aircraft, has access to the highest state secrets, and, in the past, has had contact with a British secret agent. As recently as 1938, if memory serves.'

Himmler held up a hand to forestall Bethwig's protest. 'You should know that less than eighteen months ago this same British agent was active at a factory in Liège, Belgium, which produces parts used in your experiments at Peenemünde. We know that this agent had direct contact with the criminal Belgian underground, members of which were also employed at the factory. Our investigations show that your von Braun has visited this factory several times.'

Bethwig felt his temper rising and drew a deep, if concealed, breath. Himmler was watching his reaction, his bright, protruding eyes staring fixedly.

'Of course Wernher visits the factory. As I do. When Wernher last met this man, we were not aware that he was a British spy. I say "we", as I also met the man. We learned his identity from a Gestapo officer a day later. That officer, the man who arrested von Braun, was sitting in the same room that night and did not think it important enough to warn us at the time. In fact, he waited until the man had slipped away before doing so. Now he claims – and I have no doubt that the one who prepared this indictment is that same officer – the encounter was of sufficient importance to implicate Doktor von Braun in a plot to murder his sponsor, Reichsprotektor Heydrich. I say it is nonsense and would not be permitted in any German court of law!'

Himmler walked behind his desk again and stood tapping his fingers on the wood. 'Young man, you clearly are not aware of all the facts. Your defence of your friend does you credit, but it is also quite dangerous. Because of my long friendship with your father I will overlook your arrogance. Perhaps there are oversimplifications in that document; it is a preliminary indictment and this entire matter is under administrative review at the moment.

'I am given to understand that powerful friends of Doktor von Braun, some of them of questionable loyalty to the Reich, made representations against this officer merely for doing his duty. As did your father.' Himmler raised a pale eyebrow.

'If my father did so,' Bethwig answered stiffly, 'it was without my knowledge. The man was . . .'

'His personal deportment is neither here nor there,' Himmler snapped. 'The man has been completely reinstated, and his superiors speak highly of him. As for a court of law, the SS needs no court to instruct it in its duty. Herr von Braun is accused of treason. He will be tried by an SS tribunal.'

Even though Bethwig had expected nothing else, Himmler's pronouncement shook him. The SS had the power of life and death over every party member in Germany through its secret police, the Gestapo. But members of the armed forces were exempt. Von Braun was a civilian employee of the army. Is that enough? he wondered.

Before he could capitalise on the theory, Himmler resumed his seat and, in abstracted manner – as if the subject really did not interest him – asked, 'Just what was the objective of this so-called A-Ten project? I believe it involved rockets of some sort?'

'The A-Ten is . . .' Bethwig hesitated only the barest fraction of a second as the thought occurred to him that Himmler had set this whole ridiculous drama in motion only to discover what his second-in-command had been up to.

'But surely you know, Herr Reichsführer' – he tested – 'as your subordinate, Reichsprotektor Heydrich certainly would have explained the details of the project to you?'

Himmler's eyes flashed at him, and in that instant Bethwig realised that his flippancy had made him an extremely dangerous enemy.

'Of course he explained it to me; however, I am essentially a non-technical person so I did not understand all of what he was saying,' Himmler answered smoothly. 'Reinhard trained at Kiel and understood complicated engineering and scientific concepts. Myself, I am little more than a simple country farmer, serving the Reich as best I can.'

This last was said with a completely straight face, and Bethwig coughed to smother the laugh that threatened to overwhelm him. Choosing his words with care, he explained the concept of the A-10 rocket as applied to the military situation, and ended with Heydrich's latest information concerning the uranium bomb.

After he finished, Himmler was silent for several minutes, staring at the huge party banner that dominated one wall of the immense room. 'An interesting, if risky, conjecture.' Turning back to Bethwig, he said, 'It all smacks of that silly cinema film of a few years ago in which a girl goes to the moon.' Bethwig knew he was referring to the Fritz Lang film of the late 1920s *Frau in Mond – The Girl in the Moon* – inspired by Hermann Oberth's first serious study of the problems of space travel *Rakete zu den Planetenraumen – The Rocket in Interplanetary Space.* His own first experience with building rockets had come about because of that movie. He had been part of a group of young amateur scientists and technicians, as was von Braun, hired by Hermann Oberth in 1928 to help with the construction of his famous Model B rocket, which was to have been launched in conjunction with the film's premiere.

Himmler questioned him closely for twenty minutes, showing a greater grasp of technology than he admitted. It became clear later, when Bethwig had a chance to think about it, that Himmler's questions signified some, but not a great deal of, knowledge about the project; it was as if he were filling gaps. It occurred to him that perhaps Heydrich *had* kept his boss in the dark about the project, and Himmler, never one to ignore a possible advantage, was now taking the opportunity to explore it fully – before someone else did.

Himmler appeared satisfied and hummed to himself as he made notes on a small pad. 'You could be in a great deal of trouble yourself.' He looked up suddenly.

Bethwig smiled. He had nothing to fear from this, in his father's words, 'jumped-up chicken farmer'. 'How is that, Herr Reichsführer?'

'You, my boy, are in possession of one of the most closely guarded secrets of the Reich – the uranium bomb. I believe that if our files were checked for those persons with access to such information, your name would not be among them. The penalty for such an offence ranges from ten years' imprisonment to death.'

Bethwig inclined his head politely. 'In that case, Herr Reichsführer, you would have to imprison or shoot half the scientists in Germany.'

Himmler laughed. 'Probably so,' he conceded. 'Probably so. But in any event, I must take what steps I can to remedy this situation. We do know that the Allies are also working to develop a uranium bomb, and we would not want them to learn of our progress.'

'No, we would not,' Bethwig answered, his voice smug.

Himmler stood up abruptly. 'Well, we shall get to the bottom of this. My aide has arranged quarters for you in the city. You are not under arrest, but you must not leave Berlin. I will give every consideration to the case against Wernher von Braun, but I can tell you that it does not look good. In spite of what you think, the evidence is strongly against him.' He held up a hand to prevent Bethwig's protest, and the door opened behind them.

'Right this way, sir,' the aide announced. Himmler had already resumed his seat behind the desk. Glancing up to see Bethwig hesitating, he waved a hand in dismissal.

'That is all. I will call on you if necessary.'

Bethwig stalked from the room, and the aide had to hurry after him, waving a small card with the address of a hotel written on it. Bethwig snatched it from the man and pushed through the door into the corridor as the aide tried vainly to describe the restrictions imposed on him. Bethwig had no intention of paying them the slightest attention.

Himmler kept him waiting for two days. During that time Bethwig remained at the Hotel Bauer, staring for long hours through the window at passing traffic. The weather had turned quite hot and the room was stifling, even with the windows thrown wide. On the afternoon of the second day, when he could stand it no longer, Bethwig went out for a walk. In the Liepziger Platz he watched a passing military convoy for nearly an hour – long lines of Mercedes lorries and tank carriers with their cargoes of Panzer IV tanks destined for the Russian front and the summer offensive everyone seemed to know was coming. The troops filling the transport lorries waved and shouted to the pretty girls who threw them small packets of candy, ersatz coffee, and cigarettes. Franz found that he was smiling. This is what the war is all about, he thought; Germany regaining its rightful place as it should have done long ago.

He turned away as the last of the tank transporters disappeared towards the Tiergarten, and found a small sidewalk café only half-filled. He took a table, ordered the house wine – which turned out to be French, surprisingly good, and cheap at the same time – and a plate of wursts.

The convoy had done much to restore his spirits. The war would end within a few years – no one thought it would be over within the year – and the future would be Germany's to shape. The A-10 would give them their first step to the moon. Guided rockets with uranium bombs would be followed by lunar bases manned by scientists and technicians. God only knew what benefits would be derived and how they might change the world. It was good to be alive, to be a pioneer. For a moment he was embarrassed by his private enthusiasm.

A thin-faced man in an old trench coat stopped by the next table, flipped open a wallet, shoved it under the nose of a soldier wearing an eastern front campaign ribbon, and ordered him and his girl to leave. The soldier started to protest, but the gaunt man asked the girl for her name. They went quickly then, and the man sat down and snapped his fingers for the waiter. He turned and smiled at Bethwig. Captain Jacob Walsch.

Bethwig hesitated. Uncertain, then angry, he got up and approached the table. Walsch, smiling lazily at him, stood. The other patrons had witnessed the scene with the soldier and now stopped their conversations to watch.

'Captain Walsch, I believe?'

The Gestapo officer inclined his head. 'Major, Herr Bethwig. I received a promotion a year ago.'

'My congratulations, Major. Cream rises to the top, they say. But then, so does sewage. I was speaking about you just the other day, to Reichsführer Himmler.'

Walsch nodded, on guard now. 'I am most flattered that you remembered me.'

'Yes,' Bethwig went on, his voice rising a bit so that the other patrons could hear. 'I believe I told Herr Himmler that you were an ass.' Bethwig chuckled into the sudden silence. 'An incompetent ass, I think I said.'

Tension was palpable in the tiny restaurant, and the head

waiter started as if to intervene, but another waiter wisely held him back.

'I am sorry that you retain such a poor opinion of me . . .'

'You brought the charges against Herr Doktor von Braun, did you not?' Bethwig continued. 'Only an incompetent ass would present such a monstruous series of lies in the form of an indictment. You, Major Walsch, are a disgrace to the position you hold and to the Reich.' Bethwig had carried his half-empty glass with him, and as he finished speaking he threw the contents into Walsch's face. The Gestapo officer jumped back, tripped against his chair, and fell over backwards. Bethwig calmly extracted a five-mark note from his wallet and tossed it on the table.

'That will pay for cleaning your coat, Major. Good day.'

He turned and walked out of the restaurant to the spontaneous applause of the other patrons as waiters rushed to help Walsch. One began dabbing his coat with salt and water, but Walsch pushed him away and went to a telephone.

It was a foolish thing to do, Bethwig thought as he strode along the busy street. A cloud had passed in front of the sun, easing the heat but increasing the mugginess. The city had suddenly become stifling. He returned to his hotel room and spent the rest of the afternoon and evening sitting by the window with his shirt off, enduring the heat and the uncertainty. The summons to Himmler's office came the next morning.

Himmler was standing with his back to the room, peering through the heavy curtain behind his desk. The single ray of sunlight dispelled some of the gloom, enough anyway to permit Bethwig to see von Braun sitting in the chair before the desk. A second chair had been placed two metres away, also facing the desk. Von Braun half turned to see who had entered; his face was expressionless.

'Please have a seat, Herr Doktor Bethwig.' Himmler dropped the curtain and turned, twisting the pince-nez between his fingers. He took a gold pocket watch from his trousers, snapped the lid open, and gazed off into space as if considering. Then, having decided, he shut the lid and put it away.

'Come, come. I haven't much time. I must leave shortly for a tour of our resettlement camps in the Government-General of Poland. My staff expects to demonstrate their latest procedures.' He was smiling now as he motioned to the chair.

'But then, you two gentlemen do not wish to hear about my administrative problems. I am certain that you have sufficient of your own.'

Bethwig sat down, glancing cautiously at von Braun, who was staring at Himmler with a look that Bethwig could not quite describe. There was a bandage on his forehead and several bruises about his chin. When he moved his head, he did so as if his neck were stiff. The image of Inge's battered body flashed across his mind.

'I suggest, then, Herr Himmler,' von Braun rasped, 'that we stop all needless conversation and get right to the point.'

Himmler raised an eyebrow at him but only murmured, 'As you wish.'

Von Braun turned by twisting his upper body so that he was looking at Bethwig. 'Herr Himmler has made an interesting proposition. I refused to give him an answer until you could hear it as well.' Himmler nodded in agreement. 'Basically he is offering to allow work on the A-Ten to continue, but under *his* sponsorship and direction. Herr Himmler is convinced that Reichsprotektor Heydrich was doing the correct thing when he instituted the project.' Von Braun's voice had a sarcastic tone that Bethwig had never heard before. 'We are to meet the time schedule laid down by Heydrich.'

'That's all?' Bethwig glanced at Himmler, thinking that Heydrich had won after all and that this had all been a charade . . . to a point.

'All? What more would you expect?'

'The charges, Herr Reichsführer. What about them? Does Doktor von Braun remain under – what is your fancy legal term? *Schutzhaft*, protective custody?'

Himmler waved a hand. 'Ah, the charges. Probably nonsense as you suggested the other day. In due course the investigation will be completed and, if warranted, the charges dismissed. In the meantime I see no reason why an eminent scientist such as Doktor von Braun should not, with the proper security supervision, of course, continue work that best serves the Reich.'

'With the proper security supervision? I understand that political prisoners and Jews are allowed to function under those conditions. Not eminent scientists.'

'Well, young man, you must keep in mind that Doktor von Braun has been charged with a serious crime. I would be derelict in my duty if I neglected to order such supervision, particularly when the person in question is engaged on a project of the highest importance to the Reich.'

'Of course,' Bethwig murmured. 'Derelict.' He turned to von Braun who was staring down at his hands. 'What do you think, Wernher?'

Von Braun nodded without looking up, and Bethwig noticed that a bruise on his cheek was fresh enough to show a crust of blood. 'Was that necessary?' He swung back to Himmler, who seemed to know exactly what he meant. The Reichsführer shrugged.

'You must understand that the SD deals with the worst sort of animal, the traitor. Because they are exposed to this filth so often, they tend to become overzealous.' There was no hint of apology in his voice.

Bethwig restrained a comment. 'As I understand it, then, the project will be allowed to continue as before. Will the army not have something to say about such interference?'

Himmler smiled. 'The OKW has agreed with my assessment and stand ready to co-operate. As Doktor von Braun remarked, I believe that my good friend Reinhard made a wise choice. Yes, the project must continue, on the schedule as modified by the Reichsprotektor's planning staff.'

That was too much for Bethwig and he started to protest, but von Braun held up a hand. 'Never mind, Franz, we will do our best.'

Himmler bounced to his feet then as the door opened and the ubiquitous aide stepped in.

'I apologise for my haste, but I do have to leave. An officer will be assigned to act as co-ordinator. Webel here will provide the details.' Himmler stopped half-way across the room and turned once more to face them.

'Gentlemen, I will expect your complete and personal loyalty in this matter. Complete and personal.'

The aide drew the door closed as Himmler vanished.

The aircraft left Tempelhof in advance of a thunderstorm, and for a while the violence of the flight precluded conversation; but by the time they passed over Stettin, the storm had abated and the aircraft had broken out into clear air below the clouds. As Bethwig stared through the window at the limpid, watery sky and landscape he felt for a moment as if they were giant fish gliding above an aquarium landscape.

Von Braun was silent, brooding, eyes fixed on his window. Bethwig was already regretting that he had left his car behind in Berlin for a complete overhaul. The long drive north would probably have benefited his friend.

'What happened, Wernher?'

For a while von Braun did not answer. Finally, he glanced across the aisle.

'They thought I had something to do with Heydrich's murder.' Bethwig had to strain to hear him above the noise of the engines. 'They accused me of all sorts of stupid things that first day, even as far back as those asinine charges levelled against Willy Ley in 1931. I was accused of helping him sell VfR petrol on the black market. But the most serious charge, besides murder, was that I was wasting government money and manpower on personal projects.'

'The A-Ten?'

Von Braun nodded. 'It's a political game, Franz,' he said with no sign of emotion. 'All of them – Heydrich, Himmler, and the people they control – would throw this war away to line their own pockets. They care nothing at all for Germany. I spent an hour with Himmler before you arrived.'

Bethwig glanced sharply at his friend but kept quiet.

'Do you know what this was all about? Why they arrested me and threw me in that hole that passes for a jail cell?' He took a deep breath. 'When Heydrich was killed, Himmler saw it as his chance to find out what Heydrich had been involved in. People were sent to Prague for his files, just as that SS officer friend of yours predicted. Himmler discovered just enough to whet his appetite. He had me arrested then. At first they suggested that I co-operate. The interrogator was a nice man, about fifty and very pleasant. Of course, I was too dense to realise what they were after, and told him no. So they taught me. God, how they taught me. It is amazing what a rubber hose can do in the hands of someone who knows how to use it.'

He twisted in his seat to face Bethwig. 'Franz, you cannot help yourself. They do things to you that you would not believe one human being could do to another. It is more than just the pain, it . . . it's . . . the indignity.' Von Braun fell silent and turned back to the window.

The plane shuddered in the thick air, and Bethwig's ears popped. The aircraft was losing altitude for the descent into the Luftwaffe airfield on Peenemünde. Suddenly Bethwig was no longer so certain that people like his father could deal with this new element in the party. Wernher von Braun was a famous scientist, an army employee, the son of a wealthy and influential father, yet they had done this to him with impunity. Even the army had been helpless to stop it; and for the first time the vast power of the SS was borne in upon him. The SS had become a state unto itself. All the normal constitutional and legal guarantees did not apply to their victims. What was it that Himmler had said? 'We do not need the courts to remind us of our duty.' Nor did they want them to interfere. It was so much easier to conduct business by tribunal.

The rain had begun again as the Junkers aircraft lined up for its approach. Staring at the long streamers pouring down on the scrub and pine forest of the island, von Braun murmured just above the engine noise:

'We thought Heydrich was the Devil? We were wrong, Franz. He was merely the Devil's cub.'

Retrenchment

England–Germany July 1942–March 1943

Jan Memling turned the jeep into the narrow street and slowed to examine the buildings on either side, particularly the upper-storey windows. His sergeant was doing likewise from behind a fifty-calibre machine-gun mount. Narrow two- and three-storey buildings with decaying fronts lined each side of the road before debouching several hundred feet further on into a sort of village square. He could even see the remains of a fountain that probably had not worked even before the war.

The jeep idled along, its engine rough. It was badly in need of an overhaul, but he knew there was little likelihood of its getting one any time soon. Memling nursed the pedal to keep the revs up. The silence was unnerving. Both men knew the enemy was there.

'There,' he muttered, not moving his lips. 'Third-storey window, on the right, grey-brick building, two ahead.' The familiar excitement began to build, and he found himself smiling.

'Right, sir.' The sergeant shifted his stance. Memling knew they would wait until the jeep was directly beneath, then lob grenades, supplemented by MG fire from one of the other buildings. It was a classic street ambush and a difficult one to survive. The hard choice was which to hit first – providing you spotted them: the bomb throwers or the machine-gunner?

Memling eased the clutch out until the jeep bucked and threatened to stall. He bent forward as if adjusting the throttle and made a quick survey of the buildings on the left. Just along the road and two opposite he had caught a glimpse of movement in an upper-storey window. He described it to the sergeant and pushed the clutch in.

'Hang on tight. I'll dash for the left side of the street. Put a burst through that window. I'll take the bombers. When I shout, you duck. Understood?'

'Right you are, sir.' The sergeant was a combat veteran with two years in the desert, and he did not like street fighting one bit. He wanted to be able to see his enemy, and Memling was well aware of the man's shortcomings in that regard.

'Just do as I tell you sergeant and you'll be all right.' Memling dared not risk a glance behind. 'Get ready. On three. One . . . two . . . three!'

He yanked the wheel hard left, jammed the accelerator down, and the jeep stalled. The MG exploded into action and Memling was out in an instant, crouching beside the jeep, Sten gun poking over the bonnet; but a figure was already in the window, and the stick grenade flew at them before he could open fire.

'Duck!' The sergeant landed on the cobbles beside him as the grenade hit the gun mount and bounced to the road. It rolled under the jeep and went off in a plume of choking red smoke.

A whistle blew, and Memling got up, swearing, as the referee strolled from the doorway behind. 'Afraid you chaps have bought it. Grenade exploded right under your petrol tank.' He waved his stick at the window where a grinning commando was leaning out. 'Good pitch, lad. Good pitch.'

'South Maling will be wanting him after the war.' The instructor, a reed-thin colonel with an artificial leg, offered Memling and the sergeant a cigarette. 'American, I'm afraid. All I could get at the NAAFI.' The sergeant accepted the light, then saluted and went off to return the jeep. Memling and the colonel walked along the street which was now full of enlisted men in fatigues setting up for the next practice.

'Weren't quite quick enough, were you? Next time, Jerry will be using live bombs,' the colonel observed. 'Not like you to mess up that way.'

Memling gave him a quirky smile and thought about the jeep's stalling. Excuses were never acceptable. He should have foreseen that possibility. 'If we were perfect every time, there wouldn't be any sense to having a war. No one would get killed. Then where would we be?'

'Sounds a bit Bolshie to me,' the colonel chuckled. 'I understand you go off on leave today.'

Memling nodded. 'That probably accounts for my lack of quickness back there. Hard to keep your mind on playing soldier when that nonsense is coming up afterwards.'

The colonel lurched to a stop, then with a mutter lifted his left leg and shook the knee joint back into position. 'Yes, there is that. Still I suppose it can't be avoided.'

Memling gave him an anxious glance. 'What do you think, sir? Have we much of a chance?'

The colonel flicked his cigarette away. 'Why do you ask me questions like that? You know how I must answer.'

Memling shook his head. 'Not with me, sir.'

The wind off the loch caught at his thick, fair hair, and whipped it about his head as he sighed. 'You stand damned little chance, Memling. Damned little. Your Canadians are keen enough and, I don't doubt, will give a good account of themselves. But they haven't got the training, and we haven't the equipment to support them properly. I dare say the objective is important; but in all fairness, you should remember that the real objective is a practice for the big one. London is expecting mistakes, quite a few in fact.'

The older man tapped his cane against his tin leg and studied the surrounding hills. 'It's going to be hard, boy. Damned hard. In spite of our precautions, Jerry will be waiting, and that's only one aspect. The other is lack of training. London thinks that troops can be trained in less than a month for this sort of invasion. Well they're wrong, but they won't believe it until they have their faces rubbed in the casualty lists. The problem is training a vast number of men, possibly upwards of a million or more, to invade a continent that has had four years to prepare. This dress rehearsal is designed to find out. Do you understand what I'm telling you?'

Memling nodded. 'I could be shot for hiding in a hole, sir.'

The colonel gave him a sad smile, then clapped him on the arm. 'That you could, lad. That you could. A sacrificial lamb in either case. Just like we were in the last war at Ypres.' Somewhat absently he tapped his leg. 'Didn't get this there. Happened in a car smash near Brighton twelve years ago. Had absolutely nothing to do with any war.'

'It doesn't seem to make any difference, then, does it, sir?'

The colonel gave his leg a last swat and limped on. 'No, I suppose it doesn't. Just remember,' he continued, almost as an afterthought, 'what you're about over there. No sense inviting trouble. Think about that.'

Memling did think about it as the train lumbered south from Scotland. The raid against the still-unnamed French coastal town had other objectives which they were not being told about yet. They had given him less than a month to bring his Canadians up to shape. The problem was that with very few exceptions they were fresh from training camps in Ontario. They simply were not ready – by his standards. They needed blooding, a few easy raids into Norway, nothing more than a lightning-fast hit-and-run operation to get them used to the confusion, the mistakes, and the fact that nothing ever went as planned; in short, to teach them what individual initiative really meant. But there was damned all he could do about it now.

Janet was waiting for his train even though it was six hours overdue into Euston. He saw her at the barrier, and she waved and pushed across the crowded concourse until they met under the great clock. Taking his hand, she gave him a soft kiss on the cheek and, as they drew back in mutual embarrassment, leaned forward again and kissed him soundly on the lips.

There were no taxis to be had, naturally, and they walked slowly along Woburn Place, which was thick with pedestrians. As overcast as it was, there was little chance of the Luftwaffe appearing tonight. The Bofors anti-aircraft battery they passed in Tavistock Square was manned, but the crew were relaxing on the park benches with cups of tea and laughing with the NAAFI girls.

Janet had written to thank him for his note a week after he had left in February, and he had replied, thus beginning a correspondence that had become a regular part of their lives.

He had almost ignored her first letter, as he was still haunted by Margot's death. But Memling was an intensely lonely man, had been most of his life, and the few months he and Margot had had together had worked a permanent change in him. In addition, he was intelligent enough to realise that the more time passed, the more pristine his memories of those brief months became until they had taken on an air of unreality.

Memling was surprised at the rush of excitement he had felt when spotting Janet at the barrier, a slim, pretty, dark-haired girl in a slightly shabby coat and a short victory skirt. He glanced at her now in the glow of a blackout lantern, but the blue light gave her complexion a sickly cast. She felt him looking at her and glanced up and smiled, and his heart turned over.

He struggled for something to say, but the best he could come up with was 'Did you have much trouble finding me a place in an officers' club?'

'Yes. Quite a bit of trouble, in fact.' She gave him an impish grin. 'I could not find a room in all of London.'

'Really?' was all he could think of to say.

Janet squeezed his hand. 'Really. You might think me a bit forward, but I am going to have to put you up at my flat again.'

Memling's breath caught in his throat, and Janet took the moment's silence for disapproval. 'Oh, I know what you're thinking . . . I mean, perhaps it is too soon . . .' She stopped, and as she was still holding his hand, her weight had swung him about to face her. Her expression was somewhere between apprehension and defiance, and Memling stopped fumbling for words.

Janet had arranged to have the following day off, but Memling came wide awake at 4.30 a.m., a hopeless victim of years of discipline. He was standing beside the bed before he was fully awake, reaching for his trousers, at the same time blinking at the darkened room, trying to remember where he was and wondering why his Fairbairn knife was not strapped to his leg – his usual storage place when asleep. Janet turned on the bed lamp, gave him an exasperated look, and ordered him back to bed.

'Whatever in the world possessed you?' she demanded sleepily. 'Why, it's not even five o'clock and I can sleep as late as I want this morning.'

Memling stretched under the warm blankets, feeling the softness of her back and thighs, and gathered her into his arms. 'I just wanted to have your full attention,' he muttered, and began stroking the soft smooth skin that was a wonder to him. She half turned so that her nipples caressed his chest, and his breathing nearly doubled.

'Now that you have me awake, I suppose we may as well make the best of it.' She pressed her half-opened lips against his, and her tongue darted into his mouth. After a moment she whispered, 'You must think me shameless,' and buried her face against his shoulder until he lifted her head with both hands.

'No, never. I think of you as the woman with whom I am falling in love.' He nuzzled her cheek, inhaling the soft, sleepy odour of her skin.

Carefully she spread her thighs and wriggled downwards, and they lay like that for a few moments, holding each other tightly, locking out the world of violence and pain that had surrounded them a little more with each year. Then Janet moved, gently at first, and he followed, each successive thrust coming deeper and faster until she took his face in her hands and crushed her mouth to his, their tongues locked together. It seemed that they held to each other for ever, until their shudders were simultaneous. They continued to cling to one another afterwards.

When Memling awoke the second time, it was after nine and rain pattered on the roof. Janet was asleep, one leg and arm across his body, and he eased from beneath and touched his lips to the gentle hollow in her back. He lay quietly, content with himself and the world for the first time in years. No longer obsessed with the idea that he was betraying Margot, he wondered if his wife, cool, slender and quiet, would have approved of this ebullient and daring young woman. But it no longer mattered so much.

He found his robe in the closet, slipped it on, and went out into the living-room. The flat was tastefully furnished with rather fine antiques from the Regency period, and the blue Oriental carpet was soft beneath his feet. He found the tea in the kitchen and put the water on to boil, then stood at the window for a few moments watching the summer rain fall on the city. The streets glistened as if they had been newly scrubbed. A figure hurried past, umbrella slanted against the rain. The kettle whistled softly just as a blue navy staff car stopped below. Memling scowled at this intrusion of the real world. Not today, he thought, and closed the curtains. He turned back to the stove, shut off the gas, and fixed the tea. He found some breakfast biscuits and carried everything through into the bedroom, whistling reveillé.

Just as he was settling back into bed, Janet in his arms and tea finished, the doorbell rang. They looked at each other, Memling shaking his head. 'Ignore it. It could only be an encyclopaedia salesman.'

Janet giggled as he ran his tongue along her throat. 'Don't be silly. They are all in service . . .'

'That's certainly where they belong, then,' he growled, and grabbed for her, but Janet slipped laughing to the other side of the bed. The doorbell rang again, this time accompanied by heavy pounding.

'Christ, he's going to knock the door down.' Memling leapt up and, drawing on his robe, headed for the entrance hall.

Throwing open the door, he roared, 'Look here, whoever you are . . .' and stiffened to attention. Out of uniform, he was not required to salute, and he stopped himself just in time, then whipped the robe more tightly about himself.

'Sorry to intrude at a time like this.' Colonel Oliver Simon-Benet chuckled, and stepped inside. 'But there is a war on, you know, and none of us are exempt.' He took off his raincoat, surprising Memling with brigadier's shoulder boards.

'Colonel . . . I mean, ah, Brigadier . . . what . . .?'

But Simon-Benet, looking past him, tipped his hat as Janet appeared in the doorway, not at all embarrassed that both were in their robes.

'Good morning, Brigadier,' she said brightly. 'Have you had your breakfast yet?'

Simon-Benet laughed. 'Ah, yes, some time ago, I am afraid. I do apologise for interrupting like this, but it is important. I must borrow Lieutenant Memling for an hour or so. Do you mind terribly?'

Janet gave him a sweet smile. 'Yes, I do mind. And the next time I think you might just telephone to say you are coming, Brigadier.'

Simon-Benet actually coloured at that. 'I do apologise, but there just was no time. It's a stroke of luck the lieutenant is in London at all.'

Memling rubbed the back of his neck. 'Damn it all, Brigadier . . .'

Simon-Benet scowled, and he gave up. 'All right, sir. I'll need a moment to wash and shave.'

Thirty minutes later they were sitting in a café a block away, waiting for the waitress to finish distributing eggs and tea. Memling gave the brigadier a sharp glance when she left. 'This had better be damned good, Brigadier. I am on a week's leave, you know.'

'And making the best of it too.' Simon-Benet grinned, then seriously: 'Janet's a damned fine girl, Memling. See you take good care of her.' He hesitated then and contrived to look around the room without appearing to do so. 'I wanted to talk with you a bit, in private. It concerns some work you once did for your previous employers.'

Memling picked at the egg. 'Most of that work was classified secret.'

Simon-Benet hesitated. 'So it was. But we need only to speak in generalities. Look here, you never did see eye to eye with old Englesby, did you?'

Surprised, Memling shook his head. 'What has that got to do with . . . ?'

'Forget it. Not a question I should have asked. Except that it does explain a good bit. Look here, Memling. You were trained as an engineer. There is a notation in your MI-Six file that you were selected personally by the admiral for that reason. In spite of that fact, you were put on reserve status nearly two years ago and joined the Royal Marines. I'd like to know why?'

Memling looked stubborn. Simon-Benet watched him a moment, then said, 'It could be quite important.'

'I left,' Memling replied in a reluctant voice, 'because I felt there was little I could do to help the war effort sitting behind a desk reading German technical manuals already ten years out of date. No one paid any attention to my reports anyway. My wife had been killed in a bombing raid, and I felt I needed a bit of a change. I enlisted in the Royal Marines. Simple as that.'

The brigadier played with his glass a moment, then stared through the taped-up plate-glass window at the rain, which continued to slant down even though the cloud had broken to the west and blue sky was becoming visible.

'I believe there was more to it than that, wasn't there?'

Memling shrugged. 'I'm not sure I . . .'

'But you do. You returned from Belgium with what you saw as vital information which was totally ignored. You knew that the people who helped you get out were killed, and then you discovered that your wife had died in the blitz. On top of that, a departmental enquiry into your activities in Belgium did not give you a clean bill. It was at that point you joined the Royal Marines where, in view of your reserve status with the Firm, you were commissioned and sent to Home Army Intelligence. You wangled your way into the commandos and have since taken part in several raiding expeditions.' Simon-Benet gave him a quick grin. 'Would you say that forms an accurate summary of your career to date?'

Memling had listened with a growing dislike for the brigadier. 'Yes, sir, that is correct.'

'In that case' – Simon-Benet gave him an appraising look – 'a bit more detail is in order, I think.

'In 1938 you were sent to Germany. You met a man named Wernher von Braun. How well did you know him?'

'Wernher?' Memling looked at Simon-Benet in surprise. 'You have been doing some digging, haven't you!' When the brigadier did not react, he went on. 'I met Wernher von Braun in Paris in 1934. I was still at school then and interested in rocketry. I had saved all that year to attend a congress on rocket development. Von Braun was a member of the German Society for Space Travel and about my age. I suppose we became friendly because most of the others attending were dabblers and fantasists.'

'And you two were not?'

Memling frowned. 'Yes, we were. But we were also realists in the sense that we knew it would not happen unless we were willing to acquire the proper training. I dare say Wernher had learned that lesson sooner than I. In any event, we struck up a friendship that continued by correspondence.

'Our letters were infrequent and after 1936 stopped altogether. The following year I joined MI-Six and soon had to give up my position in the British Interplanetary Society for, well . . . other reasons.'

'You did not correspond with, or see, von Braun from 1936 to 1938?'

'No. And then strictly by accident. We just happened to be staying at the same hotel. We had dinner that night, and he introduced me to a colleague, a . . . Franz something or other.'

'Bethwig,' Simon-Benet supplied.

'Yes, that's the name. I next saw von Braun in 1940 at the arms factory in Liège.'

Simon-Benet sipped his tea. 'Both times you made reports concerning Germany's research on long-range rockets?'

'Yes. I assume they are in the files somewhere.'

'The first was, yes. The second seemed to have been misplaced. Carelessness, I was told when it was finally found.'

Memling grinned. 'I shouldn't be surprised. The start of the war caught the old bureaucracy at Northumberland Avenue by surprise.I doubt they have adapted to it yet.'

'They haven't,' the brigadier replied wryly. He paused, as if arranging his thoughts. 'At the moment I am assigned a special task, that of co-ordinating information concerning Germany's scientific and technical progress in one particular field, that of rocket research.'

'I'll be damned.'

The brigadier ignored him. 'I put my staff to searching for further information among various Allied intelligence agencies, and bits and pieces began to crop up, especially from Polish intelligence.'

'Polish intelligence?' Memling murmured in surprise. 'Why ever in the world would they be interested in rockets?'

'Seems that parts of Poland are being surveyed for testing sites. In any event, there were quite a few reports stuck here and there that, when assembled, suggest that more is going on than meets the eye. And none of them were duplicated in MI-Six files. I had a talk with Englesby, and he tended to dismiss their importance. When I mentioned your reports he shrugged and made remarks that gave me the impression there was a personality conflict between the two of you.'

The brigadier waited and, when no comment was forthcoming, called to the waitress for more tea. When she had gone, he fixed Memling with a steady look. 'I am convinced there is something to this business of German rockets. What about you?'

Memling shook his head. 'I thought so at one time, before the war. But since then, no. The rocket motors I saw in Liège were part of a put-up job to trick me into leading the Gestapo to the resistance group operating in the city.' And with that admission came the familiar sickening despair that had always accompanied any memory of those terror-filled last days in Belgium.

'Nonsense! There *is* something to all this, and your estimates of the size and range of the German rocket are not so different from those made by my own staff from information obtained through other sources. A remarkable job considering the circumstances. That is why I want you to come to work for me.'

Memling shook his head again. 'I know damned well that whatever information you have must have been planted by the Nazis. Damn it, they tricked me, and God knows how many people died because of my stupidity.'

The brigadier regarded him for a moment. 'There does seem to be a certain arrogance in that statement. It suggests that since you were, or thought you were, fooled, everyone else will be as well.'

'Wait a moment . . .'

Simon-Benet held up a hand. 'I know what you meant. I am afraid, however, that you must resign yourself to the fact that you are wrong. The rockets do exist and you are going to work for me.'

'I can't . . . sir. At least not until after the next mission. My section is raw and needs . . .'

'One junior officer more or less is not going to affect the war effort all that much. This might. I'll allow you the rest of the day. Report to number Eighteen Red Lion Square tomorrow morning at 0700 sharp.'

Memling toyed with his cup a moment. 'You don't seem to leave me any option.'

'I can't afford to. This isn't a game.'

There was an uncomfortable silence, which the brigadier finally broke. 'I suppose you will stay on with Janet? Housing is very difficult in London now.'

'Good Lord, no!' Memling started. 'I can't just move in there . . . I don't even know if she'd have me.'

'If you want my opinion, she needs you about as badly as you need her.'

'But good God, man, I can't just . . .'

The brigadier stood up grinning. 'A damned puritan, hey? Let me tell you, boy, none of us may survive this war. If a bullet doesn't find us at the front, a bomb might get us here in London. So if you can provide comfort to another, do so. Personally, I think prostitution and the theatre are the two noblest professions in which mankind can engage. Both offer entertainment and, best of all, relief from the outrages of the world.'

He touched his swagger stick to his cap and ducked out into the rain. The patch of blue sky, Memling noted, had disappeared, and it was coming down harder than ever.

'October has been a busy month for us at Peenemünde,' Franz Bethwig told his gathered staff. 'The first wholly successful launch of the A-Four was made on the third of this month. I am proud of you all and the work you performed under arduous and adverse conditions.'

The staff applauded, and he smiled in acknowledgement. I'm learning how to handle them, he thought. Perhaps Heydrich was right after all. 'Today,' he went on, 'we have a much tougher job to do. With the A-Four we had behind us the assembled resources of a powerful nation – even though we lacked a meaningful top priority.' He waited for, and received, the expected laughter. 'But we are operating under even tougher conditions with the A-Ten. We all know how demanding the SS has become, and with good reason. We must push development as quickly as possible to spare the Reich the damage of a long-term, if ultimate, victory. For that reason Reichsführer Heinrich Himmler will arrive secretly at Peenemünde this morning to witness the first test flight.'

As he expected, a low murmur filled the room. The SS was never welcome; Himmler doubly so. 'I expect you all to conduct yourselves with the utmost courtesy and respect for his rank and that of his aides.' Bethwig paused a moment, then grinned wickedly. 'I myself will do my best to keep those desk commandos out of your way.'

The room remained silent, except for the muffled exclamation of a horrified secretary. No one joked about Himmler.

Scowling, Bethwig continued: 'I am pleased to announce that the countdown is proceeding well. We are holding at the moment, waiting for the reichsführer's aircraft to arrive. We have also received word from our two picket submarines in mid-Atlantic. Both are on station. The count will resume in one hour. We expect to launch this evening at 1900 hours.'

Franz and his new secretary, a pretty young land service girl named Katherine, went out into the watery autumn sunshine; a driver was waiting to take them to Launch Stand XII located near the centre of the island. The car drove off, keeping to the middle lane to avoid the pedestrians and bicyclists streaming towards the canteens for the lunch break. Few of them, Bethwig knew, were yet aware of the A-10; by this evening all would know about it. The massive test stand could be isolated and guarded in its remote, marshy section of the island, and the massive first stage could be shrouded during assembly and its move to the stand. But once the engines reached full thrust and the gargantuan vehicle rose above the trees and, one hoped, streaked down range, there would be no more secrecy. Bethwig's staff had estimated that the noise would be heard in Stettin, some ninety kilometres distant.

As the car approached the test complex they had an occasional glimpse of the massive structure rearing above the pines, and even after a year and a half Bethwig still could not shake the feeling of awe it inspired in him.

The main control centre was housed in a half-buried bunker located a kilometre from the launch stand. He made a quick series of inspections among the consoles, then went up to the bunker's roof where the cameramen were running checks on their equipment. One or two nodded, but no one spoke. Ordinarily the crews would have been excited and expectant; but the spectre of Himmler and his SS minions had dampened their enthusiasm. The A-4, a much smaller and less-complicated vehicle, had required three attempts before a successful flight was achieved. And numbers four and five, fired since, had failed. The crews realised that this was to be expected, but no one knew how the reichsführer, the second most powerful man in the country and reputedly not the most stable individual, would view a failure on their part. The A-4 was an army project, and they were no strangers to failure. The A-10 was an SS project, and the SS did not admit to failure. Himmler's reputation was on the line, and all recalled how the once mighty Goering had fallen when his vaunted Luftwaffe had failed to polish off the RAF in the summer of 1940; and how the army had sunk in esteem when the Russians shoved them back from the very gates of Moscow the previous autumn.

Bethwig tried to shake off these gloomy thoughts. The test firing sequence from static mountings had been pushed hard during the previous six months and had produced fairly consistent results. Lack of time had prevented them from incorporating the newest versions of his film cooling and fuel injection systems into the A-4 engines, but starting from scratch with the A-10, they had been able to do so. Combustion chamber overheating was a thing of the past. And only rarely did lethal amounts of fuel flood the chamber prior to ignition and cause an explosion. The construction and testing of the engines had proven easier than expected; relatively easier, he amended. The new fuel injection system made it possible to cluster the powerful engines to produce the massive thrust needed to break up and out of Earth's gravitational well and reach the moon. He shook his head unconsciously. It never ceased to amaze him when he thought how great were the technical strides they had managed in the last three years.

'Ah, here you are. Daydreaming, heh?' Himmler had come on to the roof accompanied by two aides.

Startled, Bethwig turned quickly. 'My apologies for not meeting you. I was not told you had arrived.' His staff's method of making certain that Himmler understood that he was not welcome? he wondered.

'No matter.' Himmler turned to stare out over the immense circular reach of concrete separating the bunker area from the launch table nearly a kilometre away. He stood with his hands on his hips, bouncing on his toes and smiling. 'So this is what my late friend Heydrich began, hey? Look, Hans,' he joked to an aide as he pointed at the concrete apron. 'How many West Wall bunkers could be built with all that?'

Bethwig missed the answer as the loudspeaker announced the resumption of the countdown sequence. Three hours to go, he thought to himself. Three hellish hours of waiting made worse by Himmler's presence.

The afternoon wore on at a snail's pace. Early dusk came swiftly out of the west, and with it a damp cold that drove them inside. Floodlights went on as they re-entered the bunker; and in the distance Bethwig heard the drone of fighters patrolling against Allied reconnaissance aircraft.

Inside, the atmosphere was sticky with waste heat from the electrical motors and instruments. Bethwig escorted Himmler and his staff to the glassed-in VIP gallery, but the reichsführer refused to stay there, preferring instead to roam about the vast room interrupting the technicians and scientists at their work. At less than an hour to launch, Dornberger came in, his expression disapproving yet excited. Although he had no responsibility for the A-10 project, he received a round of applause from the men at their desks and consoles. Dornberger was a popular administrator, as dedicated as any of them to rocketry in spite of his official disapproval of the A-10 project. It was understood that he was a soldier first and a scientist second.

Dornberger even smiled and had a good word for Bethwig, the first in months. He was polite to Himmler and his staff, although it was obvious that this took considerable effort.

During the long afternoon the volume of sound inside the bunker had risen gradually until now it was a continous roar and one had to speak loudly to be heard. The launch crew consisted of fifty-three people sitting at consoles in the concrete vault of a room that had all the earmarks of the Todt Organisation's hasty wartime construction. The current joke was that in spite of reinforced concrete walls several metres thick, a nearsighted fly ran into and knocked down the bunker's west wall – an obvious allusion to the vast fortifications under construction along the Atlantic coast of France, which even the reichsführer had joked about and which was the usual excuse for the lack of building materials at Peenemünde.

An armoured glass viewing window was set into the front wall of the bunker. In spite of mild distortion, the squat, can-shaped rocket with its truncated nose was clearly visible. The concrete apron glistened with evening mist, and the rocket's fuselage glowed under the batteries of searchlights. Bethwig would much rather have launched during daylight when the cinecameras could have done a better job recording the rocket's flight. But the submarines would need the daylight to spot the rocket when – not if, he thought – it flashed into the Atlantic two thousand kilometres south-east.

The clock over the viewing window read exactly 1855 hours when the countdown reached minus one minute thirty seconds. The final LOX tank topping had gone off without the expected hitches, and Bethwig called a three-minute hold. The crew relaxed visibly, and the air was suddenly blue with cigarette smoke.

Himmler had begun pacing as the tension increased. Now he approached Bethwig and demanded to know why everything had stopped. Franz's explanation – time was needed to bring various schedules into line and also to allow the submarine tracking vessel to regain station – barely pacified him.

The controller's voice was droning the count at ten-second intervals now. At minus forty seconds the wisp of steam that Bethwig had been waiting for appeared near the nose as the hydrogen peroxide generators pressurised the fuel tanks.

As chief development engineer and project manager, Bethwig had little to do during the launch sequence but supervise. No longer did the project manager design the rocket, then weld, rivet, and install electrical gear, run the cinecameras, and do a hundred other tasks because no one else could be spared. Bethwig had no more idea how to operate a six-channel telemetry bank or the new recording machines that used a plastic magnetised tape to store data, than the operators knew how to design a rocket engine capable of producing three and a half million kilograms of thrust.

'Well,' Himmler said, turning to him. 'What is your estimate of the chance of success, Herr Doktor Bethwig?' He smirked at Dornberger. 'After all, if the engineer who designed this monster does not know, who does?'

Dornberger frowned at Bethwig, a warning to guard his words. But Franz ignored him.

'This is a first trial, Herr Reichsführer,' he snapped. 'A rocket is a very complex machine. I will be most surprised if the engines merely fire all together this first time. If it rises away from its table, it will be a miracle. The chance that it will fall to Earth within five hundred kilometres of its intended target is almost non-existent.'

Before the surprised and angered Himmler could reply, the firing control officer's voice rumbled over the loudspeaker announcing the beginning of the ignition sequence.

Bethwig jumped eagerly to the window. The first tendrils of

vapour were already curling about the massive base of the rocket.

'Minus thirty seconds.'

The half-minute dragged; tension mounted in the bunker until Bethwig thought he must scream to release it. On the launch table the vapour suddenly became a steady mist; cables fell away and gantries swung back, leaving the rocket standing clear against the floodlights. The mist became a hissing pillar of flame shot through with reddish shades at the moment the FCO announced actual ignition. The cloud of burned gases swirled outwards, roiling with streaks of flame and debris. The bunker began to vibrate to the low-frequency rumble of the twenty-one M103.5 rocket engines firing in unison. Even at a kilometre's distance the rocket could be seen to shudder. The FCO's voice reading various instrument results was lost in the painful crescendo of sound that struck and hammered at their ears through the metres-thick wall.

The rocket was rising now, lifting out of the inferno of flaming gas and steam. A shaft of flame erupted half a kilometre further on where the exhaust tunnel ended, and the sky caught fire. Bethwig realised he was holding his breath, then forgot as the ungainly rocket cleared the top of the gantries. It was rotating slightly now as the internal guidance system began to prepare for a thunderous flight towards the distant Atlantic. The rocket climbed steadily, passing two hundred metres, and Bethwig had to duck to see upwards through the slit window. The television monitors were useless once the rocket left the floodlit stage; they could show only an intense pinpoint of flame without reference. He became aware that he was gripping his clipboard so hard he had torn half the sheets. My God, he thought, it really is going to make it!

Cursing, he ducked out of the gallery and, defying all regulations, raced down the corridor, shoved the startled guard aside, and dived into the night. Above, the entire sky was lit as if by an artillery barrage. A slender pillar of flame was growing longer and wider as he watched. It moved with all the inexorability of a meteor in slow motion. The magnesium-bright exhaust was visible even through the light cloud that had filtered in from the direction of Rügen. Damn, he thought, it's going to make it. It's . . . The rocket blew up with a flare so brilliant that he was blinded. The sound bellowed about his ears, and he ducked towards the doorway, blinking and cursing the retinal after-image that obscured everything.

'You have failed me. I do not like my subordinates to fail.' Himmler's voice was mild enough, but there was no doubting the threat behind his words. Bethwig, however, was not in the mood for the reichsführer's tantrums. It was nearly three in the morning, and they had just come from a post-mortem examination of telemetry data, dragged away at Himmler's express command. Von Braun had been acting as Himmler's escort since the launch and now lounged in a corner, smoking a cigarette. Several ranking engineers and department heads were watching the reichsführer with apprehension. Bethwig turned furiously on Himmler, dashing his clipboard to the floor.

'We have not failed you, Reichsführer,' he roared in uncontrollable anger. 'I expressly recall warning you that it would be a miracle if the rocket even raised off the stand. It did that and more. There are some four hundred thousand parts that must work correctly if the rocket is to complete its flight. Four hundred thousand,' he repeated. 'We are battering against the frontiers of science, Herr Reichsführer. Only three weeks ago we launched a rocket that was less than three per cent as powerful, a major accomplishment in itself. Now, we are taking what can only be described as a quantum jump in technology. When you accuse us of failure, Herr Reichsführer, *you* let us down!'

He distinctly heard several gasps, and Himmler flinched as if he had been struck. In an instant Bethwig realised he had made a mortal enemy but was too tired to care. Himmler signalled his aide and swept out of the lounge. Dornberger hustled the rest of the staff out, and von Braun closed the door and leaned against it.

'Not wise, Franz. Not wise at all,' he admonished in a weak voice.

Bethwig shrugged and threw himself on to the sofa. 'I really don't give a damn any longer.' He closed his eyes for a moment, shutting out the light and the world.

Von Braun took a cigarette from his gold case and offered one to Franz, only to discover that he had fallen asleep. He finished the cigarette in silence, then, with a glance at his sleeping friend, closed the door carefully behind him.

Memling found his new working arrangements very curious. In 1939 Dr R. V. Jones had been co-opted from Clarendon Laboratory on the recommendation of Sir Henry Tizard who then headed the Committee for the Scientific Survey of Air Defence (Great Britain). He had been assigned to keep track of German weapons research but had been granted neither staff nor secretary. Until Simon-Benet ferreted him out in the mysterious and trackless wastes of Whitehall, Jones had plugged along from year to year doing an amazing amount of work to which no one paid the slightest attention. The two men had come to an arrangement: Jones would supply the scientific expertise to evaluate new discoveries, and Simon-Benet would provide the data and, whenever possible, on-site investigation through his extensive connections with the miscellany of intelligence services that infested London.

Several times Dr Jones had tried to move them out of the decrepit building in Red Lion Square, but each time the ministry had turned him down. The walls were bowed with age, the gaps between the floorboards were large enough to hide cockroaches – and did – and the windows opened grudgingly, if at all. The building's only advantage lay in the fact that it was no more than a brisk walk from Janet's flat in Montague Street.

Memling also discovered that Simon-Benet had a powerful enemy in Professor Frederick A. Lindemann, Viscount Cherwell, the Prime Minister's scientific adviser. Viscount Cherwell maintained that Germany lacked the resources to undertake such a massive rocket project as well as to develop and supply the vast volumes of fuel that would be needed. In the first two meetings he attended at which Viscount Cherwell was present, Memling had argued that if Germany was capable of producing synthetic petrol she could certainly produce one of three possible rocket fuels – ethyl alcohol, petrol, or hydrazine – in sufficient quantity. Cherwell disagreed.

Simon-Benet then arranged for Memling to present a paper describing the selection of ethyl alcohol as the likeliest fuel. Memling prepared his notes carefully, fully conscious of the fact that Viscount Cherwell was supremely confident of his own abilities and opinions and would likely dismiss him as an uneducated upstart. It was work he had never liked, and a long succession of beautiful summer afternoons slipped past while he struggled to assemble the required facts in the reading room of the British Museum or in his dingy office. But in the long twilight evenings there was Janet to make it all worthwhile.

The designated day arrived, and Memling, conscious that he was an interloper, presented his data to a silent and, as he expected, resentful committee. Anxious to be finished, he summarised the paper quickly: 'The characteristics desired in a rocket fuel are: one, availability of raw materials; two, high combustion heat for the greatest combustion chamber pressure; three, low molecular weight of the resulting gas; four, low freezing point for the greatest temperature range of operation; five, high specific gravity; six, low toxicity and corrosiveness to avoid the need for equipment and clothing; and seven, low vapour pressures for long storage life.

'Given this set of conditions, gentlemen, ethyl alcohol appears the logical answer. The farmlands of East Prussia and Poland are particularly well suited for the cultivation of potatoes, which are easily converted to ethyl alcohol, making an easily renewable resource. Calculations based upon thrust-to-fuel consumption curves, coupled with an analysis of the number of rockets required to make a significant impact upon the course of the war – some twelve hundred per month – require fifty-seven hundred and sixty to sixty-six hundred tons of ethyl alcohol monthly. Ethyl alcohol is also easier and cheaper to produce than petrol or hydrazine, and it possesses the requisite low toxicity and high stability to make it a natural choice. It does have one undesirable characteristic,' he added, trying desperately to inject some humour into the inquisition; 'it is drinkable.' It did not work.

Viscount Cherwell, acting as chairman, thanked him for his presentation, remarked upon its preciseness, disparaged his conclusions with personal opinion, and dismissed him. Simon-Benet nodded as he stood, and as Memling shut the door he heard the brigadier's voice rising to levels it had probably never reached before.

Memling, who had been up against just such entrenched opinion since the beginning, doubted it would do much good. But the brigadier, returning from the meeting several hours later, was in an excellent mood. He clapped Memling on the shoulder, sank down in the old armchair used for infrequent visitors, and propped his feet on the desk that had been well scarred before the Boer War.

'Think we made some progress today, damned if I don't!'

Memling, still sulking, grunted.

'Cheer up, old man. Things like this take time. Your presentation was masterful. Impressed them all no end.' He lit a cigarette and inhaled with satisfaction. 'That's the trouble with scientists. They are paid to be brilliant. Because of that, they can never admit to mistakes. Who will pay them for wrong answers? So, when you do spot a mistake, don't back them into a corner. Scientists have flashing teeth, my boy. Make the Hun look like Sunday-school masters. Just let them go on hoping that no one notices their mistakes while you proceed to do what needs doing.

'They know you're right, but scientists are worse than priests. They stick together right to the bitter end – or until their own reputations are put in jeopardy.'

*

During that endless summer one major setback seemed to spawn another. Mandalay fell to the Japanese in May. Rommel advanced to Sidi Barrâni and sent the Eighth Army on the long road through Mersa Matrûh into Egypt. Sebastopol collapsed in the face of the seemingly invincible German offensive, and a huge Murmansk-bound convoy, PQ-17, was decimated in the Arctic Ocean. Only the Americans had a stroke of luck at Midway Island, and Britons rushed to their atlases to see where it was.

Memling tried several times to make contact with members of his old command, but they all seemed to have been swallowed up by the war. He was short-tempered with everyone, including the brigadier, as the date for the raid approached.

He heard the name for the first time from a newsboy hawking papers outside the Russell Square tube station. Over his head the hoardings repeated the name Dieppe in huge black letters. He snatched a paper from the pile, dropped tuppence on the counter, and sidestepped through the crowd to a quiet backwater in the constant flow where he could lean against a lamp post and devour the stories. There were photographs that made a mockery of the government's attempt to put the best possible face on what could only be regarded as the disaster the old colonel had predicted.

Ragged, exhausted men shuffled down gangways, carrying bits and pieces of equipment. Here and there a Canadian unit badge was visible, but he did not see any marking the presence of his old unit. And defeat was there in the stunned, silent faces. For a moment he experienced a curious sense of relief that he had not been on the docks and quays of that insignificant French port town to see his people being decimated. Then the relief was replaced by anger, an intense black anger that he had not been allowed to participate. It was foolish, he knew, even as the disgust and revulsion coursed through him, but if he had been there, perhaps it might have made a difference to his undertrained green troops. And then he asked himself, sneeringly, what one more junior officer could have done.

But from that moment on, his frustration began to grow with each day that he continued to sit, occupying a desk, engaging in gathering useless facts that no one believed.

If it had not been for Janet, he might not have made it. Suspecting the turmoil he was enduring, she put up with nearly all of his moodiness; but when he overstepped, she let him know about it in no uncertain terms.

After one particularly explosive incident during the first week in August, they lay quietly on the bed, not touching but enduring the heat and resenting each other's presence. He shifted restlessly on the bed, wishing the sun would go down, but it was only a quarter to nine.

'Look, darling, something has got to change,' Janet said when he had shifted position for the fourth time in as many minutes. 'You're driving yourself into a nervous breakdown and me around the bend. Some people have to fight the war, some have to stay behind and support them. You know how important your job is. And besides, you've already done more than your share of fighting.'

Memling grunted, and she went on, 'Of course you're worried about your unit, but with the extra time they had to train . . .'

She broke off and propped herself up. 'Look here. I'm damned sick of your bad temper and ill humour. Think of me for a change. I need someone to love me, not yell and shout all the time. If I wanted that, I would have joined the army too.'

Memling blinked, not quite certain whether she was serious, and suddenly the realisation broke upon him that he had done nothing for the past few months but abuse her hospitality.

'Marry me?' The question popped out, and he wondered later how long it had been rattling around in his subconscious.

Janet smiled. 'Will it improve your humour?'

'It certainly won't worsen it.'

'That's not good enough.'

Memling pretended to think about it. What Janet had said was completely true. He was feeling sorry for himself. Why? To hide something? Distant thunder rumbled, and the air was suddenly dead. A middle-aged veteran of the trenches had once told him, 'It's like that just before the barrage, mate. All still and quiet, like the world 'as gone and died.'

As if echoing his thoughts, she kissed his forehead. 'Sometimes I wonder if you're not trying to hide the real reason for your ill humour behind this need to get back into action.' When he looked at her in surprise, she shook her head. 'I don't mean it's deliberate. It might be entirely unconscious.'

Memling chuckled. 'Been talking to the new psychologist Englesby took on? Has he had a look at Englesby's drives and motivations yet?'

Janet giggled. 'As a matter of fact, we had tea the other day. He claims Englesby has an enormous inferiority complex and covers up with that damnable smug superiority. He also says that most of the upper class are that way. They know the rest of the world resents their money and privilege, and they're stuffy as a defence. Sort of like whistling in the dark to keep up your courage.'

The wind struck then, whipping the curtains into the room and banishing the heat instantly. Janet sprang to the window, spreading her arms wide to the breeze. Memling followed and pulled her aside before the neighbours could see her naked earth goddess display. The rain came swiftly behind the wind, thunder crashing and banging about the city in an almost continual symphony.

Janet tugged his head down and whispered into his ear, 'I accept your proposal, darling, whether it improves your humour or not.'

Memling laughed and pointed at the rain. 'No German bombers tonight.' Janet nodded seriously and led him back to the bed.

They had been in Berlin for three days, trapped in a seemingly endless round of technical conferences and symposia, before being summoned by Himmler. A chauffeured Mercedes limousine took them to his headquarters. As they drove through the streets they could see that in spite of regulations the festive coloured lights had not been turned off to comply with the blackout. Shop windows were crammed to overflowing with goods, and well-dressed shoppers struggled with packages on the icy sidewalks. Traffic, both military and civilian, was heavy, and there seemed to be more uniforms in evidence now than the previous summer.

Von Braun sat quietly staring out the window, until the limousine stalled in heavy traffic at a busy intersection. Then he turned to his friend.

'I saw a picture of London in that American magazine *Life*. Leiderle brought it back from Switzerland. The city is in ruins, and the people look half-starved. Yet here you would never know there was a war. Look at them.' He motioned towards a couple running hand in hand across the street, both clutching bundles and laughing happily. 'It's as if they were on holiday, a permanent holiday, and no one will ever have to pay the reckoning.'

Bethwig remained silent. Germany triumphant! A nation surfeited with self-confidence after so many years of insecurity. How much longer could it last? The British had even begun to bomb Berlin's industrial suburbs. How much longer would the British and their American allies show such restraint, he wondered, with British cities being subjected to terror bombing?

The limousine inched forward until it was stopped opposite a news-stand. The banner leader indicated fresh news from Stalingrad, and Bethwig wound down the window and motioned for a paper.

Von Braun glanced at the headline and snorted. 'Herr Goebbels is still trying to convince us that the mighty army is winning the battle of Stalingrad, I see. What foolishness. I spoke to a pilot who had flown some wounded out a few days ago. He said the situation grows more hopeless by the day.'

Bethwig shook the paper loudly and jerked his head at the driver beyond the glass window. Von Braun nodded wearily and fell silent. The car broke free of traffic then, and a few minutes later they were walking up the broad steps into SS headquarters. An officer was waiting to conduct them directly to the reichsführer who stood to receive them, smiling broadly. He indicated two chairs, then occupied a few moments with pleasantries and comments on how well the battle at Stalingrad was shaping, while the aide brought coffee – not ersatz, Bethwig noted, but the real thing.

'Well, now, gentlemen, I see by the reports that in spite of difficulties, you have made remarkable progress in the past few months. I understand that you are readying another A-Ten for testing. Fine, fine. We must keep things moving along now that the Americans are beginning to make themselves felt in the war.' Himmler hunched forward and stared at each man in turn.

'Gentlemen, I must be frank with you.' He turned first to Bethwig. 'It concerns the matter of priorities. I am finding it most difficult to supply your needs in the face of the Führer's repeated refusals to allot top priority to rocket development. I have discussed the matter with Minister Speer' – he turned to von Braun – 'and he also has had little success in obtaining materials and priorities for Peenemünde. It seems that our Führer has dreamed that rockets will not be successful weapons. Whether or not this colours his thinking I do not know, but he continues to state that he is not yet convinced that the rocket will be an effective weapon. Now, gentlemen, I understand something of the needs of research and the amount of time required to ready new weapons for use. I believe that I have hit upon a scheme to ease the matter of priorities.'

Himmler smiled his most disarming smile, and Bethwig thought he looked more than ever like an ineffectual country farmer.

'And what is this plan, Herr Reichsführer?' von Braun enquired politely.

'A very simple one, to be sure, and to your benefit. As you know, the Schutzstaffel is a separate legal entity of government within the Reich. We are essentially a state-within-a-state and therefore are exempt from the unnecessary and time-consuming foolishness foisted on the Wehrmacht by bureaucrats.' He leaned back and regarded them both with a benign expression.

'My position as reichsführer allows me a great deal of freedom. We of the SS have our own army, courts, market system, housing, transportation, and scientific sections, as you know. And I am solely responsible for the establishment of priorities within that framework.' He shot forward in his chair and peered at von Braun over his pince-nez.

'I propose that you both leave the employ of the army. You, Doktor von Braun, would become director of my rocket research programme with the rank of gruppenführer and you, Doktor Bethwig, his second in command as brigadeführer. I can assure you that everything necessary will be granted without delay. You have no idea how efficient my SS can be.'

The suggestion did not impress Bethwig. Heydrich had tried to force acceptance of a similar offer before his death, and it had been only a matter of time before Himmler did likewise. Only the high ranks were surprising. The reichsführer was not known for his generosity, and ranks equivalent to major general and brigadier general only hinted at his determination. In spite of his antipathy to Himmler, Bethwig could see the benefits of such a move. But von Braun would have none of it. He cited his contract with the Army Research Centre, as well as his personal loyalty to Dornberger. Himmler, surprisingly reasonable in the face of such stubborn opposition, turned the talk to other matters.

At eight o'clock an aide entered to remind the reichsführer of another engagement, and he apologised for keeping them so long. As they walked towards the door Himmler smiled and reached up to clap a hand on von Braun's shoulder. 'Please reconsider my offer, Herr Doktor von Braun. I am sure you will not let last spring's unpleasantness obscure your judgement.'

Von Braun snorted. 'And what of the investigation, Herr Reichsführer? Have I been cleared yet?'

'Ah, yes, the investigation,' Himmler replied, half turning to glance back at his desk as if the answer lay there. 'I read a preliminary review of the evidence only last week. Most favourable. Most favourable. Otherwise, I would not be able to offer you such a fine position, would I?'

'And when will the charges be dropped?'

'Soon, my boy. Soon. Don't give it another thought. There are more important things with which to occupy your mind.' Himmler gave them an enigmatic smile and closed the door.

*

As they were getting into the car an officer hurried out with a sealed envelope.

'The reichsführer asked me to give this to you personally,' he said to Bethwig, 'and to assure you that if further information is required, he will endeavour to assist you in any way he can.'

Bethwig stuffed the envelope into his pocket and got in. The return trip to Tempelhof was made under escort with sirens blaring. A Ju.88 was standing on the apron, engines turning, and a pretty hostess in Lufthansa uniform welcomed them aboard. After the plane was airborne, they were served wine and a gourmet supper, followed by cognac and real coffee.

All through the meal von Braun ranted angrily at Himmler, and Bethwig listened silently until he ran down and fell asleep. He remembered the envelope then, found it in his overcoat, and struggled to read the spidery handwriting. When he had finished, he refolded the letter and sat motionless.

Franz remained silent during the drive from the airfield to their quarters, barely acknowledging von Braun's comments. He pleaded exhaustion and went immediately to his apartment.

In his room, he lit the fire, poured a stiff whisky, then spread Himmler's note on his desk and stared at the words. Now he knew why Himmler had summoned them both to Berlin. The last two paragraphs made it perfectly clear:

'*Knowing of your concern, my investigators established beyond doubt that the young lady is being well cared for in a Prague hospice. It is certainly possible that if her treatment continues as successfully as heretofore, she may be released in the near future. Unfortunately, her parents have disappeared, and it is thought they may have been killed in the bombing of their small village by aircraft of the American Eighth Air Force. If so, there will of course be the matter of guardianship to be settled, as the doctors are doubtful that she will ever again be well enough to live on her own. Perhaps something can be arranged in this regard.*

'*Knowing of your concern, I take this occasion to set your mind at rest. You may be assured that I will do all I can to assist you, as I am most concerned that nothing be allowed to distract you from our great plans.*'

The implication was plain enough. Himmler had anticipated von Braun's angry refusal. So, if he delivered von Braun, Inge would be his reward. Bethwig slammed his fist on to the note and flung himself about the room. How in the name of God did Himmler find time to concern himself with something as petty as this? Was the A-10 all that important to him? It must be. Look at the lengths to which he had gone: locating and then keeping the girl locked away and somehow disposing of her parents so the question of guardianship could be raised. German law was quite strict in that regard, and while Himmler might profess to be above the civil law, he was not averse to its use when it suited his purposes.

After a while he took his raincoat and went out to the officers' club to look for von Braun. He had no other choice; and as Himmler had suggested, there were certain benefits to be derived from enlistment in the SS.

Spring had come early to London. The walk to Red Lion Square had turned pleasant in the past week, and only that morning Memling had thought seriously of requesting a few days' leave to take Janet to Devon for a belated honeymoon. But all such plans had evaporated instantly in the last five minutes. He looked up from the photograph to the RAF squadron leader who sat across from him smoking an especially foul-smelling pipe.

'Interesting, heh?'

Memling reached for his telephone and rang through to Simon-Benet. The phone clicked several times as the monitoring devices were activated, and then the brigadier was on the line.

'Hello, sir. The Central Interpretation Unit people have come up with something quite interesting. Can we come across?'

A few minutes later he was introducing the squadron leader to Simon-Benet and handing him the magnifying glass at the same time. 'Look just here, sir.'

The grainy black-and-white photograph showed an oval structure, oriented north-west to south-east, that looked vaguely like a sports stadium. The open centre was surrounded by high banks of what appeared to be packed earth. A large two- or three-storey structure was located at the eastern edge, and several smaller buildings were scattered about the area. A network of roads, appearing as white tracks in the photograph, circled the oval structure. Inside, near the south-east perimeter, was a snub-nosed greyish object resembling a torpedo with large fins; it was lying on a transport vehicle of some kind. Several dots resolved into people under the glass, and one appeared to be walking towards a rectangular building.

'I'm damned,' the brigadier said after a while. He looked up at Memling who nodded in agreement. The brigadier glanced at the photograph's scale, then took a metal ruler from his desk and measured the length of the torpedo shape. 'Agrees with your estimates, at least as far as length is concerned.' He tapped the photo with a finger.

'Any more like this, Squadron Leader?'

The man shook his head. 'Not yet, sir. But we have another high altitude flight scheduled as soon as the weather clears. The Yanks will be doing this one. We have to be careful, though. If Jerry gets the idea that we're interested in the area, he'll start taking precautions.'

'Where was this taken?'

'Place called Peenemünde. An island off the Baltic coast, near Stettin. Used to be a seaside resort before the war.'

Simon-Benet nodded as if the information were not unexpected. 'Thank you, Squadron Leader. I assume that you have given this area the highest priority?'

'Yes, sir. And we have initiated a review of past observations of the area.'

'Very good. Keep me informed. That will be all.'

The brigadier motioned Memling into a chair as the squadron leader left.

'You recognised the name of that island, sir?'

Simon-Benet nodded absently. 'First heard of the place in 1939. A report appeared at our Oslo embassy just after the Nazis attacked Poland. Everyone thought it a plant.' He sat down, still staring at the photograph. 'How do you feel, Jan, now that you have been vindicated?'

Memling cocked his head at the unusual question. 'It hadn't yet occurred to me that I had,' he answered stiffly.

The brigadier held up a hand. 'Just pulling your leg, my boy. Didn't expect it to come off in my hand. Look here, the name Peenemünde is familiar. For several months now, we've been getting reports through from various sources that something is going on up there. Civilians barred from the area, huge shipments of supplies and materials going in, a search through forced labour camps for scientific and technically trained types who are all then sent north. Tell you anything?'

Memling frowned. 'Depends on how many of those people they are after, sir. If it's only a few, it might not mean anything. But if it's several hundred . . .'

'Several thousand. And my sources believe it's only the beginning. I might add that these sources are Polish. Their Armia Krajowa has been quite active in this area, as a good many of their POWs from 1939 have been sent to the labour camp at Peenemünde. Strange reports of flying torpedoes and such like have been coming through from the Baltic coastline for months. Seems they have been confirmed now.'

'What's the next step then, sir?'

The brigadier shrugged. 'That may not be up to us. I've just had a meeting with our new boss. The Prime Minister is becoming concerned and has decided to formalise our little group. We are all now under the command of a gentleman named Duncan Sandys. Is the name familiar?'

Memling frowned. 'Seems to be . . . but I can't place it exactly.'

'Well, Mr Sandys is, or was, joint parliamentary secretary for the Ministry of Supply. He does have two other qualifications that provide me with a degree of hope. He commanded an experimental rocket battery at Aberporth and he is Mr Churchill's son-in-law. Perhaps we now have someone of sufficient stature to stand up to Lord Cherwell.'

Memling gave a low whistle. 'And when did this all take place?'

'Just the past few days. As I said, the government is beginning to take quite seriously the possibility that the Germans may indeed be developing long-range rockets. But until things clarify themselves, we must sit tight and see.'

Franz Bethwig studied the three faces and was struck by the way in which they delivered or received the news: the triumphant sallow face of Minister Gerhard Degenkolb, the apoplectic face of General Dornberger, and the thunderstruck countenance of Wernher von Braun.

Professor Hettlage cleared his throat timidly as if wanting to say something more, but Degenkolb signalled him to be quiet.

'May I ask who suggested this insanity?' Bethwig enquired politely.

Minister Degenkolb glared at him. 'The suggestion came directly from Minister Speer. And I suggest that you modify your language appropriately or you may find yourself in very hot water, sir.'

Bethwig gave him a lazy smile. 'You think so, do you?'

Dornberger intervened: 'And why,' he asked, voice barely under control, 'did the minister suggest this course of action?'

Degenkolb glared once more at Bethwig before answering. 'Minister Speer is most concerned with Reichsführer Himmler's offer to employ Herr Doktors von Braun and Bethwig. Minister Speer is certain this is a first step towards assuming control of the Peenemünde facility, in spite of the good doctors' persistent refusals. He felt that converting the entire Army Research Centre, Peenemünde, to a private stock company would circumvent the reichsführer's plans. I advise you to go along with him. Otherwise, you gentlemen' – he glared at the two scientists – 'will find yourselves in the employ of the SS, and you, sir' – he addressed Dornberger – 'will be seeking a new post!'

Dornberger waved a hand as if dismissing that possibility. 'May I enquire how the change is intended to be made?' Dornberger's famed control seemed to be deserting him. Bethwig had never before heard such anger in his voice.

'Of course. Peenemünde would be transformed into a private company with limited liability. The entire capital would remain for now with the state, while the firm would be managed by a large concern acting as trustee – General Electric, Siemens, Rhinemetall, or Krupp, whichever is found most suitable. After amortisation of capital invested, the plant would be transferred to possession of the firm.'

'Are you aware,' Dornberger asked, 'that the value of Peenemünde and its equipment is several hundred million marks? The interest payments and amortisation quotas could hardly be of interest to industry.'

Degenkolb smiled at that, and Professor Hettlage intervened, anxious that his contribution not be overlooked. 'We already have acceptable tenders in that regard. We would make a cut in capital and declare assets of between one and two million, letting the rest go.'

Bethwig burst into laughter. 'Amazing,' he finally managed. 'You will take an investment worth several hundred million marks and turn it, by a "cut in capital", into a bargain. Of course, once the shares are resold by the state to a few select individuals – including, I have no doubt, you, Herr Degenkolb, and Minister Speer – the assets would then be re-evaluated and inventoried at their real worth. How very clever.' Bethwig sat forward abruptly and snarled. 'In the meantime the hell with the war effort, heh? We must not let that interfere with the lining of your pockets, must we?'

Degenkolb's mouth worked in astonishment at being accused of outright thievery.

'Do not look so surprised, Minister. I am, after all, a banker's son.'

With an angry hiss Hettlage motioned to Dornberger to control his subordinate, but the general only stared at him. 'I assume,' he said finally, 'that this suggestion has been cleared with General Fromm. If not, then we have nothing further to discuss.'

Dornberger got to his feet and stamped out, followed by von Braun and Bethwig. Franz turned at the door. 'Minister Degenkolb, you are an excellent administrator, if somewhat of a bastard. I suggest you stick to that and leave the thieving to others.' He smiled wickedly and closed the door.

As they walked across the park to the administration building von Braun waved an arm about. 'Look at this. Laboratories, wind tunnels, construction and production facilities, housing, shops, amusement centres, and test stands, all employing and housing over four thousand people. How in the name of God can that man think this could all be turned into a moneymaking concern? Why, our budget is one hundred and fifty million marks per year. What do we sell? How can they possibly expect to make money?'

Bethwig explained patiently that the investors would make their money simply by buying the facility for a fraction of its worth, then at some later date selling it for its true worth either back to the government or to a holding company that they would invent; that company would, of course, be funded by the government.

Von Braun listened patiently; when Bethwig finished, he gave him a dubious glance but did not argue. Dornberger left to begin a series of phone calls, the first to Colonel General Fromm, chief of armaments and his direct superior.

Von Braun's secretary, Hannelore Bannasch, met them at the elevator and gave her boss an envelope bearing Himmler's personal seal. Von Braun glanced at Bethwig, then opened and read the message. He tossed it to his friend with a pleased expression.

'That seems to be that. Perhaps Speer's little game has frightened him away for now.'

The letter said only that because of changing circumstances the reichsführer's offer of direct employment had been withdrawn. The reichsführer sent his best regards and wished them every success for the sake of the Reich. Bethwig felt a chill spread slowly through him, then mumbled an excuse and rushed to his own office. The envelope waiting for him contained two notes: one, impeccably typed, was an exact copy of von Braun's. The second, in Himmler's own spidery handwriting, reported that Inge had taken a turn for the worse and the doctors had not thought it wise to release her just yet – perhaps in a few months when the situation clarified itself.

He was being punished for his failure to persuade von Braun to join the SS. The fact that he had had little chance of ever doing so would make no impression at all on the reichsführer.

A member of his staff telephoned to request an appointment to review the new procedures for the fast-approaching launch of the second A-10 rocket. Bethwig put the man off for the moment, pleading other commitments. No sooner had he hung up than the phone rang again. This time it was Dornberger, telling him to prepare for a visit to Hitler's eastern headquarters to report on their progress to date. A few moments later von Braun burst in, grinning broadly, convinced that Speer had won, had beaten Himmler at his own game, and that they would now have a chance to change the Führer's mind about the worth of rockets.

The meeting had been as stormy as the day outside, and Brigadier Oliver Simon-Benet fumed as he and Captain Jan Memling hurried along the road to their car. Jan opened the door and stepped back, but the brigadier, who held the umbrella, motioned him in impatiently. As the staff car, an American Buick – Memling still did not understand how Simon-Benet had acquired it – edged into traffic the brigadier swore and shoved the folded umbrella into its holder as if bayoneting his worst enemy.

'Damn, I suppose they're right. One more overflight at low level and the Germans are certain to know we're on to them. But we do need those data! Isn't there anything more CIU can do?' he demanded plaintively.

Memling shook his head. 'I've been over it a dozen times with them. Perhaps if the weather had been better . . .' He shook his head, recalling the grainy, underexposed pictures that were all the photorecon aircraft, at the very limits of their fuel supply, had been able to obtain. 'Unless your people on the ground can obtain the information, I am afraid we will have to go on what we now have.'

The brigadier muttered to himself, then said, 'Nothing there, I am afraid. The AK people say their only contacts inside Peenemünde are with low-level labourers.' He fell silent, staring out at the rain-sodden streets. May has been nothing more than a month of rain, he thought, all across Europe. But they had to have that data. Without specific and precise co-ordinates for the important test sites and facilities, Bomber Command could never hope to destroy the Peenemünde research centre. It was just too huge. He glanced at Memling sitting beside him, likewise staring out at the rain. He had been considering this solution for some time now but had not wanted to broach it until every conceivable avenue had been explored.

'Jan,' he began abruptly. 'We need to send someone in. Someone who has the training to understand what he's seeing. Will you go?'

For just an instant Memling thought he might vomit. He breathed slowly through his nose at the same time tightening his diaphragm to control the gag reflex. Ah, Christ, he thought, to go back again? He couldn't do it, but even as the thought was formulated he knew he had no other choice. Janet was right, he had done more than his share. But that was an excuse no one would ever accept, particularly the brigadier.

Simon-Benet grunted in satisfaction at his nod of acceptance.

Passage at Arms

Germany August 1943

The blackness was absolute until he tugged back his sleeve and the radium dial of his watch glowed like a hundred-watt bulb. Three and a half hours since take-off. Jan Memling groaned and shifted position in the cramped confines of the Mosquito's bomb bay. His legs were numb, and his back ached. The space, according to his sadistic instructor, was no larger than the famous medieval torture chamber in which you could neither sit up nor lie down at full length.

Memling shifted again and tugged on the parachute harness until the offending buckle came away from his spine. He started to curse, but gave it up, having already run through his entire vocabulary several times, and looked at the watch again. Twenty-five minutes. Of a sudden, that damnable surge of fear slashed through his chest. After two years' active service in the Royal Marine Commandos he thought he was finished with that pervasive terror. My God, he wondered, why did I never experience it in combat? Why now? Why always in situations where I must operate on my own? Memling found that he was starting to hyperventilate, and he struggled to hold his breath; then as he began to think coherently he pinched the oxygen tube shut and squeezed the rubber bulb to force carbon dioxide back into the mask. After a few moments his heart stopped fluttering and his breathing evened. This was always the worst part, the anticipation. Yet Memling also knew from experience that the fear would continue, growing more intense, until he was safely out – or dead. It did no good telling himself he hadn't wanted this mission; no one ever did.

'Are you comfortable, old man?' The pilot's voice rattled in his earphones, startling him. Memling swore and the pilot laughed. 'Ten minutes will see us passing south of Greifswald. Five minutes more will put us north of Wolgast and into your drop area.'

Memling acknowledged. At least the painful – physically and mentally – three months of training were behind. Coupled with an almost overpowering fear of going back into German territory was his growing estrangement from Janet, so that he had boarded the aircraft at Church-Fenton almost with a sense of relief.

Their difficulties had begun the evening Simon-Benet asked

him to undertake the operation. He had told Janet only that he was being sent on detached duty, but she had either guessed from his attitude, or picked up rumours in Northumberland Avenue, that he was being sent into Germany, and it had occasioned an argument that had nearly ended in a complete break. Janet maintained he had done more than could be expected of anyone, that it was plain his nerves were not up to such a mission, and, finally, that she could not go through the agony of waiting and wondering if he would come back.

During the final weeks before he left for training, the argument had recurred several times until they became afraid to speak to each other. Memling had taken to sleeping in the spare bedroom, and their parting at Victoria Station had been strained. Since then, Janet's weekly letters had become shorter and shorter until they were little more than notes concerning the weather, the same war news he heard on the BBC, and occasional comments about the increasing influx of Americans.

The ready light went on, filling the tiny space with its reddish glow. He fumbled to make certain that everything was in order. Parachute – he checked each fastening and made certain that the rip-cord ran free; chest pack containing the heavy radio transmitter, rations for three days, and his pistol, a Walther PP nine-millimetre automatic which he had obtained from a captured German officer in France. He himself had made the silencer for it from a length of conduit tubing packed with metal washers and steel wool. He buckled his leather and steel crash helmet securely and did up the laces on his boots, then made certain that the Fairbairn knife was strapped to his left boot – and waited, trying to hold the fear in check.

The pilot apologised for disturbing his rest and announced they were now passing Greifswald. 'No anti-aircraft fire and no sign of night fighters. Maybe we got through without Jerry spotting us this time.'

Memling muttered something in reply, and when the co-pilot broke in to tell him to stand by, he removed his earphones and clipped them into their rack.

The minutes dragged before the yellow light went on. Memling released the four catches holding the plywood cover over the circular hole cut through the doors of the bomb bay, and slid it aside. He struggled into a sitting position, head bent, legs straddling the hole, and squinted at the frigid windblast. The yellow light began to blink the fifteen-second warning, and Memling slid his feet into the hole. Immediately the wind sucked them back against the fuselage, and he had to brace himself to keep from sliding through. For a moment the urge to pull his feet back, re-cover the hole, and go home to Janet was overpowering. The green light came on, and without thinking, Memling straightened his back as he had been taught, and dropped.

Even with the Mosquito bomber throttled right back to stalling speed, the one-hundred-and-forty-mile-an-hour wind of their passage flung him astern, tumbling him while he sought to spread arms and legs to maintain stability. He had an impression of the dark fuselage slipping past, black paint glinting with tiny highlights; and the earsplitting thunder of two Rolls Merlin 23 engines enclosed him in fury.

Then it was over, and he was wrapped in silence. The cold air brushed his face. The ground below was barely discernible. To his right lay a body of water interrupted by a dark landmass. The River Peene, he thought, the island of Usedom, and the Baltic beyond.

He glanced at the altimeter strapped to the top of his chest pack, twisting to catch the moonlight on its dial. The needle pointed steadily at zero. Damn, he muttered, and was surprised at the sound. Warrant Officer O'Reilly's voice had dinned into his brain: 'Wait until the needle points at eight hundred, boyo, or the bloody Hun will be waiting for you.'

There was nothing for it but to pull the rip-cord. Without the altimeter there was no way to judge a low-altitude drop at night. Memling made certain he was in position, took a quick look at the river to establish his orientation, and then pulled. He felt the canvas flaps slap against his helmet, had the impression of the pilot chute snaking behind, and then there was the sudden jolt that always came as a surprise when the chute blossomed and the sense of falling became apparent.

Memling craned his neck upward to make certain the black canopy had spread properly; then searched below for the pinpoint of light that would mark his reception team. There was a small pond or lake near the landing zone, and he fastened on its moonlight surface as a visual reference. The plan had been for the Mosquito to drop him at three thousand feet. He judged that he had fallen free for no more than eight or nine seconds, which meant that he had opened the canopy at about – he calculated the sum in his head – eighteen hundred feet. Maybe.

The ground came up fast. The lake had been misleading; it was further away from his point of impact than he had thought. Memling had just enough time to spot the pine tops, yank his shrouds to the left, and force relaxation into his knees before he smacked hard enough to knock the wind from his lungs.

He lay for some minutes, face pressed against damp moss, while he sought to regain his breath. When he could struggle painfully to his feet, the full realisation that he was in Germany broke on him and he had to sit down until the nausea passed. With few exceptions, every man, woman and child he encountered from now on would be his enemy.

At the same time, he experienced the heightening of senses that fear induced. The night was suddenly alive with a myriad of sounds, and even the darkness seemed to recede. His chute had caught on a pine branch, and that had upset his landing. Working quickly, he manoeuvred the canopy loose, tearing a long gash in the silk, and stuffed the endless yards of material back into the pack. He tied the flaps together and hunched down beneath the tree, listening.

He hadn't seen the signal. And now there were only the normal night sounds to be heard: the scurrying of a small animal, the droning of insects, the bark of a distant fox, and once the flutter of wings as a night predator cruised past. He had been told as little as possible about his contact on the principle that the less he knew about the fledgling German resistance movement, the less he could betray during interrogation.

The hours inched by, and still he huddled beneath the tree, unmoving except for his eyes. Towards dawn he heard a cough some distance away and slid the Walther from his pocket, checked that the silencer was screwed on tight, and pushed the safety catch up with his thumb. A few moments later he heard a thin whistling. The sky had begun to lighten, so that he could make out large objects, but with the light had come a ground mist that softened and obscured outlines.

The whistling was closer now, and he stepped back into the trees.

It could be a woodcutter getting an early start or a routine patrol – although he could not imagine wasting manpower to patrol such an isolated section of the country. And it was not likely that a patrol sent out to find him would make so much noise.

Memling found himself staring at an apparition. The man, or woman, he could not be certain which, was dressed in a ragged jacket and pants; broken-down boots were tied on to its feet, a shapeless hat sat atop long greasy hair, and an axe was slung over one shoulder.

The apparition stopped, leaned on the axe, stared around, then asked in heavily accented English, 'Where you are, Tommy?'

The man's voice was deep, well modulated, and totally inappropriate to his appearance.

'The password be's Birmingham.'

Memling worked his way back into the trees as the man shrugged and sank down on to his haunches to wait. Memling moved silently back along his path, pausing often to listen and search the fog-shrouded trees for signs of a German patrol. The correct password was reassuring but not in itself sufficient. There had been plenty of time for the real resistance contact to be captured and the password extracted.

Memling went half a mile to the west, then described a wide circle south so that he approached his former location from the opposite direction. There had been no sign of any German activity; no sign, in fact, that anyone had been in the area in a long while. Jan came in through the trees, using the sparse underbrush as a screen, and the ragged woodcutter was still waiting. As Memling settled down to watch, the man yawned, shrugged, and stood up.

'Tommy, I have not yet my breakfasts. When you satisfy yourself, you follow my tracks. I will have breakfasts waiting you. Okay?'

The man chuckled, and Memling gave it up. He stepped into the clearing, pistol in his right hand, eyes searching in every direction.

'Oho! You are good, Tommy. Trusting nobodies. Good. Live to an old age, maybe. My name being Wolcowitz. Of Polish citizenships.'

Memling regarded him dubiously. 'Polish? In Germany?'

'Of course, and why not forever sakes? No Jew or officer. Just Wolcowitz the woodcutter.'

'Woodcutters don't normally speak English.'

The Pole bellowed with laughter, and Memling flinched. 'For the love of God,' he hissed, 'keep quiet!'

The Pole shouldered his axe and motioned around at the trees. 'Whyever do you say? Is no German nearby. None in woods. Only me, Wolcowitz. All Germans in Russia, fighting. Good place for them. Germans and Russians all kill each other, world be better place. Finn tell me once only Russian he like to see is over iron sights. For me, same with German. Come now. I quite hungries.' Whistling, the Pole led off through the woods.

Wolcowitz served Memling a breakfast of rabbit stew, although Memling suspected the ingredients included other animals as well, to judge by the variety of gamey flavours. But he was hungry enough to eat anything that did not move, and Wolcowitz urged more food on him. Afterwards, to satisfy Memling's edginess, the Pole took him on a sweep of the area.

A dirt track led into the forest from the general direction of Greifswald, an ancient town of forty thousand near the mouth of the River Ryck in the Greifswalder Boden, some twenty kilometres to the west and south. Memling studied the road carefully until he was certain it had seen no recent traffic. By noon he was satisfied that the area was as isolated as Wolcowitz claimed.

The two men stood in a sun-filled clearing. The heat-laden silence was broken only by the insistent drumming of cicadas. A bird flashed through the trees, and a squirrel chattered briefly. For the moment the constant fear was gone, and Memling turned his face to the sun and breathed deeply. It was almost possible to forget the war, but then the drone of an aircraft passing high above on its way east into Russia destroyed the mood, and the ever-present fear crept back.

Memling learned little from the Pole who, while talkative enough about non-essentials, was close-mouthed about the resistance and plans for Memling's future. After a few hours' acquaintance with the man he was convinced that Wolcowitz had once been an officer and was probably of good family as well. Even after years in the German forest as a woodcutter, he bathed and exercised regularly and his table manners were impeccable. His personal habits were in such contrast with his appearance that Memling remarked on them the first evening as Wolcowitz stood drying himself on the bank of the small stream that ran past his cabin.

'Hah! Is what you call protective colours. Fool Huns if they come about. How it look to see woodcutter with neat clothes and shaved? But I do not like dirt on me.'

Memling spent a week with Wolcowitz. On the fourth day it rained, but they went out to cut trees anyway, the Pole explaining that he must deliver so many cords by the end of the summer if he wished to be allowed to return the following year. With Memling's far from expert help, they made a large dent in the section of the forest in which Wolcowitz was expertly selecting and cutting trees. Memling began to suspect the Pole was in no hurry to pass him on.

On the sixth night a thin whistle sounded from the trees, and Wolcowitz motioned Memling to the front wall of the cabin. He went quickly, Fairbairn knife and pistol ready, noting with some surprise that the fear had receded abruptly. Wolcowitz took an automatic pistol from its hiding place and stepped outside. Memling heard quiet voices speaking in what he assumed was Polish, and then Wolcowitz called to him.

The moon was almost full, and the man standing beside

Wolcowitz was in German uniform. Memling froze, eyes searching wildly about the clearing for the shadowy figures of troops hidden in the trees. Wolcowitz laughed and urged the soldier towards the cabin.

'So you would not kill my friend, Rodalski, you must see him with me. Good friend Rodalski is in guard unit in Anklam. Is Polish. Born in Danzig. Stupid Germans join him to army. They take anyones now, send them to Russia. Rodalski not his name, so don't worry that account.'

Rodalski had come to guide Memling on the next stage of his journey. He had brought the proper clothes, and while Memling changed into the none too clean pants, shirt, and oversized shoes, the two men spoke together in Polish. As Memling was strapping the knife and sheath to his back, just below the collar of his ragged shirt, Wolcowitz broke off and came over to him.

'Is better you not take weapons. Hun will know you are British and shoot you after while. But first will try and make you tell all you know. You not be able to hurt Wolcowitz if you speak, so do not worry then. Rodalski tells me must be gone from here tomorrow. Other job to do somewhere.'

Memling shook his head. 'If the Gestapo arrests me, it won't take them long to discover that I'm not a Belgian foreign worker. My fingerprints are on file. I got away from them once, and they won't let that happen again.'

Wolcowitz grasped his shoulder and squeezed. 'You are brave man. Gestapo will kill you very slow. Better you not let them take you then.'

With bravado he did not feel, Memling grinned. 'Not brave, my friend. Just frightened to death.'

Wolcowitz's expression was serious. 'Good. You will live long, then.'

Shortly after midnight the three men left the cabin. Wolcowitz accompanied them for a few kilometres before disappearing into the darkness. Memling was not aware that he had gone until he turned to say something.

Rodalski's German was worse than his English. 'Woodcutter is' – he fumbled for the words he wanted – 'knowing wise of woods. You never see him again until war is over. I go to Russia soon. I never see him again, ever.'

As they walked on through the still night Memling thought about Rodalski's seeming equanimity in the face of certain death on the Russian front. Wolcowitz had described in some detail the extraordinary reverses both sides had taken in recent months. There had been a huge tank battle near the Russian city of Kursk a few weeks before, perhaps the largest the world had ever seen, and as a result Wolcowitz claimed there would never be another German victory in Russia. With Allied aid and their own factories relocated in the Urals, the Russians could absorb their massive losses, but the Germans could not. In response to Jan's contention that the Germans could, by virtue of their industrial base, absorb far more than a tank defeat, Wolcowitz had dismissed Stalingrad as merely an example of German stupidity matching Russian stupidity.

And here was his guide going to Russia as part of an army that endured casualties at the rate of seven in ten – ten in ten in certain foreign conscript and punishment regiments. But like Wolcowitz, Rodalski did not seem to care so long as he could first kill as many of one side or the other as possible.

It was dawn before they reached their destination, a farm near the edge of the forest. Rodalski led Memling to a small outbuilding and cautioned him to stay well hidden, as the owner was a loyal German. He left Memling two packages of field rations and a bottle of water, enough to last until someone came for him. With a cheery 'Good luck', he was gone, the rising sun outlining his sturdy figure as he strode back into the forest – that was the last sight Memling had of him.

The following days merged to form one of the strangest interludes in Memling's life. Not even his experiences in Belgium could compare. He was shuttled back and forth across this obscure corner of Germany by a succession of people who were either natives or foreign prisoner-workers released to do 'land service'. Most such moves involved hiking for miles along dusty country roads. He saw only two soldiers during this time, both on leave, friendly and willing to talk and share cigarettes, which his guides seemed to have in greater quantity than the soldiers. After a few such days Memling's constant fear eased to the point where he was able to keep his voice under control and his hands no longer shook in unguarded moments.

The sojourn began to take on the aspects of a summer holiday. The weather remained beautiful – clear and warm with mild evenings and short nights. By stages, although the route was never divulged, Memling concluded they were heading in the general direction of Wolgast on the River Peene. On the twelfth day his guide was a friendly and buxom German girl who introduced herself gigglingly as Francine. Her father, it appeared, had brought a French bride home from the Great War. She set a smart pace that rarely varied during the long morning. Memling guessed they were approaching the coast, as the air had lost its stifling summer heat and there were more people about.

Towards noon an army lorry carrying a squad of field-equipped troops went by, dipping precariously as the soldiers lined the side, whistling and shouting invitations to Francine. The girl waved and blew kisses until the lorry was safely past, then swore in German. 'Reservists,' she spat. 'All rich enough to avoid the front service. I would not mind if they were regular troops, front-line or not.'

Memling was puzzled. The girl's comment seemed inconsistent with her present occupation, but when he remarked on it, she only shrugged.

'Our soldiers are fighting to destroy the communists. If they do not, the communists will destroy Germany. It is as simple as that.' She turned to him, pert face screwed up with suspicion.

'Are you one of those English communists?' she demanded, and Memling laughed to conceal his sudden uneasiness. He realised from remarks made by previous guides that should the girl suspect he was, he might not live out the night.

'Of course not. There are a few communists in England, but not many and certainly not in the employ of the government.'

Francine snorted. 'So you think. They are there. Believe me. You should find and shoot them all. Every one of them.'

As they resumed their march his curiosity was aroused by this seeming contradiction. 'Isn't that a bit drastic?' he asked. 'After all, they are our allies.'

Francine spat again, and it began to dawn on Memling how deep was the hatred many Germans held for the communists.

'Why? They would shoot you if they had the chance. You English, you are so naïve. You have not lived so close to the Russian as we have, nor have you experienced his full treachery. They even feed upon themselves. All that shooting and killing during the past few years. And before, preying on our German citizens or those of German ancestry, like wolves, for centuries, denying us the right to eastern lands, lands needed to make Germany a great nation. Is it any wonder that Hitler and his like decided to make war on Russia? The Slav is inferior and he must give way to the German folk. But by fighting England and America as well, Hitler destroys the fatherland.'

Memling left it at that, sensing that to argue would only persuade her that he was at least a closet communist.

Late that afternoon they came in sight of a distant church steeple, and Francine led him off into a patch of woods. From her rucksack she extracted a loaf of brown bread and a large piece of cheese. Memling filled his water bottle from a nearby stream, and they ate, after which the girl scraped a mossy patch clear of twigs and stretched out, relaxing with a sigh. After a moment she opened her eyes and, seeing that Memling was watching her, smiled.

'No one will come for us until after midnight.' She patted the moss beside her.

Memling cleared his throat and glanced around at the trees, silent and filled with muted colour in the long summer dusk. 'Where do we go then?' His voice was hoarse and a bit unsteady.

Francise turned on to her back, stretching arms above her head so that her breasts rose and fell languorously beneath her thin cotton blouse. 'To Peenemünde, by boat. You will be a foreign worker employed at the works. I am to be your wife. Everything has been arranged. We will stay with another married couple, friends of our movement.'

'My wife?' Memling repeated stupidly.

'Of course. A married man is always suspected less. A foreign worker married to a German woman must be safe, the authorities will think. After all, to get married a foreign worker must be a party member, and so he must have been investigated fully. We will be given our documents tonight. The day after tomorrow you will report to work.' Francine grinned and rose to her knees, unbuttoning her blouse at the same time. 'You see, we are married. So I think there can be nothing wrong. And besides, if we are to carry out our role as a married couple, then I should not remain a virgin, should I? The Gestapo are quite thorough.'

Memling was having difficulty keeping up with this girl who had started out that morning as his guide and was now his wife. Sunlight filtering through the trees had taken on the radiance of early evening and coated her skin with gold. Francine had removed her blouse, and her large, well-shaped breasts swayed only inches from his hands as she wriggled out of her skirt. She smiled and took his hand, placing it flat against her stomach.

'In Germany it is the duty of a married couple to have as many children as quickly as possible. You must make me pregnant or it will seem suspicious.'

'Pregnant . . . ?'

Francine tossed her skirt aside. 'Oh, do stop repeating things. Yes, pregnant. It is no sin,' she assured him. 'The Nazis have become as godless as the communists. Our priest was taken away to the concentration camps two months ago.'

The girl's voice was matter-of-fact as she talked, sitting back with her hands on her knees, unconscious of her striking beauty.

Memling's breath caught in his throat. Her figure was firm, well rounded, her large breasts were perfectly formed, and her flat stomach sloped to wide hips and sturdy thighs. Her skin was smooth, milky, and scattered with freckles. Curly blonde hair capped a heart-shaped face with high cheekbones. Sitting nude before him, she seemed as natural a part of the forest as the trees or the stream nearby, and Memling knew then why the Greeks had invented the nymph.

'It only matters that the communists be stopped, not how. We work for an armistice with the English and Americans so the struggle can continue wholly against the godless communists. So, you see, this is a holy endeavour, as Father Dunn told us before they took him away.'

The girl leaned forward and began to unbutton his shirt. 'You English. You must be as cold as they say. Perhaps the sun will warm you.'

The next few hours capped the holiday events of the past days with an idyll he would not have believed possible. Although a virgin, Francine later told him that she had spent much time discussing the techniques of lovemaking with her married friends, and despite a bit of clumsiness now and then, she threw herself enthusiastically into her work – as she made him understand she viewed it. And Memling had thought only the English capable of such self-deception. But he was grateful that she had no basis on which to judge his performance, out of practice as he was and worn down from days of hiking. Francine seemed pleased enough and asked him to stay behind while she went to the small stream to wash. After a while she called to Memling, and their cooling swim ended in a much more satisfactory bout of lovemaking. Dusk had deepened by the time they left the stream bank, found their clothes, and dressed. Francine was quiet, and whenever Memling glanced at her, she smiled with such vivacity that he knew she was quite happy at the way things had turned out.

The girl kissed him once, stretched out on the moss, and was asleep in moments. Memling sat nearby smoking and wondered what he had got himself into. There were a host of conflicting thoughts vying for attention, beginning with the fact that he was married and had just betrayed his wife. Second, there was the problem of what to do with Francine, tonight and tomorrow and the day after that. What if she did become pregnant? What the devil was going to happen to her?

They had walked openly through the streets of Wolgast to the riverside docks where the fishing boats waited for a pre-dawn start. Francine moved along proudly beside Memling, her arm linked with his and one soft breast pressing his side, and he realised that she viewed this all as a great adventure.

They had seen no policemen and very few soldiers, for so remote was this corner of Germany that – if one ignored its contributions of men, taxes, and levies of crops, as well as the presence of a good number of apparently ill-supervised foreign prisoner-workers – the war could have been taking place on another planet.

A single long-faded poster advised fishermen to be on the lookout for foreign submarines. The customs house, little more than a Victorian-style shed, was shuttered and closed. The quay stretching along the river was silent. Francine found the right nondescript Baltic trawler, and the captain of the boat and his crew – consisting of a beefy wife with the same reddened face and hands as her husband, and a son so shy that he could not even look at Francine – greeted and conducted them below to an evil-smelling hold. The captain apologised for the inconvenience but thought that as they were often stopped by coastal patrols, it would be better if they remained out of sight. A few minutes later Memling heard the engine rattle into life, and the boat moved slowly out into the river.

Francine clung to his hand, but apparently the smell of the place dampened her ardour and shortly she fell asleep against his shoulder.

The journey was over within an hour. The changed beat of the engine woke Memling just as he had begun to doze. He sat up, struggling with the familiar gagging sensation of fear, and disengaged Francine's arm. He slid the pistol from his blanket roll as the hatch was thrown back and pale dawn flooded the interior. The captain beamed down on them.

'We have arrived, sir.'

Memling scrambled to his feet, shushing Francine's questions. 'Arrived? Arrived where?'

'Why at Wolgaster Fahre, sir. Just across the Peene from Wolgast. We would have come sooner, but I go down the river to make anyone watching think we are bound for the fishing grounds. You have only now to walk to Peenemünde town a few kilometres north.' He handed down a heavy envelope. 'Here are your papers, including orders to report to the research centre for assignment to duties there. You and your wife are to stay with a couple named Zinn, at number Seven Treptnow, in the town of Peenemünde.' He spread his hands in apology as if it were his fault. 'There are no accommodations for married couples at the foreign workers' compound near Herringsdorf, sir.'

Memling and Francine walked along the dusty, little-used track that led to the fishing village of Peenemünde. The island was covered with thick pine forest, much as the mainland had been, and for a long while there was nothing but the silence of forest sounds about them. They had familiarised themselves thoroughly with their new identification documents, and when they had come to a spot out of view of the river, Memling turned inland until he found a place deep in the forest. There he burned and scattered the ashes of their old documents and hid the radio.

For the next half-hour they quizzed each other on their new identities. Memling's new name was Walden Forst. Born twenty-eight years before in Herent, a small village near Louvain, he was an experienced quality control technician and had served in the Belgian army. His unit had surrendered at Namur in early May 1940. He had been released from a prison camp near Aachen a few months later, after having volunteered for labour service, and had been sent to work in a chemical factory near Bremen. A few weeks ago he had been selected for a highly technical position at Peenemünde and had accepted in return for a promise that his new wife could accompany him and a sizable increase in salary. He was now reporting for work after a two-week walking holiday-honeymoon.

Because of her distinct Pomeranian accent, Francine's history had not been altered. She assured Memling that should anyone check, they would find that she had worked in the same chemical factory in Bremen and that they had married two weeks before in Wiescek, a fishing and farming village on the Greifswalder Boden. They were both Catholic, and the marriage had been performed in the parish church and duly recorded and witnessed. 'You see,' she said, laughing, 'we really are married, even if you did not have a chance to say I do and promise to love, honour and obey me for ever.'

There was a shaded but concealed clearing in the fragrant trees, and it was mid-afternoon before the two of them reached Peenemünde village, hand in hand.

Jan Memling reported for work the following morning. They had registered the previous day with the elderly local constable at the Peenemünde village hall, and the man had assured him that, considering their long walk, tomorrow would be soon enough to visit the research centre's security staff. He leered at Francine and plucked a pine needle from her hair. They had wandered through the small fishing village then, finding it much like other such villages along the Baltic coast – a single road fronting an old wooden quay, now quite dilapidated as the war made increasing demands on local labour.

The Zinns, a middle-aged couple of sour disposition, expected an outrageous rent, for which they would get an unfinished space in the attic, a rickety double bed, and two meagre meals per day. Memling wondered who had recruited these two grasping misers into the resistance.

It was obvious from the beginning that only greed had induced the Zinns to house them. The husband whined all the first evening about their losses, as they were now unable to rent the very desirable space in the attic to one of the wealthy scientists at the research centre. Finally, Francine could take no more and railed at the man and his wife in country German, threatening to report them both to the resistance. The two whispered together for the rest of the evening, clearly frightened.

Francine wakened Memling the following morning and went off to the kitchen to make certain that Frau Zinn had prepared a proper breakfast. As he sat on the edge of the lumpy bed, it occurred to him that his unexpected holiday was over and that it was time he returned to work. It took him a while to adjust to that fact.

Herr Zinn provided directions to the research centre, Frau Zinn handed him a tin pail containing lunch, and Francine kissed him goodbye. The good husband going off to work, Memling thought to himself.

As he trudged along the road in company with others converging on the installation he was surprised at the extent of the facility. Barbed wire seemed to run for ever, and through the pines he caught glimpses of the most modern buildings, lined up one after another. Security was thorough, if relaxed. His papers were examined at the main gate where the Luftwaffe guard gave him instructions and showed him on the map where to find the personnel offices.

By nine that morning he had been processed, fingerprinted, photographed, and assigned to a job as quality control technician in the Preproduction Works Building. The research centre, or what he could see of it, looked more like the American college campuses that he had seen in photographs. There were parklands and even a sports ground that would have done credit to any town in Europe. People – many in white laboratory coats and all, it seemed, with briefcases or clipboards – walked quickly, intently, from one building to another. Small special-purpose vehicles hauled canvas-shrouded equipment. There were bicycles everywhere but few guards.

As Memling made his way towards the designated building a distant roaring grew louder, and he looked towards the north to see a thunderhead of white smoke roiling upwards and, a moment later, a pointed cylindrical shape rising above the trees. Its fuselage was painted in alternating bands of red and yellow, and in the bright summer sunshine it flashed as brilliantly as the pure column of flame on which it was balanced. For an instant he was suffused with sheer joy as he watched a dream come to life. Even when the rocket had disappeared into the cobalt sky, Memling continued to stare after it, oblivious to anything else until a bicycle bell forced him to step hastily aside.

A smiling middle-aged man in a nicely tailored suit shook hands, offered him a seat and a cigarette, and welcomed him to the Peenemünde research facility.

'We would like you to know that we are very grateful to you for accepting our position here at Peenemünde. We need all the technically minded people we can obtain, and I think you will find us willing to go out of our way to make you happy here.'

Memling assumed the proper dazed attitude; it was easy enough, as he recalled the conditions under which he had worked in Liège.

He was assigned to a quality control station monitoring the tolerances of valve assemblies which he quickly discovered were a part of the fuel control system for the rocket he had seen launched that morning. His foreman was a French national, extracted from a labour camp at Belsen and assigned to Peenemünde. Memling quickly gained overall impressions from the man which suggested that Allied intelligence regarding Peenemünde was sadly inadequate.

'You will find the Hun a totally different type here,' the foreman told him. 'These are scientists, not soldiers or SS. They are just like any of us. Four thousand people work here. I tell you, it is enough to make your head spin when you realise all that is going on. We are not supposed to know, but everyone does. You are soon swept up in the scientific spirit, and then you are no longer working for the enemy but with fellow scientists. I ask you, did you ever think that some day man would fly to the moon? Well, they will, and perhaps sooner than any of us think. And if they do, it will be right from here, Peenemünde! Talk to any of the scientists. They will tell you the same, and what is more, if you have something constructive to offer, they will listen. I tell you, this place is what Plato's republic might have been. Ah! If only there were not this damned war! But enough, your job will be to follow the specifications laid down on these sheets.' He showed Memling a series of printed pages in protective celluloid covers, and a fine set of gauges.

'The measurements must not vary by more than a tenth of a millimetre, otherwise the system must be rejected. Perform each measurement three times, recording the readings. Average the results, and if within limits, mark the card attached to each unit after reassembly and sign your initials and employee identification number. Understood?'

Memling assured him it was, and performed the first two measurements while the foreman watched, grunting with approval at the expert way he handled the gauges. Before he left, the foreman confided that this station was used to weed out the inept, and if Memling passed through successfully, he would undoubtedly be promoted to a more interesting task with an increase in salary as well.

That evening he discussed his day with Herr Zinn, who worked as a gang foreman supervising twenty Russian POWs. Grudgingly, and with much coaxing, he confirmed Memling's observations. The rocket that had been launched that morning was called an A-4. Similar to the one photographed by CIU, he said to himself. This morning's launch was apparently part of a series of tests, not all of which were successful. Some of the rockets disappeared into the sky, and some exploded either at the launching site or after they were in the air. In addition, there was a type of aeroplane that flew without a pilot; the Luftwaffe were conducting their own series of experiments on that one. Zinn knew little about them and cared less.

That evening Memling expressed his misgivings concerning the Zinns. Francine tended to dismiss his complaints, and Memling was uncomfortably aware that she was assuming a superior role. He was at a loss to know how to deal with it and cursed the unknown resistance leaders who had saddled him with this inexperienced little fool.

The Zinns, however, were a bigger problem. The man was clearly stupid and considered foreigners beneath contempt. The wife was little better, and shrewish and grasping into the bargain. It would be only a matter of time before it occurred to the Zinns to realise a profit by selling them to the authorities.

On the afternoon of his third day Memling was taken by one of the German engineers into the assembly area and shown the A-4 power plant.

The engineer, who introduced himself as Ernst Mundt, was a

pleasant young man in his late twenties, blondish and pale-skinned with freckles that made him seem even younger. He showed Memling the carts of assembled rocket motors as proudly as any father showing off his children, and when Memling expressed astonishment that so much had been achieved, the man fairly glowed.

'Before the war,' Memling told him, 'I was a member of the Belgian Experimental Rocket Society. I have always been interested in rockets and the possibility of spaceflight.'

'Aha! Another man of intelligence.' The German clapped him on the back. 'You see, the war produces some good after all. It brings us rocket scientists together. We will achieve things here at Peenemünde that will be talked about for a thousand years, Third Reich or no Third Reich.' Mundt, realising he had been indiscreet, grinned sheepishly at Memling but said nothing more.

He assigned Memling to perform final quality control checks on the completed rocket motors before they left the building for final acceptance testing. When Mundt had gone, Memling spent the rest of the afternoon reviewing the procedures manual and familiarising himself with the engine, struggling all the while to control his amazement and enthusiasm. The engines were rated to develop over twenty-five thousand kilograms of thrust – fifty-five thousand pounds – very near what he had originally estimated three years before. The general dimensions and carrying capacity – the Germans called it payload – were also quite close.

The massive hangar doors at the end of the building were opened to allow the Baltic breeze to sweep away the afternoon heat, and periodically a distant roaring sounded across the pine forest and scrub flats as engines were tested. Each time, the German engineer caught his eyes and winked, and each time, Memling responded. Enemy or not, there is something a great deal more important here, he thought, than politics and war.

That evening, much to Francine's consternation, he sat up late, making crabbed sketches and notes concerning what he had learned. At first she sat on the bed trying to coax a response and, when he ignored her, angrily demanded his attention. Everything welled up so quickly that he had already slapped her before he realised what he had done.

'You little fool,' he hissed. 'This is more important than sex.'

The girl tried to swing at him, and he slapped her again, hard. Francine shrank away, holding her face where the bright red finger marks were beginning to show, and nodded sullenly.

Memling went back to the table, and Francine continued to crouch on the bed in a sulk until she fell asleep. He worked a long time and then, feeling guilty, concealed the notes and drawing between a rafter and roof board, and got into bed beside her.

He stroked her back until she woke, and then tried to take her into his arms. Francine jerked away from him and curled into a ball. His anger at her childishness exploded, and he spun her around and forced her legs apart, seeking to relieve his own pain and fear. When he was finished, the girl was sobbing but refused to let him go. He lay awake for the rest of the night, staring at the moonlit ceiling.

The following morning Francine was subdued. Finger marks were still prominent on her cheek, and her eyes, red from crying, rarely left Memling as he ate. Frau Zinn glanced knowingly from one to the other, and she practically fawned over him until he was ready to leave.

The days then became routine for Memling. He would arrive at his station every morning at seven and leave at five-thirty when the shifts changed. In between, he spent hours painstakingly checking the tolerances of various engine parts, sometimes completing four assemblies in one day. By the time he was moved to the final check station at the end of the week, he was familiar enough with the engines to reproduce the blueprints from memory.

He had become quite friendly with the German engineer, Ernst Mundt, and on Friday afternoon was invited to Test Stand VIII to see the mounting and firing of an engine he had passed. Afterwards he was introduced to a tall, raw-boned man in army uniform with ordnance flashes and the insignia of a general-major. This was General Walter Dornberger, director of Heersversuchsstelle Peenemünde, the Army Research Centre. Mundt called him a member of the team, an appellation Memling found warming in spite of the fact that these men were enemies who intended to destroy his country with their rockets.

He took what advantage he could of the brief outing to identify the major structures he could see through the trees and along the beach. That evening he sketched a detailed map of the installation and added to it each night during the following week until it showed the centre divided into two distinct entities: one controlled by the army, Peenemünde East Development Centre; and the other under the auspices of the Luftwaffe and known as Peenemünde West. Together the installations covered ten square kilometres, as had been estimated by CIU in London. The problem for Bomber Command lay in the fact that installations were scattered generally along the eastern coast of the island from the northern tip to the town of Zinnowitz, fifteen kilometres south. Memling had gained a brief glimpse of the actual rocket launch stands, massive structures located close to the Baltic on the northern strand. Farther south were smaller stands for static testing, including Test Stand VIII, and beyond them began the engineering and research areas comprising both military and civilian headquarters, the administration buildings, canteens, officers' quarters, and maintenance shops.

Two days before, he had been sent on an errand and having taken a wrong turn, found himself face to face with a barrier manned by soldiers in black uniforms bearing the jagged collar flashes of the SS. That night Memling added the roadblock to the map and sat puzzling over what it hid. The map showed nothing but marshy grasslands beyond the pine forest covering the centre portion of the island.

Eight kilometres south of the major test stands was the village of Karlshagen, a pre-war seaside resort of some renown where most of the scientists and their families were now housed in a special compound known as the Siedlung, or settlement. Many of the foreign workers were also quartered there in barracks near the square, across from which were barracks for the enlisted military personnel. A camp at Trassenheide some two kilometres west contained the Russian and Polish POWs who were used both at HVP and at the Luftwaffe installations. As diligently as he had searched and asked dangerous leading questions, he had been unable to locate the liquid oxygen plant, which, in his and Simon-Benet's mind, was a primary target.

Memling contemplated his map late one evening as Francine came to stand beside him.

'It does look rather sparse, doesn't it?'

As on previous occasions, Memling was struck by her perception. It was hard to remember that she did have some training as a technician when she generally behaved as childishly as a twelve-year-old.

'It does. There have to be major machine shops, chemical laboratories, a wind tunnel, and especially the liquid oxygen plant, but I'm damned if I know where. Access is so limited that it would be suicide to try and search, even at night.'

'But haven't you learned a great deal anyway?'

Memling rubbed his aching eyes and glanced at the map. 'I suppose so. But so much is missing and there's so little time left to find it all.'

Francine's fingers tightened where she had been massaging his neck. 'So little time?'

'Of course. We can't stay here much longer. I want to be well out of Germany before the Gestapo turns us up.'

The girl sat down on the bed and stared at him. 'Leave? Where? How do we . . .'

Memling had the damnedest feeling that she had never even considered the possibility that she would have to leave Germany. What in the name of God was going on here? Was the German resistance that inept?

'Francine, what were you told about this assignment?'

The girl avoided his glance, and he grabbed her shoulder and shook her hard. 'Answer me, damn it.'

'They . . . they told me I was to go with you, as your wife, until you were finished with me. Then we would return to Wiescek until the war was over. I have an uncle who will hide us on his farm. I thought . . .'

'God damn it to hell.' Memling leapt off the bed. 'What in the name of God are they thinking of? We can't go to Wiescek. How long do you think it would take the Gestapo to find us?'

Francine stared at him, eyes brimming. 'I can't leave,' she whispered. 'My family, my friends, what would I do . . . ? I . . .'

Memling shook her hard. 'Listen to me, you silly little fool. This isn't a game.' He remembered Paul's angry voice describing their methods that last night in Belgium. 'Do you know what the Gestapo does to pretty little girls accused of treason? You like sex, don't you? But how would you like to have twenty or thirty men rape you, one right after another? How would you like to be hung from wires? Or have electrical shocks to your nipples? Or be given enemas and douches with sulphuric acid? And they won't stop after you've told them everything you know because those people like the job they do. Traitorous little girls are a treat for them, a reward, like candy. They can do what they want. Do you know the Gestapo uses women to torture other women because they know how to hurt you best? You'll pray for death, scream for death,' he hammered away at her, 'do anything they want on their promise to kill you and end the pain.'

Memling found that he was shouting, and shoved her away, fighting for control. Everything he had said was true; it was also a reflection of his own fears and he knew it. He turned back to the girl who was crouched in the corner sobbing. He took her into his arms, murmuring to calm her.

After a while Memling lifted her on to the bed and turned out the single bulb over the table. He undressed her slowly, caressing her smooth skin until her sobs subsided. 'Believe me, Francine,' he whispered, 'we have no other choice. Perhaps when the war is over we can return, but we cannot stay now. Do you understand?' After a moment she nodded against his shoulder, then turned her back and lay quietly until her breathing evened and she was asleep.

Memling forced himself to lie quietly until dawn, struggling to find a way out of the situation, while at the same time avoiding any thought of what he would do with her if they ever reached Great Britain. He got up as the sky was beginning to pale, and went down to the quay to watch the fishing boats leave. He had a nasty premonition that the resistance had done little or nothing to get him out of Germany. Looking back on the days of hiking across the countryside, he realised now that it was because the resistance had not known what to do with him. It was only a matter of luck that they had not met a security patrol or been stopped by the police in all that time. And that in turn suggested that the identity furnished him was worthless.

All during the day, as he revised specifications for a change in the oxidiser valving system, Memling worried over the problem of leaving the island. Their best chance appeared to be in resuming their walking tour. If their luck held and they stayed to the back roads, they might elude the search certain to result when he disappeared. The question was, where in this rural corner of Germany could they go? Neutral Sweden was across the Baltic, and the only other possibility, Denmark, with its well-organised and active resistance organisation, meant a walk of three hundred miles. The weather was good and they were both healthy enough; food would be their biggest problem, but once they got into Denmark it would be easy enough to make contact with the underground who could then smuggle them to Sweden.

As a plan it was next to useless. But he had no faith left in the German resistance and he dared not stretch his luck beyond another week.

The day, a Friday, was hot, and even with the doors open the interior of the building was stifling. The dependable sea breeze had disappeared, and by noon a heat haze hung over the entire island. He had fallen into the habit of eating lunch with Ernst Mundt who was working on a temporary basis in pre-production to resolve the high failure rate during flight testing. A few days earlier, Memling had been unable to conceal his reaction when Mundt mentioned that he worked for Dr Wernher von Braun, the director of HVP. Mundt noticed his surprise, and Memling covered hastily by mentioning that he had met von Braun some years before.

Today Mundt waited for him in the shade of an immense fir that occupied a knoll facing the Baltic. The heat was oppressive, and both men had removed their shirts.

'I'm for a swim after lunch,' Mundt remarked. 'How about you?'

'No bathing suit,' Memling shrugged.

Mundt laughed. 'The hell with that. I know a small cove on the river side. When it's hot like this the land service girls go there. No one worries about bathing suits.'

Memling grinned but shook his head. 'I'm married, remember. And besides, those specifications have to be done today.'

'I want to talk to you about that,' Mundt said. 'You're a conscientious worker and a good engineer. Is there anything in your background that you would not want the SD to uncover?'

Memling choked on his bread ration, and Mundt thumped him on the back.

'That's always the reaction when you talk about the SD.' He laughed. 'Look here, I mentioned you to Doktor von Braun and described the work you had done. He was most impressed. We have another project going here,' he went on, not noticing how Memling paled, 'much more important than I can even begin to tell you. If we had our way, the A-Four would be scrapped. If we could begin again, with what we know now the missile would be entirely redesigned. Its reliability might reach as high as ninety-two per cent rather than seventy-two point four per cent. However, enough of that. This other project concerns space travel.'

He said this last without inflection and sat back to watch Memling's reaction. He wasn't disappointed.

'Space travel! What the devil are you talking about? I thought this was a military installation?'

'It is, but some of us are looking far beyond the war. We all agree the future of the human race lies in space travel. You said as much yourself, and we need good engineers for that project. Our staffing problem is horrible, especially for non-military projects. Whenever we find someone who shows promise, we try to recruit him. So, once those specifications are finished, you will be transferred to this other project, which is being directed by Herr Doktor Franz Bethwig. I don't suppose you know him?'

My God, who next, Memling thought, just managing to shake his head.

'Franz has been with us since the VfR days. He's a damned good sort and you'll like working for him. When I go back to my laboratory tomorrow, you are to go with me. Now, this project is secret, so keep your mouth shut about what I tell you. We are developing a rocket engine that will produce one hundred and fifty-nine thousand kilograms of thrust. That's nearly six and a half times more powerful than the A-Four. The engine is simpler and a hell of a lot more reliable. The idea is to cluster enough into a single booster rocket' – Mundt glanced around quickly – 'to produce a total thrust of three and a half million kilos. Now where do you think we can go with that?'

Memling stared at him in disbelief. 'Three and a half million . . .' His voice trailed away in astonishment. 'You can't be serious?'

'But I am. We've already launched three test vehicles.'

'Three . . . !' The idea was almost more than Memling could grasp. The strides the Germans had made in the past decade were astounding. They had gone from firecrackers shot across a deserted World War I army camp near Berlin, to a rocket with six and a half million pounds of thrust.

'What altitude have you reached?' he asked, struggling to comprehend the magnitude of the technological advance, conceal his dismay, and sound vitally interested at the same time.

'It is not altitude that counts these days but range, my friend. And that is secret, so let us just say that one of our U-boats photographed the third test vehicle as it fell into the South Atlantic.' Mundt laughed with delight at his expression.

'But that is incredible! With that much power you could reach the moon.'

Mundt winked. 'I have told you enough to whet your appetite. Would you like to join us and accomplish something meaningful?'

'What would I do?' Memling stammered.

'Work with me, of course. As my assistant. I need someone to oversee the preparation of the appropriate documentation for the engines. You would also assist in supervising the test crews. Now, yes or no?'

'Yes! Of course, yes! How could I possibly say no?'

'Good.' Mundt beamed with satisfaction. 'Report to Building Twenty-three at seven a.m. The guards will tell you where to go. You'll have your own office and secretary. We even have air conditioning, and of course, as a member of the professional staff, you will have access to the officers' club. For the first few days you will not be allowed to do much, as you won't have the proper security clearances. I should warn you that this project has attracted the personal interest of someone very high in the SS. So, the SD is in charge of security, rather than the army. But don't worry about that. I knew you were going to say yes, so I submitted your name to the SD two days ago. It normally takes only three or four days to complete a security check.'

Memling could only nod weakly.

Mundt grabbed up his shirt. 'Well, now that's settled and the girls are waiting. Sorry you can't come along, but then that is what I liked about you from the start. No nonsense when it comes to work.'

Memling burst into the kitchen, grabbed Francine, and hurried her to the attic in spite of her protests.

'We're leaving tonight,' he told her. 'As soon as it's dark.'

'Leave tonight?' Francine wailed, and Memling glared her into silence.

He told her what had happened during the lunch hour. 'Mundt thought he was doing me a favour. Instead, he's put our necks in a noose. And as if that isn't bad enough, tomorrow I'm to meet two people I knew before the war.'

Francine burst into tears, and as Memling turned away in disgust he heard voices below. He stepped to the door to see Frau Zinn pull her husband into the kitchen. The old bitch must have been listening, he thought. Leaving Francine to her self-pity, he took the Walther pistol from beneath the mattress and slipped down the stairs, keeping as close to the wall as possible to avoid loose boards. From the hall he could hear easily as the woman described his abrupt return and the visit of a curious village constable earlier that afternoon. Memling swore, having no way of knowing whether that meant they were already on to him. Zinn immediately shushed the woman and began to pace. After a few moments he stopped.

'We have no choice, my dear. We must send to the authorities and tell them that we suspect our boarders are spies. If we hurry, it will look so much the better for us. If he points the finger, they will not believe him then but will think he is trying to get even. I'll go this moment . . .'

Zinn broke off as Memling stepped through the doorway, silenced pistol in hand. The woman saw him first and jumped from her chair. Memling raised the Walther, and Frau Zinn took a hesitant step towards him. Memling motioned her back and shouted for Francine.

The girl clattered down the stairs. He told her what had happened. 'Get some rope or cord. I don't want these two loose.'

Francine nodded. As she slipped out of the kitchen she struck the woman a blow so stout that she sat down abruptly in her chair, gasping for breath. Francine was back in moments with a coil of heavy fishing line, and Memling herded the two frightened people into the bedroom and had them lie on the bed. He lashed their hands and feet securely with the line, drew the blanket over them, and lashed several coils around the bed, drawing the blanket tight so that they could not move. He then rummaged through a drawer, found a pillow slip, then tore it into strips and gagged them both. After he had tested the bonds, he dragged Francine out with him in spite of her protestations that he allow her to kill both of them.

'You should have cut their throats, the swine!' she hissed.

'Stop it,' Memling snapped. 'There's no need to kill anyone. Let them explain to the SD what the hell happened. Now shut up and let me think a minute.'

Francine glared, and he sent her to fix a quick meal while he tried to work out the next move. He stood by the window, staring at the narrow road fronting the end of the quay. Before Usedom Island had become a military research centre, Peenemünde had been a tiny fishing village of a few hundred inhabitants. The village of Peenemünde faced the River Peene, and except for a new wharf across the shallow indentation that served as the harbour, it had been little altered by the war or the presence of the Army Research Centre.

Watching the wharves now, Memling could see fishing boats at anchor and several coming up river. On the far side a petrol barge and tug were tying up to the government quay, and a lone sentry paced lazily in the evening heat. Abruptly he made his decision and went into the kitchen.

'I'm going for the radio. I want you to keep an eye on those two. I'll be back before midnight and we'll leave then.' Francine started to argue, but he cut her off. 'Get this through your head,' he snapped. 'If we stay in Germany we haven't a hope of surviving. If you like the idea of a Gestapo torture cell, I'll point you in the direction of Wiescek when we reach the Danish border. Understand?'

As if out for a stroll, Memling walked along the road towards the south end of the village. He passed one or two locals who ignored his polite *guten Abend* with the usual sour charm of isolated country people, and was soon out of sight of the last house. He struck off into the pine forest then, moving swiftly through the trees parallel to the road. It took two hours to cover the seven kilometres to the sharp bend in the road and the lightning-blasted tree where he had hidden the radio.

Jan dug it up and ran the wire aerial up into the tree as high as it would stretch, then took a deep breath and flipped the power switch. He had little faith in the radio; during training he had tested it in the Orkneys and been unable to raise his contact near Glasgow, even when it was operating properly.

A green light glowed on the panel, and he adjusted the crystal until the cat's-eye narrowed to the thinnest line he could obtain. He began to transmit his call letters, but to his dismay, the power light faded abruptly. Memling swore and sat back on his haunches, then retrieved the aerial and started back towards the village. With the Zinns safely out of the way, he could use the house current.

Dusk was coming earlier now, so that by ten o'clock it was pitch black. The full moon was just beginning to show through the trees. The air was more oppressive than ever, night having brought little relief from the heat. Memling's shirt was soaked through with sweat. The village was silent, and few lights showed despite the fact that blackout regulations were in effect only in the event of an air raid. There were no lights in the Zinn house. Memling paused in the shadows and studied the surrounding area. The night was absolutely silent. No one was about, not even the usual sentry on the government wharf. He waited, sensing something wrong, the lessons drummed into him by years of commando training controlling his actions.

As he left the shadows for the back of the weather-beaten house he saw a staff car parked in the shadows. Memling froze in mid-step. After a moment he detected the reddish glow of a cigarette where a bored guard stood beside the vehicle.

For an instant panic threatened to send him into headlong flight, but fierce exhilaration quickly replaced it. They must be waiting for him inside the house, he decided. He watched for several minutes. Not even a window shade moved.

Memling circled through the trees until he could approach the driver from behind. The man carried a shoulder weapon and, as Memling drew the silenced pistol from his belt, knelt to light a second cigarette, unaware that he had signed his death warrant with the first. Memling shot him through the spine.

He hunched into the shadow of the car to wait for his eyes to re-adjust after the muzzle flash, then examined the area again. Once certain that no other soldiers were about, he dragged the body beneath the vehicle, then moved cautiously to the house to check each window. There were three soldiers inside: two in the front room and a third in the single bedroom. The Zinns were still a lump beneath the blanket. Obviously, the SD had not believed them.

The girl was his major concern, and Memling eased back to the dubious protection of the automobile. His fear had vanished, and he was now thinking coolly and logically. Whoever was in charge inside knew what he was doing; they were waiting for him to walk into the trap, and there was no way he could reach the girl without first killing all three. Spread out as they were, it would be impossible to take them all.

An idea came to him then. He dragged the dead soldier into the trees and searched his pockets until he found a box of matches and the man's paybook. Using the body as a shield, Memling struck a match.

According to the paybook, the dead driver, one Erik Grubbe, was an unterscharführer, an SS rank equivalent to a sergeant. Good enough, he muttered, and stripped tunic and helmet from the body. The cloth was sticky with blood, and he rubbed a handful of dirt into it to hide the sheen. He slipped his Fairbairn knife from its sheath and a few minutes later was standing beside the bedroom window.

'Hst! It's me, Grubbe. Be quiet and come here. There's someone moving through the trees.'

A shadow appeared beside the window. 'Where?'

'There, behind the greenhouse.' Memling pointed towards a moonlit structure partly concealed by bushes. As the man leaned out for a better look Memling yanked his helmet forward and drove the knife into the base of his skull. He pushed the man's head and shoulders down, lifting his boots clear of the floor so they would not drum on the wood, and eased the body through the window. A moment later he was standing inside. There had been some noise, though less than he had expected, drawing only a muted order for silence from the front room. He smiled to himself.

The moon rising above the trees was beginning to brighten the bedroom. He bent over the bed and Frau Zinn's eyes bulged when she saw who it was. He rested the bloody knife against her throat. Her eyes rolled up as she fainted. Herr Zinn was sound asleep.

Memling moved to the doorway. One guard was standing in the centre of the floor, a machine pistol slung over his shoulder, waiting patiently. Judging by his posture, the man was an expert at this business. Good, Memling thought. His actions would be predictable. The second man was sitting at one end of the couch, which had been moved to provide a clear view of the road through the open window. He was relaxed, one arm over the back. As Memling's eyes adjusted to the gloom he saw that Francine lay, unmoving, in the space next to him. Occasionally he stroked her thigh.

Memling eased back until he was deep in the shadows. The moonlight was now bright enough to cast a patch of silver light through the open window. Deliberately he kicked the washstand, waited a few moments, then did it again. This time the noise drew a sharp order for quiet. He remained motionless for nearly five minutes, then skittered a hairbrush across the floor. The order was louder this time, and to encourage the officer in the other room, he knocked against the porcelain washbasin. That seemed to do it; he heard the sound of boots hurrying across the floor.

As the officer came through the door he would have seen a shadow and felt stiffened fingers thrust into his mouth to prevent a cry, and the searing pain of a knife as it drove into the unprotected flesh below his breastbone and up into his heart. He might have glimpsed his killer in the instant before he died of massive haemorrhage.

Memling eased the man down, mumbling loudly enough for the remaining soldier to hear, then walked into the other room, shaking his head and muttering about incompetence. The soldier had turned as he came through the door, then swivelled back to the window as Memling knew he would. He veered without breaking stride and in a single paralysing stroke drove the knife down into the man's neck. The soldier went rigid, his back arched. Memling released the knife and put his entire weight behind a chopping blow to the throat. The man was dead before his knees buckled.

Memling had to go back into the bedroom to search the officer's body for the keys to Francine's handcuffs. The girl fell against him, barely conscious, and Memling eased her around into the moonlight. They had beaten her badly. Her blouse had been slashed with a knife, and they had used burning cigarettes on her chest and stomach. Memling slipped the gag back on, lifted her on to one shoulder and slung the dead guard's machine pistol across the other. Francine was like a deadweight as he crossed the yard to the staff car. He had no idea how long it would be until the four dead SD men were discovered, but he knew that both of them had better be damned far away by that time.

He laid the girl on the rear seat and hurried back to the trees for the radio. He started for the house, then hesitated. If the SD knew where to find him, they would certainly be listening for transmissions. If he tried now to get through to London, they would know something had gone wrong. He tossed the radio on to the floor beside the machine pistol – an MP40, he noticed, almost an old friend – and settled into the unaccustomed left-hand driving seat.

The road was deserted, and he drove on until the trees closed in on either side. It took only a few minutes to reach a point where the road ran above the river for a short distance. Opposite, a spit of land divided the river Peene. The channel was deep but rather narrow here, and he stopped the car and lifted out the girl and the machine pistol. Memling then reversed for some distance, put the engine into first gear, and shot towards the bluff. He rolled out at the last moment, and the heavy car leapt the bank, landing nose-first several metres into the river to settle beneath the surface with a sullen belch of air.

Memling covered the tyre marks as best he could, picked Francine up, and shouldered the machine pistol. The water was cold but the current less swift than he had expected. Francine gasped and struggled, but he forced her to swim the stretch of deep water to the island.

Memling allowed them only a few minutes' rest in the shelter of a clump of willows. Francine was exhausted and wanted only to sleep, but Memling dragged her with him through the trees to the far side. The channel was not as wide here, and they crossed easily. The girl was confused and on the verge of hysteria, but Memling knew that the best antidote was to keep her moving. Relentlessly he drove her along the riverbank, north towards the village of Freest.

The stillness had grown palpable; nothing moved in the night. The moon had been hidden by a bank of cloud moving swiftly out of the north, and the darkness was intense. The storm was signalled only by a blinding flash of lightning and an earsplitting crack of thunder. Wind howled suddenly across the marsh, and the deluge was total; rain lashed by the wind blew at them from every direction. Francine's fingers dug at his arm in terror, and he hunched down, trying to shield her with his body. The storm front seemed to take hours to pass, and even when it had done so, the rain continued to pour down unabated. The howling wind was unnerving, and without the river as a guide, Memling would have lost direction.

Francine had recovered enough to understand the urgency of the flight, but she was so weak that Memling was forced to half carry her. He knew she was in constant and severe pain from the burns, but there was nothing he could do.

Freest was only three kilometres from the point where they crossed the Peene, but they were forced to circle inland to avoid another village, Kroslin, where a small army garrison had been stationed. Freest was located on the Greifswalder Boden, the bay that emptied into the Baltic proper, above the boom that closed the river to traffic. He had no clear idea what they were going to do when they got there, other than try to steal a boat and move along the coast, away from the immediate vicinity. For the moment the necessity for getting as far away as possible before dawn overrode all other considerations.

It took them an hour to cover the last kilometre to the village. Memling allowed a few moments' rest crouched in the shelter of a building. He was exhausted, soaked to the skin, and shivering violently. The girl seemed to have slipped back into a mild delirium, and he had difficulty rousing her. Memling was not familiar with the village, so he could only follow along the top of the low bluff edging the bay. The terrain rose slowly. The wind seemed to have steadied from the north. Suddenly a light flashed, and he heard shouts only a few metres ahead. The girl stumbled and slipped from his grasp as he stopped; her cry was lost in the wind, but the sound scared Memling badly.

He sank down on his haunches, covering the girl's mouth with one hand and holding her down with the other. The light flickered in their direction and then swung to show a soldier helping several men tie up a fishing smack that had worked loose from her moorings. Memling had a brief glimpse of a stove-in hull and guessed that she would be on the bottom by morning. Beyond the damaged boat were several others barely visible in the thin beam. He lay down then, covering the girl's body with his own, resisting her feeble struggles until she was quiet. There was nowhere else he dared go.

As the rain beat upon his back and mud seeped into his clothes, a plan was beginning to take shape. Sweden lay one hundred and fifty kilometres or less due north. He had not considered attempting escape in that direction because of aircraft and naval patrols. But this storm gave every appearance of working up to a near hurricane. If they could make four knots an hour, they would be in Sweden in less than twenty-four hours. The storm would likely keep the Luftwaffe grounded at least that long. And any naval patrols would have their hands full just staying afloat.

Memling's experience with small boats was limited to his commando training, but there was no other choice. The trek to Denmark across three hundred miles of enemy territory was not only unrealistic but suicidal. And with four dead SD agents to his credit, the Nazis would not rest until they captured them both.

The men on the pier checked the moorings on the other boats and then moved off. Memling picked up the unconscious girl, stumbled through the blackness to the pier, and crossed slimy wooden planks to the third boat in the line. He eased down on to the deck, hanging on for dear life as the waves, even in the sheltered inlet, tossed the boat about. Checking quickly to see that the craft was unoccupied, he laid the girl on the deck in the shelter of the wheelhouse and found the engine compartment. The cover slid back with a squeal, and he froze. But the storm was loud enough to cover the firing of an eighty-eight-millimetre cannon.

Fifteen minutes of feeling about the greasy, fume-ridden space and he had found and set the magneto and opened the fuel petcock, all the while blessing his trainers for their hysterical insistence on operating machinery under the most adverse conditions. It took several tries before the engine coughed into life, and he left it to warm up then while he carried Francine down into the cabin. Even here he dared not risk a light. The cabin smelled of long occupancy and little cleaning, but it was dry. He stripped off her sodden clothing and chafed her cold body, covered her with dirty blankets found by touch in one of the lockers and tied her into the bunk with torn strips of cloth. It would be some time before he dared leave the wheel.

He then dried the machine pistol and left it under the other bunk. The Walther must have slipped from his pocket some time after he had left the house, but it made little difference now.

Balancing on the heaving deck, he tried to recall details from the map he had studied so carefully over the past weeks. The Greifswalder Boden was free of most navigational hazards except for the scattered sandbanks that edged this tideless inland sea. They would be the greatest problem, as all channel markers would have been removed at the start of the war. There was, however, no other choice. Accordingly, he slipped the bow mooring, ran back and lifted the stern-line off the cleat, and, as the boat swung about under the battering of the waves, raced for the wheelhouse. There was a grinding crash as the boat collided with the one to starboard, then a second, and he had the engine full astern and the wheel spinning over.

The boat responded sluggishly to the helm at first, its bluff coaster hull wallowing heavily, and as they cleared the point the gale-force winds laid her right over. Memling fought the wheel, pulling the throttle further and further open until the engine screamed in protest. The boat came reluctantly under control, and he reduced the rpm's. He had no idea how much diesel oil there was in the tanks, but knew it would be damned little. There was a sail furled professionally about the boom, and he suspected it saw a great deal of use given the shortage of fuel in Germany.

By accident Memling found the switch that started the circle of glass set in the windscreen spinning to provide a semblance of visibility. Huge seas, only half-hidden by the darkness, reared about the boat, and spume snatched from the wave crests was flung away by the violent wind like shotgun pellets. Summer gales in the Baltic were doubly dangerous because of its shallowness, and Memling wondered if they would survive.

The sky began to lighten near dawn, revealing heaving white-flecked mountains of water towering in all directions. Irrationally Memling had expected the storm to moderate, but instead it seemed to increase in fury. The compass showed a north-easterly course. The fuel indicator was broken so there was no way of judging the distance covered or the magnetic correction factor to be applied to the compass; yet he felt they must have come far enough to have cleared the island of Rügen, which formed the northern rim of the Greifswalder Boden, and to have left the dangerous sandbanks behind. Memling was forced to guess at the magnetic correction as he altered course due north, turning the wheel a bit at a time until the compass needle was oscillating north, north-west. He was hazy about the exact directions and distances involved but recalled that the island of Bornholm also lay to the north of Usedom and was less than sixty kilometres from the Swedish coast. But Bornholm was occupied Danish territory, and he had no idea how to distinguish between it and neutral Sweden without actually landing. With the fatalism that his present predicament encouraged, he decided to worry about that if and when the time came.

The gale slackened a bit towards noon, and he was able to lash the wheel and hurry below. Francine was still in the bunk, but the blankets had been churned into knots. He found and lit a lantern and swore the souls of the four SD men to damnation. Any regrets over their killing disappeared at the sight of her breasts – where they had concentrated the cigarette torture. Bruises on her thighs suggested she might have been raped. When he eased her over, he discovered large crisscross weals on her back where they had used their belts.

Memling rummaged through the lockers but found nothing with which he could treat her burns and the cuts from the belting. He made her as comfortable as possible in the narrow bunk and retied the restraints. Her pulse was slow and weak, and her breathing noisy.

The gale picked up in violence again during the afternoon and raged on into the night. He was on the verge of total exhaustion, and some time during the night he fell asleep. A violent twisting, corkscrewing motion shook him awake, and he stared out at the phantom shapes rearing above. The rain had stopped, but the wind had worked up to a screaming frenzy, piling up water in unstable masses that struck down on the boat, threatening to smash her under at any moment. Memling realised that unless he could turn and run before the sea, they would be swamped. He shoved at the wheelhouse door, but it refused to open, held shut by the wind. He wasted no more time then. The waves were silhouetted against the night sky, lighter now that the rain had stopped. He waited until the boat forced its way to a crest, then risked a quick look at the following wave and spun the wheel hard over hard to port, yanking open the throttle at the same time. They dropped below the crest, sheltered from the wind for a brief moment, and the boat fought around. There was a moment's sickening vertigo as the deck fell away and then a jolt, and the bow buried itself to the hatch cover. For one agonising moment Memling was certain the boat would go right under, but like a terrier, she shook herself free and bounded upright. With wind and wave now dead astern, her motion became easier. Memling slumped on the wheel, gasping for breath, exhausted beyond endurance. For the remainder of the night he fought the seas that threatened to turn them broadside as they raced south-east towards Germany.

Dawn brought an easing of the violent gale, although the seas were as wild as ever. Again he struggled to bring the boat about towards Sweden. The boat responded well enough and settled down to doggedly bashing a way through the waves. Once more Memling found it possible to lash the wheel and go below for a few moments. Francine's condition did not seem to have changed, except for her breathing, which had become noisier, making him fear pneumonia. There was not much he could do but try to feed her some of the small supply of food he had found in one of the lockers and make her as comfortable as possible.

The day wore on into afternoon, and still the boat chugged on into seas that never seemed to change. Memling napped whenever possible and between times stared, hypnotised, at the heaving water. When the engine died, he was surprised but not disconcerted. As the bow fell off he slipped the cord over the wheel and dashed on to the deck.

He had prepared by tracing the sail's hauling mechanism and the sheets that controlled its movement. He slipped the lashings that held the canvas sail to the boom, inserted the handle into the winch, and cranked like a madman. The sail came up freely on to the mast, bellying out in the thirty-knot wind, and the boat heeled to windward. Immediately she became easier as the huge cat-rigged sail balanced her, allowing her to heel so that a minimum of hull was in the water.

Memling found the boat amazingly responsive to the helm. This was what she had been built for, to bend the elements to her will, not to potter along under the impetus of a smelly diesel. There was an impression of great speed as the little boat shot along, bow wave creaming and wake stretching behind, and Memling, exhausted as he was, began to enjoy himself. He checked the engine and found that a cooling line had snapped, allowing the engine to overheat and seize up. But as long as the wind held steady, they were probably making better time under sail, and so he did not mind the loss of the engine. For hours they raced northward close-reached, wind steady over the starboard quarter. At four the weather and the seas had moderated, so he felt it safe enough to go below.

Francine was in a deep but restless sleep. Her face was flushed, her hair damp with sweat, and her skin hot and swollen. She tossed against the restraints, fingers plucking weakly at the blankets. When he examined her burns again, he found that several of the deeper ones had turned a puffy grey. Her breathing, Memling was certain, indicated that she had pneumonia. He covered her as best he could and rummaged through the cabin stores, finding only a dried, stringy sausage and a piece of cheese. There was a bare spoonful of tea in a canister, and he heated water over the recalcitrant alcohol stove and tried, without much success, to get her to sip a little. Her murmuring had turned to country German in which only the name Karl – a brother, he supposed, or a friend – was understandable. He made certain the lashings were secure before going back on deck with the rest of the tea. He knew she was going to die, and found himself cursing the fools who had sent her to this fate; then he stopped, recognising the futility of it all. He finished the tea slowly, making it last, and chewed on the tasteless sausage and cheese.

In late afternoon the sun broke through to cast long pillars of light on to to the sea. At seven o'clock he sighted a smudge of land. For a long moment the old fear rushed back. Neutral Sweden or Nazi-occupied Bornholm? There was nothing to do now but wait. He went below then to check on the girl and clean the machine pistol.

Francine was comatose; her skin was hot and dry to the touch, and her mouth worked with the effort to breathe. Fluid was filling her lungs with unbelievable rapidity. He sat helplessly on the bunk, holding one limp hand. There was nothing he could do other than to keep watch while she died.

When he went back on deck an hour later, the skies had cleared almost completely. The wind had dropped, and the sail slatted sullenly. The aircraft had apparently been circling for some time, engines throttled back. Memling grunted; its appearance had been inevitable. The plane had twin booms, three engines, and stabilising pontoons slung beneath the wings. He identified it as a Bv.138 naval reconnaissance seaplane – an aircraft the Swedes did not use. Half-heartedly Memling waved, hoping they would think he was a Swedish fisherman. The plane made one more circuit and climbed for altitude until he lost it in the darkening sky. Radioing for instructions, he suspected.

The smudge of land had taken on definition in the time he had been below. A low range of hills were visible, as were one or two lights along the shore: Sweden, he realised, as Bornholm would have been blacked out. Not that it mattered much now. He judged that he was well within neutral Swedish territorial waters, but he also knew that such niceties would not deter the Nazis who could not allow him to escape with the information he had gathered at Peenemünde.

Memling began the preparations he had thought through earlier. He took the hatch cover off the engine compartment and punched a hole in the fuel tank, hoping that enough fuel remained to do the job. Earlier he had gone down and prised boards away to let the oil seep into the aft hold. He found two bulky cork life-belts and took them into the cabin. Francine was delirious and much weaker now. A matter of hours, he thought. He balanced the knife in his fingers and bent over her, easing her chin back. It would be so much kinder to slip the blade in quickly; death would be instantaneous. But he could not bring himself to do it. He did not even like her very much, and he doubted if she cared at all for him. They had been given a job to do. As she had seen it, sex was a part of that job, a part she enjoyed, but a job nevertheless. He, in turn, had used her, partly because she was willing, partly because he was reacting to his own problems with Janet, and partly because her magnificent body offered a relief from his own fear. Each had been a convenience to the other, nothing more.

He cursed himself as he slid her arms through the cork jacket and tied the thongs securely. He could kill when it was an enemy and there was no other choice, but not a helpless woman who had shared her body with him, for whatever reason. If there was any chance at all, he meant her to have it. Jan lifted her from the bunk, then, grunting in the confined space, carried her up and placed her on the deckhouse floor. He went below again for the alcohol stove and the dead SD man's machine pistol. He poured a panful of diesel oil on the limp sail, lit the stove with difficulty, and sat down beside the feverish girl to wait.

The reconnaissance plane made its first attack from dead astern at sea level. Machine-gun fire chewed across the deck, and the aircraft swept past so close that Memling saw the pilot staring down at him. The gun turret forward of the cockpit swivelled as the pilot sideslipped to give the gunner clearance, but the burst went wide. The plane banked sharply, fell off one wing, and swept down on them, again at sea level. Memling knelt behind the engine compartment and held his fire until the last possible moment; a split second before the twin machine-guns opened up, he fired a long burst that exhausted the Schmiesser magazine. The turret shattered and the aircraft swept past without response. One dead gunner, he hoped.

Memling rammed home the other magazine and watched the aircraft sweep away low, then climb swiftly. The pilot would not make that mistake again. Regretfully he dropped the machine pistol and picked Francine up, easing her over one shoulder. She muttered something through cracked lips, and he held her tightly for a moment, then bent, picked up the stove, and opened the valve until the flame roared.

Far above he could see the Nazi turning towards them. Sun glinted for a moment, highlighting the aircraft, and he could even see the racks of bombs slung under each wing. As the pilot began his run Memling walked to the after hatch where he had put a cloth-wrapped stick that he had soaked in oil. He lit the torch from the burning stove.

The seaplane droned nearer, and he saw the first bombs drop. The pilot had chosen his altitude well. The bombs would strike before the boat could answer the helm. They landed so close that when they exploded, the boat shuddered. The stove was knocked into the hold, and at the same moment Memling threw the torch against the sail. The canvas flared and he slipped over the side. Francine struggled a moment as the shock of the cold water bit through her delirium, then she was still.

The boat was pulling away rapidly, sail flaming brightly, providing an unmistakable target for the seaplane and perhaps a beacon for the Swedish coastal patrols. Two more bombs plummetted, and Memling held his breath, waiting for the concussions. When they came, it was as if a huge fist had clamped, then flung him away. The oil in the hold ignited, and the flame ran back to the fuel tank. The boat leapt clear of the water with the force of the explosion and fell back, a seething mass of flame. Still moving forward under her own momentum even though the sail had disappeared, she plunged beneath the waves.

The aircraft made a final low-level pass across the burning boat, then, as Memling had hoped, sought altitude and turned south towards Germany before Swedish pursuit planes could come to investigate.

Two hours later a Swedish coastal patrol launch found them. Memling was barely conscious, and although the girl must have died within minutes of entering the water, he was still clinging to her.

Sweden September 1943

'I say, are you Captain Jan Memling?'

Memling turned over on the bunk and regarded with suspicion the thin, pale young man in a well-tailored suit. He rubbed a hand over his face, grimaced at the three-day stubble, and nodded. 'Yes.'

The man smiled with satisfaction and dropped down on the bunk opposite. 'Had the devil of a time finding you. Must have been over this camp three times. None of these chaps want to help. Think I'm a spy.'

'Are you?'

'Good heavens, no! I'm the naval attaché at the Stockholm embassy. Name's Ian Fleming.' He handed Memling a leather case with his identification.

Memling decided that Fleming was who he claimed to be. A German impersonator would not have failed to mention his rank even though it was listed on the ID card as lieutenant commander, RN.

'What can I do for you, Commander?'

'I'd say it's rather a matter of what I can do for you. But first, let's establish your bona fides, shall we?' He took a photograph from his case and held it beside Memling's face. 'Well, you look like Captain Jan Memling, late of the Number Two Commando. Perhaps you could tell me your mother's maiden name?'

Memling grinned for the first time in three weeks. 'Wells. Anything else?'

'Oh, quite a bit.' Fleming consulted a pocket notebook. 'I believe your father was a Belgian gunsmith?'

'My father was a British citizen, born in London,' he corrected.

'Oh?'

'Yes. My grandfather left Belgium in 1872.'

'I see. Well then, in 1928 he made a certain type of gun for a rather famous personality. Perhaps you could describe it?'

Memling blinked. His father had made dozens of fine rifles and shotguns for his customers, many of them famous. He took a chance, knowing first-hand just how thorough MI6 could be.

'He made a ten-bore double shotgun for Lord Esterbrook to use on his East African farm. Lord Esterbrook wanted a serviceable weapon with a steel skeleton stock. It had cast-steel barrels to make up the weight thus lost to reduce recoil.'

'Very good.'

'How did they find out about that gun? My father considered it an abomination and even refused to sign it. He made Lord Esterbrook promise never to reveal its maker.'

The naval officer only smiled at the question. 'You know better than that.' He slipped the notebook into his pocket, then took a small leather bag from the case and extracted an ink pad and a sheet of celluloid. He pressed Memling's middle finger to the pad and then to the celluloid sheet and stepped to the window where he superimposed the celluloid over a transparent photocopy of Memling's fingerprints and studied the results with a magnifying glass.

'Well, that's that. You do appear to be Captain Memling.'

'So. Now what?'

Fleming packed up the kit. 'Now we get out of here. I have a car outside.'

Memling shook his head. 'Maybe you haven't heard, but I've been interned for the duration.'

'I did hear something to that effect.' Fleming tossed him an envelope with the Royal Swedish cipher embossed discreetly in the upper left corner. 'Royal pardon. Seems a mistake was made. You were thought to be an Allied combatant when your boat was sunk in Swedish territorial waters. The police should never have arrested a member of the embassy staff. Diplomatic immunity and all that. What's the world coming to, I wonder? Ready?'

The day was exceptionally mild, and Fleming drove at breakneck speed through the rolling countryside. Somehow he had obtained an elderly Bentley that had obviously been restored in painstaking detail. With the top down it was difficult to talk, and Memling lay back against the leather seat and closed his eyes, revelling in the fresh air, warm sun, and semblance of freedom the car's passage provided.

He could remember little of the first three days after the Swedish patrol boat fished him from the water, other than a successive flicker of static scenes; a jouncing ride in an ambulance, soft sounds and sterile walls, a woman in white uniform bending over him, and then nothing.

He awoke in the Allied detention camp at Korsnäs, north of Västerås, in central Sweden. A week later had come a hearing presided over by a civilian and attended by Swedish military officers and one representative each from the British embassy and the International Red Cross. The British diplomat impressed upon him the importance of keeping his mouth shut. At the end of the hearing, conducted entirely in Swedish, he was remanded to the detention camp for the duration of the war. Since then, all his attempts to contact the British embassy had been fruitless.

Routine, he was told in the officers' billet to which he had been assigned. His fellow internees were mostly aircrew, pilots and one or two Norwegian MILORG officers who had come overland from Norway after finishing a mission.

'They'll get us all back in time, never fear,' one of the RAF types had told him. 'Until then, just relax and enjoy life.'

But he could not. Memling was aware that time was running out. Bad weather would set in shortly over the Baltic, and when it did, the RAF would probably cancel all plans to bomb Peenemünde until spring. So he fretted and fumed and made a nuisance of himself at the administration centre trying to contact someone in the embassy.

The internees pretty much had the run of the camp, he discovered, but the perimeter was well guarded by armed sentries and dogs. The food was excellent, and the officers' club functioned like its counterparts in Britain, even to mess bills. Nor was it difficult to obtain a pass into Korsnäs, a village of a few hundred people, or even for a day trip around the countryside. But to obtain a pass, you had to give your parole and he had not been prepared to do that.

Fleming slowed the car and turned off on to a farm track that led back into a field. He kept on until the track bent double and disappeared into a grove of trees where he stopped the car. The naval attaché walked into the field towards the road to make certain they were concealed sufficiently, then strolled back.

'How about a spot of lunch?' Fleming opened the trunk, removed a wicker hamper, and spread a blanket beneath a massive beech. 'Had the hotel put up a basket. Much more pleasant than a roadside café. And we can talk here.'

After years of wartime strictures, Memling was amazed at the variety of food that appeared from the hamper: sandwiches of all kinds, canapés, cheeses, sliced and potted meats, and sweets.

'Had the devil of a time teaching the chef to make a proper sandwich,' Fleming remarked, offering one. 'Kept insisting it was sacrilege to put a slice of bread over the top.' He produced a chilled bottle of wine and pulled the cork with a flourish. 'A nice Château Margaux 1928. Bought several bottles from an old gentleman in Strängnäs by the name of Iwan Morelius.' He sniffed the cork and held the bottle up to the sun. 'Not bad,' he muttered, examining the colour with a critical eye, 'for wartime.'

They ate in silence. The sun filled the glade with light, reminding Memling of his first week in the Mecklenburg forest with the strange Polish woodcutter. Insects droned lazily, and a light breeze rustled trees. A distant cicada thrummed; a small stream ran nearby, and the water chuckled over moss-covered stones. The sounds of summer, he thought.

Fleming glanced at his Rolex wristwatch and broke the silence. 'I must apologise for taking so long to pull you out of there. The Hun is very well organised in Sweden, and he has a great deal of support from certain types. They know you are alive, and they seem to want you quite badly, which caused no end of furore at the Foreign Ministry. Seems Jerry claimed you were not a British citizen at all but a Belgian working on contract for them. Claimed you murdered some policemen, and wanted you returned to Germany for trial.'

Memling snorted, but Fleming held up a cautioning hand. 'Wait. It was damned close. There is strong sentiment for Germany in certain quarters of the Foreign Ministry. The warrant had actually been issued, and several policemen and a German Gestapo official were already on their way when I found out about it. You may actually have seen him at the camp. He looks cadaverous.'

A sudden chill ruined the beauty of the day. Memling stared at the thin officer sprawled beside him. His coat had fallen open, and he saw that Fleming was wearing a chamois-skin shoulder holster and what looked to be a twenty-five-calibre Beretta. 'Very thin? Gaunt actually. A face like a skull's?'

'Yes, that's the one. There certainly can't be two alike. Do you know him?'

'Yes . . . I do.'

Fleming looked up sharply at the tone in his voice but asked no further questions.

'Anyway, I got the ambassador to ring up the Justice Ministry and get you off the hook, but it was a near thing. If the camp commandant had not insisted on double-checking the warrant, you might be sitting in a Nazi concentration camp at this moment.'

Fleming sipped his wine and unwrapped another sandwich. 'That's why the government wants you out of Sweden today.' He chewed with evident pleasure and swallowed. 'My orders are to see you on to a plane for London as quickly as possible. An American transport leaves this evening for Iceland. You can transfer there for a flight to London. We don't dare try and set it up from here because Jerry's radio interception is excellent. But you should have no trouble finding a flight in Reykjavík. Dozens go out every day in both directions. Otherwise, there are plenty of British naval vessels in the harbour.' He got up then and fetched a manila envelope from the Bentley.

'Diplomatic passport and all that. You can read it on the way. Take good care of it as the FO gets quite upset if one is lost. They only agreed as you are an MI-Six reserve officer.'

Memling took the envelope and slipped it into his jacket pocket. 'Thanks very much for all you've done. I . . .'

Fleming waved a hand. 'All in a day's work. Think no more about it.'

Fleming fetched another bottle from the Bentley, this time a fifth of Haig and Haig. 'Just the thing with which to celebrate.' He produced two small cups, filled them, and offered Memling a silent toast. 'Now, tell me who the young woman was?'

Memling hesitated, then shook his head. 'No, Commander. I don't think I had better say anything at all.'

Fleming nodded. 'Probably the wisest course. However, we have little choice in the matter. She is the only gap in the story, and the Swedes are pressing for an answer.'

Memling finished the Scotch and stared at the silver-plated cup. 'Look here, she was a member of the German resistance assigned to help me. SD thugs tortured her, and, well, she contracted pneumonia and died. That's all there is to it.'

Fleming gave him a level stare. 'I see. I suppose the "SD thugs", as you call them, are the four dead policemen?'

When Memling stared off at the forest instead of answering, Fleming nodded, laced his fingers behind his head, and closed his eyes. After a long while he murmured sleepily, 'I suppose I should tell you they did let me in on the purpose of your mission. You might be interested to know that in 1939, shortly after the war began, our embassy in Oslo received a package containing a report that described much of Germany's secret war research, including radar and rockets. The report was carefully studied, but no one could decide if it was a plant or not. So nothing was done.

Seems there was something to it after all.' Fleming was silent for a while.

'London had given you up for lost, and Bomber Command laid on the Peenemünde raid a week ago. The official word is, they did one hell of a lot of damage.'

Memling was stunned by the news. Christ in heaven, it had all been for nothing, then, he thought. Francine's death, everything they had gone through, his estrangement from Janet, all of it wasted.

'How in . . . they must have known I was in Sweden . . .'

Fleming gave him a sympathetic nod. 'Yes. We notified London that you were here but it looked as if the Germans might get you and the weather was deteriorating and someone decided they couldn't wait any longer. But' – he brightened – 'you should be of immense help in interpreting the after-action damage photos, as you were there, on the ground, so to speak.'

Memling could only nod in bitterness.

No one was at Croydon to meet him; but then, Memling hadn't expected it. He found the military transport office and, after an argument over the priority accorded him by his diplomatic passport, gave up and bought a ticket on the London-Brighton Line for London Bridge. He still had to wait an hour on the dripping platform. At London Bridge Station the crowds streaming down the tube platform deterred him, and he walked north across the bridge and past Saint Paul's towards Holborn.

The bomb damage was appalling. Whole blocks had been destroyed and cleared away to leave gaping holes in the line of buildings. For some reason he had not noticed before how ragged the city had become. Shops, however, were open, and the streets crowded, particularly with children, who seemed to have filtered back in spite of the government's efforts to keep them in the countryside. It rained steadily, but the air was warm and he didn't mind. No one paid attention to his shabby clothing and run-down shoes; he looked more or less like the majority of Londoners around him, except that most men his age were in uniform.

As he started up Gray's Inn Road a teenage girl darted up, thrust a white feather at him, and disappeared, giggling, into the crowd. An elderly woman clucked and turned away as he stared after the girl, too outraged even to swear. Suddenly all the frustration, all the fear and misery he had endured for so long, crashed upon him. People stared with mixed expressions at the tall no-longer-young man dressed in shabby civilian clothing swaying on the kerb; most thought him drunk.

The block of flats on Montague Street seemed unchanged; the unpleasant image of an earlier homecoming had been in his mind the past few days. The flat was locked and, as he expected, Janet was out, probably still at work. Memling considered going across to Red Lion Square and reporting in, then decided against it. Tomorrow was soon enough, and he was exhausted. He sat down on the top step and leaned against the banister. It was four-thirty, and Janet wouldn't be home until after six. He closed his eyes, seeing the foolish little girl with her bunch of white feathers and no idea in her silly head except to . . . to . . . To what? he wondered. They were about the same age, that silly girl and Francine. The futility angered him all over again before he realised that he was canonising her. Francine was no different from that girl with the feathers. She too had considered it all a great game, until it had killed her.

So much had happened since he left that it might have been someone else who lived here. The memory of his terror was rapidly being sublimated as events of the past month receded. He did not understand them and doubted he ever would. Nor did he understand himself or the fear which infected him, and of which he was ashamed. He knew he would never be able to discuss it with anyone, not even Janet.

He forced his mind away from that line of introspection as he had done so many times in the past, and thought about the strides the Germans were making in rocketry. My God, he breathed, as the wonder of it struck him again. A rocket powerful enough to reach the moon! It was incredible, but the thrill died abruptly when he remembered that a rocket that powerful could also deliver thirty metric tons of explosive on London in one blow.

Any sympathy, any understanding, any liking for the Peenemünde personnel, had evaporated with the girl's murder. The scientists may have had nothing to do with her killing, but they had acquiesced in it by tolerating the sadists infesting the SS and the Gestapo. And he knew with fierce pleasure that even though there had already been one bombing raid, there would be many more when he made his report. The fact that massive enemy rockets existed could no longer be ignored.

Janet found him two hours later when she came up the steps searching her handbag for her keys. He was sound asleep against the banister. In the dark she took him for someone who had wandered in out of the rain in search of shelter. But after turning on the hall light, she sat down abruptly, confused and conflicting thoughts swirling through her mind. She studied his face, wondering at the deep lines carved in the forehead and cheeks and the streaks of grey above the temples. He is too young, she protested silently. Too young! She knew then that she would neither give him up nor let him go again.

Peenemünde August–October 1943

Franz Bethwig stared at the yellow telegram sheet.

> REGRET STANDARTENFÜHRER EDGAR ULLMAN, NO. 3254678, KILLED IN ACTION, EASTERN FRONT.

He crumpled the flimsy sheet, dropped it in the wastebasket, and left the administration building. The day was exceptionally hot and still. A storm was brewing, but Bethwig was oblivious to his surroundings. He went along the paths leading to the beach, wanting only to be by himself. People scurried past, so many that their faces did not even register. Once he had known everyone on the island, including the military guards.

He found a deserted stretch of beach and threw himself down on the sand. The sun blazed down, and after a while he removed his shirt. With Ullman dead, his last link to Inge was broken. A great emptiness surged from his chest to encompass his entire body. He was aware of sullen wavelets lapping the shore, the iron sun burning his skin, the gritty sand, all at the same time that the knowledge he might never see Inge again struggled to blot everything from his mind. Why? he thought suddenly. She was a prostitute, and a half-wit into the bargain. But none of that mattered. Heydrich had understood, perhaps even arranged it; certainly he had tried to use it against him and had nearly succeeded.

And now Himmler. Did Ullman die in combat, as a matter of course, or was he the pawn in this perverted game? Himmler had twice now tried to force him to replace von Braun, and twice he had refused.

Yet Bethwig could not bring himself to believe that something as petty as this would be important enough to occupy the attention of a man in Himmler's position. Could he not understand that Bethwig did not have to be blackmailed into doing his best to make the A-10 project a complete success? There was nothing more important in this world to him than landing a human on the moon. The thought struck chill as it came unbidden into his mind. Was Inge?

A messenger found him an hour later, and he trudged back to the administration building to settle a jurisdictional dispute over the use of four automated lathes in the experimental machine shop.

The staff meeting began at two o'clock even though Wernher von Braun had not yet arrived. The department heads, most of them members of the original Kummersdorf or Greifswalder Oie teams, sat in a semicircle, listening intently.

Since that strange meeting with Hitler at Rastenburg in July most of the bottlenecks had disappeared. They had shown the Führer movies of the A-4 in flight and had briefed him on the capabilities of other projects such as the Wasserfall anti-aircraft missile and the A-10 multi-stage rocket. Hitler's sudden enthusiasm for the new weapons was in striking contrast with his previous lack of interest. He had declaimed for more than an hour on the effect such weapons would have on the course of the war, promised to make von Braun a full professor as a reward, and ordered Minister Speer to see that top priority was afforded the army's rocket projects. In spite of Dornberger's dire predictions that priority at this late date could not make up for the years of neglect, work had been pushed ahead at Peenemünde with renewed zest.

There had been no overt reaction from Himmler, but word had reached Bethwig through the grapevine that the reichsführer was furious that von Braun had discussed the A-10's capabilities with the Führer. A series of petty annoyances had begun, including the seemingly endless addition of SS security forces to the research centre. Apparently Hitler had queried Himmler about the extent of his interest and had issued a mild warning about overreaching one's position. According to his father, the Führer was more than a little disturbed by the actions of his reichsführer lately. Bethwig suspected, therefore, that von Braun's demotion would come swiftly and that he would have no choice but to accept the position. Brooding, he listened with half an ear to the engineering department's report on the new liquid oxygen valve servos.

The double doors slammed against the wall like gunshots. Everyone jumped, and a file of SS troopers double-timed into the room and spread along the walls, weapons at port arms. Shocked silence filled the canteen. Bethwig, as the senior official present, strode to the SD officer who stood with hands on hips surveying the startled scientists.

'What is the meaning of this interruption?' Bethwig's voice

whipped through the silent room, and the officer, a hauptsturmführer, surveyed him lazily. 'I have orders to . . .'

'Stand to attention when you address a superior,' Bethwig snapped, and the captain stiffened in reflex. Technically Bethwig's pay grade as an army employee made him equal to a full colonel, but the SS was subject neither to military nor civilian control.

'The next time you distrupt a scheduled meeting with your childish tactics, you fool, I will make you regret it to your dying day. Now, state your business immediately!'

The SS officer's face went red as he struggled to retain control of himself.

'State your business, sir,' Bethwig demanded again, staring directly into the man's protruding eyes.

'I am ordered to arrest engineer Ernst Mundt immediately.' The captain choked.

A shocked murmur ran through the room, and Mundt stood in confusion. Immediately two SS men ran forward to grab him, but Bethwig's angry shout brought them to a halt as they began to hustle Mundt from the canteen.

'You, sir – ' he addressed the officer – 'will state the reason for this arrest and the authority by which it was ordered.'

The hauptsturmführer was on firmer ground here and knew it. 'Engineer Mundt has been accused of aiding an enemy of the Reich, complicity in the murder of four security personnel, and consorting with the enemy. My orders are to bring him to SD headquarters for interrogation.'

Bethwig exploded. 'Your orders are shit, Captain!' he roared. 'You have no jurisdiction here. Mundt is not a party member; only the state security police may charge and arrest him. Leave this canteen at once or I'll see you on the eastern front by tomorrow night!'

The SS captain hesitated. He knew who Bethwig was, and his connections were rumoured to be extremely powerful. But he had his orders and they allowed no equivocation.

'Stand aside, sir,' the captain snarled, one hand going to his holster. The movement only enraged Bethwig further, and he would have grabbed the officer by the throat had Dornberger not arrived at that moment. Accompanying him were the senior SS officer at the facility and another man in civilian clothing whom Bethwig immediately recognised as Major Jacob Walsch. Bethwig ignored Walsch and made his protest to the senior SS officer. Dornberger joined in vigorously, the officer mumbled an angry order, and the SS troops filed out. Walsch had watched with a cynical smile, and when the SS had gone, he arrested Mundt and took him away. The staff meeting was cancelled. Dornberger and Bethwig dashed through the rain to a waiting car and drove in silence to Gestapo headquarters down the coast at Zinnowitz.

A massive storm of near hurricane proportions had broken during the night, and as they drove along the flooded coastal road broken and uprooted trees were everywhere, as were ragged POWs working with saws and axes to clear the debris under the watchful eyes of SS guards in rain gear.

'Bastards,' Bethwig ground out, slamming a fist on the dashboard. 'How dare they . . .'

Dornberger started to observe that he and von Braun had brought it on themselves with their insistence on obtaining high political backing for their pet project, but wisely kept silent rather than provoke a further outburst. Covertly he studied Franz; over the past months the scientist had become increasingly morose, to the point where his attitude verged on sullenness. He had tried more than once to discover the cause, but Bethwig refused to be drawn. Even his relationship with von Braun had been badly strained of late. His work had not suffered yet, but his standing with staff was deteriorating at an alarming rate. First that outburst at Himmler last spring, and now this. He had better learn, and soon, that the SS was untouchable. He could not continue to attack and obstruct unless he wished to end up in a concentration camp. Bethwig was correct in his judgement that the SD had no jurisdiction over Mundt, that this morning's nonsense was no more than another ploy to increase their power at the expense of the army. But there were other, more effective means of handling that kind of situation. Dornberger had no doubt that if Bethwig had continued to interfere, the captain would have shot him dead on the spot – and, under SS guidelines, would have been perfectly justified in doing so.

Rain lashed the windows of Gestapo headquarters, and by leaning against the glass Bethwig could watch the waves crashing against the breakwater below. He was only half listening as a very confused Ernst Mundt described his conversations with a Belgian contract worker who, it appeared, had murdered four SD security men and was now missing. When Mundt finished, the thin Gestapo officer gave him a ghastly smile, meant to be reassuring, and indicated the stenographer.

'Your statement will be typed shortly, Herr Mundt. I would appreciate it if you would wait to read and sign it. I will then have one of my drivers return you to your office. I appreciate your candour, and you really have nothing to worry about. It would appear that your actions were correct and that nothing has been revealed that should not have been. In any event, we will soon have the man, and that will take care of that.'

Mundt, now greatly relieved, was ushered out, but the Gestapo officer signed to Dornberger and Bethwig to remain. When the door closed, Walsch regarded them both with a trace of contempt.

'That man is a fool. He has no conception of the political realities of war. It seems I have made this point to both of you before,' he finished, eyeing Bethwig.

'That man is an engineer and a scientist,' Dornberger snapped. 'He is not concerned with politics. That is your department.'

'No, Herr Generalmajor. It is our collective responsibility. You and your staff . . .'

'Enough of this nonsense,' Bethwig snapped. 'Tell us what harm if any has been done, so that we will know what actions to take.'

The Gestapo officer stared at him for a long minute, then indicated the chairs before his desk. 'Sit down, please.' A long rumble of thunder muttered in from the sea, and the rain beat down even more insistently.

'Perhaps you do not recall that in 1938 I had occasion to warn you about an English agent and loose talk?'

'Yes, quite clearly. Your manners were insufferable then, and . . .'

Dornberger cut him off sharply and Walsch smiled. 'Also, last year in Berlin you, Herr Doktor Bethwig, and I had a conversation in a café about a similar subject. I recall that you called me an incompetent ass. Well, Herr Doktor, it would seem that this same espionage agent has been here, at Peenemünde, working for Doktor Mundt. He is the man who murdered the SS officer and the three enlisted men who attempted to arrest him.' The greyish light served only to heighten Walsch's extreme gauntness by carving great hollows beneath his eyes and in his cheeks so that, for a brief moment, his face became a leering skull.

Bethwig recalled the weedy young man he had met in Arnsberg before the war. He would never have credited him with the ability or the courage, yet three times now this Memling, by his activities, had managed to involve them with the Gestapo. How much time have we lost because of him? Bethwig asked himself angrily.

'He was employed,' Walsch continued, 'in the pre-production shops. He worked there for nine days, and during that time was promoted twice to positions of greater responsibility by that fool

Mundt. We also know that he was employed for nine months in 1940 as a quality control technician at the Manufacture d'Armes in Liège. Couple that with your own indiscretions in 1938 and you can be certain that the English are very much aware of what is going on at Peenemünde.'

Walsch paused long enough for them to absorb the impact of his statement, then said in a thoughtful voice, as if it had just occured to him, 'It would seem that someone at Peenemünde may be assisting an agent of an enemy nation to obtain information about the rocket development programme.'

It was Major Jacob Walsch's turn to stand at the rain-streaked window. Tapping his teeth with a finger – an old habit he had given up trying to break – he watched the automobile plough through the flooded streets towards the northern end of the island, and wondered if perhaps they were not chasing the wrong phantom after all. Politically von Braun was too stupid to be attracted by British promises. After all, what could they offer? But Bethwig? Perhaps. He certainly had sufficient cover: important family connections, a long and honourable party record, and friendships in high places. He would bear closer watch. He must be on the lookout, Walsch decided, for a way to control him: perhaps a thorough search of his records? Records – he tapped his front tooth with a pencil. Of course, his records. Now that he thought about it, there had been more than the usual number of requests from Berlin, in fact from SS headquarters, to review Bethwig's file. Why? Did they already suspect him of something, something they were not yet ready to divulge? How ironic – Walsch chuckled at the thought – if one responsible for the blot on his record should be the one to erase that with a blot of his own and perhaps, just perhaps, an execution?

Having made up his mind, the major picked up the telephone and ordered his aide to release Mundt. Perhaps a small trap could be set. If it failed, no harm done, as no one would know. If it succeeded, well and good. This man Mundt was, after all, Bethwig's employee; in fact, he had noted in the man's records that it was Bethwig who had insisted that he be hired, even though the man was considered politically unreliable. One never knew these days.

Two weeks had passed with no further word concerning the supposed English spy or the alleged murders of the four SD agents, and after trying several times to obtain additional information from Walsch, Bethwig forgot the matter.

On this cloudless Tuesday afternoon in the third week of August, he strolled slowly towards Building 40, the bachelor quarters where he still resided. It had been a frustrating day, beginning with the report of another failure in the A-10's valving system, which would delay the launch three weeks. Then had come lunch with a very disheartened Wernher von Braun. Apparently there had been an early meeting with Degenkolb and his staff at which the minister had set forth impossible demands for A-4 production, refusing to recognise that the rocket was still in the advanced stages of design testing and nowhere near ready for production.

'"Gentlemen, don't tell me such stories,"' von Braun had mimicked. '"I am not interested in them. I produced a thousand locomotives a month in the interest of the Reich, after being told it was impossible."

'I pointed out to the fool that the principles of locomotive construction have been known for a hundred years. If one encounters a problem, one has only to consult a book for the answer. He refuses to recognise that we are still writing our book!'

Von Braun's evident frustration brought a rare smile to Bethwig's face. 'Go on and laugh,' von Braun muttered. 'You'll be getting the same pressures soon enough. And to make matters worse, Doktor Theil tried to resign. Walter refused to accept the resignation, but I am afraid the old man is on the verge of a nervous breakdown. If that happens, your project will be in jeopardy also.'

Both had declined Dornberger's invitation to go shooting, although Bethwig had been sorely tempted. The general was spending so much time in Berlin these days that when in residence, he grabbed every opportunity to tramp the island's thick pinewoods in search of deer or grouse. Then that afternoon a cable arrived that closed off the final avenue in Bethwig's search for Inge. The Prague hospital reported that she had been moved to an unknown treatment centre in May of that year. Himmler had lied to him again; he spent the afternoon trying to decide what to do next.

A note had been slipped under his door inviting him to dine with Hanna Reitsch that evening. Surprised, he checked the date; he hadn't known she was at Peenemünde. Normally he looked forward to dinners with his old friend, an attractive and sophisticated woman who was considered one of Germany's top test pilots, but tonight he wasn't in the mood. He telephoned the visitors' quarters to leave a message declining, but found one waiting for him which stated that Hanna would be very much put out if he did not attend.

Strangely enough, he felt a great deal better then, and whistling he went to bathe.

Bethwig enjoyed himself more than he would have expected. The dinner at the officers' club was superb, and the head waiter presented several bottles of Château Latour 1924, remarking that they had just arrived, having been 'purchased' recently from the château itself. As always, Hanna's presence put everyone on his best behaviour, and Dornberger's dinner was pronounced a success.

Towards midnight Hanna drew Bethwig aside, and they went on to the terrace. The evening was soft and quite warm; a full moon glowed above the island and coated the buildings with silver. Dance music filtered softly through the half-open french doors, and the only reminder that they were at a military research and development centre was the muted roar of an engine being tested somewhere to the north. Bethwig lit a cigarette and leaned against the balcony.

'Hanna, if I didn't know better, I'd think you brought me out here for immoral purposes.'

She laughed and placed a hand on his shoulder. 'Perhaps another time, Franz, I might. But – ' she grew serious – 'I need to talk to you.'

Below, there was a flurry of laughter and goodbyes as Dornberger, leaving early, walked across the square towards the guest quarters. Bethwig drew on the cigarette and let the smoke escape slowly.

'What about, Hanna?'

'You. And your attitude.'

Franz pushed himself upright. 'Oh?'

'Now look here, Franz. None of that "You are meddling in my business again, Hanna," silliness. We've known each other too long for that. The stories about you circulating in Berlin are verging on the ridiculous. When that happens these days, it's time for a friend to take a hand. The rumours are that you've been quarrelling with Himmler. Is it true?'

When he didn't answer, she shook her head impatiently. 'Franz, stop acting like a little boy. If it is, you are a fool. You cannot possibly win. I'm told you refused to allow the SS to arrest a scientist. That you actually threatened to strike an officer. Is that true?'

Bethwig stared at her a moment, then flicked his cigarette away and watched it spiral down to the lawn where it disappeared in a miniature explosion of sparks. 'Certainly it's true. The SS had no jurisdiction and no reason to arrest him.'

'Now wait a moment, Franz.' She laid a hand on his arm. 'Are you the best judge . . .'

'I tell you, Hanna,' Bethwig interrupted, knowing what she was going to say, 'we must stand up to these thugs before they take over all of Germany.'

'Franz, you are a fool!' Hanna blazed. 'You don't realise it, but if your father had not heard in time, you would have been arrested and shot. Himmler ordered your arrest within hours, but your father went directly to the Führer who was not only furious over your actions but even more furious with your father for forcing him to oppose Himmler. You may not know it, Franz, but the Führer detests Himmler and tries to have as little to do with him as possible. Now he is indebted to the reichsführer. I do not believe your father can ever call upon the Führer for assistance again.'

Franz listened to her with mounting shock. It could not be; how else could Himmler's pet project move forward . . . The man would not dare . . . His thoughts were a jumble.

'Do not make the mistake of thinking you are indispensable to Himmler, Franz. No one is.' She lowered her voice and leaned towards him. 'There is strong evidence that Himmler may have conspired with British intelligence in the murder of Reinhard Heydrich. At the very least, it is almost certain that he knew of the attempt and did nothing to stop it. If he could throw Heydrich away, he would not think twice about disposing of you.'

Bethwig realised then that she was speaking the truth; it was something he had suspected for a long time. Even Ullman had hinted that Himmler was responsible for Heydrich's murder. And he was dead now himself. He decided then to tell Hanna about Inge; at least Hanna, as a personal friend of Hitler's and Goering's as well as a public hero, would be immune to Himmler's manipulations. And if he were murdered by Himmler, there would be someone else who knew about her. Hanna might even be able to help him find her . . .

He plucked the packet from his pocket and took another cigarette. Hanna noticed that his hands were shaking as he fumbled with his lighter. 'There is a girl,' he began abruptly. 'I have never told anyone about her before. I met her in Prague. She . . . she was an SS hostess.' He darted a quick glance at Hanna, but her expression did not change even though he realised she knew what the term implied. Everyone did. 'Heydrich found out and used her to keep me in line.'

He went on to tell her about the girl, how Heydrich had ordered her beaten to show him that he could not disobey an order, how an SS officer on Heydrich's staff had managed to get her out of the castle in the confusion surrounding Heydrich's assassination, and finally how she had been incarcerated in a mental hospital. 'Himmler probably found out about her shortly after Wernher and I offered to continue the A-Ten project under his direction. When I refused to support his idiotic charges against von Braun, he had her taken away. Since then, I know only what Himmler allows me to know about her. Even Ullman is dead now, killed on the eastern front. Himmler is using Inge to force me to accept the position of A-Ten project director so that he can fire Wernher. I suppose he thinks I will be more amenable to his stupid whims.'

Hanna took a deep breath. As far-fetched as Franz's story sounded, it was not beyond the realm of possibility; anything was possible today. The question was, would it do any good to tell General Dornberger?

Bethwig was staring at the silvered beaches half a kilometre away. The Baltic was calm, and he could see a patrol boat idling along the coast. He thought of his sailboat, unused since the previous summer.

Air-raid sirens sprang to life, destroying the stillness. In the distance, between wavering notes, they could hear the dull, nearly inaudible drone of heavy bombers.

'The RAF again,' Hanna murmured. 'Forming up south of Rügen for another run on Berlin. God help them there,' she added.

Lights were going off all across the island. The drone of approaching aircraft was louder now. Flashes appeared to the north where the Luftwaffe anti-aircraft defences had opened up on the approaching bomber stream; something they were forbidden to do . . . unless the Centre were under attack. The crash of the exploding bombs rumbled towards them, and the sky above the trees began to glow red.

'My God,' Bethwig exclaimed in amazement, 'they're after the Centre.'

Peenemünde had never been bombed before, and it took him a few moments to absorb the idea; then he grabbed Hanna's arm and ran back into the dining-room and across the floor to join the last of the crowd jostling through the doors. They raced down the stairs and out across the square to where air-raid wardens were waving blue lights and urging people into shelters. The explosions were continuous now, and pillars of flame and debris could be seen as the aeroplanes laid a carpet of bombs across the island.

Inside the shelter Bethwig found a spot against the wall and dragged Hanna down beside him, but she pulled him away. 'Not against the wall. The concussion of a near miss will kill . . .'

Her voice disappeared in the devastating roar of bursting bombs. People screamed and struggled, and a blast of furnace-hot air whipped inside as the door splintered. Dust exploded, choking them into fits of lung-tearing coughing and the temperature shot to unbearable levels. The floor shuddered and more dust was shaken loose as the walls vibrated. The red emergency lamp burst, and Bethwig's head felt as if it might implode as the concussion squeezed. His lips were covered with something hot and sticky, and he experienced the nightmare sensation of quaking earth and vibrating air.

The bombing stopped as suddenly as it had begun, and Bethwig lifted his head, trying to penetrate the absolute darkness. A flashlight went on, and its beam swung around the interior to reveal a fog-thick haze of dust and plaster. Figures appeared in the beam as it swept past – ghostly, staring beings, many with mouths open in soundless screams. He had a glimpse of Hanna wiping a dark stain from her lips and realised that the hot gush he had felt when the bomb exploded was blood from his nose. The concussion had ruptured blood vessels.

Twice more, bombs fell across the island, although none came as close as the first wave. The bombers seemed to be concentrating on the very northern tip and the south-eastern coast, midway along the island's length, where staff housing was clustered. By design or luck? he wondered bitterly.

The shelter door was hammered open and lamps flashed into the interior. 'All men outside now!' The angry shout sounded far away. 'Women and children to remain inside until the all clear.'

Bethwig had been holding Hanna's hand, and she gave him a quick kiss as he stumbled to his feet. An SS squad was checking each man for injuries and forming them into work parties. Bethwig found himself in one composed entirely of Russian prisoners.

The SS officer flashed his light over Bethwig's face and clothing. 'You, are you German?'

Bethwig, still partly stunned by the violence and terror of the past few hours, could only stare at him. The officer shouted the question once more, and he nodded then, understanding.

'You damned civilians,' the officer stormed. 'You should all serve on the Russian front for a month . . . Take this group to Building Fourteen. Put out any fires, rescue anyone caught inside, and save what you can. Go on now, damn you!'

He pushed Bethwig towards the building and raced off with his squad to the next shelter. Franz stumbled through the trees, the Russians following apathetically until they broke out on to a rubble-filled square in front of the two-storey building housing the measurement labs. The area was deserted, with not even a soldier in sight, and when Bethwig turned, struggling to shake off the effects of the bombing, he found that half or more of his prisoners had disappeared. It makes no real difference, he thought, and ran up to the front door to find it locked. A tall Russian in a filthy striped prisoner's pullover and trousers shouldered him aside as he shook the door, and, with a delighted grin, smashed the glass with a stone. They pushed into the hall, coughing in the dense smoke. The fire seemed confined to the first floor, and they raced up the stairs to the corridor above just as the ceiling fell in. A jet of flame lashed the corridor, and the Russians ducked and beat a hasty retreat. They began to kick open doors and rush around gathering up armfuls of equipment. Bethwig, his wits returning with activity, pointed out the most important pieces to be saved. They had gone little more than half-way along the hall before the ceiling burst open with a crack like a cannon shot. As one man, they raced from the building only seconds before it collapsed.

The next building, housing the chemistry development laboratories, was also in flames. Bethwig led them across the lawn at a run to repeat the performance, and this time they managed to bring the fire under control with the building's own fire-fighting system. While three men played hoses the length of the hall, some prisoners broke into the labs to salvage what they could while others covered equipment and files against water damage. Time after time Bethwig was astonished at the risks the prisoners took to fight the fire or to salvage equipment. He was also struck by their gaunt, wasted appearance and the rags they wore. Most were barefoot or had only the poorest cardboard sandals.

As dawn approached and the fire came under control, he had time to look around. With the exception of the Measurements Building, which had been destroyed, relatively little damage had been done to the area in which the laboratories were clustered. To the south-east the sky above the pine forest pulsated with the reddish hell of raging fires ignited by incendiary bombs, while to the north, in the direction of the test stands where the first strike had been centred, there were only a few isolated columns of smoke visible against the dawn sky. To the west, at mid-island, there was no smoke or flame visible at all, and Bethwig felt momentary relief. Apparently the immense test facilities for the

A-10 were well enough camouflaged to have escaped detection.

With the fire out, Bethwig decided to send one of the prisoners to look for transport to take them south to join those fighting fires in the housing areas, but before he could do so, SS troops burst from the trees and with kicks and blows rounded up the Russians. Bethwig grabbed the non-commissioned officer who seemed to be in charge.

'What the hell do you bastards think you're doing?' he demanded. 'Order your men to stop beating those prisoners now!'

The hauptschauführer jerked his arm away and, ignoring Bethwig, started for the truck. Bethwig ran after him, screaming in anger, the terror and tension of the night released all at once in a blind rage. He yanked the man to a stop and swung him around. 'You rotten son of a bitch, these men have risked their lives . . .'

Without a change of expression, the hauptschauführer struck him in the solar plexus with his Mauser pistol. Bethwig fell to his knees, paralysed, unable to speak or even to breathe. Two SS men picked him up and threw him into the back of the truck with the Russians.

Heinrich Himmler stared down at Franz Bethwig with ill-concealed satisfaction. Behind him, General Dornberger glared and two SS officers waited, their faces carefully non-committal.

'My dear Franz, I seem to find you in the strangest places. Would you care to tell me how you got here?'

Bethwig glared at the reichsführer – at his carefully tailored uniform, at the shining patent boots, at the carefully formed officer's cap perched daintily on his head – and a series of answers, most of them blasphemous, occurred to him. Instead, he got wearily to his feet, trying not to allow the pain to show. He swayed a bit but pushed away the hand one of the SS officers extended. Dornberger's angry glare switched to Himmler.

'Herr Reichsführer, I demand an explanation for this . . . this . . . outrage. It has taken four days to locate this man. Every effort made on his behalf has been frustrated by your . . . your minions. Unless a satisfactory answer is forthcoming immediately, an apology made, and the guilty parties punished severely, I shall register charges against the SS with the OKW. The Army High Command, I can assure you, will be most concerned that such treatment has been accorded one of their employees.'

Himmler heard Dornberger out, nodding now and again as if in agreement. 'Quite right,' he murmured when Dornberger finished. 'Quite right. In fact, I have already begun such an investigation.'

The two officers took Bethwig by the arms to help him from the cell. His legs were weak and threatening to give way, but he shook them off and forced himself to walk down the corridor. Waiting at the end was the hauptschauführer who had arrested him the night of the bombing and gleefully joined in the first beating. Without a change of expression, the man jumped to attention as the officers approached, then reached over and threw open the door. The daylight made Bethwig blink as he turned to the sergeant who stared past his shoulder as if he did not exist. The light brought tears to his eyes, and he saw the sergeant's lip curled in contempt. It was all Bethwig could do to keep from ramming a fist into the man's stomach, but he controlled himself, knowing that he was too weak to make much of an impression.

'You and I have something to settle, don't we?'

The sergeant continued to stare past him, pretending not to have heard. Bethwig lowered his voice and leaned closer:

'Watch out for dark nights and make damned certain I never find you alone, you swine.' Bethwig straightened and, as the sergeant's eyes moved in his direction, said, 'And that, Hauptschauführer Gassner, is a promise.'

Outside, Himmler's limousine waited, but Bethwig passed it by and headed for the tram stop. An officer ran after him, but Bethwig swung around, fists clenched.

'Touch me, you filthy SS swine, and I'll break your back.'

The SS officer stopped abruptly, his astonishment plain, and Bethwig limped to the tram stop and sank down on the bench, refusing to look in the direction of the men clustered around the automobile. After a moment Dornberger detached himself and came over to the bench.

He lit a cigarette and offered it to Franz. 'You know you are only making things worse,' he said as he lit another.

Bethwig inhaled deeply, silently cursing his shaking hands. 'I don't give a damn. Just keep that filthy bastard and his bullies away from me.'

Behind them, the village lay in ruins. The English bombers had done a thorough job. Even in the prison it was possible to find out what had happened by listening to the guards. He knew that his old friend, Walter Thiel, was dead, killed because he had not the heart to continue working under SS pressure any longer. The old man had been too dispirited to attend the dinner for Hanna and so had died in his house with his family. His own test facilities had escaped with no damage at all, and the major test stands along the north coast had been only slightly damaged. The worst disaster had been visited on the Russian POW camp nearby. Eight hundred prisoners had been killed, and Bethwig wondered just how hard the men who saved the Chemistry Building would have worked if they had known that their reward was to be a beating at the hands of the SS or that eight hundred of their number were being killed by their own allies.

'What do you intend to do now?'

Bethwig shrugged. 'What in hell can I do but continue on as before? Himmler had never any intention of letting me come to trial. He would need a better charge than interference with an official in the performance of his duty. In theory, I outrank that bastard hauptschaufũhrer and could charge him with disobedience to, and striking, a superior officer. He could be shot for that. You put Hanna up to trying to talk me into behaving, so you have an idea what this is all about. Himmler was only taking advantage of that fool's mistake to provide me with a warning.' Bethwig fell silent then, considering what would happen should he disobey Himmler once more. He had no doubt that Inge would be the one to suffer, and horribly.

He stood up; the damned trams were never on time and his protest was being spoiled. It was five kilometres or more to his quarters, but he was determined to walk the entire distance rather than ride with Himmler. He was damned if he would provide him another victory. Dornberger watched him shuffle towards the road, then angry as much at himself as at Bethwig, he hurried to catch up.

Himmler stared after them for a moment, considering, then signalled the driver to go on.

Three weeks later the reichsführer appeared unannounced at Peenemünde. Bethwig swore as his secretary told him that there was to be a meeting that afternoon at two o'clock. But at one-thirty the door to his office was thrown open and Himmler strode in. He greeted Bethwig, motioned his aide out, and pulled a side chair around to face him, smiling pleasantly all the while.

'My dear Franz, how good to see you again.' He chuckled with ill-concealed irony and shifted in the chair until he was comfortable. 'You will no doubt have heard that the investigation I instigated concerning your arrest has cleared you completely. Those responsible have been disciplined, so there's an end to it. I know you will not hold it against me, or the SS; any organisation as large as mine has a few misfits who find it difficult to exercise good judgement.'

Himmler smiled again and removed his cap. His nearly bald

head and rimless spectacles only served to increase his resemblance to a toad.

'I have been quite pleased with your work over the past few weeks. I felt that given time you would work out your own problems.' He glanced expectantly at Bethwig who continued to stare at him.

Himmler shrugged. 'I see there is still some animosity on your part. Again, I can do nothing more than apologise for – '

'What have you done with Inge?'

Himmler blinked at him. 'Inge?'

'There is no need to play games, Reichsführer. You know to whom I am referring.'

Himmler sat back and regarded Bethwig. 'You are an outspoken young man. A dangerous tendency these days. Very dangerous.'

Bethwig remained silent, and Himmler nodded. 'Also a courageous young man. I like that. The matter of your concern for the girl was brought to my attention by a mutual friend, and I must admit that with the press of work lately I had quite forgotten about her. Fortunately I have an excellent staff who more than make up for this tendency of mine to forget the human side in the greater concern for the war effort. You will be pleased to know that my staff has seen that nothing has been spared in her continuing treatment. When your concern was brought to my attention, I was informed that she had been removed from the Prague hospital to a more modern treatment facility in Germany. She is now in a country atmosphere with the most modern facilities to hand. She certainly does not lack for attention, and her activities are supervised day and night. I am told she is making excellent progress and has proved most popular with the staff. Recreational activities are considered most important, and there are frequent impromptu entertainments at which the young lady is considered a star performer. I assure you, you need have no worries concerning her well-being. When I enquired as to when she could be released, the director assured me it would be soon, perhaps within a few months. Her progress is that good.'

Himmler smiled and sat back, noting the evident relief that swept across Bethwig's face. He nearly thanked the reichsführer but caught himself in time. 'However, I did not travel here today to discuss your personal life. You will be appointed director of the A-Ten project today. Herr Doktor von Braun has agreed to assume complete control of the A-Four project, and General Dornberger will assume overall administrative control of the entire research centre.'

Bethwig started to protest, then, realising how useless it would be, shut his mouth. Himmler nodded, pleased.

'I fear that among these pleasant announcements there is one that will not be so well received. It is necessary that the A-Ten project be redirected. The moon will no longer be your target. That phase has been cancelled.'

Bethwig stared, as if not quite believing what he had heard. He shook his head. 'Cancel the A-Ten . . . ?'

Himmler nodded, his pince-nez flashing in the autumn sunshine pouring through the windows. 'I am afraid so.'

'But why, in the name of God? The project is Germany's best hope for winning – '

Himmler cut him off. 'Normally I do not condescend to explain my actions,' he snapped. 'But as you have worked so hard, you do perhaps deserve that much. You are aware, no doubt, that heavy water is a vital ingredient of our atomic research programme?' Without waiting for an answer, Himmler went on:

'We obtain our supplies from the Norsk Hydroelectric Plant in Norway, or did until recently. This past spring Allied and Norwegian saboteurs succeeded in destroying the Rjukan facility. As a consequence, the Führer has, and quite rightly, removed all priority from atomic research. Therefore, even if your moon rocket were ready in time, it would be weaponless. No need, therefore, to continue with the monstrous expense the project entails.'

Bethwig was speechless; the last thing in the world he had expected was cancellation of the Lunar phase of the project. Himmler spread his hands. 'I am sorry, but there is nothing I can do. The Führer himself has given the order.'

'But . . . but . . . the project, the lunar base does not need the atomic bomb to be successful.' Bethwig tried to protest. 'I explained that in the beginning. Any high explosive will have its destructive force magnified by the – '

'Yes, yes.' Himmler waved a hand. 'A rock, a plain ordinary rock, would also have a great destructive force because of the speed with which it strikes the earth. I understand all that. However, my staff have conducted extensive economic studies and have concluded that the money would be better spent on a less cumbersome and cheaper system. Now, you recall I said only that the moon landing phase of the project has been curtailed. For one thing, your time estimates are far, far too optimistic. The war will have been won by the time your first rocket lands on the moon. However, if the project is returned to its original objective – that of launching massive quantities of high explosive against the eastern coast of the United States – the A-Ten rocket can, according to revised projections by my staff, be made ready by late 1944 or early 1945. The atomic bomb will not be needed, as thirty thousand kilograms of high explosive, which I am assured can be placed aboard these large rockets, will do the job, particularly when they strike in large numbers. American commitment to European wars has never been strong, and in any event, the moral fibre of the American nation is far too weak to withstand such a sustained bombing attack. In the meantime Professor von Braun's A-Four rocket will be devastating England.'

'But there is no sense, no reason, to cancel the lunar base phase. We are on schedule. In fact, we will test the fourth in the series, the final rocket, in two months. It will be launched into an orbit around the earth with . . .'

Himmler stood up, all traces of good humour now gone. 'I have given you an order, Herr Doktor Bethwig. You will be good enough to carry it out.' He picked up his cap and headed for the door.

'We will talk further of the changes to be made in both the A-Ten and A-Four projects at this afternoon's conference. I wanted you to be aware of the direction of my thinking so that you could prepare yourself accordingly.

'I believe, sir, you owe me your utmost loyalty. I have quashed very serious charges against you, and against Doktor von Braun at your request. And at great personal expense I have taken it upon myself to see that this half-witted woman of whom you are so fond has been given the best possible care. Accordingly, I will tolerate no further outbursts or disagreements over my orders. Do I make myself entirely clear?'

Bethwig, still reeling from the casual announcement of the cancellation of the moon landing, could only nod. Himmler gave him a final stare and, without another word, left the office.

London October 1943

It has the feel of the last day of Indian summer, Jan Memling thought as he crossed Bayswater Road and sought, among the maze of streets north of Hyde Park, the address he had been given by Brigadier Simon-Benet the afternoon before. The sun burned down with unexpected heat, and a lazy stillness hung over the city. Traffic noises seemed distant, and here and there he could hear children laughing as they played. He was sweating in his wool uniform and feeling quite light-headed before he found the correct address in Norfolk Crescent.

From the outside it seemed like any other Victorian town house. The bombing had not devastated the West End as it had other parts of the city, and the area retained the feeling of 'pre-war England' which the papers were beginning to write about as if it had been a distant and shining time rather than the tail end of a worldwide depression.

He rang the bell, and the elderly porter who opened the door nodded him inside where a heavily armed Royal Marine sat in shadow. An officer stepped out of an anteroom to check his credentials and compare his name and photograph with those on his list. When the officer was satisfied, the porter conducted him along the hall and opened the door to the library.

Six men sat around a polished table spread with maps and photographs. Simon-Benet jumped up when he spotted Memling, and came forward with a smile. 'Gentlemen, this is the young officer I was telling you about.'

He introduced Memling to the men sitting at the table. He recognised only two of them: Viscount Cherwell, the Prime Minister's scientific adviser, and Duncan Sandys, Churchill's son-in-law and head of the new committee charged with the investigation of German rocket development under the code name *Operation Crossbow*.

Sandys smiled and stood to shake his hand. 'Congratulations on your promotion, Major. I am certain you earned it. Brigadier Simon-Benet has told me of your latest adventure. An amazing piece of work. Gentlemen' – he turned to the others at the table – 'in case you are not aware, Major Memling has just returned from a sojourn in Germany.'

One or two eyebrows went up at that, and Sandys added, 'From Peenemünde, to be exact, where he actually worked for two weeks before escaping to Sweden.'

There were mild exclamations of surprise.

'Since his return,' Sandys continued, 'unfortunately too late to advise Bomber Command on the selection of targets, Major Memling has been reviewing the after-raid photographs. I have asked him here today to comment on his conclusions in light of his recent visit, and to describe to us what he learned at Peenemünde.'

'I am certain,' Simon-Benet suggested in a dry voice that told Memling all he needed to know about the tensions around the table, 'that when the major has finished, we will have a few surprises to deal with.'

'I dare say,' Cherwell murmured, and nodded towards Memling. 'Perhaps the major would begin?'

Memling spoke for an hour, describing in detail the design and number of rocket engines produced on a monthly basis, noting that the figures were still on a pre-production basis; the type of testing to which they were subjected; and their specifications, including materials. He also described the launching he had observed and the engine test firing.

Memling hesitated before continuing. He and Simon-Benet had discussed the advisability of mentioning the new rocket project he had uncovered. The brigadier was insistent that he do so; but Memling was reluctant, recalling the reaction given his earlier reports. With a glance at the brigadier, who encouraged him with a smile, he related his conversations with Ernst Mundt and presented his estimate of the size and capabilities of the new rocket. Memling could see by the pained expression that passed across Viscount Cherwell's face that his report was being received much as he had expected. When he suggested that such a rocket might have a transatlantic range, it was only Simon-Benet's stern glance that prevented an interruption.

When he finished, Simon-Benet did not allow the briefest lapse and immediately launched into a description of Memling's escape. The brigadier had somehow got hold of his after-action report to Commando 2, to which he was still officially attached, and narrated in detail all the events, including his killing of the four SD men. There was polite applause and smiles from the military men present, while the civilians looked a bit uncomfortable.

A slim, quiet man in elegantly tailored clothes asked to direct a question to Memling, and Sandys nodded agreement.

'This new rocket you speak of sounds quite an advance over the smaller one the Germans refer to as A-Four. I would assume it would require a great deal more in the way of support services, such as increased launching areas. Those used for the A-Four are readily detectable, now that we know what to look for. Why is it, then, that we have not spotted such an area for – I believe you called it the A-Ten?'

Memling took a deep breath. He had expected this question. 'Such a launching site does exist. I found indications of it in earlier photographs. The site is in the central southern portion of Usedom, well away from the Luftwaffe or A-Four launch sites. It occupies an area normally referred to on our maps as marshland. Few photos have been taken of this area, as overflight time is necessarily limited, and the concentration has been on known launching sites and test facilities on the northern and Baltic coastal sections of the island. The Germans are, as we all know, masters of camouflage, and the wide marshy area is easy to disguise. We have asked that the next recon flight include this area.'

The man studied him for a moment, then nodded, clearly unconvinced, and Memling felt a flash of anger at the man's dismissal of the information simply because it did not fit his pre-conceived theories. Sandys started to ask his assessment of the bomb damage, but Viscount Cherwell interrupted with a question.

'Major, correct me if I am in error, but are you not the one who first reported the work in Germany on large rocket engines, in, I believe, 1938?'

'Yes, sir.'

'And again in 1940, as the result of another daring mission behind enemy lines, this time in Belgium, I believe. At that time you supplied an estimate of the capability of rocket engines seen in, I seem to recall, Liège, was it not?'

Memling nodded, glancing quickly to Simon-Benet who was scowling down the table at Viscount Cherwell.

'Major, you and I have debated the status of the Nazi rocket programme before, and you are well acquainted with my opinion that Germany cannot spare the economic resources for a research and development programme of such magnitude. Now I freely admit' – he smiled in condescension – 'that my opinion may be coloured by my own prejudices in this matter, and I would ask you to stop and consider whether, in view of the amazing series of coincidences by which you have ferreted out what you believe to be the secret of enemy rocket research, your own opinion and conclusions are not coloured by your personal prejudices as well?'

'I say!' the brigadier exploded, but Memling's calm answer stopped his further objections.

'You may be right, Viscount Cherwell. And in your position I would be inclined to ask the same question. Since you first raised your objections nearly a year ago I have given it a great deal of thought. As you may recall, I described in a formal paper how sufficient alcohol could be produced for fuel, and I believe my estimates have since been verified by independent intelligence means.'

'Not to my satisfaction, I'm afraid,' Viscount Cherwell interrupted.

Memling ignored the comment and continued: 'What you say

about limited resources and their distribution among various war-effort goals is quite correct. My only objection to your conclusions is that they presuppose a logical and efficient effort directed towards planning. If that were the case, I am certain the rocket, at least at this stage of development, would not be seen as economically feasible.'

He could see that Cherwell was taken aback by his answer, and pressed on: 'I have spent nearly a year's time in German-controlled territory, and during that time I never once saw a single bit of evidence to suggest that efficient and effective planning had taken, or was taking, place. Rather I saw the exact opposite. Foreign workers in most industries are treated little better than slaves. The Peenemünde organisation is the single exception, and I would suggest even that will change as the SS becomes more deeply involved. I could begin to detect the same fear there that I found in Belgium . . . and believe me,' Memling blurted in a rare moment of candour, 'I am an expert on fear. Ernst Mundt was an exception, and I hate to think what has happened to him because of me. As additional support for my theory that planning is neither logical nor efficient in the Third Reich, consider the fact that Jews are persecuted in Germany despite the fact that the Jewish population formed the single largest pool of industrial and scientific talent Germany possessed. Instead of being allowed to play a part in the war effort, they have become ruthlessly exploited slave labourers confined to concentration camps. That suggests a system groping through a tangle of political and ideological nonsense.

'The rocket project and its extent are consistent, in my view, with the Nazi predilection for grandiose schemes. It is being called a terror weapon, but I have serious doubts, from what Mundt told me, that the Army High Command views it as such, or even as the secret weapon that will win the war. Instead, they seem to think it a useful, if expensive, adjunct. But it will see service, and win the war or not, it will cause great damage to our cities and populations. I have seen it rising above the trees with its engine flaming, and it frightened me to death. If Mundt is correct and the even more powerful rocket is successful, then all major cities within its five- or six-thousand-mile range are doomed to complete destruction.'

Viscount Cherwell stared at him for a moment, but before he could ask a further question one of the other men at the table, a civilian official from the Home Office, asked for Memling's assessment of the bombing raid on Peenemünde and how it might have affected operational use of the weapon. The air vice-marshal representing Bomber Command stared long and hard as he began.

'You must realise that what I say comes only from studying photographs and relating it to what I learned while on the ground. Briefly, the raid, while it appears to have been pressed home with great skill, missed damaging the vital installations on the island only because they were skilfully camouflaged, a fact I did not realise until I saw the aerial photographs. My assessment, then, after two weeks of study, is that development has probably been slowed only three to four months at best.'

Memling gave Viscount Cherwell a long steady look. 'I recommend, therefore, that three projects be put in motion as soon as possible. First, organise an effective tactical fighter bomber force to seek out and destroy the rockets before they can be launched. Second, warn the Americans and Canadians about the A-Ten. And third, bomb Peenemünde again and again until it is utterly destroyed. To fail in any of these three will subject – '

'Preposterous!' The air vice-marshal snorted. 'CIU assures us that incalculable damage was done and that the work will have been thrown back by at least a year if not more. Our own Air Intelligence assessment concurs.'

'Were any of your people on the ground at Peenemünde, Air Vice-Marshal?' Simon-Benet murmured.

'You know damned well they were not, sir. However, they are trained in the assessment of bomb damage from photographs and have had a great deal of experience at the job. With all due respect to Major Memling, even though he has been there he does not have the skills required to interpret after-raid photographs. My people do.'

'Is that why Bomber Command's raids on aircraft plants have resulted in increased production of German fighter aircraft?' As he made the remark the brigadier got to his feet, expression angry. 'I would suggest, gentlemen, that we stop trying to protect our own backsides in this matter. Time is running out. Soon those damnable rockets will be raining down on Britain and God knows where else. How are we to explain to the British people that we were not prepared? Since 1938 we have had warning after warning, and all have been ignored. MI-Six, of which you speak so highly, Air Vice-Marshal, buried Major Memling's reports because they sounded too far-fetched to be believed by his superior – who, I might add, read classics at Exeter College. This in spite of the fact that MI-Six received copies of a document delivered to our embassy in Oslo in September 1939 which outlined the entire Nazi military research programme. In addition, both Polish and Czech resistance groups have sent reams of wireless data bearing out what Major Memling has learned. And just this past spring MI-Six distributed the transcript of a conversation between Generals Thoma and Cruewell in the London Cage in which Thoma expressed surprise that London was not yet in ruins from rocket bombardment. He even described to General Cruewell the rocket launchings he had witnessed at a firing range in Germany!'

Simon-Benet glared around the table. 'This man has risked his life twice now – no, three times – to bring us information concerning Germany's rocket work, and so far his only thanks have been a questioning of his motives.'

Afterwards it seemed to Memling that no one's mind had been changed even the slightest. All three proposals had been rejected completely, and he felt the meeting, like his mission in Germany, had been a waste of time and effort.

Sandys asked both him and Simon-Benet to remain after the others left, then disappeared with the brigadier, leaving Jan in the library. He was exhausted, but the tension engendered by the meeting would not leave him and he paced the room as the shadows deepened.

Part of him yearned for refuge in the flat in Montague Street, yet, at the same time, he was not all that anxious to go back to the strained atmosphere present since his return. Janet had tried hard to recreate their first days of marriage; that much he recognised. The truth of the matter, if he would only have allowed himself to admit it, was that he was suffering from shock. He had had far more contact with the enemy than most other soldiers and for far longer, and the nature and cruelty of those incidents had all worked on his subconscious, twisting his perceptions and straining his capacity to remain a thinking, rational being. Memling, like other soldiers constantly exposed to killing, was discovering that it had become too easy, that one had to struggle against the temptation to kill for the sake of killing or simply sparing oneself the trouble of dealing with prisoners. The deliberate torture and murder of Francine, coupled with his own execution of the four SD men, had driven him to the verge of nervous exhaustion in the Swedish detention camp. He had not recognised the symptoms for what they were, but had ascribed them to nervousness and apprehension as a result of his narrow escape and the pressure of the information he carried. Once Commander Fleming had told him that the bombing raid had been carried out, a great weight had been lifted from him, and a deep lethargy had set in on his return to London.

Janet was the first to notice. He had slept for twenty-six hours after she had found him in the hall, and when he had awakened late the next night, she had brought him tea and scrambled eggs. Afterwards he had bathed and shaved and, returning to the bedroom, found the window thrown wide and the room filled with the soft summer air. Janet had wanted to recreate the night he had proposed to her, and grinned impishly as he got into bed beside her, only to find himself impotent. The shock to his self-esteem was crippling. Since that night, he had avoided her, finding excuses to be absent or taking refuge in anger to hide his fear. He did not know what to do to break the impasse, short of admitting to her that he was frightened to death, and that he would never do. Not to anyone.

Sandys returned an hour later to find Memling asleep. He woke him reluctantly, and after a quick bite, the three of them sat long in the drawing-room discussing the implications of the German rocket programme and their inability to make the committee realise the great danger it posed to the entire Allied war effort. Both Sandys and the brigadier were pessimistic, and the discussion turned to ways they might circumvent Viscount Cherwell's influence on the Prime Minister.

'I don't understand it.' Sandys smacked the table in exasperation. 'He is a brilliant scientist. Brilliant! But for some reason he is totally blind regarding the German rockets. Even after seeing the photographs. It is beyond belief.'

Simon-Benet gave Memling a smile to remind him of their discussion.

It was after midnight when they emerged, and Memling was drained. Sandys and the brigadier stood talking beside the car, and Memling leaned against the railing drawing deep lungfuls of cold night air. The wind had stiffened and was now whirling dead leaves across the square. The stuffy library had left him with a raging headache, and in spite of the liberal infusions of whisky and water that Sandys had poured, his throat ached. A chill shook him, and he pushed himself up and took a few steps along the gravelled walk, wishing the two would finish their conversation. He was dead tired and wanted nothing so much as his own bed and sleep.

Sandys said good night to them a few moments later and returned to the building. Simon-Benet motioned Memling into the car and gave the driver the address.

Memling lay back against the upholstery, eyes closed as the brigadier droned on about the impression he had made on Sandys; his head was spinning and he was half-asleep when the car drew up in front of his door. He mumbled a good night to Simon-Benet and shuffled towards the steps. Jan found his key and got the door open with difficulty. The flight of stairs seemed endless, and he could not make his key fit in the door to the flat. Janet heard his fumbling and came to open it. She took one look at his perspiring face and helped him directly to bed, undressing him and then covering him with a quilt. By this time he was shivering and his teeth were chattering. Janet got into bed beside him and took his shivering body in her arms. The room seemed to spin and bob, and for a moment Memling was frightened that he was still aboard the fishing boat caught up in the storm. Then Janet's face swam into view and he relaxed, knowing everything had come out right.

The next morning Janet phoned the hospital, and Memling was removed from the flat for treatment of exhaustion and incipient pneumonia.

Berlin March 1944

Military police were everywhere, waving batons and shouting at drivers, urging them through the tangle of debris, and cursing civilians and soldiers alike. Peering through the mud-spattered window, Bethwig caught sight of an army officer arguing heatedly with an SS obersturmführer at a roadblock. The army officer was pointing to three of his men being held at gunpoint. The obersturmführer waved him away and, when the army officer continued to argue, turned abruptly to his squad and snapped an order. Before the astonished officer could react, the SS had surrounded his company. As his car finally broke out of the crush, Bethwig had a last glimpse of the soldiers being disarmed.

'The breakdown is beginning,' General Dornberger grunted, peering over Bethwig's shoulder. 'The SS is overstepping itself, and the army is powerless to stop it – lacks the courage to do so.'

They had been driving since eight that morning, moving through heavy snow and rain, dodging military traffic, and enduring frequent stops at Gestapo checkpoints where their papers were examined and re-examined until they had become dog-eared. It was a revelation to Franz how far out of esteem military personnel had fallen of late. The Gestapo and SS were contemptuous of their documents and frequently made them wait while telephone calls were placed to obtain approval to allow them to pass.

Munich had suffered heavily from a British bombing raid the night before, and fires still raged inside the city. Only bad weather prevented the American follow-up raid, Franz thought. They spent two hours inching through traffic before the driver was able to turn off on the road to Berchtesgaden, which they reached just before 6 p.m. As soon as they were in their hotel room Dornberger rang up General Buhle, chief of the Army Staff at Hitler's headquarters, to announce their arrival. He was told to remain where he was.

Dornberger gave Bethwig a puzzled glance as he replaced the receiver. 'I would certainly like to know what this is all about, Franz.'

Franz had been in Dornberger's office in Schwedt-on-Oder that morning, ready to begin a long-delayed discussion about priorities and personnel which promised to last most of the day, when the summons to Berchtesgaden came. Rather than waste the opportunity, Dornberger asked Franz to come along, and they had conducted their discussion in the back seat of Dornberger's Opel Admiral. It was the first time in months that Bethwig had been further away from Peenemünde than Schwedt, and he was shocked at what he had seen. Their route had taken them through Berlin to Hof and on to Munich, and he was startled to see that vast sections of the capital were in ruins. The newspapers and radio had reported the bombing of the cities but always the raids were said to be failures and the toll of enemy bombers exceptionally high. Yet the industrial suburbs were bombed-out ruins, and the city centre devastated. Bethwig could not get over the sight of shrapnel holes in familiar city buildings and bomb craters in the Park am Zoo. The autobahns seemed to have been targeted as well, and on the drive south they had passed a military convoy stopped by the side of the road. Several vehicles were burning, and a line of snow-dusted bodies could be seen beside an ambulance, proof that in spite of the Luftwaffe, Allied fighter bombers were managing to penetrate this far into the country.

Fifteen minutes later General Buhle entered their hotel room. His heavy face was grim, and he wasted no time on preliminaries, barely acknowledging the introduction to Bethwig.

'This morning at eight o'clock,' he told them abruptly, 'Professor von Braun, Ernst Mundt, and another engineer, Helmuth Gottrup, were arrested for sabotage. They were removed to Gestapo headquarters in Stettin.'

The news stunned both men, and they stared at each other as Buhle went on to tell Dornberger that he was to meet with Field Marshal Keitel at nine the following morning. Buhle offered his sympathy and privately told Dornberger not to expect much help from Keitel. Having refused a drink, he left abruptly, as if by remaining longer he would be contaminated.

As Buhle predicted, Dornberger's meeting with Keitel was a farce. 'He told me point-blank he was afraid for his position,' Dornberger stormed as the heavy automobile raced north again.

'"Himmler is waiting for me to make one mistake,"' Dornberger mimicked Keitel. '"He will have me removed and the officer corps will have lost its last direct pipeline to the Führer. Then the reichsführer will have it all his way."' The general slammed a hand on the seat of the car. 'Keitel has not yet realised that Himmler already has everything except the Führer's position. Then, heaven help Germany, we will have a madman at the helm.'

Keitel had, Dornberger told Bethwig, agreed to arrange with Himmler's aide for Dornberger to see the reichsführer, but Himmler had refused, preferring instead that Dornberger meet with SS General Ernst Kaltenbrunner, Heydrich's successor. When Dornberger then demanded that Keitel issue an order for the release of the three scientists on grounds that as army employees they were not subject to Gestapo arrest, Keitel refused, claiming he could not interfere in an ongoing investigation.

Kaltenbrunner, SS chief of security for Berlin, was not available. Instead his deputy, SS General Heinrich Müller, was waiting for them in Kaltenbrunner's office. After Dornberger stated the reason for his visit, General Müller rolled his eyes towards the ceiling, as if seeking sympathy, and denied any knowledge of the circumstances surrounding von Braun's arrest. He was a huge, florid-faced man who obviously depended more upon physical size and demeanour than brains. Bethwig watched him in fascination, thinking that in his presence one had the feeling that a physical assault was imminent, and admitted that he was, indeed, intimidated.

Dornberger adopted a reasonable tone, explaining that the three men must have been arrested by mistake, that they were absolutely indispensable to the A-4 project which was in its most critical phase. He asked for their immediate release. When he finished, Müller eyed him carefully, then turned towards Bethwig.

'And what is the reason for your presence in my office, Herr Bethwig?'

His tone was belligerent enough to make Bethwig bridle, but he kept his temper under control. 'Simply to support General Dornberger. I am a scientist and an engineer and can – '

'Yes, yes.' Müller waved a hand. 'I know all about you, Herr Doktor. In fact, I am surprised that you were not arrested with von Braun. Our file on you is even thicker than his, or General Dornberger's,' he finished with a smirk.

'If you are attempting to intimidate either of us, let me remind you that as military personnel we are – '

'Not subject to the authority of the SS. Yes, I know.' Müller waved a weary hand. 'And I would remind you of the position in which Doktor von Braun now finds himself, for the second time. I would have thought one warning sufficient.'

Bethwig could endure the man's arrogance no longer. He sprang to his feet, slammed a fist down on Müller's desk, and had the satisfaction of seeing the SS officer jump.

'Not those ridiculous sabotage charges again! You fool!' he shouted. 'Do you work for the Allies or for Germany?' Bethwig leaned forward until his face was inches from Müller's. 'Well, two can play this game,' he snarled. 'Perhaps an investigation into your own activities would show who the traitors are. What do you suppose a thorough investigation of all those fine houses, expensive automobiles, and greedy women you surround yourself with would disclose? The Führer himself might even take a personal interest, especially when he contrasts his own way of life with the hedonism so beloved by the SS.' The accusation was simply a shot in the dark, but the odds were on his side; and when he saw Müller's expression transformed for an instant he knew that he had struck home.

Dornberger stared at Müller, making no attempt to calm Bethwig who was close to raving. The SS general had leaned back in his chair under Bethwig's assault, and Bethwig leaned closer still and jabbed a finger directly into his face.

'You issue orders for the release of those three or I will go directly to the Führer. It will give me a great deal of pleasure to see you squirm as you try and explain why you are delaying the development of a weapon which the Führer himself has proclaimed will win the war for Germany. I am certain he will also be interested in an examination of your personal finances and those of other officers in the SS!'

As he subsided into his chair, exhausted by his outburst, Bethwig could see indecision grinding its way through Müller's brain, and he thought with contempt that in the Machiavellian world of the SS one could never be certain where one's support lay.

The SD commander stared at the angry Bethwig, wondering just how much fact there was in his accusation and how much guesswork. He knew that Bethwig's father had high connections in the party, and it was rumoured that the younger Bethwig worked directly for the reichsführer on a secret project; something also to do with rockets. There were too many loose ends, Müller decided. Since he had no direct orders from Himmler on how to proceed – there had been only a telephone call from an aide instructing him to see Dornberger – he decided to stall until he could clarify the situation.

'Gentlemen' – he tried a winning smile – 'I apologise for my abruptness. It is a bad habit caused by overwork. If I seemed insensitive, it was because I have had little sleep in the past two weeks. As to this matter of your scientists, let me say that I will look into it immediately. As you may know, they were arrested by the Gestapo and are currently in custody in Stettin. The SD had nothing to do with their arrest. It is my understanding, though, that they were arrested because they spoke publicly of the fact that it had never been their intention to build war rockets, that everything they had done was directed towards their personal goal of travel in space.'

Müller was beginning to regain some of his confidence as he talked; and studying both men, he decided that a touch of the lash was in order to remind them who he was.

'They have, in effect, admitted to swindling the Reich out of millions of marks to further their own ends. I might add that the first notation in the file was entered personally by Reinhard Heydrich, in August of 1941. If convicted of those charges, I need hardly tell you gentlemen of their fate. The wire noose is reserved for traitors.'

Bethwig stared at him in astonishment as he recalled that dinner discussion with Heydrich in Swinemünde three – no, by God, only a little over two years before. As long ago as that, the SD had been preparing . . .

This time it was Dornberger's turn to explode, repeating his demand that they be released immediately or, at least, turned over to civil authorities for investigation of the charges. The argument grew vicious with Müller threatening to bring charges against both men based on their own extensive files, which he kept tapping with a large, meaty forefinger, until Dornberger challenged him to do so. At that point Müller, recalling his previous decision not to be pushed into mistakes, backed off and once more became conciliatory, promising to do what he could to have the three men released.

They drove from SS headquarters in Prinz Albrechtstrasse to Tempelhof where Bethwig boarded a transport for Peenemünde, while Dornberger returned to the city for a hurried meeting with Major Klammroth of the OKW Counter-intelligence Department. As the aircraft made its way north at low level to avoid marauding fighters Bethwig stared out at the blank greyness, wondering if Himmler had somehow learned that their carefully guarded lunar project was still very much alive. If so, there was more than a grain of truth in the Gestapo charges, and God help them all.

A car was waiting for him at the airfield. Franz was tired beyond belief and went directly to his new house overlooking the storm-lashed beach north of Trassenheide, the only positive result of his association with the SS. The house was cold, and he lit the fire laid by the Polish housekeeper. Warming himself before the fireplace, he watched the waves tumbling on to the beach, depressed by all that had happened.

The A-10's fourth launch, his first as project director, had been a near disaster. The new directional gyroscope had worked perfectly both in static tests and on the A-4 vehicle that had been made available to them. It had failed, however, in the A-10, causing it to veer off course in the first seconds of flight and head inland over Germany. The controller had no choice but to destroy the rocket. The power plant had performed flawlessly, and that in itself was some consolation. His engineers had subsequently discovered that the gyroscope mounting had given way under the unexpectedly high vibration from the new turbo-pumps used to pressurise the fuel tank. Steps had been taken both to reduce the vibration and to increase the strength of the mounting. In a marginal notation on his last report Himmler had professed himself satisfied with his explanation, yet now there was this business with von Braun less than a week later.

An open Mercedes touring car of the type the Gestapo was so fond of drew up outside the house at three-thirty that afternoon, just as dusk was closing in. The rear door was opened by the driver, and a figure emerged clutching a small bag. The driver pointed at the house and, without waiting, got back into the car and drove away. The failing light was uncertain, and the gathering fog obscured detail. Puzzled, Bethwig waited on the porch as the bent figure limped up the path. It was a woman, he saw, and as she looked at him through her heavy black veil Bethwig realised it was Inge. For an instant he could not believe it; he stood as if frozen while the woman stared at him with no sign of recognition. She lifted the veil, and a stray lock of hair escaped from beneath her hat; it was no longer the lovely amber he remembered so well but a coarse grey. The dull light served to emphasise her lined, wasted skin, and when she gave him a tentative smile, he saw that her teeth were badly discoloured and broken. As if in a dream, Bethwig helped her into the house and sat her down before the fireplace. The cruel drive in the open car had left her cold and shivering, and he poured tea from the kettle resting on the hob. Inge held the cup in both hands and, staring about her at the comfortable furniture, the clean rugs, the firewood neatly stacked on the stoop, began to weep. When Bethwig helped her remove her coat, he saw that she was wearing only a short-sleeved dress of coarse sacking. Inge coughed, a deep racking cough that doubled her frail body, and when he helped her into a chair, he saw the eight-digit number tattooed on her left arm.

Himmler's mocking assurances flooded back: 'Nothing has been spared in her continuing treatment . . . does not lack for attention . . . recreational activities supervised day and night . . .' In his fury he could think of no curse, no defilement sufficient for the reichsführer. All the time that he was being reassured, she must have been in a concentration camp, a plaything for the guards.

He looked at the wasted, dying woman, and a mixture of sadness and anger surged through him at the knowledge that he lacked the power to sentence Himmler to eternal damnation.

Scotland–Germany–Poland June 1944

When Brigadier Oliver Simon-Benet found Major Jan Memling at the small training camp deep in the hills above the Firth of Forth, he was seated on an upturned jerry can studying a map. The brigadier noted as he slithered down the slope that exercise and sun had agreed with Memling. He was tanned and had filled out his uniform again. The brigadier recalled what Memling had looked like four months before when released from hospital: all skin and bones, and with a pallor that would have shocked an undertaker.

An enlisted man called Memling's attention to the brigadier's approach, and Jan stood slowly. Simon-Benet tapped his cap with his swagger stick. 'Morning, Major. You're looking quite fit.'

'Good morning, sir.' Memling's manner was polite and icily formal, and he expressed no surprise at seeing him here in the north of Scotland. Obviously, the brigadier thought, he still blames me for that nonsense with the *Crossbow* committee last winter.

He looked around. Two non-commissioned officers were seated nearby. Both men had noted the red shoulder tabs denoting staff assignment and lost interest. The other man, a lance corporal, was busy repairing some type of electrical gear. The midsummer sun burned in an absolutely cloudless sky, and the temperature was in the mid-eighties. There was no breeze at all. Brownish heather covered hills that rolled away in every direction. Dark-green stands of trees filled the valley below. Simon-Benet wiped the sweatband of his service cap with a handkerchief, then his perspiring face.

'Can you be spared for a few moments, Major? I must speak with you.'

Memling gave him a resentful stare, then nodded and called to one of the sergeants to take over. They went on down the slope to the valley floor where a small stream trickled and chuckled over mossy stones, and Simon-Benet lowered himself to the ground in the shade of a twisted oak.

'I should get away from London more often,' he commented in an attempt to break through Memling's reserve. 'Too many fine restaurants. I'm getting fat and sadly out of shape.'

Memling, who had squatted down nearby, now and again glanced up the slope. 'What can I do for you, Brigadier?' he asked finally.

'Stop acting like a silly schoolgirl, for one thing,' Simon-Benet snorted.

Memling glared but said nothing.

'I was not responsible for your removal from the *Crossbow* committee, nor was I to blame for their discrediting your reports. You know as well as I that Viscount Cherwell is convinced Germany cannot support the effort to construct war rockets, and nothing is going to change his mind until after the first of them falls on London. The other faction on the committee feel that you had originally underestimated the size and capacity of the German rockets. They point to their own reports showing the A-4 to have a carrying capacity of ten tons or more of high explosive as determined by photographic measurements. Until we actually capture one, there will be no convincing them. Your removal was effected because you were in hospital while I was in Washington trying to convince the Americans of the dangers of the new rocket you uncovered. Those people, I might say, are even more pigheaded than our own. Even with General Eisenhower's endorsement, I couldn't make them understand.'

The brigadier paused a moment. At least the man is listening, he thought, even though he refuses to look in my direction. 'Look here, Jan, I know that you were under an intense strain, but the doctor gave you a clean bill of health. On that basis Combined Operations agreed to put you back on active duty. So I think it time you stopped acting like a wounded prima donna. You know as well as I that London committees are intensely political animals. It was a clear-cut trade where you were concerned. Certain people on the *Crossbow* committee felt that you were not technically competent, and you must face the fact that without a union card, in other words, a diploma, they will always think that. No one spends years taking specialised training, only to admit that a non-trained person might be as competent as he. Therefore, in order to gain support for the London anti-aircraft defence and the tactical fighter sweeps, I had to go along. You were the trade goods, Jan, and as much as your feelings were hurt, I do not regret my decision for one moment. The defence of London and its ten million people is of far more significance than your wounded feelings.'

Memling nodded as he finished speaking, but said nothing. Simon-Benet looked away. 'I suppose I do sound like a headmaster, my boy, but damn it, it's true.'

Memling stood up, a trace of a smile struggling through. 'I must admit I have spent the last few months feeling sorry for myself. The spurned hero relegated to Coventry, I suppose.' He stared off towards the slope where his CP had been set up. 'I suppose Sergeant McElroy has the situation well in hand. Let's walk a bit, loosen you up.'

They hiked along the stream in silence until the slope turned sharply upwards.

'Are you going to tell me what brought you up here, or do I have to play guessing games?' He simply could not stay mad at Simon-Benet. There was just something irresistibly likeable about the man.

The brigadier chuckled. On the flight up from London he had rehearsed all manner of appeals ranging from patriotism to self-interest. Now, on the spur of the moment, he decided to be straightforward:

'We've discovered the Germans are firing numerous A-Four

rockets on a range established in Poland. It is MI-Six's guess that they're training operational crews, and Polish Intelligence seems to bear this out. In late May, the twenty-fifth to be exact, a rocket was fired from near a town named Blizna. It apparently went a bit off course and crashed beside the River Bug. The Poles got to it first, hid it from the Jerry recovery team, then spirited the whole thing away. From the reports we have, the damned rocket is completely intact, if a little bent. I've proposed to the committee that we bring it out of Poland. They agreed, and the Prime Minister endorsed the mission. Special Operations Executive has agreed to lay on a special aircraft. I want you to go along as the committee's representative and take charge of the affair.'

Memling listened in silence, then shook his head. 'Sorry, Brigadier, but the answer is no.'

Simon-Benet had expected a bit of hedging, perhaps some argument, but certainly not a firm, outright refusal. His temper got the best of him then. 'Damn it all, Jan, I thought I'd made it clear it was time to stop playing the jilted schoolgirl. This is – '

Memling interrupted: 'Brigadier, I don't give one good Goddamn in hell what the committee thinks, or what they don't think. I won't go! I can't,' he finished lamely.

After a moment the brigadier asked, 'Why ever not?'

Memling had turned away, his shoulders hunched, refusing to say anything more. Simon-Benet waited, not quite understanding. After a moment he said softly, 'I saw Janet just before I left London. She's looking well.'

Memling gave no sign of having heard.

'She asked me to give you her love.'

'Look here,' Memling shouted, 'let's leave Janet out of this, shall we? She has nothing to do with your being here.'

'All right, Jan. Let's get back to the subject at hand. Why are you refusing? As a superior officer, I'm entitled to an explanation.'

Memling walked off a bit, then turned and came back. 'Damn it all, what more do you want from me? If you want to know so badly, I'll tell you! I won't go because I've bloody well lost my nerve. The idea of going anywhere near a German gives me the shakes. I'm scared to death, damn it!' Memling was on the verge of tears as he stared at Simon-Benet.

So that's it, the brigadier thought. My God, and he hid it so well. No wonder . . . and he began to laugh.

Memling blinked in astonishment. 'You think cowardice is funny?' he demanded in outrage.

Simon-Benet had to lean against a rock for support, and it was a few moments before he could bring himself under control. 'No,

Jan,' he finally managed. 'I don't. I don't at all. And I am sure I do not know whatever gave you the idea that you were a coward. Good God in heaven, you have to be one of the bravest men I've ever met. If I could, I'd recommend you for the Victoria Cross.' He paused to examine Memling's anguished face.

'Everything makes more sense now. Janet suggested that you had been having . . . ah . . . certain difficulties, and she felt that was why you – '

'Jesus Christ, isn't anything considered private any more? What right do you – '

'Major!' the brigadier's voice cracked like a whip. 'Shut your mouth. You are speaking to a superior officer, or have you forgotten?' He glared the younger man into silence, then waited a moment more.

'It might interest you to know that I am a physician and a psychologist. I held a professorship in medicine at London University Hospital before the war. So, I know what I am talking about when I ask you, by what possible conceit do you conclude that your problems are unique? Perhaps if you had discussed them with your doctor while in hospital you would have discovered they are not confined exclusively to you.

'Of course you are scared and your nerves are shot. They should be after what you've been through. That does not mean that you are a coward. What it does mean is that you have a healthy respect for danger and your body will not allow your brain to overrule common sense. Fear is simply a warning of danger. Nothing more. If those damned fools at Combined Operations had listened years ago, we would be teaching courses in how to deal with fear, and as a consequence we would have far fewer officers and men institutionalised because of so-called battle fatigue. The lessons of the First World War were clear enough. Unless men are taught to respect and use fear as a self-protective device, they will . . .' Realising that he was beginning to lecture, the brigadier broke off.

'Look here, Jan. When in danger, any sane person is frightened. Often that fright persists after the danger has passed. Body and mind together must deal with the effects of fear, and to do so, a great deal of energy is expended, generally in situations that are stressful. Over time this is very debilitating and causes a form of exhaustion, both physical and mental, and certainly nothing to be ashamed of. Better to be ashamed of yawning, which is a natural response to an excess of carbon dioxide. Instead such reactions should be cultivated and trained as warning systems and used to increase strength and response levels to a high degree. The Vikings recognised, and trained their warriors in, the phenomenon we know today as a berserk rage. A Viking could turn it on and off at will. Its basis was fear, but fear channelled into a useful course. If you were a coward, as you suppose, nothing could have dragged you into the Royal Marines. Do you understand what I am saying, Jan?'

When Memling nodded, the brigadier sighed. 'All right, then, to the next item, your so-called impotency, as I am certain that is what Janet was so delicately alluding to. She felt your trouble was exhaustion, and in that she was entirely correct, but I assume her response was to be embarrassed for you, and you in turn felt that you had failed. Correct?'

When Memling nodded angrily, he rolled his eyes skyward.

'The ignorance of this supposedly enlightened generation as regards sex, a perfectly natural function of the human body, is at times beyond belief. Your impotency was *originally* due to exhaustion brought on by the stress of a lengthy sojourn in a fear-producing situation. If it continues at all now, it is because you have convinced yourself that there is something quite wrong with you, namely, this ridiculous idea of cowardice.'

Memling shook his head. 'You're wrong there, Brigadier. Damned wrong. Not everything that happened in Germany was in my report.' Memling described Francine's insistence that they live as husband and wife. 'I don't know why I went along,' he admitted, his face flaming. 'I was a married man . . . it was just that Janet and I had been having trouble before I left, and she was there and, well, I had no trouble with her, Brigadier. Absolutely none. So you see . . .'

Simon-Benet stared at him in amazement. 'My God, boy, I find it hard to believe . . . I thought you had been married once before . . .' He shook his head. 'Look here, you need straightening out and badly. I've been married three times. I am also considered an expert in the psychology and training of combat soldiers, and I served in the first war. In fact, I survived twelve months on the Somme. So I think I know what I'm talking about. You left England, guilty over your problems with Janet, fell into the clutches of a nubile and probably oversexed teenage girl. What could be more natural than your reaction? From the way you describe her, she would have tempted Christ himself. There is nothing wrong in that, or in your taking advantage of the situation. If you hadn't, I would have been worried. I would also think that under the circumstances, Janet, if she should ever find out, would be the first to dismiss it for what it was – mutual need. Now, as for being able to perform with this little German girl and not, afterwards, with Janet, you told me yourself that you stopped sexual relations after reaching the village because there was too much to do.

'If you think back, you will probably find that your desire for sex had diminished. The young lady's remained high because she, as you yourself maintain, did not appreciate the danger of the situation.'

The brigadier pushed himself away from the rock. 'Look here, Jan. This isn't simple cocktail psychology. The effects of stress on the human body have been carefully studied. Certainly this damnable war provides no end of subjects. One thing we know for certain – stress is cumulative over time and can and does cause temporary impotency. We are also finding that its cure is often quite simple, requiring nothing more than the patience and help of a woman who loves you.' He hesitated, then decided that it was all or nothing.

'I want you to run this operation for me, but only if you feel completely up to it. I suspected something like this after speaking to Janet, although certainly not the extent of the problem. Before I left London, I made arrangements to have you transferred back to my command, if you were willing. The only condition I now impose is that you speak to a certain doctor in London. I think he can help you appreciate what I've told you. Think about it. If you decide yes, ring me in Glasgow at this number.' He handed Memling a card on which he had scribbled a telephone number.

'If you decide no – well, then no hard feelings. But I must know within twenty-four hours. Otherwise it will be too late to get things organised properly.'

Simon-Benet punched him lightly on the shoulder and strode away, knowing that he had best have time alone.

As they walked along the path leading from the tiny Peenemünde cemetery to the waiting car Wernher von Braun caught Bethwig's arm and steered him away from the others so that they were screened by the pines.

'Franz, you know how sorry I am about this. I just wish . . .' His voice trailed off, and he glanced around at the dripping branches and hunched his shoulders against the rain.

Bethwig nodded but did not reply, and after an awkward moment they resumed the walk to the car. The SS officer who had accompanied Bethwig stared sullenly as they approached, oblivious to von Braun's glare; he opened the rear door, and once settled inside, Bethwig leaned against the seat, face carefully composed even though he was still clutching Himmler's telegram expressing sorrow at his loss.

Bethwig was long past either sorrow or anger; both had ended with Inge's death. The Peenemünde staff physician, an old friend, had offered no hope from the beginning.

'I'm sorry, Franz, but there is nothing I can do other than to make her as comfortable as possible. She has advanced tuberculosis. A week, perhaps a month. Certainly not more. Since the war began, there are just not the medicines available, not that they would be of much use at this stage. The Allies are said to have a drug that will help but . . .' He shrugged in helplessness.

The car turned into the drive. It had made little difference, he thought. Inge had no recollection of him. The house, the warm bed, food, and hot tea were enough. Whatever had been done to her in the camps had destroyed her already damaged mind. It was impossible for her to carry on even a short conversation; she had great difficulty composing the simplest sentence. His housekeeper, a taciturn Polish woman of middle age, assumed immediate care of her and even moved into the house to be with Inge at night. Bethwig found himself on several occasions studying this strange woman as she sat bundled in blankets on the enclosed porch, searching for even a vestige of the beauty that had so entranced him. But there was nothing left of her former self in this wasted frame. When she died quietly one night after a severe bout of coughing, he could only feel vast relief that she was now spared further agony. His consolation lay in Himmler's defeat. Dornberger had persuaded Hitler himself to free von Braun, Gottrup and Mundt. Von Braun was now safe, by order of the Führer, and Inge was beyond reach.

Franz opened the door without waiting for the driver and stepped out. A sentry standing by the gate presented arms, and Bethwig turned to see the Gestapo officer Walsch stepping from the front seat of a touring car.

'What is this man doing here?'

Walsch nodded towards the front of the house where another guard waited. 'You are quite fortunate, Herr Doktor Bethwig. The reichsführer takes great interest in your safety. It has been reported that a Russian assassination team has been sent into the area. The sentries will assure your safety.'

It was a barefaced lie, but Bethwig was too disgusted, too exhausted, to feel outrage. That fool Himmler should know by now that he could not be intimidated with threats to his life. Walsch, smiling now, continued. 'Our counter-intelligence forces have established that the Russians have marked you and your family for murder, Herr Doktor. The reichsführer has therefore extended the same protection to your father.'

The blow so stunned him that Bethwig could only gape. As if from a great distance, he heard Walsch explaining that precautions required that his father be placed in protective custody, that the Führer had personally approved the plan, and that the reichsführer hoped he could now continue his work with his mind eased. Bethwig turned away and stumbled up the path as Walsch smiled and nodded after him.

'I tell you, Franz, this may very well be our last opportunity.' Von Braun kicked at the sand, then picked up a stone and hurled it towards the waves. It skipped twice and sank. 'You can't resign. You can't give up now!'

Bethwig shook his head stubbornly. 'I can and I will. If I have to leave Peenemünde, I'll do so.'

Von Braun snorted. 'Ever since that spy scare last summer, SS control has tightened like a noose. You could no more leave here than a front-line soldier could desert his unit.'

Bethwig shrugged, and von Braun muttered to himself in exasperation. 'Damn it, Franz, you are badly needed here, now that Dornberger has been transferred to Berlin. Ever since that fool Keitel and the Army General Staff refused to support him a few months ago, it's become clear the army is giving up all claim to rocket development . . . and Himmler is moving quickly to assume control. The attempt to kill the Führer only strengthened his hand.' He stopped and swung around to face Bethwig. 'You've met General Doktor Hans Kammler, the SS's own wonder boy, and you know what he thinks of the work being done here. Well, tomorrow he assumes complete command of the programme and the Peenemünde facility.'

Bethwig looked at him in surprise. 'How do you know this?'

'My brother, Magnus, has a friend at OKW. A few days ago he was sent to General Buhle's office to take notes on a meeting between Buhle and Kammler. Kammler described Walter as a public danger and told Buhle he ought to be court-martialled. Buhle refused, of course, but not strenuously.'

'Degenkolb won't stand for it,' Bethwig protested. 'Peenemünde is a private concern. That makes it immune to military takeover.'

'Damn it, Franz, can't you understand? This is not a military takeover. This is the SS. Himmler can do just about anything he pleases these days. It is said that even the Führer dare not oppose him now. My God, his personal bodyguard are SS troops. As for Degenkolb, when was the last time you saw him here? At least

Kammler made one correct assessment when he described that man as a hopeless alcoholic.'

Bethwig shrugged.

Their walks had become much less frequent of late, and the conversation usually concerned political matters affecting their work. Rarely did they discuss technical or speculative matters related to science as they had done in years past.

Von Braun followed a pace or two behind, studying his friend with concern. Since the death of that strange woman and the arrest of his father, Bethwig had subsided into a world of his own, one in which he continued to function as effectively as ever, directing the final development of the A-10 transatlantic bomber rocket with skill but no personal interest. The drive that had so characterised him had disappeared. For weeks now Franz had taken little interest in staff debates concerning technical problems, preferring instead to issue directives from his office. How did that madman gain such control, von Braun wondered, that even Franz's father, among the party's earliest and most ardent supporters, could be thrown into a concentration camp like a communist or a Jew to keep Franz in line?

They turned inland after a while and strolled through the nearly deserted production buildings, which were quickly falling to ruin. No repairs had been made since the bombing a year ago. Windows remained broken, and sliding doors hung at odd angles. Rubbish littered the area, and weeds grew between the concrete slabs. The actual production facilities had all been moved into Germany proper, to an underground factory near Nordhausen where most of the work was performed by prisoners from the local concentration camps under, it was rumoured, appalling conditions. Von Braun had no reason to doubt that. Since the SS had assumed control of Peenemünde's security, the quality of work obtained from both foreign contract workers and POWs had fallen well below standard; and he was certain that Dornberger's imminent arrest stemmed in good part from his repeated protests against the starvation and brutality to which they were subjected.

Von Braun caught up with Bethwig as they approached the middle of the complex. Massive buildings frowned at them from the mist, and huge puddles were forming wherever stopped-up drains acted as miniature dams.

'Franz, tomorrow I'm returning to Poland for more test firings. They may keep me there for several weeks, and you know this is the critical phase. One more A-Ten test launch is all Kammler will allow. Unless it is a complete success, he will close the project down and we will lose for ever any hope of a lunar flight.'

'But if he does,' Bethwig answered in a bitter voice 'at least my father might live. There would be no reason for Himmler to continue to hold him.'

Von Braun uttered an obscenity. 'Perhaps. And perhaps the opposite. The man is mad; you cannot expect him to act rationally. What if he takes it into that stupid head of his that further failure is due to sabotage on your part? You know as well as I that he is capable of that kind of thinking. You only have to see what he is doing to Walter Dornberger. He has no scientific background and no conception of how such research is conducted.'

Bethwig looked at von Braun, his face a mask of anguish. 'Wernher, how can I? How much longer can my father survive? The best information I have is that he is at Ravensbruck, which is supposed to be a special camp for important political prisoners. As long as I do exactly as I am told he has a chance. You saw what they did to . . . Inge.' Bethwig had to force himself to say her name. 'I just cannot go on, Wernher . . .'

Bethwig started to walk away, but von Braun called to him to wait. Something in his tone stopped Bethwig, and his shoulders slumped. He waited, apprehension growing, as von Braun came up and slipped an arm about his shoulder.

'Franz' – his voice was soft – 'I wanted to spare you this, but too much is at stake and you should know. I am certain that Himmler has taken steps to see that you do not find out. As I told you, Magnus has a friend, a clerk at OKW.' Wernher's arm tightened and Bethwig knew then what he was about to say.

'Your father died of congestive heart failure on September eighth. Franz, I can't tell you how sorry . . .'

Bethwig nodded, then straightened his shoulders and walked off. His mind was clear now, icy and calm. He remembered von Braun after a moment and turned to see his friend looking after him, coat clutched about his neck against the rain and hair plastered about his face.

He nodded. 'I'll be ready, Wernher.'

Jan Memling trudged across the wet tarmac to the operations office where RAF Flight Lieutenant Stan Culliford was just finishing the weather summary. Jan leaned against the warped door and waited, hands jammed in the pocket of the Yank bomber jacket he had won in last night's card game.

'Looks like we might go tonight, old boy,' Culliford grunted when he turned away from the board. 'Weather's clearing over the landing site until shortly after dawn, the Met boys think. Word is the ground's firm enough to support the wheels.'

'Whose Met boys?' Memling asked sceptically.

Culliford grinned. 'The Poles' of course.'

'Do we know where we're going yet?'

Culliford nodded and pursed his lips, his expression pessimistic. 'Place called Motyl, near the village of Zabrow. It's an old landing field. The AK will provide the security.'

The Polish home army, the Armia Krajowa, operated under impossible circumstances, yet according to Simon-Benet's assessment, they were the best in the business. The AK was a duplicate of the pre-war Polish army and perhaps the best organised of all resistance groups in Europe.

The two men walked outside. Culliford, noticing that they had glanced at the dawn sky together, chuckled. 'Won't do us any good to be looking around up here. We have six hundred miles to go and then some.'

Memling nodded, staring at the flaming Italian sky. Over the hills to the east, the sun was edging above the horizon in splendours of reds and blues, and the high cirrus glowed and danced in the growing light.

'It's your decision, Stan,' he said after a moment. 'You have to fly that thing.' He gestured towards the waiting Douglas Dakota. In its coat of dead black paint, the aircraft was barely visible on the tarmac.

The New Zealander glanced again at the sky, then at the yellow flimsy in his hand, scratched his jaw, and nodded. 'Let's go. We probably won't have a better chance for another couple of weeks and I sure as hell don't want to hang around here any longer. You might lose that jacket and then I'd never get a chance to own it.'

They took off at 20.00 hours, with four officers and nineteen suitcases of equipment aboard. Three of the officers had flown in with Memling two weeks before but had remained segregated in separate quarters. He heard them speaking Polish among themselves and surmised that they were couriers or Special Operations Executive agents. The fourth, who had arrived the previous week from London, was a Captain Leslie Reynolds whom Memling knew vaguely from his work with R. V. Jones's group the year before. The man had been a physics professor at Leeds University before the war and was an admirer of Viscount Cherwell's.

The last few lights were disappearing below as they droned into the Adriatic. Memling climbed forward to the cockpit. The navigator gave him coffee from a Thermos, and Culliford pointed out a dark mass against the horizon.

'Yugoslavia. I've flown across her several times. A few night fighters about but nothing serious as long as you keep below their radar. Our bombers work their coastal stations over quite regularly, and in case of serious trouble, the partisans will be glad to see us, or so I'm told.

'By the way, we've lost our escort, I'm not sorry to say. Bloody great lumbering beasts. Attract Jerries like flies to sugar.'

'Lost them?'

'One had engine trouble. Never left the runway. We've simply outflown the other. Not to worry, though. In case of trouble, we'll just turn around. That second Liberator is about fifteen miles behind. Anyway, he'll be leaving as soon as we cross the coast again, on a mission of his own.'

Brindisi had been chosen as the jump-off point for the flight into southern Poland. Memling gathered that SOE had been making good use of the Italian fields to insert agents all over occupied Europe. While it was nearly twelve hundred miles from Britain to southern Poland by the most direct route, the existence of Allied airfields in central and southern Italy enabled them to shorten the flight by half. The route took them up the Adriatic to cross the Yugoslav coast south-east of Split, then on across the Dinaric Alps to skirt the Hungarian-Rumanian border, across eastern Czechoslovakia and into southern Poland.

The Polish co-pilot, Kazimierz Szrajer, was saying something to Culliford which drew a laugh, but the noise of the engines prevented Memling from hearing. The flight settled into routine, and Memling left the cramped cockpit after a while. One of the Polish agents looked up from the Sten gun he was cleaning and smiled, happy to be on his way.

The Dakota had been stripped of all non-essential equipment to open up as much room as possible for the cargo they would be bringing back. The only seats, as a result, were unpadded benches bolted to the wall, and the curving side of the fuselage forced one to sit hunched forward. The accommodations, he remarked, were only slightly better than those of the Mosquito in which he had been flown into Germany the year before.

After much soul-searching Memling had visited the psychiatrist recommended by the brigadier.

'He did telephone you were coming, and we discussed your case to some extent.' The doctor smiled and offered a cigarette which Memling declined.

'From what you have told me, I see nothing to suggest that his diagnosis was incorrect. If you will pardon my bluntness, your problems were created by ignorance. There is nothing to be ashamed of in that unless, of course, you persist in that ignorance. As to the treatment – unfortunately there are no magic cures: only patience and the determination to face up to the situation as it exists. Do you love your wife?'

The question had come as a complete surprise, and Memling's reaction was automatic:

'Of course I do. It's . . .'

The doctor held up a hand. 'No need to go into the matter now. If you want my advice, you will listen to Dr Simon-Benet. He seems to like you very much, and he has your best interests at heart. He tells me that you have a decision to make, one that may place you in a stressful situation similar to the one that appeared to be your undoing last autumn. I can only advise you to be certain you are physically strong enough to undertake the activity. If you are not, you cannot expect to deal successfully with the mental and emotional aspects of the problem. Other than that, I can only repeat what the brigadier has already told you. You must face the situation resolved to be the master of your own body. Fear is a powerful weapon, one you can use against an enemy or against yourself. Think it over carefully.'

Hunched uncomfortably in the old Dakota, Memling felt the familiar fear renewing itself. He thought he had mastered it before, after four separate commando raids, only to discover that the excitement of battle was far different from the corrosive agony of illicit activity behind enemy lines.

Captain Reynolds had fallen asleep and Memling was grateful for small favours. The captain had spent the last hour pointing out the errors in Memling's A-4 rocket analysis with all the smug assurance of an academic whose closest contact with the industrial world had been polite discussions in immaculate conference rooms with executives who hadn't been near a production floor in years. He had been quick to point out that as science and technology were systems of logic, their application in research, development and manufacturing were bound to follow logical procedures. One had only to list the steps to be taken, isolate those requiring the longest time to complete and arrange the remaining tasks within those parameters. The project would then be completed in the shortest possible time – the sum total of the longest tasks. He was, he admitted modestly, one of Britain's leading experts in the new discipline called operations research.

'I am certain, Major' – Reynolds's voice dripped superiority –

'that it must have been difficult to obtain accurate measurements when you were at Peenemünde, but those measurements were, after all, the basis for your subsequent calculations, were they not? Now, if you were out as much as a foot, your estimates would be all skewed towards the minimum, would they not?'

Memling restrained the urge to swear.

'I understand that you were not graduated from your technical course, so even though you did your best, one must be careful of over reaching oneself, what?'

'You bloody bastard,' Memling muttered, but Reynolds did not hear over the engine noise.

'I do not mean to dwell on your shortcomings, Major Memling, but it is essential that you understand your mistakes so that the divisive debate of the past months can be ended. The payload of the rocket you term A-Four is inconsistent with the measurements you reported. A simple mistake in measuring has apparently led you to conclude that this rocket is incapable of carrying more than a ton, while your mistake with the other, the A-Ten, is of the same magnitude, only in the opposite direction. Why, the very size is . . .' He started to say 'preposterous', then thought better of it: '. . . extraordinary. A rocket of that size could lift more than thirty metric tons.'

'I see,' Memling answered in a thoughtful voice. 'You dismiss my estimates as nonsense but agree with the committee's analysis which suggests the A-Four is capable of carrying ten tons of explosive as far as London?'

'Well, yes of course. It was my analysis that corrected your figures, you know.'

'And your analysis was made strictly from photographs – photographs, I might point out, neither detailed nor clear enough to enable Bomber Command to pinpoint targets – yet you arrived at accurate figures on which you then based your assumptions?'

'Well, of course. I estimated the actual weight of each major component and used sophisticated statistical and mathematical modelling techniques, naturally.' The captain's voice was full of confidence as he warmed to his subject in the face of Memling's unexpected interest.

'For example, you estimated the weight of the fuel tanks based on their fabrication in steel. You must realise, old boy, that the use of steel in such a situation is illogical. Weight is everything in the rocket. Steel is far too heavy. Aluminium, which possesses sufficient strength, would provide a great weight saving. Also, and this is my greatest point of disagreement with you, old man, you suggested the rocket fuel consists of a mixture of alcohol and liquid oxygen. My dear fellow, that would be equally ridiculous.' The captain chuckled to himself.

'It has been well established by these Polish fellows, who do indeed possess a few good scientists, that hydrogen peroxide is being used as the oxidiser. Hydrazine, then, would be the logical fuel. Its specific impulse – you are familiar with the term – is far greater than what can be obtained with alcohol and liquid oxygen . . .'

Memling had taken enough. 'Captain,' he had interrupted the tirade, 'you are an ass. I was at Peenemünde where I worked as a member of the quality control department. I witnessed a test firing. Logic is all well and good, but sometimes it has to bend in the face of reality.'

Reynolds began to bluster, but Memling bored on. 'I am willing to bet you my figures are more correct than yours, Captain Reynolds. In a few hours we will have an A-Four rocket aboard this aircraft. You and I should be able to determine, just the two of us, if the fuel tanks are made of steel, as I said, or of aluminium, as you maintain. If they are made of steel, I win that part of the bet and you get one good swift kick in the arse. If, when the Farnworth wizards finish their analysis, they determine that my estimate of the payload is closer than yours, you make a public and abject apology to me before the committee. I am well aware of what you told them regarding my work, and it only reinforces my belief that you are an arrogant know-it-all as well as an ass. Now, as an officer superior to you in rank, Captain, I am giving you a direct order. Shut your mouth!'

The Dakota lost altitude abruptly, jolting Memling from his reverie. He turned to the window to see a bright path of light below and swore angrily. His watch showed just after midnight. They were over the landing site, and the flares lit by the Poles were bright enough to draw every German within a hundred miles. Apparently the Polish officers aboard thought so as well, to judge by their exclamations of dismay.

The aircraft side-slipped, lost more altitude, and bucked in the turbulence. As they came around to line up for the approach more flares were set off until the makeshift landing site seemed as bright as day. Memling rebuckled his seat strap as the jolting grew more severe.

They were losing altitude rapidly now. A stand of trees – only inches below the wings, it seemed – fled past. Then the first flare shot past, and in its glow Memling saw the wing flaps go down, then, unexpectedly, grind up again. Engines screamed and the aircraft shuddered. For an instant he was weightless as the plane staggered, then they were rising with agonising slowness. What the hell, he wondered; but the Dakota was banking hard to port to go around again. The noise added to the lights would surely bring the Germans swarming.

This time Culliford took them straight in. Once over the trees, the aircraft dropped so abruptly that Memling gripped the seat, willing them not to crash. Afterwards he was certain he had left finger marks in the wood.

The Dakota came down hard, bounced twice, and staggered across the field. As the plane turned at the end of its roll, Memling saw a man with a torch point to the right, then chop down abruptly. The engines shut off, and a moment later someone was pounding on the hatch. Memling drew his Colt automatic and heard the unmistakable snicks of four Sten gun bolts being cocked. Gingerly he unlatched the door, remembering a deserted landing field in the Ardennes, and swung it open.

'Hello, Tommy!' A bearded man dressed in worker's clothes and a cloth cap greeted him, one gnarled hand clutching a Mauser rifle. He broke into rapid Polish directed at the four men standing behind Memling, and they shouldered him aside with shouts of greeting, jumped down with their suitcases, and disappeared into the press of people milling about the aircraft.

Culliford materialised at his shoulder. 'My God,' he roared above the noise, 'don't they know there's a war on?'

Orders were shouted, and the crowd dispersed. The bearded man climbed inside and shook hands with Memling and Culliford, then threw his arms wide at the sight of the Polish co-pilot. For a moment the two men embraced, laughing uproariously.

'He says to tell you,' the co-pilot told them above his friend's laughter, 'welcome to Free Poland. He is General Kaspar Kierzek and he commands the Twenty-second Home Army Regiment.'

'Yes, but for how long?' Culliford demanded. 'Those lights will have every damned German garrison in the area about our ears.'

When this was translated, the Pole laughed and went to the hatch. He gestured expansively and broke into a speech.

'He says there is only one German garrison in the area. His people surrounded the barracks earlier. When the Germans opened the door to see what the noise was about, they heard rifle bolts being cocked and decided they were better off not knowing.

'He says the Russians are pushing hard less than a hundred kilometres east, and the Germans are retreating through this area. They do not want trouble. He thinks we are safe for another two hours. The only threat is an SS panzer unit twenty kilometres north-west of here.'

'He thinks?' Culliford muttered.

A line had been formed, and bundles and packages were being passed along from hand to hand. An engine racketed to life, and a German armoured car lurched across the field dragging a makeshift trailer piled high with large, canvas-wrapped bundles. General Kierzek hustled Memling and Culliford out of the way while the Poles set about loading the aircraft.

The co-pilot, Szrajer, who had been pumping the guerrillas for information, wandered back. 'It is amazing how much they have done with so little. This unit has been stationed in this area for two years now and has monitored all the rocket flights. When this one crashed in May, they got to it first and found it on a riverbank, virtually intact. They simply rolled it into the river and had a local farmer drive a herd of cows into the stream to muddy the waters. The German recovery team finally went away convinced they had been given the wrong location. General Kierzek then captured an armoured car and used it to extract the rocket from the river. The major components were disassembled and sent to the university in Warsaw for thorough study, and reports were submitted to London. When the decision was made to fly the rocket out of Poland, the components were repacked and returned right under the noses of the German security forces. The drawings and copies of reports were stored in Holowczyce-Kolonia, a nearby village, to wait for favourable weather.

'A German infantry group came to practise here this afternoon, and two aircraft landed, but they all left before sundown. The general says the Nazis own the countryside during the day but hardly dare venture out after sunset.'

Kierzek came over to them. 'Everything hokay.' He nodded at the Poles lifting the last package aboard. 'You go now.'

With the rocket aboard the Dakota, the Poles became subdued and tense. After perfunctory handshakes all around and a hasty farewell to the four intelligence agents who were staying behind, Memling hurried the others aboard and swung the oversized cargo door shut while Culliford went forward to the cockpit.

The engines exploded into life, and Memling strapped in. The noise mounted as the engines were run up, but the aircraft remained stationary. Culliford reduced power, then ran up again. Twice more and he shut down and stuck his head into the cabin.

'The brakes are locked. Have you a knife?'

Memling handed over his Fairbairn knife and glanced into the cockpit. 'What are you doing . . . ?'

The co-pilot was levering a plate from the floor. He took the knife and ducked head and shoulders into the hole.

'He's cutting the hydraulic brake line. Without hydraulics, the brake shoes open automatically.'

A few moments later the engines were started again, but still the aircraft refused to budge. Culliford tried jockeying it back and forth, but the plane would not roll forward.

Finally he shut the engines down and came back. 'Damn it all. Fifty pounds of boost and she still won't budge. Everyone out!' He flung open the cargo door and jumped down. The co-pilot followed and they went to examine the wheels with an electric torch. The engine vibration had caused them to sink into the wet soil.

'Damn,' Culliford swore. He paced about the area, kicking at the muddy ground with his heel, then he stopped and scratched his head. 'Look here, I think we should try and dig out.'

Memling's orders were to burn the aircraft and its contents if anything went wrong, then attempt to reach Russian lines. But he had little faith in their ability to find the Russians before the Germans found them and even less in Russian hospitality.

'Dig!'

A line of men with shovels formed up quickly, and twenty minutes later two shallow trenches had been excavated. In the meantime another group unloaded the aircraft while a third disappeared into the night to cut brushwood.

The co-pilot took over, shunting Memling and Culliford aside. Memling felt like the proverbial fifth wheel and said so to the worried New Zealander who only grunted.

'If they dig us out of here, you must realise that our troubles are only beginning.'

Memling closed his eyes. 'Why?'

'Well, we're past schedule now, so we'll be in the air, over enemy territory, during daylight. For several hundred miles. With the landing gear down. And,' he continued remorselessly, 'we won't have any brakes for the landing.'

Memling stalked off with what he hoped was a semblance of dignity. A few minutes later he noticed that Captain Reynolds was struggling with a canvas shroud that covered a piece of the rocket. Memling started towards him, but Reynolds dropped the cover and walked away. The canvas was neatly tagged, but in Polish, and its lumpy shape was unidentifable. Puzzled at Reynolds's actions, Memling had started after him when Culliford shouted.

The Poles were already reversing the loading procedure. Culliford was casting worried glances at the sky. A high cloud cover had begun to move in, obscuring the moon and the brighter stars visible through the glare of the landing flares.

The pilot jerked a thumb at the sky. 'Rain, before dawn.'

General Kierzek hurried up and drew the co-pilot aside. His head snapped up, and he glanced around for Culliford and Memling.

'Lorries have been sighted leaving the SS camp near Bialystok. They are headed in this direction. The road has been mined, so it will take them at least an hour to get here.'

'Let's go. Now!'

The bearded Pole grunted and shouted to his followers. The reloading was accomplished in fifteen minutes, and Memling swung the door shut. The starter cartridges went off with a bang, and both engines ran up easily, but again the aircraft refused to move. Through the window Memling saw one of the resistance men waving his arms frantically, and he flung the cockpit door open, grabbed Culliford's shoulder, and pointed at the Pole. Cursing at the top of his voice, Culliford shut the engines down.

This time the wheels had gone in up to their hubs. Culliford stared at the bisected wheels, too angry even to swear. Finally, he took a deep breath. 'Without brakes, we couldn't run up to full power, and so she just vibrated her way in again. Goddamned ground!' He kicked at the mound of soil that had piled up on either side of the landing gear.

Memling studied his watch. The SS detachment was now twenty minutes nearer. Culliford took his arm and pulled him aside. 'I think we had better burn her and take to the hills, old man. We'll never get her off the ground now. It's going to start raining any moment, and even if it holds off a bit, the Hun is going to arrive.'

For a moment Memling was on the verge of nodding agreement, but then something made him hesitate. 'Damn it, no. We've been through too much to . . . to . . .' He took a deep breath. 'Look here, Stan, we'll dig out once more, only this time we'll use boards rather than brush under the wheels.'

General Kierzek arrived with more bad news. The co-pilot listened, his face growing longer with each word.

'Outposts have spotted the SS detachment now less than three kilometres away,' he told them. 'It's apparent the mines did not slow them as hoped. They have also rallied a small army garrison and sent them to circle around the far end of the valley. The general thinks they will reach here in about thirty minutes. His people report no artillery, but they are certain to have mortars and automatic weapons. The general suggests that unless we can take off immediately, we destroy the aircraft and go with his people.'

An argument in two languages broke out, but Memling shouted for silence. When he got it, he had the co-pilot question the general concerning the probable tactics the SS would employ. Kierzek answered impatiently at first and then with growing interest as the pattern to the Englishman's questions emerged.

'The general would like to know, Major, where you received your training?'

'Royal Marine Commando,' Memling grunted, and knelt to examine the map one of the general's aides had produced. Kierzek knelt beside him and pointed to a road which Memling could barely see in the dim torch light. His answers now held a certain respect.

'How much help do you think the general is willing to give?'

The co-pilot looked dubious but put the question anyway. The answer must have surprised him because he grinned and then translated. 'He says that will depend on how long we would require to free the aircraft?'

Memling glanced at Culliford, who shrugged. 'Judging from what they did before, twenty minutes maximum is my guess.'

'Tell him,' Memling ordered, but the general nodded.

'I speak little English.' He seemed to be thinking a moment. 'Twenty minutes, no more. Burn airplane then. Hokay?'

Memling stared at the men surrounding him; even Captain Reynolds had wandered over to listen. 'All right, twenty minutes it is.' Memling ordered Culliford to organise the digging parties while the co-pilot saw to repairing the hydraulic line. He then turned to the general. 'Can I help?'

The general laughed and clapped him on the shoulder. 'Hokay, Commando. You come see how we do.' He stood up and began to bellow orders. As the partisans formed up into units Reynolds approached Memling and coughed apologetically.

'Ah, Major Memling, I did receive a basic training course. I can shoot a rifle. May I go with you?'

Surprised, Memling glanced at the scientist. He was obviously frightened; his eyes darted here and there, and his hands were tightly clenched, yet he wanted to do his part. Memling nodded. 'Get a Sten from the aircraft.'

The general bellowed orders in Polish, and the guerrillas divided into three columns and moved out. One column was to backtrack to the end of the valley and ambush the army garrison pushing up the road.

The second and third columns were organised to form a trap. A thin screen, part of the second column, would be thrown across the road a kilometre north of the aircraft. They would allow the SS unit to burst through, into a fire field laid down by the remainder of the column. Again the SS would be allowed to break through, thus providing the impression that they had breached the partisans' defences. While their confidence was high, but before the motorised column could resume speed, they would be slowed again by trees felled across the road. The general was confident that the column's commander, rather than wait to clear the trees, would order the lorries on to the verge to bypass the roadblock. The soft ground would slow the troop carriers and the armoured car reported with them. At that point the partisans' single thirty-seven-millimetre anti-tank gun would fire on the armoured car while soldiers with Molotov cocktails would destroy the lorries. With the way blocked front and back, the rest could be dealt with at leisure.

It was the classic guerrilla tactic against armoured vehicles, devised by the Finns during the winter of 1939–40. Even the weapons were the same: the thirty-seven-millimetre anti-tank gun and Molotov cocktails. Memling watched doubtfully as the partisans trotted off into the darkness. The tactic was well known; it might work against the invalided troops coming up in the rear but not against the battle-hardened Waffen SS who would have perfected their anti-guerrilla techniques on the Russian front. The general must have sensed his thoughts, for he clapped him a stunning blow on the shoulder.

'His hokay. You see! German always do same thing.'

With Reynolds panting behind, Memling followed the fast pace set by the partisans. Loud cracks sounded just ahead, and a moment later he saw tree trunks crash across the single track. Memling and Reynolds dogged the general as he checked his forward positions. The ground on either side of the trees was even spongier than the landing site, and Memling's boots squished. The Poles had excavated shallow trenches which were already filling with water. Memling slid in without hesitation but had to reach up and yank Reynolds after him. He took a quick look at Reynolds, but the darkness hid his face.

'Ah, Major?'

'Just keep your head down and you'll be all right,' Memling answered absently.

'No, it's . . . I had a look at the rocket. There was no sign of any radio guidance system, and the fuel tanks . . . well . . . they were, ah, made of steel. Just as you said they would be. I certainly owe you . . .'

An exchange of gunfire broke out with the sharp bursts of SS machine-gun fire predominating. The shooting stopped, and the engine noise of the lorries was clear in the night silence. General Kierzek chuckled and clapped Memling on the shoulder.

A moment later firing sounded again, only sharper and more prolonged this time. The lorry engines were louder, and suddenly the armoured car loomed in the darkness, silhouetted against the sparse trees. Its machine-gun chattered off a burst, swivelling across the road to either side, a tactic originated by Erwin Rommel during the 1940 blitzkrieg.

The partisans ignored the probing gunfire, and a moment later the driver saw the trees lying across the road. The machine-gunner fired a long burst into the area, and spurts of dirt and flying rocks kicked across the top of their trench. Memling heard a shout, and the armoured car turned on to the verge, followed by the first lorry. Both ground forward and bogged down. The anti-tank gun to their right went off with a bang, and the armoured car's turret burst open. Troops tumbled out of the leading lorry, and the partisans opened up with everything they had. The thirty-seven-millimetre gun barked again, and the lorry exploded. A flaming bottle arced down on to the second lorry still on the roadway and splattered against the canvas top. The fourth and last in line received a similar barrage and blew up quickly.

The partisans who had manned the two forward lines appeared out of the trees to pour fire into the meagre defensive line the SS troops had managed to establish, and it was over in minutes. Scattered shots sounded as partisans finished off the wounded and dying SS troopers, then set about stripping the dead of weapons, ammunition, rations and boots.

The general is well pleased with himself, Memling thought as they trotted back towards the landing site at an easy pace. A runner had come up in the last stages of fighting to report the army troops successfully ambushed at the other end of the valley. There were no survivors. Thirty Waffen SS and twelve regular soldiers were dead, as against three slightly wounded partisans. And Captain Reynolds. Memling carried his ID tags in the pocket of his battledress.

Culliford met them, but the look of triumph and relief on his face disappeared quickly when Memling told him about Reynolds.

'We've dug the Dakota out and repaired the hydraulic line. We can fill it with water and make it work well enough to get the landing gear up.'

The Dakota was already reloaded for the third time. They had exhausted their supply of starter cartridges, and when the last bundle was secured, Memling stood outside with the fire extinguisher while the partisans lined up to turn the port-side prop to start the engine. The co-pilot had gone to great pains to impress upon them that they were to jump aside as soon as the engine fired, but he needn't have worried. Three times the nervous men had to reform before the engine caught with a bang.

When the second engine had been started, Memling tossed the fire extinguisher aboard, shook hands solemnly with the general, and, as an afterthought, removed his pistol belt and handed him the Colt automatic. The general was delighted and pressed him to take his own nine-millimetre Radom.

'Have plenty guns now. Get them from Nazi. You take, remember me.'

Memling grinned then and buckled the belt and holster on and climbed aboard. He slammed the cargo doors on the partisans' cheers and hurried to the cockpit to clap Culliford on the shoulder. 'Make it good this time,' he shouted.

The pilot's face was grim, and the co-pilot, at his nod, eased the twin throttles back. The engines ran up smoothly, and Memling watched the rpm needles mount until they were hovering near the red line. The Dakota vibrated, then, with a Maori war cry, Culliford released the brakes and the Dakota bounded forward. For just an instant Memling could feel the wheels sink as they came off the boards, but the aircraft's momentum was too great and she raced on. At forty-seven pounds of manifold pressure, the tail came up and Culliford began to pull back on the control column. The aircraft lifted easily for all its load, and they were airborne. The treetops flicked past, and the Dakota went into a climbing turn.

Culliford brought them around to fly down the field waggling his wings then climbed for altitude to the south-east.

Jan Memling landed at a new airfield west of London, near the suburb of Heathrow, having changed planes three times in two days. Rain swept across the tarmac in gusts as he trudged into the Nissen hut that served as reception. Two red-capped MPs escorted him to a damp office.

Memling broke into a grin when he saw the brigadier seated at the desk smoking a cigar, and he tossed the leather satchel containing the Polish reports on to the desk. 'There they are. Safe and sound. You did receive my preliminary report from Brindisi?'

Brigadier Simon-Benet nodded and opened the satchel. His abstracted air as he glanced through the first report puzzled

Memling. 'You did very well, Jan. It was too bad about Reynolds. Very bad. But I'm sure it couldn't be helped.' He glanced significantly at his aide who took the hint and stepped outside.

'I take it you experienced no special personal problems?'

Memling looked at him in surprise. For the first time in thirty-odd hours, he thought about his fear, or rather the lack of it. From the moment they had touched down in Poland, he suddenly realised, there had been the usual apprehension but nothing more; in fact, he had even been able to understand Reynolds's fear and admire the way he overcame it. Perhaps that was an end to it, then.

'No, sir, none.' He grinned. 'You were right.'

'Good,' Simon-Benet answered gruffly. 'I am happy that something came of all this. While you were waiting in Italy an A-Four rocket crashed in southern Sweden. We obtained it from the Swedish government in return for two destroyers and some radar sets. The bloody thing's at Farnborough now where the wizards are taking its guts apart. I don't want to suggest that this mission of yours was not worth while; far from it. The more information we can gather, the better off we are.'

The brigadier studied him. 'You've already been vindicated by the Swedish rocket, my boy. Preliminary reports indicate the fuel is alcohol diluted to seventy-five per cent with water and liquid oxygen. Hydrogen peroxide is used to drive a turbo-pump which pressurises the fuel tank – constructed of steel, as you reported. That and other uses of steel rather than aluminium account for the great weight discrepancy between Captain Reynolds's analysis and yours.'

Memling nodded, his face suddenly haggard.

'What's the matter, boy. I would have thought you'd be happy to be proven right?'

Memling nodded. 'I am . . . I was just thinking of a bet that I don't have to collect now.' He brushed a hand over his eyes, seeing Reynolds crouched beside him in the muddy trench firing his Sten at the third lorry in line, short bursts in the approved manner. He had reloaded even though his hands were shaking so badly that he had to rest the gun on the lip of the trench and ease the magazine into the breech. The next time he had looked, Reynolds was sitting against the back of the trench as if resting, his face shot away.

'. . . found one difference between the Swedish rocket and your report,' he heard the brigadier saying. 'I suppose it can be counted as one for Captain Reynolds, since it was his pet idea. The Hun has apparently added a wireless type of guidance. One was found in the rocket. Now that we have it, it should be easy enough to develop a method to assume control of the rocket in flight and direct it away from inhabited areas, as he proposed.'

It was a moment before Memling absorbed what Simon-Benet was saying. Then he shook his head. 'They don't use a radio control system. The rocket is a ballistic missile. No provision was made for a wireless guidance system. Reynolds had a look at the rocket and admitted that himself.'

The brigadier smiled and clapped him on the shoulder. 'Now don't you fret about that, Jan. Even Jerry changes his mind occasionally. This rocket had a very sophisticated guidance system. You can see it for yourself tomorrow. But first I suggest you get to bed for a good sleep. You look as if you could use it.'

As he talked the brigadier led Memling to the door. For a moment a curious sense of déjà vu passed over Jan, and he wondered if it was starting all over again. The brigadier was speaking to him in the same condescending tone that all the others had used when refusing to accept his suggestions or evidence. But before he could say anything, Simon-Benet had opened the door and he saw Janet waiting for him in the corridor.

Descent and Resurrection

Holland–Germany December 1944

Franz Bethwig dived for the slit trench as the Mustang leapt over the hedge. Four distinct lines of machine-gun bullets raced across the frozen mud towards the V-2 squatting on its erector. As he plopped into the mud there was a dull boom and a flash that lit the waning afternoon. Pieces of metal showered the area, and when he dared raise his head above the lip of the trench, the rocket, its erector, and the firing and tracking caravan were little more than flaming masses of twisted metal.

An officer ran towards him shouting, trying to make himself heard above the blowtorch roar of flaring alcohol. His message was clear enough, and Bethwig vaulted from the trench and dived into the woods, while more aircraft raced in to drop their bomb loads and machine-gun the launch site.

Franz stumbled to a halt and sank down beside the trunk of a fallen beech. He huddled into himself, breath rasping, and stared dully into the declining twilight while the explosions went on and on. Somehow during the headlong run he had torn his army overcoat so that it gaped along one shoulder. He had also twisted an ankle.

A stiffening wind was getting up, and a few desultory snowflakes drifted past. Aircraft raids had become a way of life to V-2 launch crews. No matter how far they retreated into Holland, American Mustangs and Thunderbolts and British Spitfires and Typhoons sought them out. They always came like that, he thought, low over the forest so that they seemed to jump down on to the launching area, their only warning a snarling engine and stuttering machine-guns. The launch crews were so thoroughly demoralised that the SS had found it necessary to add a contingent of guards to stop the high rate of desertion. Just in the past two weeks there had been three executions within his own battalion. Two SS guards had been found with their throats cut, victims of army retaliation. Bad feelings between SS and army troops were developing into open warfare. No SS man dared walk about by himself, even in daylight.

The light was fading fast, and Bethwig knew that he should find his way back to the assembly point before darkness fell completely. He fumbled for a cigarette, found one that was comparatively dry, and lit it, shielding the match against the wind. He drew the smoke into his lungs and coughed; the tobacco was foul and musty-tasting. He stared at the glowing end with distaste but did not snuff it out.

'You in there! Come out immediately and with your hands up.'

Startled, Bethwig peered through the branches to see two men in dark overcoats and coal-scuttle helmets watching him. One had a rifle levelled.

He muttered a curse and fought his way out of the tangle of branches to glimpse the lightning-bolt device on one man's collar.

'SS!' His voice dripped contempt.

The tall one smirked. 'Another deserter, Clement.'

Bethwig shook his head. 'I am a civilian, an army employee. And you have no jurisdiction.'

'Is that so.'

Bethwig could identify the rank now; the tall one was a sturmmann and the other an SS-mann, equivalent to lance corporal and private, respectively, in the army.

The sturmmann reached forward to rub the material of Bethwig's torn greatcoat between his fingers. 'This looks like an army issue to me.'

Bethwig knocked his hand away. 'It is, you idiot.' He unbuttoned the coat and flung it open. 'But no uniform underneath.'

'Not so unusual. Most deserters get rid of their uniforms as quickly as possible. They think to fool us that way.'

Bethwig shook his head in disgust. They were one of the SS patrols detailed to search behind the front lines for deserters. Soldiers caught away from their units without proper authorisation were summarily executed by men like these.

'We are at least twenty kilometres from the front lines. Are you two skulking back here because there is no one to shoot at you?'

The private chuckled. 'For someone about to be shot, your mouth certainly flaps a lot.'

Bethwig snorted. 'I am an engineer assigned to a V-Two launch team, B company. Four hundred eighty-fifth Battalion, about a kilometre from here. It was shot up twenty minutes ago by an Allied aircraft.'

'And so you ran away?' the other sneered.

'Of course, you fool. Those are standing orders, written by SS General Kammler himself. The Allied aircraft always try to kill as many of the launch crew as possible. The general's orders are to scatter and return to a specified assembly point within sixty minutes. We have few enough trained technicians as it is.'

The sturmmann laughed. 'Well, if that is the case, the Four hundred eighty-fifth is about to be one fewer.' He looked around the clearing. 'This spot is as good as any, I suppose.'

He undid the holster flap and drew his Walther pistol. Bethwig was so cold and exhausted that for a moment his actions did not register. To be shot almost seemed a welcome idea, but he forced himself to make the effort.

'You damned fool. How do you think you will explain my execution to your superiors?'

'Quite simply. We complete the report forms when we return to our unit. Whatever we say is accepted. Right, Clement?' The SS-mann nodded in solemn agreement.

Oddly enough, Bethwig felt absolutely no fear, only curiosity as to the outcome, and he could not decide if this was a result of exhaustion or self-confidence. 'You do have to submit the executed prisoner's identification tags and paybook, do you not?'

'Of course.'

'Then before you shoot, you had better search me. You aren't going to find either.'

The sturmmann shrugged. 'It is not unusual.'

'What you will find are my identification papers that show clearly I am an employee of the Army Weapons Research Centre, now under the direction of the SS. I report directly to General Kammler and through him to Reichsführer Heinrich Himmler.' He tilted his head to one side as the man released the safety.

'You really should check, you know. If I am killed you and your friend are liable to hang – from a meat hook. Himmler prefers that method of execution, I am told.'

The other SS trooper, Clement, put a hand on his companion's arm. 'Wait. I think we had better check, just to make certain. What if he isn't lying?'

He pushed Bethwig's arms up, yanked open his coat, and searched until he found the wallet and dragged it out. Using his electric torch, he examined Bethwig's papers.

'See, just as he said.'

The sturmmann shook his head. 'Probably forgeries. I'm cold, damn it. I'm going to shoot him now, and then we are going back . . .'

Clement shook his head. 'If these papers are correct, we will hang. If not, we can shoot him later.' He turned to Bethwig. 'Where is this assembly point? Will there be anyone there to identify you?'

Bethwig nodded. 'Of course. In the village of Vreden.'

The sturmmann muttered to himself, but Clement shoved Bethwig around. 'Get started.' Bethwig suppressed a snort of satisfaction and began to retrace his steps in the fading light. Apparently the sturmmann, although superior in rank, was deficient in brains.

It took them almost thirty minutes to find the clearing, and when they pushed cautiously into the deserted area, they found the remains of the launching site still burning. Bethwig trudged on across the trampled field towards the distant village of Vreden without waiting for them.

Bethwig had spent the previous month living a gypsy-like existence, moving from one raw launch crew to another in support of the offensive in the Ardennes. Peenemünde had been stripped of experienced personnel to direct the barrage of rockets launched against Antwerp, Brussels and London in an effort to disrupt Allied supply lines and kill reserve troops and headquarters units. For two weeks they had operated in the comparative safety of bad weather, but a few days after Christmas the weather had begun to clear, and they were being hunted again.

He had slogged from one frozen, wind-blasted forest clearing to another, following the same exhausting drill. The crews were all ill-trained, some lacking any idea of what they were about. He had only a few key veterans to assist him, and the spate of air attacks had killed the last of them two days before, leaving him with the sole responsibility for moving the train of vehicles from one location to another, checking the rockets, seeing that the necessary repairs were made – often doing them himself – then supervising the erection and launch procedures. Even so, with certain shortcuts he had managed to whittle down the time between launches to less than six hours. He could have improved on that, he knew, but the quartermaster corps seemed to have given up on the war, and as a result, his men were constantly hungry, cold, and exhausted. Then there were conflicting orders from Berlin and Kammler's headquarters, all of which were interpreted by a succession of arrogant SS officers whose loyalties to Germany rarely seemed to coincide with their loyalties to obscure superiors who had other objectives in mind.

Now he sat on his bunk in the unheated caravan housing the launching and tracking equipment and stared stupidly at the piece of paper shoved at him by an orderly who had just wakened him from the first bit of sleep he had had in more than two days. It took several moments for the message to make sense.

He was to return immediately to Peenemünde. Nothing more. The order was signed by Kammler. Bethwig stepped to the door and pulled the curtain aside. Bright sunlight forced him to squint as he looked across the Dutch barnyard towards the amazingly flat fields beyond. He knew they were somewhere west of the River Ems, but had not had the strength to ascertain exactly where when they had arrived shortly before dawn. Wherever it was, they were nearing the absolute limit for V-2 operations against England. It must be true, then, he thought. The Ardennes offensive had failed. If so, troops would soon be falling back into Germany and the effectiveness of the V-2s would suffer accordingly.

He packed his few belongings and went over to the mess tent for a hurried breakfast of coffee – burned toast steeped in boiling water – hard bread, and ersatz jam. He showed the orders to the SS officer commanding the unit. The man was the fourth in as many weeks, and Bethwig had not even bothered to learn his name. The officer stared with glazed eyes at the yellow sheet of paper, then nodded. Franz went out and hitched a ride with a lorry heading east towards the Ems. Less than a kilometre along the road a Spitfire flashed towards them, waggled its wings in derision, and a few moments later they heard the explosions begin.

'Herr Doktor, the Führer has granted the A-Ten operational status as a retaliation weapon. It is to be known as Vengeance Ten, and you are to see that its deployment is accelerated!'

Bethwig shook his head. 'General Kammler, it is impossible.'

'Nothing is impossible to a member of the German . . .'

Bethwig laughed. 'General, do not waste my time with party slogans. I was a veteran party member while you were still at university. Slogans no longer impress me and do you know why? Because people like you have destroyed the party and, in the process, destroyed Germany.'

Kammler thrust his head forward and glared at Bethwig. 'Defeatist talk! For that you could be shot!'

'And then you would lose all hope of deploying the V-Ten, wouldn't you?' Bethwig shot back. He opened the box of cigarettes on the general's desk, took one, and glanced at the name printed on the paper.

'These are American.'

'Help yourself,' Kammler sneered. 'They were taken from a convoy of American supplies a few weeks ago.'

Bethwig smiled. 'That is my point, General. You, safe, warm and well fed in a rear area, have good American cigarettes, while the frontline soldier dies on the battlefield, with dried leaves for tobacco.'

Kammler's face flushed, and he started to retort, but Bethwig, weary of arguing, held up a hand. 'General, I did not say that I would not, I merely said that it was impossible to ready the V-Ten batteries in the time you expect. I am not averse to trying; I merely wish it to be understood that I do not expect to succeed. There is no longer a possibility of establishing four batteries by May thirtieth. My preliminary studies indicate that they will not be ready until September even if the priorities you claim could produce the raw materials. And a miracle would be needed, even for that late date. With the loss of the Dutch industrial areas, we cannot even produce sufficient liquid oxygen to fuel the existing four battalions of V-Twos, let alone four more of V-Tens. And you know as well as I how meaningless priorities now are. Where are the two railway locomotives I requested months ago? They are heading to the east, pulling wagons loaded with Jews. Why do these people, enemies of the German Reich, take precedence over the survival of Germany?'

Kammler turned to the window, his expression hardening. 'I do not know. And I do not concern myself with matters that are not my responsibility. You would be well advised to follow a similar policy.'

'Sound advice, General. And very necessary in our Germany today. However, please remember, it was you people in the SS who created the Germany in which such practices are accepted.'

Bethwig stared at Kammler who returned his look without flinching. Finally, Bethwig shrugged.

'Perhaps I can furnish that miracle, General Kammler.' When he was certain he had the general's attention, Franz went on. 'Three V-Tens were near completion when you sent me to Belgium. I told you then that given another month I could have had them ready for launching. If you had left me alone, perhaps now your batteries of transatlantic missiles might be nearing readiness.'

Kammler remained silent. His stare would have disconcerted anyone but Bethwig, who now had little to lose.

'I can have one ready by the end of January, the remaining two by mid-February. The pilots have been selected, and fortunately their training has not been interrupted. While I no longer believe that America can be forced from the war unilaterally by a few rockets landing on her soil, I do believe that two or three such, with the promise of more to come, might send them to the negotiating table, dragging their British and French allies along. If an armistice can be achieved, Germany could turn its attention solely to the east and the defeat of Russia. An old tune, General, but it is Germany's last hope, and the only reason I comply with your demands.'

Kammler's silence indicated that he accepted this rationale, and without a further word, Bethwig left the office. This is the last opportunity we will have, he thought bitterly, and we'll damn well make the most of it. The old dream was far from dead.

Peenemünde January 1945

On New Year's Day Bethwig knocked on the door of the test office in the air tunnel laboratory. A moment later a technician clad in a fireproof asbestos suit opened the door and handed Bethwig a similar suit to pull on over his working clothes. The suit was hot, smelly, and heavy. Muttering to himself, he followed the technician across the room to a steel door and waited while he fiddled with the lock, swung it open, and motioned him through. Bethwig ducked and wriggled past the heater cells behind the stationary wind-tunnel vanes. Three other men waited for him, none of them in protective clothing, and he removed his helmet.

'Keep the suit on, Franz,' Wernher von Braun told him. 'This won't take long.'

Bethwig nodded. He had worn the suit only to persuade the Gestapo guard who followed him everywhere to remain outside. 'All right, Wernher. What's going on?'

Von Braun glanced at the other two men – his brother, Magnus, and Ernst Mundt. 'I'll come right to the point, Franz. We've had a meeting with the department heads still at Peenemünde as well as those we could reach at Nordhausen. It is clear that the war is lost, and it remains only for the Allies to occupy Germany. Even your V-Ten will not delay that for long.' He looked anxiously at Bethwig who nodded.

'I agree.'

Von Braun looked relieved, and the other two exchanged puzzled glances. 'We know that Kammler has orders to begin planning an evacuation. Rumours from the most reliable sources say that the facility is to be completely destroyed. No trace is to be left of the work being done here. I suppose those fools in Berlin believe it possible. There is another rumour to the effect that Himmler has ordered the SS to shoot all scientific and technical personnel. While I don't quite believe it, I do not dismiss it either. We have all seen how the POWs have been treated since the SS took over, and I can tell you that Peenemünde is paradise compared to conditions at Nordhausen.'

He looked uncomfortable for a moment. 'I must also tell you

this, Franz. Most of the other department heads were against bringing you into our plans. Many of them feel your loyalties are to Himmler and that you cannot be trusted.'

Bethwig remained silent, and von Braun struggled on. 'You know what I think about such nonsense but . . .'

Bethwig nodded. 'I understand.' He paused a moment. 'I doubt there is anything I can say to convince them otherwise.' He shrugged. 'I suppose you could shoot me. That seems to be a common solution to problems these days. Otherwise, you will have to put up with me.'

The three men exchanged looks, and von Braun muttered, 'I think there is no question of that.'

Magnus broke the uncomfortable silence. 'Franz, we have all decided to arm ourselves, just in case this rumour about executing all scientists and technicians should be true. When the Luftwaffe left last fall, they abandoned a great deal of equipment. Several cases of automatic rifles, ammunition and hand grenades have been located and shifted elsewhere, in case they are needed. In addition, the decision has been taken, unanimously, to surrender to the Americans or British. Under no circumstances will we allow ourselves to be captured by the Russians.'

'I should think the English are to be avoided at all costs,' Bethwig replied dryly. 'Surely they would not lavish much love on people who helped destroy their capital city with long-range rockets.'

'No more so than our bomber crews, yet by all reports they are treated as well as, if not better than, English airmen in our prisons.' Magnus hesitated, then at a nod from his brother he continued. 'We have reason to believe that the British would welcome us if we surrendered to them.'

'Reason to believe? Nothing more than that?'

Magnus shook his head. 'No. Nothing more than that. Nor would I say more if I could, except that we have also been approached by the Russians.'

'What do you want from me?'

'Your agreement,' Wernher told him, after a moment of consideration in which the strain was evident in his expression. 'Your staff will follow you. Until now, we dared not approach any of them because of the disagreement over . . .' He hesitated, and Bethwig nodded.

'I understand. When is the evacuation to take place?'

'We don't know. As I said, most of what we have learned is rumour. But everything points to the end of January. The Russians are well into East Prussia, and it is almost certain that they will make a concerted effort to take Peenemünde before it can be destroyed. The best guess is they will reach here no earlier than mid-February, if their present rate of advance continues.'

'There is the V-Ten to launch. I cannot go until that is completed.'

Von Braun's expression was full of sympathy as was Mundt's; they both shared his dream, but Magnus broke in with an exclamation. 'How can you think of the V-Ten now, Franz? It can do nothing to help the war effort. The Russians will have arrived even before the second rocket can be launched. To attempt to do so would jeopardise us all and contribute nothing to a war that is already lost . . .'

Bethwig's voice was calm when he spoke, but von Braun and Mundt understood his determination. 'The V-Ten, Magnus, is no longer a war weapon. And I am no longer concerned with the war effort, nor have I been since my father was murdered. People like Himmler and Kammler have betrayed the Führer and Germany with their greed. Prolonging the war only serves their purposes. I am concerned only with launching the V-Ten. I have given it seven years of my life, and now I have nothing else to live for.'

His expression was still calm as he gauged their reaction. 'The rocket will not be launched against the United States. Wernher, do you remember what we resolved on that evening on the Greifswalder beach, before the war began? Then again last fall when you tried to talk me into this one final time?'

Von Braun stared at him. 'Franz, the moon? Are you crazy?'

'Am I? It can be done, Wernher. Kammler would not know the difference – until too late. The requirements are virtually the same but for the fuel load.'

The three men stared at him in shock; finally, Magnus broke the silence. 'Franz, it would be suicide – even if successful, how would the pilot get back? Who would fly it under those circumstances?'

'I have two volunteers even now. Both understand clearly what the outcome will be. There is no need to be concerned. Both are party members, both fanatics, and they will die gladly for the greater glory of the Reich.'

Ernst Mundt and Magnus von Braun exchanged dubious glances, but Wernher was grinning broadly as he clapped Bethwig on the shoulder.

'You can depend on us,' he cried, thus confirming Bethwig in the decision he had made privately the week before in Kammler's office.

Von Braun followed Bethwig up the scaffolding to a narrow

platform some seventy metres above the launch stand. To the west they could see across the island to the snow-covered fields on the mainland where farms and forests were etched diamond-sharp in the clear January air. To the south the pines almost hid the buildings that housed the laboratories and administrative offices and, beyond them, the staff living quarters. Lost in the distance was the prison camp, most of its buildings deserted. The prisoners had been shipped to the underground factories of Nordhausen deep in the Harz Mountains where, under the direction of the SS, the V-2s continued to pour off the assembly lines for shipment to western Germany and the shrinking areas of occupied Holland.

To their left the cobalt-blue reaches of the Baltic stretched north to Sweden and Finland. Only a few naval patrols dared move on the Baltic now. Most of the merchant ships that had survived the Russian and British submarine onslaught were busily engaged in the forbidden evacuation of German troops from East Prussia and northern Poland.

'We will be ready before the end of January.' Bethwig broke the silence. 'Unless something completely unexpected develops, there is nothing of a technical nature to stop us.'

They had ridden the elevator to the top of the gantry and climbed the rickety scaffolding to the pilot's cabin in the third stage of the rocket. There had not been time to extend the gantries, or the material to do so, and the makeshift platform teetered dizzily in the wind.

Von Braun gave him a worried glance, then, grasping the hand bar bolted above the hatchway, lifted himself, inserted his feet, and slid in. He settled down, released the gimbal brake, and the couch swung freely to assume a horizontal position.

'My God,' he exclaimed, 'this chair is comfortable. If everything wasn't going to hell, I'd have one made up for my study.' Von Braun rocked the couch a moment, then reached up and began to finger switches and tap dials, making certain the needles moved freely against their stops.

'You've designed well, Franz. Nothing more than twenty centimetres away from the hand.' He tapped another dial, then remarked off-handedly, 'I was going over the flight plan last night and noticed you increased the initial G forces to six. Do you think that's wise? Won't it be too exhausting?'

Bethwig shook his head. 'I don't think so. We need that increased speed to eliminate the need to carry so much fuel into orbit around the Earth. I would rather expend it going up than reduce our manoeuvrability on landing. Anyway, I have spent several sessions in the centrifugal chamber at higher G rates myself. The increased gravity does exhaust one quickly, but I have been able to function in an acceptable manner well in excess of the time required.'

Von Braun turned on the couch to face him. Since the death of the elder Bethwig, von Braun was not certain he knew Franz any more. He had hardened to the point of abrasiveness. Every moment of his life now seemed to centre on the damned rocket. The risks he took with Kammler and the Gestapo security staff were appalling; it was as if he were challenging them to discover what he was up to. He also knew that Bethwig had taken to carrying a Mauser pistol, and von Braun had no doubt that he would use it if pressed.

'Franz,' he said after some hesitation. 'You and I have been friends for a hell of a long time now. We can talk about things that . . . well, you know what I mean. I want you to tell me now why you are doing this. You know what Kammler will do if he finds out, as he is bound to. If not before, then certainly after the launch.'

Bethwig nodded. 'Are you suggesting he will shoot me? Of course, he will. But I suspect that by the time he finds out, it will be too late to take such action. If the rocket lands on the moon, the impact on the Allies might well be so great that Berlin will consider me a hero. If the rocket fails, well, then we have only to claim that it has crashed in mid-Atlantic, and go on to try again – providing there is time left to do so.'

'Franz, you have been away for over a month, you don't know . . .'

'Damn it, Wernher, you will not talk me out of it. If you don't wish to be involved, say so now and let me get on with it alone.'

Von Braun looked abashed for a moment. 'I . . . I am sorry, Franz, I didn't mean to imply that . . .'

'Let's forget about it, then, all right?'

As he followed Bethwig into the elevator von Braun found himself even more troubled by his friend's off-hand dismissal of Kammler and his SS and Gestapo thugs.

During the next two weeks the total resources remaining at Peenemünde were mobilised to prepare the V-10. In mid-January a barge docked at Peenemünde village, and under heavy SS guard, a steel cylinder five metres in diameter by four in length was unloaded and moved by specially constructed trailer across the island to the V-10 launch complex. The cylinder contained the thirty metric-ton warhead of Amatol high explosive. The assembly crews took two days to substitute a set of auxiliary fuel tanks for the explosive and mate the final stage of the V-10 to the second. The cylinder containing the explosive was then removed from the launch complex and hidden.

The V-10 had assumed its final configuration: a tapering cylinder more than fifty metres high, twenty-five wide at its base, and consisting of four main sections or stages. The first contained twenty-one M103.5 rocket engines, each generating one hundred and fifty-nine thousand kilograms of thrust, plus two immense fuel tanks which were kept pressurised at all times to support the weight above, and which would contain ninety per cent of the total weight of the entire assembly in liquid oxygen and alcohol. The second stage was a miniature version of the first, powered by four of the same engines and containing five per cent of the vehicle's weight in fuel and liquid oxygen.

Bethwig had worked out the equations for the Earth-moon trajectory in 1939, and he and von Braun had spent many hours since refining and polishing them, even to the point of modifying a Luftwaffe pilot's circular slide rule to calculate the effects of changes in velocity and weight quickly and accurately. With sufficient fuel load and power, the moon, a target constantly visible to an observer in space, could hardly be missed – providing the initial orbital injection speed fell within defined limits.

The third stage contained the relatively crude pilot's cabin above the fuel tanks. Designed originally for transatlantic flights lasting no more than thirty minutes, it had little to offer in the way of pilot comfort. No body waste relief facilities had been included, and the system cobbled together by the Peenemünde staff presented one insurmountable problem – there was no way to test it under weightless conditions. The usual test procedure required an aircraft to fly a shallow outside loop, but now all flights had to be approved by Kammler's office, and no one could think of a sufficiently believable excuse.

The warhead had originally been designed to separate from the third stage containing the pilot, which would then re-enter the atmosphere well behind the warhead. A steel mesh parachute would be deployed to slow the third stage sufficiently to permit the pilot, who would be carrying a pack including a rubber raft, small radio, and rations for several days, to bail out. If the pilot survived, it was hoped that he would be picked up by a U-boat stationed for that purpose in the area approximately one hundred kilometres off Long Island. If he was not picked up and it appeared that he would be rescued by an Allied ship, the pilot was to take his own life. Under no circumstances was the pilot to allow himself to fall into Allied hands. Each pilot, therefore, had been selected from the ranks of the SS especially for dedication as well as ability.

The entire Peenemünde staff had been drafted to ready the V-10, and they fell to with a willingness that surprised Kammler and his aides. Von Braun eased his suspicions by suggesting that as this was probably the last rocket launch they would ever conduct, the staff was eager to give its all. That seemed to satisfy Kammler, so that on the twelfth he shifted his headquarters south to the outskirts of Berlin, leaving the final details for the evacuation to be completed by a special staff which included a one-hundred-man SS security unit to supplement the five-man Gestapo team already well ensconced in Trassenheide.

The following day Bethwig set the launch date for Saturday, 27 January 1945.

Jan Memling could hear Janet humming in the tiny kitchen; the rattle of dishes and the clink of silverware acted as counterpoint. When she came out a few moments later with a wine bottle for him to open, he was standing by the telephone, one hand on the receiver.

'Who was it, Jan?' She threw one arm around his back, tickled his neck, and pressed hard against him. When he did not respond, she drew back, puzzled. 'Jan . . . ?'

He turned slowly, expression strained. For a long moment he stared as if she were not there. Janet had swept her hair up into a roll and was wearing a sheer negligee and high-heeled slippers. They had turned down invitations to several Christmas Eve parties to spend the night alone, and he had obtained a rare bottle of French champagne and two steaks from an American friend with access to a commissary officer at SHAEF.

'I predict this as the last Christmas of the war in Europe,' he had announced a week before. 'So let's celebrate properly.'

Janet had paused for a moment. 'If it really is the last year, then I want a special Christmas present.' When he had asked what it was, she grinned. 'Throw away those damned rubbers. I think Christmas Eve is a good time to start a family.'

He shook his head, muttered, 'Just a wrong number,' and kissed her soundly, then nuzzled the hollow of her throat.

'The steaks,' she protested, the phone call and his expression already forgotten. 'We should start them, shouldn't we?'

'When I was a boy,' Memling offered impishly, 'we followed family tradition and always opened our presents on Christmas

Eve, before supper.' He undid the gown's single tie and slipped it from her shoulders. 'I believe in tradition, don't you?'

Janet lay quietly against his chest. Her breathing had evened, and he thought she might be asleep. For a long moment he revelled in the silky feel of her body and its gentle pressure, but only for a moment, as the memory of the telephone call came crowding back.

As much with Janet's help as the psychiatrist's, he had come to terms with himself, and with her, after his return from Poland. Not even the committee's disappointing rejection of his contention that the A-4 rocket was not radio-guided, as the rocket recovered from Sweden suggested, could surmount the satisfaction and contentment that Janet had brought to him during the past months.

Both the doctor and Simon-Benet had suggested that he take a long holiday in the Irish Republic, away from the 'alarms and excursions', as Simon-Benet had phrased it. For once, he had done as he was told, and Janet's patience and humour had helped him overcome his imagined impotence. Looking back then, he was astounded that he could have taken fear so seriously, could have built it into such a mountain. He realised that continually dwelling on one's own problems was the height of selfishness and that to do so until they assumed such awesome proportions as to block every other consideration was worse than selfish – it was the path to insanity.

Surprisingly, the doctor had agreed with his self-analysis, and as the weeks passed, Memling had gradually cancelled so many of his appointments that two weeks had gone by before he realised he had completely forgotten the last one. When he phoned to apologise, the doctor pronounced him out of danger.

The V-2, or Vengeance Weapon Two – as the A-4 had been renamed – offensive began on 8 September 1944. The first rocket fell on Paris, near the Porte d'Italie, and caused minor structural damage. The following morning two V-2s smashed into London, one on Chiswick Road and the other in Epping Forest, killing three people and smashing water and gas mains.

Eight more V-2s fell on or in the neighbourhood of London during the next five days. At first the Ministry of Home Security's Research and Experiments Department tended to dismiss the V-2 as a no more effective, and a good deal less accurate, weapon than the V-1 unmanned bomber aircraft. Memling had argued, but without success, that the German launch crews needed time to break in, and that for the first weeks it would be impossible to judge the effectiveness of the V-2s, much as it had initially been difficult to rate the effectiveness of the V-1s. But his argument had been dismissed, and Home Security had presented a chart of the first week's operational use of the V-2 showing that the average number of people killed or wounded was similar for both the V-2 and V-1: 2.7 killed and 8.5 wounded per launch, as against 2.7 and 9.1, respectively.

Because of his active and very loud opposition to measures being taken to defend London, Memling's involvement with V-2 analysis came to an abrupt end. A week later, direction of the 'New Battle of Britain', as the newspapers were calling it, was transferred to a special committee, code-named *Big Ben*, that was charged with the responsibility of ferreting out launch sites and perfecting defences against the rocket. Before his transfer to Combined Operations Headquarters in London where he was to begin planning commando-style actions against the Japanese home islands, Memling had the distinct pleasure of seeing his original suggestion for a concerted bombing campaign against operational launch sites of both the V-1 and the V-2 put into operation by direct order from the Prime Minister. He had only just received orders to report to Honolulu in April and had been saving that, and the news that he had wangled Janet a place on his personal staff, as a Christmas present.

Now everything was shattered by Simon-Benet's phone call. As before, it had been put to him as a voluntary operation. He could accept or refuse as he wished; yet the general had known he would go.

Janet mumbled something and lifted her head. She smiled sleepily at him. When he was certain she was asleep again, he got up and went out to the kitchen. The steaks lay ready on the sideboard, and he picked up the bottle of barbecue sauce given to him by a ranger captain from Lubbock, Texas.

He shook his head impatiently. Why delay any longer? The general had said three hours. He looked at his watch, then sat down at the writing desk and thought about what to tell Janet. After a few moments he scribbled a brief note to the effect that he had been called away and would be back in a few weeks. He thought briefly of telling her about Hawaii, decided that it sounded too much like a bribe, then did so anyway.

Memling dressed quickly in the bathroom, found his overcoat in the closet, and felt along the top shelf for his knife. He paused in the bedroom doorway for a moment while he strapped it to his leg. When he left the flat, the gleaming Buick was waiting for him in Montague Street.

As they sped north out of London the general gave him a quick rundown on the mission. 'The Russians have had agents active in the Peenemünde and Nordhausen areas for several months now. We believe they made their first contact with the German scientists in Poland and are trying to follow up. In any event, your friend Englesby at MI-Six is of the opinion that unless we take immediate action, we may come out of this with little more than a handful of broken rocket parts while the Russians carry off everything else. He pushed very hard and General Eisenhower is concerned enough about this matter to give it the go-ahead. SHAEF has set up the mission and code-named it *Project Paper Clip*. When SHAEF asked SOE for an agent, they suggested you. The *Big Ben* committee and MI-Six endorsed the suggestion, and SHAEF asked me to sound you out.'

Memling swore violently enough to cause the driver to jump. 'For seven years everything I've said has been ignored. Each time I've been proven correct and still no one cares. Now they come up with this ridiculous idea and everyone points to me. Why, for God's sake?'

'Don't be a damned fool,' the general snapped. 'There is no one else with your qualifications. You know Wernher von Braun personally and you've been to Peenemünde. Because of that, von Braun might listen to what you have to say.'

'Or throw me to the Gestapo.'

Simon-Benet snorted at that. 'You will be wearing your uniform. They can't shoot you as a spy. For God's sake, the war is almost over.'

It was Memling's turn to snort. 'Has anyone told *them* yet?'

'You will do it, won't you?' Simon-Benet said.

'You know damned well I will.'

'Good.' The general sat back, satisfied. 'You'll be given brush-up training at Northolt and then sent over by air. They'll drop you right on the island this time. Agent reports and reconnaissance indicate the place is nearly deserted. We've infiltrated a few people who will be able to help you. All you have to do is persuade von Braun to come to us and bring anyone he, and you, trust. A submarine will be standing by in the Baltic to take you off. If for some reason the submarine cannot come in, there will be an aircraft standing by in Sweden. We have the full co-operation of the Swedish government in this matter. They don't want to see the Russians in possession of these people any more than we do.'

'There is one thing you have to do for me,' Memling said, turning to face the general. There was a full moon and the sky was ice-clear; he could see Simon-Benet watching him.

'I want you to tell Janet where I've gone and why.'

When the general started to protest about security Memling cut him off. 'Damn it, don't give me that nonsense. She's worked for MI-Six for four years. If I don't have your solemn promise that you will see her first thing tomorrow morning to explain where I'm going and why, then you can turn this car around now.'

Simon-Benet studied him for a moment, then nodded. 'You have my word.'

Memling sat back against the cushions, relieved. The car sped north between hedgerows glistening dark against the snow-covered fields and grey hills.

27 January was cold, overcast, and threatened rain. Kammler telephoned early to check on the V-10's progress and promised to fly in by mid-afternoon. Bethwig then drove to Administration Building 4 which had been established as V-10 headquarters. He trudged wearily to the third floor, as the elevator was out of order. Everything is falling apart, he thought. Just like the war effort. Department heads waited for him in the director's conference room, and he took his place at the head of the table. Von Braun came in a moment later, and as Bethwig stood to begin, the door opened and an out-of-breath Gestapo agent looked in.

'Come in or stay out, you fool,' Bethwig roared, 'but don't leave the door gaping. It's cold enough in here as it is.' The man gave him an embarrassed glance and stepped in while the others in the room contrived to look elsewhere.

'Sit over against the wall there' – Bethwig pointed – 'and keep your mouth shut.' He turned back to the table, glanced at the clock, and began:

'Gentlemen, it is now nine in the morning. We have exactly fifteen hours remaining before the launch. You know your jobs and you know the importance of this mission.'

He grinned, and eyebrows went up. This was the first time in weeks they had heard anything from Bethwig that even approached humour.

'You might even say this is the culmination of a dream we have shared for more than fifteen years. Tonight, before midnight has come, we will have taken man's greatest stride into the unknown reaches of space. You all know what this mission represents and why it is important.'

Bethwig stole a glance at the young Gestapo officer who was watching with a puzzled frown, and nodded to the propulsion plant chief to begin his report on the oscillation problem that had plagued the project from the start.

'We completed successful firing tests at four this morning,' he concluded with a wry grin. That part of the announcement was unnecessary, as the roar of the twenty-one engines had been heard for miles. 'The solution is patchy at best, but I believe it will work.'

The other department heads gave him a tremendous round of applause. The solution was a brilliant piece of engineering accomplished under the most difficult conditions. After the oscillation problem, fuel had been their greatest concern. With the loss of the Dutch liquid oxygen plants and the great damage done to German facilities over the past year, obtaining the full 3.9 million kilograms of fuel and oxidiser had become a tricky proposition. Peenemünde's own liquid oxygen plant had been put back into service late in the fall, and the last refrigerated tank cars were at that moment moving on to sidings for loading. Fuelling was scheduled to begin at 6 p.m. An additional half million kilograms had been diverted from the Nordhausen V-2 production plant at Kammler's reluctant order. The Russian offensive had overrun East Prussia and western Poland before the autumn harvesting of potatoes – the raw material from which the alcohol was distilled – had been completed. The Logistics Supply Department had been forced to use meagre reserves of hard currency to buy sufficient potatoes from Sweden, but the shipments had never arrived, delayed first by the Allied Baltic submarine offensive and then by a Swedish ban on all strategic raw materials to the Reich. Alcohol reserves, as a consequence, were down to less than fifty thousand kilograms stored in a single tank in the almost deserted Luftwaffe storage yards. No one worried any longer about a second launch attempt.

The meeting broke up at noon, and everyone scattered to offices and command centres to begin the final vigil. The most intensive stage in the launch operation had begun, and there would be no rest for anyone before midnight.

Bethwig gathered up some papers while he and von Braun discussed last-minute details. As they were leaving, the Gestapo agent called to Bethwig and motioned him to the table. Annoyed, Bethwig shook his head and started to follow von Braun, but the man ran around the table and grabbed his arm.

'You had damned well better listen to me,' he whispered angrily.

Bethwig jerked his arm free, but the young man kicked the door shut and thrust a photograph at him. 'Do you know this man?'

Bethwig was surprised, and his anger now changed to puzzlement. The face seemed familiar, but he could not recall when or where he had seen it before.

Before he could respond, the Gestapo agent said in a low voice, 'I know what you people are up to.'

Bethwig stared at him. 'What the devil are you talking about?'

The agent shrugged. 'The war is lost. Perhaps you can still accomplish something useful.'

'What . . . ?'

'I am talking about the rocket you are going to send to the moon.'

Bethwig's face was a mask of astonishment.

'Herr Doktor, there is no time for games. I am not stupid. I may not be a scientist, but I did spend two years at university. You people always overrate the ignorance of non-scientists.'

He went to the door to listen, then glanced at his old-fashioned pocket watch. 'We haven't much time. I believe in what you are doing and will do what I can to help. My superior, Major Walsch, is watching you closely, more so than you think. There are others besides me. The man in this photograph is an English spy named Jan Memling. He was captured early this morning with three others, just after landing by parachute in the salt marshes to the south. Walsch seems to know him personally. I had time for a quick look at his file. He is a friend of Doktor von Braun's from before the war. There is also a notation that you and Doktor von Braun met him in 1938, in the Ruhr.'

'Good God,' Bethwig muttered. 'Not again.'

'Walsch hates you and Doktor von Braun for some reason. The Englishman and the three others are undergoing interrogation. Afterwards, I am certain, Walsch will send to Berlin for your arrest warrants.'

Bethwig groped for a chair. Everything he had planned for, worked for, in spite of the ignorance and stupidity emanating from Berlin all these years, was crashing in a heap about him, owing again entirely to the same stupid, ignorant, grasping fools who put their own greed and desire for power ahead of the Reich. People like Walsch, Kammler, Heydrich, Himmler – he raged silently – they were the ones who had betrayed the Führer and Germany, and even now, in the fatherland's death struggles, they were doing their best to twist the knife.

The agent pulled a chair around to face Bethwig. 'Look here, I said I would help and I will. Walsch will not finish the interrogations before tonight. Even if one breaks, he still must break the others. One man's testimony will not be sufficient to arrest someone of your stature. But even then, it will take time to get a warrant for your arrest. The teletype transmission lines have been broken. He will have to telephone to Berlin, persuade someone in Himmler's office, if not the reichsführer himself, to issue the warrants, and then they must be flown or driven here before he dare move. He cannot approach Kammler, as the general is counting on the V-Ten to restore his prestige with the Führer. If the rocket is successful, Walsch will not be able to touch you, so he must do so before it is launched.'

Bethwig took a deep breath. When he lit the cigarette offered by the Gestapo agent, his hands were rock-steady. Now that the first shock had passed, he was thinking clearly once more.

'All right. You have obviously had time to think this through. What do you suggest?'

The agent lit his own cigarette and blew a stream of smoke towards the windows. 'You must launch the rocket well in advance of the announced time.'

'Impossible! The sequence is extremely complex and is dependent upon the completion of parallel activities. It can be delayed but not accelerated by more than a few minutes.'

The agent did not waste time arguing. 'Then you must go about your business as usual. I'll have a word with Hauptsturmführer Schulz who commands the SS security unit in Kammler's absence. He and Walsch are at odds, and I am certain he'll be most happy to make Walsch look bad. He is also in line for the position of aide to Kammler, which would mean a promotion and fat graft before the war ends.'

Bethwig nodded in an absent fashion, then glanced up sharply. 'Look here, what's your name?'

'Prager, sir. Thomas Prager.'

Bethwig studied him a moment, noticing for the first time the thin scar that ran from his hairline, then down his left cheek, to end beneath his chin. Prager stood hunched slightly to one side.

'Why are you doing this, Prager?'

The Gestapo agent looked momentarily abashed. 'Until a year and a half ago I was a front-line soldier and proud to be so. Then I was wounded in Sicily. When I recovered, the army discharged me as unfit. My father had been a policeman in Hamburg before the war. He was killed in a bombing raid in 1943, but he still had many friends there. They needed men, and I was hired. A few months later I was transferred to the political police.'

His expression became angry, and he shook his head. 'I don't like what they have done to Germany, or the German people. I joined the Hitler Youth and the party at thirteen. But it's all changed since the war. All the goals have been forgotten, all the good things. Now everyone is out for himself. The worst are the SS. After those army fools tried to murder the Führer, we were given lists of people to arrest. Most had nothing to do with the plotters. They were people who knew someone or had once been friends of, or even went to school with, others who had been arrested. Every name squeezed out by the Gestapo was added to the list and that person arrested. Trials were a farce. The accused were rarely allowed to defend themselves. Those who were not sentenced to death were sent to concentration camps. I escorted many such, and I can tell you that when the war ends, the German people will see how we have been disgraced.'

Prager was silent a moment. 'Perhaps, if you succeed in this attempt to travel to the moon, you will show that not all Germans are like the SS, that we are still capable of great accomplishments.'

He stopped abruptly then, as if embarrassed, and went to the window. 'Will this weather interfere with the launching?'

Bethwig stared after him, wondering how many other people there were like him in Germany. If they had only revealed themselves earlier, perhaps . . . But then, Himmler was a shrewd enough judge of human nature to understand that. His answer to such a threat was the systematic terror that his SS and Gestapo had unleashed. Why had the Führer not stopped him? he wondered; and then the old rumours of Heydrich's files filtered back. Perhaps they are true, he thought. Even the Führer could be afraid of such men.

'Why did the Englishman come to Peenemünde?'

The Gestapo agent turned to rest against the windows and rubbed his head against the cold glass as if to relieve a headache. 'Only rumours so far. I was told that one of the people helping him, a woman and a German national, confessed that this Major Memling had been sent to try and persuade you, Doktor von Braun and the scientific staff to revolt against the SS and defect to England. Foolishness! But that is what Walsch believes, or wants to believe. The man was probably sent to sabotage the V-Ten project.'

Bethwig wondered. He lit another cigarette but said nothing more. He suspected that Walsch was closer to the truth than he knew, and if so, all of them were in real danger. Himmler could very well be persuaded to carry out his threat to shoot all scientific personnel. Wernher was convinced that he was badly frightened of their capture by the Russians. Something would have to be done, but what?

The interior was pitch-black. There was no sound. They designed it this way, he told himself over and over until it became a chant. They designed it this way to make you concentrate on your own terror. Memling gagged and tried to vomit again, but his stomach was empty and the retching went on and on. When the spasm subsided, he lay back on the wet cement floor and tried to breathe through his nose.

It was a set-up, Memling thought for the hundredth time. They were waiting; the SS troops rose, seemingly from the ground, as he was gathering his parachute. Within seconds he and the three Germans were disarmed, handcuffed, blindfolded, and pushed and kicked towards waiting lorries. The Germans even knew how many of them there would be, as there were exactly four empty lorries.

They were driven for what seemed like hours over rough tracks before the lorries stopped and they were taken one by one inside. Blinded by the lights, he was stripped and searched, photographed and fingerprinted, then taken naked into an administrative area where three female clerks had giggled and darted glances at him as he was shoved on to a hard bench and ignored for an hour or more before a door opened and a tall, very gaunt man in a black, ill-fitting civilian suit emerged. Memling went rigid.

'Major Jan Memling, I believe. We have met before, if you recall. Twice in fact. You worked for your secret service, MI-Six, at the time. At our first meeting you jumped from a train to avoid a conversation with me. The second time you ran away from a very fine position in Liège.' He chuckled. 'Unfortunately you do not have those options this time.'

Memling remembered the skeletal figure unfolding from a seat to pursue him through a crowded train racing towards the Belgian border, a grinning death's-head leering at him from across a scaffolding in a factory yard. He rarely dreamed, but for the past seven years he had endured nightmares in which Walsch's face predominated.

'My name, in case you have forgotten, is Major Jacob Walsch, of the Secret State Police Office, Division Three. I would suggest that a great deal of time and pain can be spared if you are prepared to co-operate and answer my questions.'

Memling nodded, fearful that his voice would betray his terror.

'Good. Then perhaps you will tell me about your mission here on Peenemünde – most particularly, the names of the three traitors who agreed to assist you, and any others of whom you may have knowledge?'

'My name,' Memling began, speaking softly to disguise the tremor, 'is Jan Memling. My rank is major, Royal Marines. My identification number is S5698034. I am a member of the regular military establishment of the United Kingdom and, as such, am entitled to the treatment accorded to prisoners of war under terms of the Geneva Convention.'

'That may well be true, Major Memling. But you must realise that you have forfeited all rights to such protection, as you are out of uniform.' Walsch chuckled at his own joke. 'I suppose you will make the usual protest that your clothing was taken from you, and so it was. I did instruct my people to make certain that it was properly labelled and stored. I can show you if you wish, but you will find, I am afraid, that they are still civilian clothes. In any event, Peenemünde is not a military installation but a secret research centre owned and operated by the SS and therefore not subject to civil or military law. I might also add that I have had a request from the local SS commander to have you released to their custody. It seems they wish to settle an old score.'

Memling had expected nothing else when they had taken his uniform away. He strove not to allow his fear to show.

'I am concerned most with three traitorous German citizens,' Walsch continued, 'arrested while aiding an enemy of the Reich. I intend to root out and eliminate the rest of their pack. You can spare yourself a great deal of pain, very severe pain, and perhaps even death, if you co-operate. You will have time to think the matter over while I discuss the situation with your comrades.'

As Walsch turned back into his office, Memling was yanked to his feet and hustled down a bare corridor to a heavy wooden door. A uniformed guard unlocked it, and he was shoved inside. The door slammed shut, and Memling sank down on his haunches, enduring the recurring waves of fear that washed over him with an intensity he had never known before.

The cell door was opened without warning, and two guards jerked him up and dragged him out into a small yard. Floodlights glared at each corner of the enclosure. Against the building stood two uniformed SS men with rifles slung. Opposite, a badly chipped brick wall edged the yard. At first its significance did not register, but then Memling realised that the scars and chips had been made by bullets and that the two soldiers were executioners. The omnipresent fear receded for a moment; they were going to shoot him immediately, rather than subject him to torture. An emotion approaching gratitude swept through him. Memling took a deep breath, bracing himself as he was pushed against the wall.

It was dark; an entire day must have passed since he had been dragged into the prison at dawn. Rain spattered intermittently, and he shivered horribly in the freezing cold. A dull roaring noise puzzled him; it came from beyond the wall, advancing and receding, but he could not identify the sound even though he concentrated with all the intensity at his command. What were they waiting for? he screamed silently.

An eternity passed before the door opened again and Walsch appeared. He stopped in the centre of the yard and glanced at the riflemen, then at the half-frozen man drooping against the wall. He smiled and motioned towards the building.

A non-commissioned officer pushed something sprawling into the mud. He bent, grabbed a handful of hair, yanked and ran across the yard to slam the figure against the wall beside Memling. Only then did Memling see that it was the woman. Shock coursed through him at the sight of her. Blood streamed from several places beneath her hair. Skin had been flayed from her back and buttocks, and there were burn marks on her breasts and abdomen. She was only half-alive, and they had to fasten a chain around her neck to hold her upright. For a moment she looked at Memling; there was no recognition in her eyes, only the starkest, staring terror.

Walsch had sauntered over then. 'You may be interested to know, Major Memling, this piece of swine flesh has told us everything.' He drew deeply on his cigarette, then reached out and yanked the woman's chin up. 'As a reward, we are going to give her a surcease from her labours. She has worked quite hard, you know. And it shows.' He laughed. 'Pity. She was rather attractive. My men appreciated that.

'Ah well, as we no longer need her services, of any kind . . .' He chuckled at his joke and nodded to the unterscharführer who slowly drew his pistol.

The woman's eyes fastened on his movements, and in spite of what must have been terrible pain, she mouthed over and over again, 'No, please, no.'

The unterscharführer raised the pistol and brought it down to rest on the bridge of her nose. The chain collar prevented her from twisting her head away, and the man smiled and pulled the trigger. There was a loud click, and feigning astonishment, the SS man turned to Walsch who shook his head in mock dismay.

'Once again, Unterscharführer.'

The performance was repeated, and again there was a loud click. Memling lost his head then, dived for the sergeant, and was clubbed to the ground by his guard. Walsch knelt and twisted his head around, forcing him to watch.

'Once again, please.'

The woman had collapsed against the chain and was choking. The unterscharführer slid a magazine home, racked the breech back, and gently held the woman up while he aimed the pistol once more and pulled the trigger. The gun went off this time, and blood spattered Memling. The bullet had shattered her skull, and she slipped through the chain into a crumpled heap.

Walsch smiled down at him. 'Perhaps it will be your turn next. Are you strong enough to endure what she did?'

Twice more, at long intervals, Memling was dragged forth to witness similar executions. Each time, Walsch smiled at him around his cigarette and promised that his turn was next.

The countdown stood at minus six hours. Bethwig turned away from the controller's ready board, crossed the room, and stepped out into the windblown night. The sea air eased his headache, and he lit a cigarette, ignored by the SS guard huddling in the corner of the entryway for shelter from the wind.

As the launch drew nearer, a curious lassitude had settled on him, and it was with great difficulty that he forced himself to continue. The countdown had gone like clockwork, days of intense rehearsal paying off. No major problems had arisen, and the tricky liquid oxygen tanks would be topped in the final hour.

So far, Prager had reported nothing of serious consequence from Gestapo headquarters in Trassenheide, and Bethwig was beginning to think they would beat Walsch in spite of the odds. He was puzzled then as to the origin of the depression engulfing him. He was about to realise the dream of a lifetime, despite insurmountable difficulties. The countdown had proceeded so smoothly they were ahead of schedule by some fifty-four seconds. For a moment he smiled to himself in the darkness, remembering the early days at Kummersdorf and Greifswalder Oie where they had struggled not only to launch rockets but to develop orderly methods for doing so.

And what would happen to their carefully constructed countdown procedures, to the painfully learned concept of built-in holds, included as much to allow everyone to catch their breath as to cope with unforeseen emergencies. An entire vocabulary had been evolved and would be lost after tonight. The Peenemünde crew would never launch another rocket. The Russians would overrun the area before his next V-10 could be readied. But that had not affected his decision in the slightest. The war would soon be over and with it experimentation with rockets. If the crew has learned one thing, he thought, it is that rocket research is so expensive only a government can afford it. And they would do so grudgingly, even under the exigencies of war.

The fact that the Allies might have sent an agent to make

contact with von Braun suggested their interest. But Bethwig also suspected that interest would be short-lived; as soon as the war was ended, the various democracies would revert to peacetime pursuits, and economic depression would follow, as always happened after a major war, and the cycle would repeat itself as endlessly as in the past.

Bethwig threw his cigarette away and walked out to the service road. Hands in pockets, he stood with his back to the wind looking down the paved surface to the floodlit gantries surrounding the cone-shaped tower that was his V-10. He could see its entire length, including the two sharply raked wings on the third stage. He stood there for a while, feeling no urgency to return; the launch team was thoroughly drilled. He was like a ship's captain, needed only for emergency decisions. Unless something completely untoward happened, six more hours would see it finished. For a moment he was close to praying.

Prager was waiting for him in the blockhouse. The Gestapo agent nodded, and a few minutes later Bethwig crossed the room to the lavatory. Prager followed him in and locked the door.

'Walsch has finished with the three traitors. All confessed and have been executed. He will start on the Englishman soon. I won't go into details, but if he resists for even one hour, then he is made of iron.'

Bethwig fought down the urge to scream, to swear, to smash his fist against the wall. They were so close, so damned close. Instead, he held himself rigid, under iron control, until he could think coherently once more.

'How long?'

Prager shook his head. 'I don't know. Walsch has nearly exhausted himself. The man is sick and may decide to rest a while.' Prager shrugged. 'Every minute he delays makes it that much easier to break the Englishman.'

'But didn't you tell me that it would still take time to get arrest warrants from Berlin?'

Prager nodded, his defeat evident now. 'So I thought. But as soon as he had the first confession, Walsch persuaded Himmler's office to issue a conditional warrant. Now he only needs the Englishman's. He would prefer to do it legally.' Prager shrugged. 'But believe me, if for some reason Walsch fails to break the Englishman, he will falsify the confession and kill him.'

Bethwig stooped over a sink and drenched his face with cold water. 'I just cannot believe that Himmler would allow us to be arrested, at least before the V-Ten is launched. There is too much . . .'

Prager pushed himself away from the wall. 'Stop thinking like that. Logic has no bearing on the matter. Himmler realises that neither the V-Two nor the V-Ten can affect the war any longer; in fact, I doubt he is even aware you are attempting the V-Ten launching.' When Bethwig stared at him in astonishment, Prager nodded.

'He is much too busy gathering together the final reins of power. As commander in chief of the Replacement Army, as well as reichsführer and head of the SS, he virtually controls Germany. Why should he spend time worrying about another secret weapon when the previous ones have failed to live up to expectations?'

'But who . . . ?'

'Kammler.' Prager answered his unfinished question. 'General Kammler chose incorrectly when offered a choice between command of the Vengeance weapon battalions and a division on the eastern front last year. It is said that even Himmler's staff members no longer accept his telephone calls. Kammler is desperate to regain favour before Himmler remembers to hang him from a meat hook for sabotaging the war effort. He believes the V-Ten will save him.'

Bethwig thought about that a moment. 'But Kammler was supposed to arrive this afternoon and did not. How much importance can . . . ?'

Prager dismissed the objection with an abrupt gesture. 'Tempelhof was badly bombed. The runways are not usable at the moment, so Kammler is driving to Peenemünde. Walsch found out and alerted friends at Gestapo headquarters in Berlin. Roadblocks have been established to delay him. Again, all this is without Himmler's knowledge; but then, it makes no difference in any case. Walsch is determined that von Braun and you be arrested before the rocket can be launched. Having failed yet again, you will both be discredited and no one will raise a voice in your defence. And do not forget that Walsch also has a hole card – the old charges of diverting war materials to personal ends are still pending against your friend. As soon as the arrests are made, the same charges will be made against you, using the V-Ten as evidence. An SS tribunal will find you guilty, and the sentence will be carried out. Kammler will have no choice but to agree or be charged as an accessory.'

'What about the SS commander here? You said he might be persuaded to intervene?'

Prager shrugged. 'He refused. He won't help Walsch, but he won't hinder him either. Hauptsturmführer Schulz knows that Kammler may be for the high jump, and wants to make certain he doesn't go with him.'

There was no reason, Bethwig knew, to doubt Prager's analysis. It made sense according to the Byzantine style of thinking that characterised the upper echelons of the SS.

His mind was working now at a feverish pace. There were two alternatives remaining. He could press ahead with the launch in the hope that it could be completed before Walsch received the warrants, but as soon as the thought was formulated, he saw its hopelessness. If, as Prager said, Walsch was that determined to stop them, he would merely have them arrested and held until the confession and the warrants were forthcoming. The man was a fanatic; he had known that since their first meeting in 1938. Logic did not affect his thinking. Walsch was determined to destroy them, to demonstrate his own power in return for the slights he had suffered, or supposed he had suffered, all these years.

That left the second alternative. Walsch had to be destroyed. They might then survive long enough at least to complete the launching. After that, nothing else mattered.

All these years he had built weapons of mass destruction, had worked willingly, joyfully and skilfully to do so, while enjoying the camaraderie that such difficult and complex tasks engendered among teams of specialists. He had seen such weapons move from his imagination to drawing board to test stand. He had participated in and directed operational launchings of the V-2 on London and Antwerp and Brussels with hardly a thought for the thousands of civilians he was killing by remote control. But now the moment had come when he must kill with his own hands, at close range, close enough to see into the eyes of the man he was murdering. The thought was sickening, and Bethwig experienced a rare sensation of futility and indecision.

Surprisingly enough, Prager did not protest the conclusion. 'How would you go about it?' he asked. 'You couldn't get near enough to Walsch now, nor could I.'

A scheme was already forming in Bethwig's mind. 'How many SS troops are left on Peenemünde?' he demanded.

Prager glanced at him, then shook his head. 'I'm not certain. Perhaps a hundred. Certainly not more.'

'Would they obey orders given by Walsch?'

'No!' Prager's answer was emphatic. 'Not even if the Russians were crossing the River Peene.'

'But they would defend him if he were attacked?'

'Of course . . .'

'How many Gestapo agents?'

'Five including myself, plus another eight clerical staff.'

'And where do you stand?'

'With you,' Prager answered simply.

'Even if it means killing the policemen you work with . . . ?'

'I am a policeman. They are murderers,' he answered simply.

'Then we must work fast and finish them before the SS can interfere.' Bethwig told him then about the Luftwaffe arms. Prager's eyes lit up at the news, and for the first time the defeated slump was gone from his shoulders. They left the lavatory and drove the eight kilometres to the tracking station on the north shore where Magnus von Braun was at work.

Memling heard boots moving restlessly outside. He tensed, waiting for the painful flash of light and the shouted commands, which did not come. Perhaps this was more psychological pressure to intensify his fear.

He had only the haziest idea how much time had passed since his capture. He knew for certain that at least twelve hours had gone by. The woman's execution had taken place in darkness; the man he knew only as Hans had been shot during the daylight, although the heavy overcast made it impossible to judge the time of day, and the final resistance agent had been killed in darkness again; there had not even been time to learn his name.

As he crouched in a corner of the cell he began to examine the possibility of extinction dispassionately. Memling recalled the relief he had felt when he had thought they were going to shoot him. He had been grateful then that he could escape the pain, that it would end simply in the crash of a bullet.

His parents had insisted on a parochial school in spite of strained circumstances, but the religion the nuns had endeavoured to impress on their charges had been wasted in his case. Even now, he realised, his thoughts did not turn to salvation. He also found it curious that he thought little about Janet . . . as if she belonged to another time and had no business in this present. It was, he knew, a result of his intense preoccupation with his own fate and another manifestation of the selfishness that could drive one to madness.

When he had been returned to his cell after the first glimpse of Gestapo justice, he had made a singular discovery: he was not afraid of dying. He had never been subject to paralysing fear in combat situations, because he knew death, if it came, would be quick. What he did fear, to the point of gibbering nonsense, was pain and torture. When he thought back to the times he had been frightened into panic, it was because torture seemed an imminent possibility. That first time on the train, then in Liège, during the long walking trip to Peenemünde – and now. He knew the pain would be prolonged and excruciating. No matter what he told them, no matter how he begged, Walsch would see that the torture continued until he died.

The solution to his fear was therefore simple enough. Suicide. Even though they had stripped him naked, it was possible to kill himself – not pleasantly – but possible. A major vein ran close to the surface of the wrist. A knife or sharp edge would be less painful, but one could bite through the vein and bleed to death in less than thirty minutes.

Under other circumstances the pain involved would have repulsed him, but compared with Gestapo torture techniques, such pain would be minor. Once he had made that decision, the fear that paralysed him, that had nearly driven him insane in the darkness, receded to a controllable level. And as it did he began to think about alternatives.

Each time they had come for him, one guard had swung the door open and the other had entered to haul him out, clearly expecting no resistance. In fact, the one guard had remained in the doorway the last time, looking off down the hall as he joked with someone out of sight. Death in action, however feeble, was preferable to gnawing through one's own wrist, Memling decided.

A second pair of boots stopped outside, and a key was jammed into the lock. It happened so quickly that Memling barely had time to crouch into position against the far wall before the door swung open. He anticipated the blast of light and shut his eyes tightly. A hand grabbed his left arm and yanked him up, but Memling was limp and the man swore under his breath and reached for his other arm. As his knees came under him Memling straightened abruptly and shot his left arm out straight to break the soldier's grip. As it reached full extension he doubled his fist into a hammer and whipped it straight back and down to smash into the man's testicles. The blow was so sudden and powerful that it paralysed him for the vital second needed to spin, flip the holster open, and extract the heavy Walther pistol.

Memling had thought each move through during the endless hours, rehearsing them over and over in his mind. His thumb sought the safety catch and shoved up as he turned, crouching and pushing the agonised soldier out of his way. A startled exclamation from the guard in the corridor gave him the last bits of necessary data. He fired once, blindly, lining up by instinct and sound. The blast of the nine-millimetre cartridge was deafening, drowning the results, but Memling was already moving sideways. He parted his eyelids the tiniest fraction to focus on the darkness inside the door. Even so, the glare was intensely painful after hours in pitch blackness, and he could distinguish nothing more than a blotch of light as the echoes died inside the cell. There was no answering shot. He covered his eyes with his left hand and peered through slitted fingers. Legs sprawled across the doorway, and shouting could be heard somewhere in the building. Feet pounded towards the cell-block.

Memling jumped to the door and dragged the body inside. A scraping sound told him that the guard's machine pistol was still slung over his shoulder. The Walther P-38 held eight cartridges, one now gone. There was no time to check the magazine, but no experienced soldier would keep his weapon less than fully loaded. He eased to the cell door, extended the pistol into the corridor, and fired six shots, three in either direction. A scream told him he had scored at least one hit, and a door slammed. There was now one cartridge left for himself.

Jan pulled the door partly shut. In the near darkness his sensitive eyes could see enough to strip the machine pistol from the dead man's shoulder. The guard he had struck was trying to get to his knees, holding his groin with one hand, scrabbling at the wall with the other.

Memling kicked him down again and in the shaft of light, saw that it was the same unterscharführer who had shot the three resistance people so brutally. Without thinking, Memling jammed the muzzle of the machine pistol against the man's throat.

'You bastard,' he snarled in English, pushing on the gun so that the man gagged. The SS officer tried to plead with him. There was another shout in the corridor, a door was slammed open, and a burst of automatic rifle fire ricocheted the length of the hall. Memling stared into the man's eyes and pulled the trigger once. The body convulsed, and hands tore at the ruined throat.

Someone had turned out the corridor lights, but his eyes were still hypersensitive, and he could see clearly the two men crawling towards his cell from the courtyard entrance. He waited until both were well along, then fired two short bursts that struck them head-on. A long period of silence followed. Memling slumped against the wall, unmindful of the icy stone on his naked skin. He drew a deep breath, revelling in the loss of his terror. The time had come, he knew, but at least he had accounted for four, possibly five, Nazis, and he knew then how the two Poles he had met in northern Germany an endless time ago had felt. He was ready to die now. Memling took a deep breath and bit down on the pistol barrel.

An explosion whip-cracked through the building. Automatic

weapons erupted and there were more explosions, until the noise and concussions drove him to bury his head in his arms.

It took Magnus von Braun an hour to assemble four former front-line soldiers at the radio direction station. They came as quickly as they could be detached from their duties, and replacements found, without incurring the suspicions of the SS guards. The four men – one oberfeldwebel, or sergeant major, one stabsgefreiter, or corporal, and two grenadiers – were members of the Versuchskommando Nord, or Test Command North, technically a combat unit assigned to guard the Peenemünde installation, but in reality a device used several years before to assemble six companies of technically trained men to ease the severe manpower shortage. Oberfeldwebel Harmutt Sussmann had served for three years in the Twenty-first Division of the Africa Corps. Wounded at Kasserine Pass, he was among the last to be evacuated from North Africa. After recovering from wounds, he had been assigned to command the VKN, most of which had now been reassigned elsewhere; only a few dozen from a ration strength of one thousand remained at Peenemünde. Sussmann's eyes glowed when his assignment was explained, and when they were assembled, Magnus left to telephone the news to his brother.

With a few rapid strokes Sussmann sketched the location of Gestapo headquarters in relation to the village of Trassenheide.

'As you see, the building is separated from the town proper by the sand dunes,' he explained in gruff Bavarian accents. 'They are not high but provide the privacy the Gestapo requires for its activities.' Sussmann stared at them and singled out Prager.

'Lay out the interior,' he snapped. There was a distinctly hostile tone to his voice, which Prager wisely ignored.

'The building is little more than a large box, thirty metres on a side,' he began. 'The front portion is devoted to offices and administrative areas. The files are kept in this locked room here. There are six cells, all three by three metres, on either side of this hall which runs like so.' He sketched a narrow corridor leading from the centre front to back. 'There are two rooms on the north wall for interrogation, and all are equipped as physicians' examination rooms.

'There is a garrison of eight SS and four Gestapo officers. The SS are part of a special unit attached to Division Three. They take their orders from Walsch and not from Kammler's command. There are also eight more employees, none of them armed, and most will have been sent home for the night. The building is constructed of cement blocks. The interior is plyboard. The cells are reinforced ply and thoroughly sound- and light-proofed. In the rear, separated from the sea by a wall three metres high, is the courtyard where the resistance traitors were executed.'

'Where will we find Walsch?'

'We?' Prager and Sussmann both asked simultaneously.

Bethwig nodded. 'We.'

'You can't go,' Sussmann told him flatly.

Bethwig leaned across the table. 'No one has a better right than I do. I intend to kill Walsch myself.'

Sussmann and Prager exchanged glances, and Prager, knowing why Bethwig felt as he did, nodded with reluctance. Sussmann saw the nod and started to protest, but Magnus von Braun, who had returned a few moments earlier, also agreed. Sussmann gave in and signed Prager to continue. The Gestapo officer placed a fingertip on a room off the administrative area.

'Walsch will either be here or in one of the interrogation rooms with the prisoner.'

'Which is the Englishman's cell?'

'The middle one, to the left or south side of the corridor.'

Bethwig glanced at each man in turn. 'You know what we have to do and why,' he said simply. 'Let's get started.'

The fitful snow had stopped by the time the six men drove up to the gate of the deserted Luftwaffe test area known as Peenemünde West, on the north-west tip of the island. A bored and half-frozen sentry was on duty at the dilapidated barrier, one of the few remaining Luftwaffe personnel on the island. He was in no mood to question Bethwig's demand for admittance, and they drove on past rows of empty buildings that seemed like evil mountains in the furtive moonlight.

Sussmann led him to the side door of a two-storey warehouse, produced a key, and got out to unlock the door. They clattered up iron stairs to the loft, and Sussmann showed them several packing boxes labelled for machinery. Four long wooden crates were stacked on a pallet behind. Sussmann levered open the top crate, peeled back the greased paper, and exposed ten MP40 machine pistols to the gleam of the torchlight. The corporal passed them out while Sussmann opened another case and extracted ammunition already packed into thirty-eight-round magazines. A third case held potato masher-style hand-grenades.

'Enough to start our own war.' Prager grinned as he hefted one of the machine pistols and cocked the action. 'It feels good to handle one of these again.'

*

Sussmann directed him to park the car half a kilometre from the beach, and they went over the plan once more, then started off. They hiked along the beach towards the isolated building, depending on the sand dunes and the weather to conceal them. Two hundred metres from the building they came to the remains of the old fishing pier. They split here, Prager and Bethwig continuing along the waterline to the rear of the courtyard while Sussmann took the other four up on to the sand dunes. The sergeant major had been adamant: Bethwig would not be allowed to participate in the frontal attack. Prager had supported Sussmann, and Bethwig had given in. Their task was limited to seeing that no one escaped over the back wall. Faced now with imminent action, Bethwig was relieved at Sussmann's decision. He discovered that he was scared to death in a way he had never been while serving with the V-2 battalion. There, death had seemed a random process of selection, much as a traffic accident would be. Here, it was entirely too personal.

The wind whipped at them as they crouched in the wet sand. The floodlit courtyard gave them sufficient light to see by, while at the same time providing concealing shadows. Even though both men wore heavy duffle coats, the wind slipped through folds and crevices to set them shivering.

Bethwig glanced at his watch again. The radium dial showed nearly 8 p.m. Less than four hours remained; and although he knew that Wernher was more than capable of carrying out the sequence without reference to him, if he was to complete the rest of his plan, he could not spare more than another forty minutes here. Yet he could not bring himself to leave until he was certain that Walsch was dead.

Two grenades exploded in quick succession, followed by burst after burst of machine-pistol fire. Bethwig and Prager could see the flares and concussive shock waves rippling outward from the building, although the wind, blowing away from them, muffled the sound. Shouts and screams mingled with the gunfire, and Bethwig was in a fury of apprehension. The battle was loud enough, he was certain, to bring SS reinforcements, even though Sussmann's first task had been to cut power and telephone lines.

Prager nudged him; a head had appeared level with the wall. A moment later a figure dropped and, crouching, reached up to grab a weapon that someone was handing over. Prager's hand was on his arm. 'Wait until they are both over,' he whispered hoarsely. 'Aim low and fire short bursts.'

Bethwig nodded and pulled back and up on the bolt handle,

as Prager did, trying to remember his long-ago Hitler Youth training.

'Now,' Prager shouted, and fired.

Over the sights Bethwig saw one man turn towards them; his face was hidden in shadow, but Bethwig could imagine the surprise that died as he fired two short bursts. The figure pitched forward, and Prager took the other as he dropped over the wall. Then Bethwig was running, propelled by the desperate need to reach Walsch. He ripped a grenade from his coat pocket, twisted the igniter, counted to three, and tossed it into the courtyard. Prager drew up, panting, machine pistol in hand, and mouthing blasphemies as he flung his grenade over as well. They both ducked against the base of the wall, and the bombs went off one after the other.

Bethwig started up, but Prager yanked him back and threw another grenade to make certain the courtyard was clear. After it exploded, Prager swung himself to the top of the wall, inched his head up, then swarmed over. Bethwig followed, shouting uncontrollably with excitement.

A man in black uniform lay dead. That made three. Prager held up a hand and edged towards the open doorway. From the front of the building sustained gunfire shattered the night. Sussmann's rush had not carried the building as planned. Could they obtain reinforcements? he wondered. An explosion came, sharp and crisp against the wind – but from outside, not inside the building.

'We've got to move!' Prager shouted, and Bethwig peered along the dark corridor. He could just make out a partly opened door and, with a jolt, realised it was the cell in which he had been held the previous autumn. Two bodies were huddled on the floor of the hall. Prager jerked a thumb at them.

'We didn't kill those two. Who did?'

Bethwig started to shake his head, then smiled in sudden understanding. 'Inside! Is that Jan Memling?' he shouted down the corridor. 'This is Franz Bethwig. Do you remember me?'

'Franz Bethwig?' a voice called back doubtfully.

'Yes, Wernher von Braun's friend.' Bethwig had switched to rusty English and was forced to search his memory for the proper words.

'We were at Hotel . . .'

'I know who you are. What do you want?'

The Englishman must have armed himself somehow. That could be the only explanation for the two dead men in the corridor. 'How many have you . . .' He could not find the English word he wanted and awkwardly substituted one in German: '... *töten*?'

'The hell with you, you bloody bastards!'

'God damn you for a fool, Memling.' Bethwig was so angry he began to stutter. 'We must . . . we need to know how many . . . remain in . . . are left, you damned ass.'

The English swear-words must have convinced him, for Memling answered after a moment. 'Four,' he shouted. 'What the hell is going on?'

'There is not time . . .' Bethwig began, then switched to German. 'There is no time to explain. Do you have a weapon?'

Memling hesitated. It made no sense . . . but then nothing had for as long as he could remember. 'Yes,' he shouted back.

'Some of us are attacking the front. We must come in through the back. Do not shoot us.'

Bethwig did not wait for an answer but raised his machine pistol over his head and stepped into the corridor. Prager lunged for him, but Bethwig twisted away and started forward, heart in his throat, skin crawling, as he waited for the bullet's impact. After a few steps he saw a hint of movement behind the partly opened door.

'If you kill me,' Bethwig blurted in sudden fright, 'you will lose your last chance.'

He was beside the cell door now, facing a crouched figure nearly invisible in the shadows. He pushed the door wider. The fear was as evident in Memling's eyes as he knew it was in his own, but the machine pistol the Englishman held was rock-steady and aimed at his mid-section.

'Get some clothes and come help,' Bethwig said quietly, and put out a hand to halt Prager as he came up behind.

'The Englishman?' Prager asked, and Bethwig nodded.

Prager stared at Bethwig, then went back down the corridor and removed boots, jacket, and trousers from one of the dead soldiers, tossing the clothes to Memling who began to pull them on as if in a daze. When Prager handed him two stick grenades, Memling clutched them a moment, then shook himself and braced his shoulders.

'How many are left?' he demanded in excellent German.

'Possibly eight,' Prager answered. 'I think we should go around the side and . . .'

'I hold a commission as major in the Royal Marine Commando.' Memling's voice was crisp. 'This is your show, but I advise you to go through that door and fast.'

Prager and Bethwig exchanged glances, and Prager nodded. 'Tell us what to do.'

'How are your men disposed in front?' Memling demanded as he moved down the corridor towards the door, keeping well to one side.

'Head-on attack by two men and one more on each flank. Grenades and machine pistols.'

That explained the explosions, then, Memling thought. He had not the slightest idea what was going on, and there was no time to find out. Already the volume of gunfire was slackening. He waved the two Germans to either side of the door; there wasn't even time to ask if either had combat experience. Jan tried the door, and when it gave, a rictus of anger slashed across his face. He slung the machine pistol, twisted the screw covers from the grenades, and pulled their igniting cords.

'Damned careless of them,' Prager grunted as he threw the door open.

Memling stepped forward and lobbed the grenades with easy underhand throws, aiming to bounce them from the walls so that the blasts would fill the long room with shrapnel. He hesitated long enough to see them strike walls; a white face turned towards him, the mouth forming a warning scream; a man in a suit paused in the midst of cranking a field telephone. Then Memling slammed the door. Twin blasts vomited through the front of the building and bulged the iron-reinforced door from its frame. It took the three of them to wrench it open.

The room was a shambles. The cement-block wall had contained the explosion and turned the blast inward, leaving the walls and every piece of furniture gouged and splintered by shrapnel. There were five bloody, torn bodies, one of them barely recognisable as a woman's. He had once seen an American Sherman tank in Sicily. A grenade had been dropped down the hatch, and the shrapnel had spun and ricocheted around the interior, so that the crew had looked as if they had been blasted over and over with buckshot. These bodies looked the same.

A groan came from a small room off to one side, and Memling kicked the shattered door wide, almost losing one of his too-big boots in the process. Walsch was slumped on the floor. Blood ran down one side of his face, and his arm dangled at a strange angle as he tried to get to his feet. A small Mauser pistol lay on the floor nearby. From behind, Prager was shouting through a smashed window that they had succeeded. The wind howled in sudden fury, and papers flurried.

Bethwig pushed past him into the room.

'He's mine,' he said, swallowing hard to contain the bitter sickness. 'He killed my father and . . .' He could go no further. Walsch looked up and unexpectedly laughed in genuine mirth.

'And the little whore. Please do not forget her. The reichsführer gave her to my charge. So, you will kill me now,' he choked. 'You must kill me.' Walsch slumped but recovered himself and stared up at Bethwig. 'You see, I have a cancer in the lungs. I will die soon in any event. You will spare me the pain.' He tried to laugh again but collapsed on the floor instead, coughing harshly.

Bethwig raised the pistol. 'I don't give a damn for your cancer, you sadistic bastard,' he screamed.

Memling caught his arm. 'Have you ever killed before?' he demanded. 'Shot a man to death in cold blood?'

Bethwig shook his head. 'This isn't a man, he's . . . he is an animal.'

'Then let me do it. It's not an easy thing to live with.'

Bethwig hesitated just as Sussmann staggered in. Walsch read the uncertainty in Bethwig's eyes and tried to laugh at him. He knew.

'It will live with you for ever,' Memling warned.

Sussmann leaned against the door-frame to watch. Walsch started to speak, but Memling turned then and shot the Gestapo officer once, through the forehead.

'One more can't make my nightmares any worse,' he muttered.

Bethwig parked the car on the northern boundary of the deserted POW camp. He and Jan Memling got out while Prager worked to bandage the surviving grenadier's shattered arm. The corporal and the other grenadier had been killed, and Sussmann had received a shrapnel wound in the stomach. The pain and loss of blood were sending him into shock. He lay back in the front seat breathing heavily, his face pale.

The wind whipped tatters of snow at them once again, and Memling shivered in his ill-fitting uniform. They stood just below a small rise where the trees had been cleared, and talked for what seemed a very long time. Bethwig told him of the work they had done, passing lightly over the details in his haste to cover everything. He wanted this quiet, capable Englishman to understand what had brought them to this night; more, he wanted his help.

Memling nodded when he began to describe the V-10. 'I know. I was here.'

Bethwig hugged his coat about himself. 'It was rumoured you killed four SS soldiers.'

'How do you know about that?'

Bethwig laughed humourlessly. 'Peenemünde abounds in rumours. They were confirmed when the Gestapo arrested Wernher von Braun, Ernst Mundt and Helmuth Gottrup.'

'Arrested . . . then . . .'

'No, all three were subsequently released. The SS wanted to hang them, but in those days we still had a few connections that meant something.'

He took Memling's arm and urged him up the slight rise until they were standing on the crest. Below them lay the immense sprawl of the V-10 launch complex. The area seemed a fairyland of lights and broad avenues leading to the towering conical shape of the V-10.

'Jesus,' Memling breathed.

The rocket was immense. He had never imagined anything so huge in his life. It was as if he had stepped into another world, another time. Even at this distance it was staggering. A lorry moving past the rocket's base snapped the scene into scale. The rocket was wider than the lorry was long. Technicians swarmed like ants over the three-stage rocket and its scaffolding. Against the moonlit sky the thrusting, brilliantly lighted shape glistened as if alive. Looking into the shallow valley formed by the surrounding hills, Memling knew he was witnessing for the first time in the history of the human race a scene that would be repeated endlessly into the future as man struck out from the tiny, cramped world of his birth in search of his ultimate destiny. That barely remembered French scientist had been right after all; they all, he and Franz Bethwig and Wernher von Braun and all the other scientists and technicians at Peenemünde shared a magnificent dream, which even the savagery of total war could not destroy.

'The V-Ten.' Bethwig leaned sideways to make himself heard over the wind. 'It was designed to bombard the eastern coast of the United States with atomic explosives.'

Memling turned to him, eyes growing wide, but Bethwig shook his head before he could ask the question.

'Our atomic projects were cancelled long ago. But not the V-Ten. We have test-flown four of them. This is the fifth and final rocket.'

'Then you are going to launch it?' Memling found his voice at last.

'Yes. Tonight. But not at the United States.'

'Where?' Memling asked the question even though he already knew the answer.

A sudden current of happiness shot through Bethwig; he could not explain it, but he laughed and clapped Memling on the back and pointed at the moon. 'There, my English friend, to the moon, as we talked about all those years ago in Arnsberg, remember? Tonight, we shall do it.'

Memling watched the car recede until its tail-lights disappeared. He then hitched on the sling of his machine pistol and started off towards the northern end of the island. Prager scratched his head and, as if reaching a decision, strode after him. The Englishman grinned as he came up, but said nothing. Both men were busy with their own thoughts.

He had an idea of Prager's mental struggle; he had been through it himself. It was conceivable, he had decided, that this rocket might have some military value, even though at this late date it could have no real effect on the course of the war. In any event, what Bethwig intended to do was far bigger, far more important to the human race, than any of its petty and – after tonight – outdated squabbles. He really had nothing to lose, Memling decided. His own chances of survival were slim in any event, and he might as well see that something came of this damned war. And besides, he admitted, he wouldn't miss the launch of the first rocket to the moon for life itself. After a while the trees hid the launch site, but the glow remained in the sky as a beacon and they trudged on towards the petrol and fuel storage tanks.

No one turned to look at Bethwig as he entered the control room and stood for a moment watching the orderly chaos. This was the part he loved, these final hours when everything came together and a thousand men worked as one towards a single goal.

Tangles of cable ran across and along the aisles, taped to the floor here and bundled together with lengths of flex there. A huge ready board was mounted on the wall where it could be seen from every corner of the room. Bethwig scanned the coloured markers quickly; everything was proceeding on schedule. As he watched, a technician scurried across the metal platform to replace a yellow marker with a green diamond indicating that the return stage liquid oxygen tanks had been pressure-tested successfully.

A twelve-year-old boy skidded to a halt before him; the son of a test engineer, he was serving as a messenger. His face was flushed with exertion, and he could barely contain his excitement. 'Please, Herr Doktor. There is a telephone call for you. From Brigadeführer Kammler. He has been waiting fifteen minutes.'

Bethwig followed the boy to the main console where Wernher von Braun scowled at him. Bethwig nodded and drew a finger across his throat. Von Braun's scowl deepened, but he offered the receiver, one hand across the mouthpiece.

'I told him you were on the launch stand, checking the second stage gyro assembly.'

'Herr Brigadeführer Kammler? How nice to hear from you. Have you been held up? We expected you this afternoon.' Bethwig made his voice drip.

'Never mind that now.' Kammler was shouting, his words almost lost in the roar of atmospherics. 'What the hell is going on there? I am being prevented from reaching Peenemünde . . .' The next few sentences disappeared in the crash and pop of static.

'I am sorry, Brigadeführer,' Bethwig said into the mouthpiece. 'The line is so bad I cannot understand you.'

'. . . status there? Will you . . . ?'

Bethwig was able to guess at the question. 'We will launch on time. All stations have reported in. The submarine is on station and everything appears ready at this time. Please do try and get here,' he finished, and handed the phone to the boy.

'If Brigadeführer Kammler comes back on the line so that you can understand him, son, tell him what's happening. Otherwise, hang up.'

The boy's eyes went wide as he accepted the phone; he stammered something, but Bethwig had already turned away, motioning von Braun to follow.

'What the hell is going on?' von Braun demanded, grabbing his arm as they reached the corridor. 'Magnus telephoned an hour ago to say that Sussmann was arming some men to deal with a problem. What problem, damn it?'

'The problem of Inspector Jacob Walsch. Do you remember an old friend of yours, Jan Memling?'

Wernher von Braun blinked in surprise. 'Of course . . . oh no, not again!'

Bethwig nodded. 'Yes. He was sent to Peenemünde to persuade you and the staff to surrender to the British or Americans, rather than the Russians.'

'But we've already decided,' von Braun protested, and waved a hand as Bethwig started to point out that London could hardly know that. Then he blanched under the impact of Bethwig's news.

'My God, if he should be caught . . .'

'He was,' Bethwig told him calmly. 'With three German citizens, all members of the resistance. Early this morning.' Quickly he described to von Braun what had taken place over the past eighteen hours. 'Two hours ago it came to a head. My contact in the Gestapo reported that the three traitors had signed confessions, and been shot. That left only your English friend. If he confessed, which I was assured he would, you and I and a good many others would be dead by now.'

Von Braun slumped against the wall. 'Where do we stand now?' he asked finally. 'You said if he confessed. If? What about Kammler? Surely he won't . . .'

'Forget Kammler. He's in enough trouble himself.' He reviewed what Prager had told him of the SS's own intramural squabbles 'The Gestapo was our major enemy, primarily because Walsch hated us both. But it doesn't matter any longer. Walsch is dead.'

Von Braun perked up at that. 'How?'

'Your English friend Memling shot him. Saved me from doing so, for which one of these days, I am sure, I will be grateful. I don't know how, but Memling had a weapon when we arrived and had already killed four of the SS. If it had not been for him, we might not have made it.'

'I don't believe any of this.' Von Braun shook his head. 'It sounds like a thriller story.'

'Never mind that now. We are not out of the woods by any means. The SS will soon discover what happened in Trassenheide, and if they should find out who was responsible, we are all dead. But we could also have them about our ears anytime now if someone gets cold feet and decides to stop the launching or if Kammler screws up his courage and bulls his way through the roadblocks. Don't forget that his orders about shooting us are still in effect.'

Von Braun pushed himself away from the wall and took a few steps down the hall, then spun and came back. 'How in hell can we stop them? What about Sussmann? He was supposed to be setting up some kind of defence . . .'

'Sussman was wounded quite badly. He's in hospital right now, but I persuaded Memling to keep the SS busy. Your English friend, it turns out, is a commando officer.'

'I thought he was a spy, worked for that . . . I don't remember . . .'

'So did I.' Bethwig shrugged. 'In any event, I made a deal with him, one it will be up to you to honour.'

Bethwig glanced at his wristwatch. Time was running out. 'I promised that after the launch you would help hide him. He speaks excellent German, and it shouldn't be difficult to pass him off as a middle-level technician for a while. Everything is falling apart here, and with the entire Gestapo staff dead, security checks are certain to fall by the wayside, at least for the moment. Memling said there is a submarine standing by for him and anyone else who wants to leave, but you can deal with that. I gave him directions to your house in Zinnowitz. He will be discreet. Now, I have one more thing to do. Stay on the control console for me a while longer, please?'

Bethwig was half-way down the hall as he asked the final question. Von Braun started after him, demanding to know where he was going this time and why he couldn't take care of the Englishman himself, before he realised Bethwig had already gone. Von Braun tore off his cap and slammed it to the tiled floor in frustration.

Outside, Bethwig hesitated, then turned away from the car park. There might be roadblocks and he could not afford the delay. The SS guard normally stationed at the blockhouse door had disappeared; he did not know if that was a good sign or not, but as there seemed to be no one about, he plunged through the shrubbery and began to run.

Jan Memling crouched in the shadows beside the fence while Prager, a few metres on, pushed up a strand of wire and wriggled through. The few incandescent lamps mounted on high poles swayed with the wind, flinging shadows and light in every direction. Memling slipped through after him, and they trotted towards the looming bulk of the tank farm. There were only two guards, one at each entrance – the first asleep in his hut, the other sheltering from the wind and staring glumly into the night. It was obvious that neither expected the slightest bit of trouble. And why should they? Prager observed. In the six years of its existence, the Peenemünde facility had had only one actual taste of war: the bombing in 1943. And here they were, a year and a half later, guarding a useless farm on a miserably cold January night while they waited for the Russians.

'The tank contains approximately fifty thousand litres of alcohol,' Bethwig had explained. 'Not enough to do more than make a big flash. Wernher's brother, Magnus, is in charge of our security, and he made it his business to see that if we needed it, a suitable distraction could be produced. The thirty thousand metric tons of high explosive removed from the V-Ten warhead has been stored inside a deserted petrol tank near to the alcohol tank. If it could be exploded, I am certain it would keep the SS far too busy searching for Russian saboteurs to interfere with us.'

Prager hissed, and they both went to ground. A shadow passed on the single-track road, and a moment later they heard the racketing sound of a motor fading into the night. The two men exchanged glances.

'Let's get this over with fast,' Memling muttered, 'before they come back. Do you have your bearings yet?'

Bethwig had given them the code number of the alcohol tank and described its location on the seaward side of the farm. Their way was impeded by a tangle of pipes, fire barriers and deserted buildings, and it was 21.39 hours when they reached a concrete wall that overlooked an isolated cluster of tanks squatting above the beach. The moon, jousting with broken cloud, silhouetted their target against the sullen Baltic.

They vaulted the wall and trotted down the slope. Memling explored the surrounding area for the fill pipes, which he then traced back to the metering valves mounted on the tank itself. The piping was stainless steel – to prevent contamination of the alcohol – which only made their task that much more difficult. The joint where the piping ran into the tank proper was well protected by a heavy riveted iron flange.

He backed off then and stared upwards. The tank was made of cast-iron sections, and therefore it had to be lined with glass or stainless steel to prevent contamination; somewhere inside would be the emergency drain valve. Memling found the ladder on the north side, jumped, caught hold, and went up quickly.

The top of the tank was gently rounded and covered with a glare of ice. He crouched against the wind and made his way along, clutching the handholds for dear life. The cloud was broken enough to make visible the entire northern end of the island. In the vague moonlight he could see the smaller, squatter petrol tank downslope and a hundred metres or more distant. He thought about the thirty thousand kilos of HE stored inside, and shivered. The damned thing had to be full of petrol fumes; it was a bomb waiting for a spark. Yet he had to be certain. Amatol was incredibly stable and damned hard to ignite. Only because of that had they dared hide it in the abandoned petrol tank.

He ducked his chin into the collar of his jacket. To the south, five kilometres or more distant, the launch area glowed as if aflame. Behind, the wind-whipped Baltic disappeared into the invisible horizon; somewhere out there was a submarine waiting for his signal. They would wait for a long time; the Gestapo had taken the 'Joan' radio transmitter lent by the OSS. For a moment the old uncertainty and fear swept him. Once the tank exploded, the SS would be out in force. Unless he and Prager kept moving and were exceptionally lucky . . . he stopped the wild, random thoughts. Bethwig and his mad scheme. The man was crazy, or was he? Wouldn't he do exactly the same if he had the chance? This was perhaps the final opportunity of their generation to fulfil one of man's oldest dreams. He had been asked to play a very small part and would do so no matter the cost. Bethwig was right. A man's dreams are all he ever really has.

Memling found the access door leading into the interior and went down into pitch-blackness. The intense odour of raw concentrated alcohol was overpowering, and by the time he found the emergency drainage system near the base of the liner, adjacent to the fill-pipe junction, he was wobbling. He fumbled the clips holding the access door open, overrode the exterior lock, and swung the door wide, scaring Prager half to death.

Memling opened the emergency drain petcock wide and ducked out quickly as the liquid spurted. With Prager's help he climbed the slope and crouched behind the retainer wall. The fumes were beginning to clear from his head, and after a few moments he pushed himself up beside Prager. Liquid had already overflowed the hatch sill and was coursing slowly down the slope. As he watched, it gathered in a small hollow, changed direction, and then resumed its course. It took ten minutes before sufficient alcohol reached the abandoned petrol tank to show in the fitful darkness.

'Do you think there is enough there?'

'Go ahead,' Memling said, and Prager took the battered Walther flare pistol from his belt, loaded it, and hesitated.

'Are you sure?'

'Damn it, unless you have a better way to do it, go ahead and shoot.'

Prager shrugged, aimed carefully, and fired.

The flare arced in a shallow parabola and burst below the tank. Memling held his breath, but nothing happened. Prager swore, broke the pistol open, and loaded another round. This time he aimed well above the hatch.

Memling had an impression of a tongue of flame spewing upwards from the alcohol-soaked ground, and then all hell broke loose. The tank disappeared with a dull *whump*, vaporised into a perfectly round ball of flame. The concussion slammed them backwards, and a moment later a gale snatched the breath from their lungs as air rushed in to fill the void where the tank had been. The fireball rolled skyward, so bright that they could not look at it. It seemed to be standing on a single column of flame and smoke, and then bits and pieces of metal whirled out of the night.

'God damn,' Memling heard Prager muttering over and over

again as they crouched behind the scorched wall. He grabbed his shoulder then and pointed. The base of the old petrol tank was ringed in flame.

'Let's get the hell out of here . . .'

They vaulted the retainer wall and raced up the slope, running desperately for the shelter of the far side. Memling had tried to memorise the way they had come, but the tangle of piping and jungle of tanks and columns were confusing in the moonlight, and he gave up trying to do anything more than maintain a heading. Prager ran beside him, clutching his side, his breath coming in harsh gasps. The anticipation was exquisite. They had no idea how long, if ever, the intense heat of the flaming alcohol would take to ignite the high explosive.

They could see the fence and the Luftwaffe guard shouting into a telephone when the sudden flare of light warned Jan. He dived for the ground, but the concussion caught him in mid-air and sent him sliding across the gravel surface. He buried his head in his arms as the world ended.

Explosion after explosion rocked the island; pillars of flame arced into the blazing sky. The tank farm had become an inferno of sound and fire. A searing wind raged across the sand waste, and Memling felt it scorch his back even through the wool jacket. He half turned then and stared with awe at the incandescent mushroom of smoke and gas erupting beyond the hilltop. He got to his knees, still staring, awestruck at the destruction they had caused. Nothing remained of the tank farm but twisted steel and flaming buildings. Prager was urging him up, dragging him towards the fence, shouting at him, and suddenly Memling began to shake. That cloud could have hovered over New York, or London. Janet could have been one of its many victims. He vomited, harshly.

Bethwig showed his pass to the SS guard, pushed through the glass doors, and hurried along the corridor. The few people about glanced at him in surprise, but he ignored them all. When he entered the ready room, a technician completing a pressure check on an oxygen bottle did a double take at finding the chief project engineer here and not at the command centre. Bethwig pointed to the dressing room, and the man could only nod.

Inside, the pilot was putting on the heavy pressure suit. Surprised, he tried to snap to attention and toppled into the arms of a technician.

'Is everything ready, Artur?' Bethwig asked the chief technician who was helping to right the pilot.

'Yes, sir. The suit checks out properly. Everything is set. The command centre reports on schedule for boarding at T-minus-forty.'

'Very good, gentlemen. Will all of you please leave us for a few minutes? I'll send Lieutenant Gross out to you in a few moments.'

The four technicians, their white uniforms soiled with the exertions of the past twenty-four hours, exchanged puzzled glances but trooped out. The pilot tried to fix an earnest look on his face but failed miserably. Bethwig suspected that for the first time the man was beginning to comprehend the odds against him.

'I understand the submarine is in place,' the pilot began, thereby betraying his apprehension, but Bethwig cut him off.

'Never mind that now. You will not be flying tonight.'

The pilot's expression showed a combination of relief, surprise and disappointment. 'Not . . . but why . . . ?'

'The flight is cancelled.' Bethwig spread his hands in apology. 'Wind conditions are near gale force at eight thousand metres. We are rescheduling for tomorrow night. I thought I should come and tell you in person, knowing what a disappointment it must be.'

Bethwig slipped from his pocket the syringe prepared earlier. 'Well that's a relief, I'll bet,' he said in a hearty voice. 'Let's have that suit off, then.'

The pilot's hands went automatically to the zipper, and as he peeled the suit over his upper arms, Bethwig slipped the needle through the layers of woollen underwear and into the muscle. The pilot jerked back, but it was too late.

'What the hell . . . ? What are you doing . . . ?'

Bethwig spoke softly: 'It's just a sedative. You'll wake up in a few hours . . .'

The pilot's eyes rolled, and his knees collapsed. Grunting, Bethwig stripped the suit off, strapped the unconscious Lieutenant Gross to a guerny, and hauled him into the storeroom.

Back in the dressing room, Bethwig removed his own clothes and pulled on the two layers of woollen underwear. He had to sit down on the floor to wriggle into the cumbersome leather and rubber pressure suit, a modification of the high-altitude pressure suit worn by Luftwaffe pilots in the Me.163B rocket plane. When the zippers were closed and fastened, Bethwig tugged on the close-fitting cotton flying helmet, adjusted the earphone pads comfortably, and lifted the heavy plastic helmet over his shoulders, settled it into the rubber gaskets, and gave it a partial turn to lock it in place. Immediately the glass vision plate steamed over.

Moving clumsily in the heavy pressure suit, he made the connections to the cart containing the air bottles and air-conditioning unit and started up the systems. Bethwig sighed with relief as air began to flow into the helmet through the perforated shoulder piece. The air brought with it the smell of stale sweat, rubber, solvents, leather, and a host of other odours. The suit was amazingly stiff in spite of its cleverly articulated joints, and the twenty-five-kilo weight dragged at him. Bethwig took a deep breath, dragged the cart with him to the door, and knocked. The chief technician opened it quickly. He clipped a wire lead to the helmet and slipped his own earphones on.

'Are you cert – ' he began, then broke off, and shrugged. 'A bit too late to be worrying about that, isn't it?' The voice was tinny and distant through the built-in headset.

Bethwig lifted a ponderous arm and clapped him on the shoulder. When the technician asked where Bethwig had gone, he waved vaguely in the direction of the inner office and stepped into the corridor, at the end of which, beyond the glass doors, he could see the lorry waiting to drive them to the launch site. Technicians and well-wishers, family members of the staff and non-technical employees, had gathered to applaud the pilot as he passed. Bethwig waved, thankful that the vision plate was tinted, so his features could not be seen. The doors were opened for him, and he stepped out. A brilliant flare lit the northern horizon at that instant, and moments later sound struck them with the ferocity of a hurricane.

Prager's estimate of the SS garrison's ability to respond was obviously faulty, Memling thought with some bitterness. He had lost sight of the Gestapo officer just after they had slipped back through the fence and started towards the woods. A rifle shot snapped past, and the wind brought the sound of a lorry engine racing towards them. Memling made it to the cover of the trees, but Prager had disappeared in the darkness.

He could not see the soldiers crossing the field, but he could hear them: an officer's whistle, the sound of booted feet on frozen ground, an occasional shout. When he was satisfied that they were in an extended skirmish line, suggesting that they did not know their quarry's exact location, Memling trotted a few hundred metres into the scrub pine, switched direction abruptly, and headed north-east towards the coast, which, unless he had badly mixed his directions, was two kilometres away. There was nothing he could do for Prager except to hope the man had got clear.

There were no longer any sounds of pursuit as he came up over the crest of a sand dune, yet he continued to move carefully. The moon had slipped farther towards zenith, and heavy cloud was moving in for good this time. Memling studied the sky; it would snow before morning, he decided. The watch he had taken from one of the dead SS troopers in Trassenheide showed 10.55. Less than an hour to go. If they kept to schedule.

As he hunched into the shelter of a bush Memling found himself wondering at Bethwig's confident assertion that the launching would not be stopped because of technical problems: had the Germans come so far that he could be that certain, or was it all an act for his benefit? He recalled the weeks and months of repeated failure in the years before the war, when he and Phil Cleator and Arthur Clarke and all the rest had struggled time and again to get their flimsy balsa and tin creations off the ground.

And that raised the question of why Bethwig was involved in this mad scheme to begin with. He was one of Germany's premier rocket engineers. How in the name of God had he become involved in a gun battle at Gestapo headquarters? Was the dream strong enough, he wondered, to drive a man into open conflict with his government, even to the point of treason? He shook his head. It was damned unlikely that he would ever know.

But Bethwig had told him he was going to ride that shining monster to the moon, and his breath caught in his throat at the memory of the rocket towering from the centre of the launch complex. Only someone like himself, like Franz, like those of the Peenemünde staff, could ever really understand the lure of the dream that had driven them all these years. And given the slightest opportunity, Memling knew he would have taken Bethwig's place without a second thought.

A figure materialised on the edge of the deeper blackness that was the pine forest. A smear of cloud slid away from the moon, and he saw Prager plodding in his direction. He watched as the Gestapo agent reached the fence edging the narrow track, stooped, and began to crawl through. A spotlight snapped on, catching Prager full in its beam, and a machine-gun stitched a dead-straight line of dirt explosions towards him; Prager's coat caught on the barbed wire, and the stream of bullets marched past and left him dangling on the fence. A moment later soldiers ran down the road, and the lorry mounting the searchlight and machine-gun followed.

It happened so fast that Memling could do nothing but watch. Someone had made a correct guess and sent a detachment to wait in ambush. Sickened at the senseless cruelty of it, Memling edged down the flank of the dune as they dragged Prager up the road. An officer met them half-way, unholstered a pistol, and fired a single round into his head.

'You bloody bastards!' Memling ground out as two of the SS squad pulled Prager's body to the side of the road and kicked it into the ditch. Memling reached the hard sand beach and began to run.

The plan had come into his mind fully formed. The track ran along the beach, just back of the dunes, as he remembered the map. Less than half a kilometre on, it snaked down into a gully and up again, making a sharp turn inland as it emerged. Memling reached that gully as the lorry came into sight, travelling slowly and rocking from side to side on the badly rutted road. The glare of its headlights whipped over him, and he flattened himself against the ground. The lorry lurched down the slope, gears grinding angrily as the driver fought the transmission and the steering wheel at the same time, and the soldier at the machine-gun hung on with both hands. As the lorry started up the short slope and entered the turn Memling twisted the cap off a grenade, pulled the igniter, and waited two seconds before tossing it into the open back. He heard someone swear, and then the grenade went off.

The blast swung the lorry half around; the petrol tank erupted and the rear became a mass of flames. The driver's door flew open and Memling shot the man as he slid out, then shifted quickly and killed the gunner as he scrambled over the side. A figure leapt from the back, uniform blazing like a torch, and Memling ignored him as he rolled about on the ground for a moment, then lay still. A bullet kicked up dirt as he got to his feet, and instinctively he swivelled, finger squeezing short bursts from the MP40. The officer who had shot Prager jerked and fell across the hood of the lorry.

Memling climbed down into the gully. A series of pops sounded beneath the blazing canvas as ammunition exploded. He kept his eyes on the officer who was groaning and trying to push himself upright. The man saw Memling standing across the hood and lifted a hand as if to shield himself. Memling reached forward and picked up the officer's pistol from where it had fallen into the open hood vent. The SS officer tried to speak, but Memling shook his head and shot him dead.

Memling crossed the road. By the time the first soldiers arrived to investigate the blaze, he was deep in the forest, moving south.

'Right foot here, sir, then left foot on the couch. That's it, sir, now ease in and down.'

The technician's big hand pushed down on the helmet, forcing

Bethwig's chin against the rim, so that he spluttered in protest before he popped through the hatch like a melon seed, caromed off the far wall of the cabin, and bounced into the seat. With an air of exasperation, the technician leaned across and reset the three switches he had knocked out of position.

Franz lay back in the contoured seat while the technicians worked to secure him to the acceleration couch and hook him into the control panels. He could hardly believe that he had pulled it off, yet the couch rocked gently on its gimbals and there was the main instrument panel above his head. He was so excited that he no longer noticed the sweaty, oily smell of the pressure suit; nor did he notice that it chafed. The suit was just about one size too small, but that could not be helped. And his neck was just that much longer than the original owner's that the top of his head rubbed against the padding.

The technician rapped on his helmet, and Bethwig came to with a start. The man was motioning for him to switch on the radio. For an instant, panic gripped him; if he turned his radio on, his voice would be transmitted over the intercom to the launch area and the command centre. If they discovered that he had substituted himself for the pilot before the hatch was sealed, the SS would certainly end the launch attempt. The man pointed again, but the chief technician elbowed him aside and plugged his headset directly into Bethwig's helmet.

'Sorry, Lieutenant. Got delayed. Small problem in the instrument bay, but it's fixed now. Some idiot left a bolt just loose enough to keep the hatch from closing.'

Bethwig suppressed a sigh of relief. Over the tinny intercom the chief technician would be unable to tell who was inside the pressure suit. He rocked the seat back until he could see the chronometer in the main panel. The two dials showed local and elapsed time. There was less than thirty-five minutes to go now.

They finished the instrument check, tested the oxygen and other support systems, checked the engineering and fuel systems, and ran through the final inventory of food and water stores. At the end the chief technician handed in the special tool kit made of non-sparking aluminium and bronze. When the hatch was closed and sealed, the air inside the cabin would be replaced with pure oxygen. Bethwig was not happy about that, but the original design had envisioned a flight of not more than fifty minutes' duration for which oxygen was the cheapest and most efficient system. Now, in the event of a fire, even normally non-flammable materials, such as the kapok stuffing in the couch, the leather of his suit, the composition board of the instrument panel, and even the aluminium panelling, would burn furiously in a one-hundred-per-cent-oxygen atmosphere.

'That's it, then, Lieutenant Gross.' The technician clapped him on the shoulder and set the gimbal brake. The couch immediately swung into a reclining position. The chief technician hesitated, as if he wanted to say more but could not find the words. He contented himself with a mumbled 'Good luck' and unplugged the headset. A moment later the interior of the cabin went dark as he lifted the hatch panel into place and began to bolt it down. Franz turned his head as far as the cumbersome suit would allow, and caught a final glimpse of the chief technician peering in at him. The thought occurred to him that the technician's face was probably the last he would ever see.

Bethwig was alone. The silence was total but for the faint whisper of oxygen inside his suit. He took a deep breath, feeling the excitement rise, and grinned. He had expected to be terror-stricken at this point. Instead, he was elated.

The chronometer hands stood at minus thirty minutes. The winking red light indicated that the command centre was trying to contact him. He reached up and inserted his helmet radio leads into the main panel. There was nothing that could stop him now.

Memling was crouched in a stand of pine less than thirty metres from the SS headquarters in Zinnowitz. Two five-ton lorries were parked on the gravelled parade, and he counted forty SS men drawn up in two columns. An officer ran from the building shouting orders, and the men hurried to their trucks. The officer leaned from the cab to give last-minute instructions to a sergeant, and the lorries lurched and bumped across the parade and out through the gate. Memling watched, waiting to see which direction they would take – north-west to the launch area or due north to the coast where he had ambushed the patrol. There was little more he could do if the SS had decided to halt the launching, but the lorries reached the main road and sped north.

The noise of engines dwindled, and he turned back to the barracks where the sergeant was still looking towards the road while the sentry behind stood at rigid attention, trying to make himself as inconspicuous as possible. According to Sussmann, the garrison had been reduced, in anticipation of the final withdrawal, to one hundred men. He had killed six and one officer twenty minutes ago, forty had just left, and there were at least another thirty, according to Prager, guarding the launching area and the various command centres. There would be ten to fifteen more SS still searching for him in the vicinity of the tank farm and a few guarding the burned-out Gestapo headquarters several kilometres to the south in Trassenheide. So there should not be more than a few left in the barracks.

There would also be radio equipment that might enable him to make contact with the submarine. He decided it was worth a try.

The parade was twenty metres in diameter and fringed closely about with trees that reached to the building on either flank. The intent obviously had been to create the same park-like surroundings found throughout the rest of the Peenemünde facility. Memling found it incongruous. He worked his way through the trees to the south-east side of the building, checking each window. The construction was cement block, as was nearly every building on the island, and the ground-floor windows were at eye level. Most of the interior was dark and the few lighted rooms empty. The central dormitory for enlisted personnel extended the length of the building at the rear; it was empty. What weapon racks he could see were also empty. He had then to depend on his single remaining grenade, the machine pistol and three magazines.

Memling completed the circumnavigation of the barracks. The single sentry and the sergeant seemed to be the only ones left, but he couldn't be certain of that. He studied the sentry from the trees. Now that his sergeant had gone, the man had relaxed and was sneaking a smoke. His rifle, however, was still slung muzzle downwards, ready for instant use.

He faded back into the shadows and worked his way to a darkened room with an unlocked window on the south-east side. Cautiously he worked it up by pressing the frame back against the casement and lifting. It rose in jerks, binding on either side, and Memling swore silently. When he had it up as far as it would go, he passed the machine pistol through and eased himself into the room.

Memling knelt at the partly opened door for several minutes until satisfied the corridor was empty. The building was a single-storey cube, and there was no way to find out how many people were left inside except by checking each room. He opened the door carefully and stepped into the hall. The first door on his right opened easily. The room was dark, and when he turned the light switch, he found himself in a mess hall. The room was huge and, combined with the dormitory, probably accounted for half the available floor space.

He checked three more rooms, each empty, before reaching the end of the corridor. Two had been quarters for officers, and he wondered which had belonged to the man who had executed

Prager. The hall made a right-angle turn across the front of the building. He knelt and peered around the bottom edge of the wall. Two doors were open, and light flooded into the corridor. He could hear voices and radio static but could not tell from which room they came. Jan quickly retraced his steps to the end of the hall. There was another corridor, as he had expected, running across the rear of the building. Three doors led off to rooms on either side, and he realised the two on the left would lead to the canteen and dormitory. The single door to the right was locked. There wasn't time to open it, and he hurried on to the end of the corridor, repeated the minute examination from a prone position, then checked two more unlocked and empty offices. Again he found one door locked and another leading to the dormitory.

Satisfied that the building was empty but for the room in front, he crouched at the junction of the corridors. Again he could hear the same voices and static. So that was it, he thought. It was like France or Norway all over again. He felt the sudden surge of exhilaration and, realising that it was little different from fear, almost laughed aloud at himself. Memling walked past the entrance – two sets of double glass doors beyond which he could see the sentry – and stopped beside the first doorway. A burst of static sounded and someone swore. Another voice demanded silence. Two at least, he thought, and how many more in the next room? The radio was in there, so he dared not use the hand-grenade.

Memling hesitated. So far he had managed to pull the SS away to the north as Bethwig had asked. He could head into the southern part of the island and disappear in the marshes and thick forest, and it would take them days to find him. What the hell was he doing here, then? Even if he could make contact with the submarine, there was only the faintest chance they would get to him before the SS. Wasn't it better to wait a few days, until the uproar died, then find a way to Sweden? He had done it once . . . But he was grasping at straws. The SS knew who he was. A few Gestapo personnel killed, a company of SS shot up, would not deter them in the slightest. There was an old score to settle, and he had only added to their anger in the past two hours. Nothing had changed. There was still no other way out.

He realised then that there was something heady about mastering one's fear, something that made suicide a bit too attractive, and sobered, he stepped around the doorway. Two black-uniformed men leaned over a desk. The operator's back was to Memling as he hunched over a microphone. A fourth man, an elderly officer with stooped shoulders, looked up as he appeared, his expression changing from annoyance to shock as the muzzle of the MP40 came towards him. He clawed for the pistol at his belt, too late. Memling fired a single burst as he swept the pistol diagonally. The officer collapsed, and the two others hunched over and fell together as the man at the radio slid out of his chair. The room was large, with two entrances – which accounted for the two doors. There was no one else inside, and, without hesitating, Memling knelt and lined up on the entrance doors. The guard burst into the corridor looking wildly in both directions. Memling killed the man with a single shot. Behind him the radio crackled with tinny static.

Jan checked the bodies at the desk. All were dead. He dragged the sentry into the radio room and took a few moments to replace his overlarge boots and trousers. He then stepped outside the building to listen but heard only the steady ululation of wind through the trees and the booming surf on the beach a few hundred metres distant. He glanced at the sky. The cloud cover was almost total now, and the wind seemed to be mounting. He had no idea what weather conditions were required to launch a rocket as large as the V-10, but he doubted if anything short of a full gale would stop Bethwig and von Braun tonight.

Returning to the radio room, he collected weapons and ammunition, moved the chair to face the door, and tuned the radio to the proper frequency. He had decided to give the radio fifteen minutes, and that was cutting it fine. He pressed the microphone switch and began to transmit his call sign.

Stunned silence held the command centre. Every eye had gone automatically to the speaker mounted above the status board.

Wernher von Braun stared at his microphone, then reached a hand forward, as if in a dream, and pressed the transmit bar. 'Franz . . . ?'

'The main control board is showing every indicator at positive.' Bethwig's voice rumbled from the speaker. 'My chronometer has T-minus-fifteen minutes,' he added, as if prompting a response.

'T-minus-fifteen minutes,' von Braun repeated, and looked about the room helplessly. Everyone was staring at him.

'I have a light indicating fuelling completed and pressure holding.' Bethwig's voice came through the speaker again. 'What is the status of the count? I foresee no further holds.' His calm, matter-of-fact voice eased von Braun from his daze; but before he could respond, the SS officer supervising the launch pushed through the crowd around his console.

He thumbed the transmit button twice, hoping that Bethwig would pick up on the warning, before the sturmbannführer grabbed his arm.

'That voice, it belongs to Herr Doktor Bethwig!' The man was practically screaming. 'Where is he?'

Von Braun jerked his arm away. 'Obviously inside the rocket, you ass! Get away from here! You are interfering!'

The SS officer was livid. 'Get him out of there, immediately! What are you fools up to? I can have you all shot!'

He grabbed for the microphone, but von Braun leapt to his feet and shoved the major so hard he tripped and fell. Von Braun yanked him up. 'I've wanted to do this for a long time,' he grated, shaking the man like a rag doll. 'You will not interfere again or I will kill you with my bare hands, do you understand? It is too late to stop now. Too late to stop the launching. Go telephone your boss Kammler for instructions.'

Von Braun flung him away and turned to the console as the major recovered his balance and clawed at his holstered pistol. A technician hit him with a wrench, relieved him of his pistol, and, grinning, dragged the inert body into a corner. Other technicians leapt for the SS guards posted around the room and took their weapons. Von Braun picked up the microphone.

'Franz, what in hell do you think you are doing?'

Bethwig's laugh floated from the speaker. 'Care to change places with me, Wernher?'

'You have to be mad. You are committing suicide!'

'Of course. And how better? There is nothing left for me but this. Please, old friend, it's much too late for recriminations. We both know there is nothing for it but to continue. There will be plenty of time to talk later.'

Someone pushed a note at von Braun and he spared a second to glance at it. 'My God,' he muttered, forgetting the live microphone. His voice bounced from the speaker, and everyone in the room turned to him.

'Peenemünde is under attack,' he announced, struggling to control his voice. 'The fuel storage area in Peenemünde West has been blown up. An SS detachment was ambushed.' This last brought a loud cheer, and the captured guards exchanged apprehensive glances.

Bethwig's voice broke in on the babble in the control room. 'Peenemünde is not under attack, at least not by the Russians. A friend is causing a diversion to keep the SS too busy to interfere with this launching. This is our last chance. Get on with it!'

For a single instant every eye was on the loudspeaker, then, as if of one mind, they set to work again; each technician present understood without explanation. Although he too understood and would gladly have traded places, von Braun shook his head in despair and announced the revised mission objective. Within minutes those of the launch crews whose tasks were completed began filtering into the empty VIP gallery, their excitement plain. A hoarse cheering broke out, all fear was forgotten.

The firing control officer announced T-minus-five minutes, and von Braun ticked the final entry in his log and relinquished control. His job was finished; the FCO had charge now. He watched the activity in the room with the detachment of someone far removed in time and space. For a moment he felt as if he had never had any part of the gruelling course that over the past fourteen years had led inevitably to this moment. And then the sensation was gone, and he realised they had done it. Now they would prove that man could travel to the moon. For just an instant there was a flood of bitter jealousy at the thought that he would never be first, but then he realised that for all his hopes and longing he had never really expected that he would be. Had Franz, he wondered, ever doubted? Had he ever thought, all those years ago, what this pact they had made with the Devil would cost? Had he suspected but gone ahead anyway, knowing that this was the only chance? Bethwig had given everything of value for this dream, far more than he, and now he was about to give his life.

The FCO's voice broke in to announce T-minus-three minutes. Von Braun wished that he could talk to Franz now in these last few moments before the launching, but it was impossible. He could hear Bethwig's calm, unemotional voice relaying an endless series of data readings to the FCO's staff to confirm the telemetered readings. Already he could see the repeater dials on his console flickering. Telemetry had always been one of their biggest problems. Franz has chosen the correct course, he thought. Perhaps the Allies would want their services after this damned war ended. If they were still alive, that is, and the sight of the unconscious SS officer in the corner made him doubt that. Even so, no matter what, they would never again have the complete control they had here. If ever again they or anyone else was offered a similar opportunity, the bureaucrats would hound them to an extent that would make Heydrich's and Himmler's interference seem like child's play.

There was so much to learn, to accomplish, so much that could be given back to humanity, but the fools and the bureaucrats would never understand that. Von Braun put his face in his hands and sobbed, as much for the loss of their dream as for his friend going willingly to his death.

Bethwig was relaxed in the couch, ignoring for the moment the constant stream of chatter flowing from the earphones, and hugging the idea to himself as the elapsed mission time chronometer hand wound down. With less than two minutes remaining, there was no way to stop him. Everything necessary to launch the rocket was under his control. He glanced again at the control panel; all lights were glowing green except for the launch sequencer and the first-stage turbine pumps. In another thirty seconds they would be started and those lights would turn from amber to green.

His thoughts turned to the Englishman Memling. He too had agreed to give his life for one final chance at a dream. Why? Was it the same demon that drove him? But how could it be? he wondered. Memling had experimented with rockets in an amateurish way, as they all had, but certainly such limited experience could not . . . or could it? For a moment the frustration and hope, the lack of money and food, and the camaraderie he had experienced as a member of the VfR during the primitive Rakentenflugplatz days were more real than the smell of the pressure suit or the glowing control panel above him. And he understood. The demon was the same.

Had they made a pact with the Devil as they so often joked, or had they merely recognised its existence in themselves? Was there any difference between Hitler and Himmler with their dreams of a world empire led by the Aryan race, or between himself and Himmler? He had his own dream as well. And each of them damned the cost, both human and economic, while citing the greater good that would result.

Intentionally or not, he had sold his father and Inge, Memling, Prager, and all the rest, even Wernher, to fulfil his ambition. Bethwig struggled to turn his mind from that line of thought as his elation faded and he realised that he was no better than Himmler or Heydrich after all.

The grinding vibration of the first-stage turbine pumps whining into operation far below brought him back to present awareness. Automatically his gloved hand went to the arming switch, lifted the protective tab, and pressed down. A voice sounded in his earphones, but he did not understand the words.

The chronometer stood at exactly T-minus-sixty seconds. Deep in the instrument bay among the tangle of painfully assembled resistors and transformers and wires and meters, a series of rotary switches were turning in final sequence. Franz watched their progress as lights changed from red to green on the status board to his left; the hydrogen peroxide generator tanks being charged, the auxiliary valves snapping open and the turbine pumps whirring to provide on-board power and pump the metric tons of liquid oxygen and alcohol towards the twenty-one engines of the first stage. Other valves flew open as the fuel and LOX coursed through an intricate net of piping which frosted instantly as damp night air condensed on frigid metal. The same rotary switches sent signals coursing through kilometres of copper cable to the command centre where technicians pressed buttons and turned switches as lights winked from red to green and the umbilical cables that were Bethwig's last connection with Earth fell away and the spider-work gantries pulled back. Another light prompted a technician to start the massive pumps that pulled sea water through an inlet fifty metres under the Baltic and five kilometres of pipes before emerging in high-pressure sprays to cool and protect the tunnel and flame baffles channelling the near-plasma blast of the twenty-one rocket engines into the sky half a kilometre away.

The vibration was growing, and Bethwig was frightened, not of his own death but of what he might have paid to achieve it.

Jan Memling found the path leading to the ridge, which, though less than ten metres high, offered a clear, uninterrupted view of the launching site. He sat down and laid the machine pistol across his knees, too exhausted to run farther. He found the crumpled packet of cigarettes Bethwig had given him. There was one left, and he lit it, shielding the match with both hands.

Memling, forgetting how cold, exhausted and hungry he was, stared at the floodlit space – it was as large as a dozen football grounds – a kilometre away. The gantries had been pulled aside, and the rocket towered against the sky in the full glare of massed searchlights. Its polished fuselage, painted with red stripes, gleamed and scintillated through some atmospheric trick. He wondered if Bethwig had been able to carry through with his plan to board the rocket in place of the pilot, but he did not wonder why.

Something flickered along the rocket's side, and he found himself wishing for a pair of field glasses. A red flare arced above the area, and he guessed the launching was imminent. He glanced at the dead SS guard's watch, but somewhere in the past hour the crystal had smashed. The hands were stopped at 11.25, about the time he had shot the SS people in the barracks. It had all been wasted effort in any event as he had been unable to contact the submarine.

A mist rose around the base of the rocket, and he drew on the cigarette, watching with narrowed eyes as if that would help him to see better.

Wernher von Braun watched the clock hand begin its final sweep. The babble in the command centre had risen to its highest level, as always in these final seconds – the result both of excitement and a last torrent of reports. He saw several lights change from green to red indicating problems and just as quickly switch back again. Bethwig was overriding them as they occurred, and he closed his eyes a moment in fear. One light had remained red for several seconds now. It flamed beneath the gauge indicating that pressure in the oxidiser system had failed. The flight control officer was calling over and over into the microphone, trying to bring that fault to his attention, but either Bethwig was ignoring him or the communications link had failed. Then he realised that Bethwig could not have missed the indicator on his own board. He was simply overriding the system to stop the FOC from calling a launch hold.

Von Braun pressed the transmit bar on his microphone and broke into the FCO's increasingly frantic calls. He struggled to keep his own voice under control.

'Franz, can you hear me?' He paused a moment, hoping that Bethwig would respond to his voice. The sweep-second touched the numeral twenty.

'We have a light on the board indicating a LOX turbine pump failure. Do you have the same?'

He released the transmit button and held his breath.

'Yes. I think it's nothing more than a short in the sensor.' Bethwig's voice seemed crisp enough.

'It should be checked. It might be a true report.'

'It might,' Bethwig agreed, 'but it would take three days to stand down and restart. We could all be dead by then.'

The second hand was passing forty. 'You could be dead in seconds if the pump has failed.'

'Maybe. But the amount of vibration here suggests both turbines are working properly. We'll soon find out in any . . .'

A thunderous roar began to grow as the second hand touched sixty, and white light from twenty-one screaming rocket engines flooded the command centre.

The explosion deafened him, and the monstrous rocket shook him like a mouse in the teeth of a cat. Lights blinked on the board, green to red and red to green again, and he closed his eyes, waiting for extinction. The shaking grew as the bellowing was transmitted through the rocket's fabric until it had become physical pain. He was being crushed; he could not breathe, and he opened his mouth to scream and realised in that instant that the pressure was gravity crushing him as acceleration mounted. He was blind and deaf, wrapped in a cocoon of his own terror, unintelligible voices in his earphones screaming in defiance of the roaring that was filling his head with pain as he lapsed into unconsciousness.

The noise was greater than anything Memling had ever dreamed possible. He pressed his hands to his ears and bowed forward, mouth open in a soundless scream to ease the pain. The rocket engines roared and bellowed and thundered and screamed in every conceivable register, and slowly, gently, the squat tower began to rise on a white column of flame brighter than a welder's torch. For an instant he had an impression – one that would remain with him for the rest of his life – of the V-10 balancing on a column of pure flame, screaming like all the banshees of hell, rotating slowly about its axis so that one delta-shaped wing appeared from the darkness, shuddered for the merest instant, and was gone. He blinked at the after-image and tilted his head back, but the rocket was already a point of flame in the night sky fleeing through the cloud rack. He lay back flat on the ground then and stared hungrily as the flame grew longer and longer, tipped towards the south-west, and continued to lengthen, flaring into a widening cone that surprised him until he remembered that the gases would expand as the air thinned.

Memling watched the point of flame until it vanished in the thickening cloud and his own tears.

The silence was blessed. As was the absence of vibration and the sensation of motion. Bethwig lay in the couch, mind drifting aimlessly, body exhausted to the point of collapse. His eyes drifted to the chronometer hand, and he groaned as he saw it sweep inexorably to the point marking second-stage ignition. He tensed as the hand passed across the point, and deep in the bowels of the rocket the vibration began again, sound and fury exploding to press him deep against the couch with a huge, padded, smothering hand. The raving went on and on, but the vibration and the screaming were less severe this time and the acceleration was bearable. As he waited for the trial to end he turned his head with difficulty to the tiny view port.

At first he saw nothing but the window itself, and then a

brilliant diamond drifted into view. It was a moment before his mind grasped the implication. He was the first human to see a star without the interfering blanket of earth's atmosphere.

An endless time later something shot past and a bluish haze filled the port while Bethwig's mind grappled with too many unexpected inputs. It has to be Earth, he thought, has to be; but it was so different from the way he had always pictured it. Where were the continents, the oceans, the clouds? It was all run together in a sapphire mist. He struggled against the restraints, trying to get closer, to see more, before he remembered the buckles, and that recalled him to his senses. Where in hell was he? What had happened? Was he in orbit? These and a thousand other questions nearly overwhelmed him. He closed his eyes to force his mind blank. When he opened them again, the transmission light was winking and someone, von Braun, was shouting into his earphones. He pressed the chin switch and acknowledged.

Memling stubbed his cigarette and carefully buried it in the sand. Old habits, he thought. He stared once more at the launch area, now curiously empty. Water fountained above the launch stand, and steam rose in rolling clouds to the west. The area was still flooded with light, but it seemed as if the entire island had been abandoned. When he turned to the north, he saw that even the dull reddish glow on the horizon from the burning tank farm had died away.

He slung the machine pistol over his shoulder and hesitated. Mankind had, in the midst of its most destructive war, taken its most civilised step towards the future – he hoped to God. Whether Bethwig survived or not made little difference in the long run. The step had been taken, and it could not be denied. Where one man had gone, others had to follow. He glanced upwards, searching for a tiny pinpoint of flame, but the cloud cover was solid to the west. He started to salute, then laughed at himself, turned, and went down the ridge towards the marshes to the south.

Von Braun walled himself off from the clamouring, cheering people by sitting quietly at his desk and staring at the dials and gauges that registered the condition and progress of the rocket. No one dared intrude; he had become an island of despair in the midst of celebration. Even Magnus was standing quietly to the side, watching his brother, not wanting to infringe on a private grief.

Dawn slid silently, inexorably out of the South China Sea and began to slip across the Indochina landmass. Borneo, a faint mixture of browns and greens, was in view on the horizon, and soon the second stage would fire a final time before being left behind. Australia could have witnessed the event, Franz thought, if anyone had known to look. He had finished the final computations that would regulate the firing, and had pinned the several sheets to the control panel where he could see them, even though the results were as logical and obvious to him as street signs.

He had been sick for a while, but the Dramamine tablets had helped to settle the nausea, even if they had left him drowsy and content to wait and watch the Earth turn beneath. From six hundred and seventy-three kilometres' altitude, there was no sign that two-thirds of the globe had been mobilised into competing killing machines of which he had, until lately, been a part. His mind shied away from that thought; he had made a pact with himself not to dwell on such subjects. Instead, he watched the splendour of the blue world beyond the port.

Von Braun's voice woke him. He acknowledged and laughed at the concern in his friend's voice.

'Just resting, Wernher, while I still have a few moments. I've set the chronometer alarm, and there are two minutes to engine ignition.'

'Franz, our calculations show you have three minutes twenty-three seconds on my mark . . . mark! I suggest you recheck your calculations.'

Bethwig chuckled. 'Have you ever known me to make an arithmetic mistake? What relative speed do you show?'

Von Braun relayed up the information, and Bethwig acknowledged. 'You see, Wernher, that is the problem. You give me seventy-eight kilometres more than I have. Fifteen minutes ago I took a series of triangulations to measure my actual relative speed, whereas yours are only estimates. The next time, a chain of radar stations with the capability of detecting a spacecraft at several thousand kilometres would be very helpful . . . we are coming up to the ignition sequence, Wernher. Pardon me for a moment.'

Von Braun started to protest, then stopped. Even though he was troubled by the dreamy quality of Franz's voice, he realised that as the pilot Bethwig must be the final authority. From nearly seven hundred kilometres' altitude he could measure his speed quite accurately with the aid of a sextant.

'The next time,' he had said, and von Braun shook his head in despair. The needles flickered and then began to move across their dials indicating that ignition had begun. He watched them mount, aware of the tension growing in him. On both this final performance of the second stage and Bethwig's abilities as a pilot depended his fate. Unless the rocket gained a specific speed within very defined limits, it would either crash back to Earth when its orbit decayed or bypass the moon and fall into orbit around the sun. He stared fixedly at the dials, which provided his only connection to the mote speeding away from the planet, conscious also of the intense silence in the command centre as the crews watched with him. A needle jumped on the telemetry signal strength link, steadied, then fell to zero.

Von Braun continued to stare at the dial, willing the needle to move, but it never did.

The explosion had damaged the instrument bay, Bethwig decided. Half of the system board was blank, and here and there on the control panel dead gauges and signal lights told the rest of the story. At least one engine had exploded on ignition, but the damage must not have been extensive, as the other four had continued to fire. He moved the switch that caused the gyros to speed up. For a moment nothing happened and he thought they had failed as well, but then a star slipped past and a moment later Earth swam into view. He was somewhere over Central America, he decided as he shot a series of bearings. A few moments of figuring gave him his speed, now barely at the lower edge of the margin. Another decimal point or so . . . He concentrated on doing what he could to repair the damage.

After an hour's extensive work Bethwig knew that while the craft was continuing to operate, its performance was disintegrating steadily. From what he could calculate based on oxygen consumption, fragments of the engine must have ripped at least one pinhole somewhere below, or perhaps started a seam. The loss was not great, but it was steady, and at this rate the tanks would be exhausted in less than fifty hours. The fuel tanks had apparently escaped injury, as had his food and water stores. But the telemetry systems and the linked radio were out for good, as were the twin radar units he needed to perform the landing seventy-three hours away.

Bethwig chuckled to himself, and the sound was grim inside his helmet. He could be out of air before then, so it might make little difference. What he regretted most was the loss of the radio. Wernher would never know how far he had got, or that the rocket would reach the moon, whether he was dead or alive.

There was a choice; by shutting off the cabin atmosphere and feeding the oxygen into his suit, he could assure himself sufficient for another six days, three beyond what was needed to attempt the lunar landing but not enough to wait for re-supply. And he laughed aloud at the thought. Re-supply? he asked himself. There would be no re-supply. How in God's name would they ever accomplish that? The SS would swarm all over Peenemünde, if they weren't already there. In his arrogance he had calculated for everything but failure, and now von Braun and the rest would be lucky to escape with their lives. And with the radio gone, he could not even let them know that it hadn't all been in vain. He smiled then at the punishments the gods were capable of inflicting upon man.

Bethwig made the decision and shut down the cabin pressurisation. He loosened the restraints so that he was floating, weightless, a few centimetres above the cushions and turned carefully, letting the friction of the straps hold him in position as he stared at the slowly receding planet beyond the view port. He would land on the moon if at all possible. Radar or not, he still had his eyes, damn it. Earth hung against a velvet blackness of incomparable richness, an amazing jewel. He was finally at peace with himself.

Peenemünde 31 January 1945

'Don't switch on the light, Wernher.'

Von Braun froze, arm partly extended.

'Is anyone with you?'

Von Braun tried to speak, but his throat was suddenly dry and he had to swallow hard.

'Well?' the voice prompted.

'No. No one. I . . . who are you?'

A table lamp went on, and von Braun blinked in the sudden glare before he made out the figure sitting on his couch, holding a machine pistol. The man was dressed in a uniform so ragged that he did not immediately recognise it as SS battledress. The face was stubbled and as dirty as the clothes, but the eyes drew von Braun the most. Pale green in the yellowish lamplight, they were steady and implacable. Von Braun had a feeling the man would kill him at the slightest sign of disobedience.

'Who are you?' he managed to croak.

'Jan Memling.'

Von Braun sagged. 'Good God in heaven, you scared the hell

out of me.' He straightened and motioned to a cabinet. 'I need a drink.'

Memling nodded, and von Braun walked carefully across the room. He paused before he opened the door. 'Do you wish to check first? There may be a gun.'

'I have already.'

'Yes.' Von Braun rubbed his lower lip. 'You would have.' He poured two glasses of cognac and brought them across to the coffee table. He was stumbling with the fatigue of three days spent in the command centre, working until it was clear they could do no more.

'What happened?'

He took a swallow, and then another, letting the liquid dissolve the cold in the pit of his stomach before he answered. Memling waited.

'We don't know.'

'What are you talking about!'

'We lost contact after second-stage ignition, as the engines were being fired to shift the rocket out of Earth orbit. We know the engines ignited, but after that . . .' He shrugged.

'It's been three days . . .'

Von Braun shrugged again. 'We just have no idea what happened. Radio contact was lost. This morning we tried to find him with radar as Earth rotated so that our antennas had a clear view, but we could not achieve a signal. If he had continued on the course prescribed, Franz would have . . .' Von Braun's voice broke, and he had to take a deep breath, then '. . . would have landed two hours ago.'

Memling took the glass and drank most of the cognac in a single gulp. He leaned back on the couch and closed his eyes. 'So it's over,' he said after a moment, and von Braun was struck by the sadness, the sense of loss, in the Englishman's voice.

'Yes.'

'What happens next?'

Von Braun walked to the window and stood looking out into the darkness. He was conscious of the beginning of a strange alliance that would have been unthinkable six months ago but which now seemed perfectly logical, the culmination of the random insanity that had held the world in thrall for seven years.

'SS General Doktor Hans Kammler has given orders to evacuate immediately,' he said. 'The Soviets are less than fifty kilometres away. He is convinced that Russian commandos were responsible for the damage caused the night of the launching. There was a submarine sighted off the coast that night.' Von

Braun turned back into the room to study the gaunt Englishman, so different from the boy he had known before the war. 'Franz told me you agreed to help. Were you responsible for the damage?'

Memling ignored the question. 'Will you go?'

'I have no choice.' Von Braun shrugged. 'We are ordered to make our way to Nordhausen, in the Harz Mountains, where the SS can protect us . . . or kill us if necessary.' Von Braun paused. 'I understand that you may have brought us an alternative.'

'I did.' Memling described SHAEF's offer of employment following the war, providing the Peenemünde scientists surrendered to the Western powers. 'On no account will the offer hold,' he warned, 'if your surrender is made to the Russians.'

'I assume there are both political and practical implications to that statement,' von Braun observed dryly, and Memling nodded.

'Then you need have little fear on that score. No one wishes to disappear into Russia. Most of us are fighting the war to prevent the spread of communism to . . .'

Memling held up a hand. 'Your motives do not concern me. I'm just the messenger. Arrangements were made to take some of you out immediately, but I doubt if they hold any longer. You will have to find another way to make contact.' Memling nursed his drink for a long moment while staring into the shadows. 'What will you tell them about the V-Ten?'

Von Braun sighed as he replenished his glass. 'Nothing. The dangers of such a weapon, the temptation to use – '

'No one has,' Memling interrupted, 'and I doubt anyone ever will, resist the temptation to use any weapon, no matter how deadly, if it will ensure his survival. It may sound naïve after what we've been through, but perhaps we should make damned certain the next time that the correct side has the V-Ten. And there will be a next time.'

Memling's eyes were hollowed by fear and privation, and von Braun shuddered. This man is war, he thought, a war which I had no idea existed. 'Perhaps,' he said then. 'In any event, the SS collected all project films for destruction, so there is nothing to discuss. In addition, the Führer is said to have given orders to resist to the last man, woman, and child. This is clearly nonsense, yet how many will and thus prolong the fighting? What will be the attitude towards Germany then? As it was the last time? Or will forbearance be shown? What inroads will the communists make?' He sat down abruptly. 'I am tired to death. For now, let us agree to say nothing until we see the shape of the future. We do not know what happened to . . . Franz. Perhaps he died when the rocket motors exploded. Perhaps he did land on the moon. God in heaven only knows.'

On 2 May 1945 Magnus von Braun rode an old bicycle down a mountain road to make contact with a leading element of the American Army, the 324th Infantry Regiment, 44th Infantry Division, in the village of Schattwald, near the Austrian border. A few hours later a party including, among others, Magnus, Wernher von Braun, Major General Walter Dornberger and Jan Memling – disguised as a German technician – surrendered to First Lieutenant Charles L. Stewart, an intelligence officer assigned to the 44th Infantry. Memling was flown to London the following day.

Jan Memling and Wernher von Braun met for the next and last time on 15 July 1969 in a Cocoa Beach, Florida, motel room, and the following day, the two greying, middle-aged men stood beside one another in the VIP gallery as Apollo 11 began its historic journey to the moon. The photograph taken after the launch shows them standing arm in arm, tears clearly visible in their eyes.

Author's Note

I have taken some liberties with events in Germany between 1935 and 1945 and with the characters in my story. Some – the obvious ones – were real people. Others are composites or else made up out of whole cloth. In either event, I trust I have treated those well who deserved it, and ill those who deserved that.

In 1960, President John F. Kennedy announced before the United Nations General Assembly that the United States of America would land a man on the moon before the end of the decade. It was not, as many critics charged, a publicity stunt but rather a notice to the world that the future of man lay beyond this planet. Over the past twenty years, the money, time and effort expended to land Apollo 11 on the moon has been returned a thousand-fold in new technology, business opportunities, and scientific and medical advances. Just as Wernher von Braun predicted in 1939.

It is a tribute to the men of Peenemünde who, although they built war weapons, never lost sight of the ultimate goal, space travel. The American lunar landing programme was solidly based on technology developed first at the Raketenflugplatz, at Kummersdorf and Peenemünde in Germany and later refined at White Sands, Huntsville, and Cape Kennedy.

It is more than possible – given logical decisions at the right times, efficient organisation of industry, military, and science, and a coherent leadership in Berlin – that Germany might well have sent the first human being to the moon. It had always been the intention of Wernher von Braun and his closest associates to do so, as his arrest in 1944 showed.

Twenty-four years later they proved it.

Joe Poyer
Orange, California

1980

By his own admission, Joe Poyer has been fascinated with the possibilities of space travel since he was a small child. The late Wernher von Braun, with whom he corresponded, was a personal hero, and the idea for Vengeance 10 *was suggested by something Dr von Braun once told him. Mr Poyer brings personal experience to* Vengeance 10, *having worked during most of the 1960s on various phases of the Apollo Space Programme. He is the author of eight previous novels including* North Cape, *of which Alistair MacLean said, it's the 'best adventure story I have read for years'. The* Washington Post *called* Tunnel War, *his last novel, 'a marvellously detailed and suspenseful fiction', and the London* Financial Times *described it as 'a really excellent example of an action novel . . . exciting and intelligent all the way through'.*